PRISONER

Also by S. R. White

Hermit

PRISONER

S. R. WHITE

HEADLINE

First published in 2021 by
HEADLINE PUBLISHING GROUP

1

Cataloguing in Publication Data is available from the British Library

Hardback ISBN 978 1 4722 6845 7
Trade paperback ISBN 978 1 4722 6848 8

Typeset in 11/15.25 pt Adobe Garamond Pro by Jouve (UK), Milton Keynes

Printed and bound in Great Britain by Clays Ltd, Elcograf S.p.A.

Headline's policy is to use papers that are natural, renewable and recyclable
products and made from wood grown in well-managed forests and other
controlled sources. The logging and manufacturing processes are expected
to conform to the environmental regulations of the country of origin.

HEADLINE PUBLISHING GROUP
An Hachette UK Company
Carmelite House
50 Victoria Embankment
London EC4Y 0DZ

www.headline.co.uk
www.hachette.co.uk

This book is dedicated to my friend Kate:
grace under pressure, and a good heart

PRISONER

Chapter 1

Willie Fitzgibbons nearly ran off the road trying to change the radio station. His hand lurched for the button and missed, catching it the second time. He cursed. Swerving back onto the tarmac, the rear of the Navara shimmied as it sought traction. One day, he told himself, you're going to kill someone doing that. Or worse, damage the ute.

The road chicaned through a copse and past the old quarry. Its limestone had created Carlton's main civic buildings, their edifices implying solidity and integrity. But even in 1900 local rivalry was such that the quarry was banned from selling any limestone to Earlville. *Their* public finery was brick, brought by wagon and train from upstate. The quarry's closure was met with a gleeful double-spread by the *Earlville Courier*. The two towns had fought over a scrubby hole now filled with tawny grass, triodia and bird droppings.

Content now he could hear the local news, Willie drove with two fingers, crisp morning air fluttering into the cab. No one ever came down here anyhow: he could probably drive on the wrong side and never hit anything. There were three rarely-used side tracks between the old quarry and the main road; but wide, flat splays meant he could see a car fifty metres early.

Solo time let Willie slow down. He was fast-twitch by nature. A quick eater, walker, talker; everything in a burst. He'd been jittery at school; a whirl of tics, a scurrying rat around superior beings. People and their judgements bothered him; pissed him off, in fact. Better to minimize contact than embark on something doomed to confrontation. Doris, his wife of thirty years, got it. *Let him go off and simmer down, leave him be.* It was why they were still together and why, deep inside, he loved her so much he'd split in two if she ever left.

He visited here seven or eight times a year; four or five good spots that he rotated, fearing exposure or intercept. He never passed anyone on the road itself. The quarry shut years ago and they hadn't even bothered to flood it. Thick shrubs and wild grasses now held tenaciously to its rocky faces. Each year it part-filled with rainwater and some snow melt; enough to suck up poison from below ground and turn the sitting water a lurid green, yellow scum around the edges.

The news said last night's weather had caused some minor flooding. Didn't he know it. The forecast 'showers' had turned into three or four hours of heavy, saturating downpours. Most of the traps he'd laid had been drenched, and the rain kept too many animals hunkered down. He'd spent half the night listening to rain clatter off the tent, then to fat drips off the branches. Waking in a foul mood, he didn't get any happier traipsing around the glade recovering the traps. Two small prizes, now stuffed into a giant ice box in the rear tray. He should have stayed in the cab and got drunk.

The road climbed past several clumps of pines, the sun glinting through the branches. Willie needed to be home soon: had to make his shift at the refinery. He still had five years to go before he could afford to punch his ticket – the thought of looking for a new job made his stomach twist. Fifty-seven, antisocial, sour-faced and left school at fifteen; he simply wasn't going to get anything else.

As he reached the S-bend he saw a flash of yellow from the right-hand side. He braked, and risked a glimpse as he passed. There was definitely something. Perhaps equipment had fallen off another pick-up: something usable, or sellable.

Not sure he'd seen or processed it right, he executed a wide U-turn, bumping over squelchy grass on each side of the road. He eased to a halt, the sun revealing streaks across the windscreen. The engine hummed, nicely warmed now, and he could hear the agitated cackle of birds. There was a brief hiss as a breeze sifted through the trees to the left.

He tried to roll a cigarette, but he was all thumbs and agitation. The paper stuck to his fingertips; he was sweating and had no spit. He threw the packet into the tray by the radio and checked his mirrors without truly knowing why. He looked around for signs that someone was watching: the glint off binoculars, the exposed hind of a badly hidden car. The breeze sighed again and nothing moved but the birds. They drew him back.

There was a man. More correctly, a dead body. The yellow was the rope that bound him to wooden posts, in a cross formation. *Lyin' like Jesus*, came his dead father's words, unbidden. The dark red was the blood from the man's chest, which had congealed black by his left side and along one half of his face. Crows jumped around excitedly, taking turns with the viscera and hopping towards the man's eyeballs.

He got out, primarily to scare the crows before they took the guy's face off. They fussed grudgingly to one side and regarded him with malign stares. He was close enough now to see marks on the wrists and ankles. Willie wasn't good at this: he'd seen a guy burned by gasoline fire at the refinery, and it had haunted him for months.

He ran his hands over his face; hot and clammy. He rubbed his jaw, sandpapery with a couple of days' growth. He ought to move on: let someone else deal with it, call it in. That shift at the refinery wasn't flexible, although finding a mutilated corpse might be a valid excuse for being late. Even so, he'd built his kind of life through looking away, and walking away. Willie had grown up in a neighbourhood that turned a blind eye to just about anything, and it still marked him. Now was not the time to change that. Plus, he had illegal catch in the ice box. He shouldn't be anywhere near here; shouldn't be calling the cops.

But, even so.

He looked back to the body. The dead bloke didn't care if cops showed up now, or this afternoon. Someone else would spy it eventually. It was not his responsibility. But . . . he might be *held* responsible. Who else could the police prove had been here in the past twelve hours? Willie hadn't seen or heard anyone; he had no alibi. His tyres had just left a trail through muddy grass. The old man from the petrol station might recall him, or have him on camera.

The birds were still dancing, something triumphant about their movements. They tugged at sinews and muscle on the abdomen, even as he stared. The engine still purred, and nothing else moved. He had to tell himself to breathe.

The thought of driving off and letting the crows have the eyes did it for him. He took a deep breath, reached for his phone, and dialled.

Chapter 2

By the time Dana Russo arrived, suited-up forensics officers were foraging beneath a white tent: disembodied wraiths moving silently. Six cars, three vans and a beaten pick-up lined the verges, diagonal to a road which essed through an interrupted treeline and disappeared into shadow. The road was closed in both directions, which Dana guessed might inconvenience about three people all day. The nearby quarry was where firearms teams used to practise shooting with new-issue revolvers; so it was hardly busy. She turned the car and pulled up facing away from the crime scene – a running joke with Mike that she always 'parks for a quick getaway'.

To her left a medical examiner's hearse waited, its rear door gaping like a basking shark. The two staff sat on the bumper, one flipping through phone apps, the other puffing stoically at a vape. The 'twins'. Lucy – her redoubtable admin officer – had investigated over the past few weeks and found that they were completely unrelated, despite being virtual doppelgangers. Their starched white collars, tightly-styled copper hair and thin black ties made them look like Mormon missionaries. The app-flipper squinted as she passed, and raised one finger to his temple in greeting. Dana gave an acknowledgement.

Detective Mike Francis was already there, directing human traffic, eyeing the clouds in case they needed to protect more evidence ahead of rain, and preparing the handover documents for her arrival. This was, she reflected, the one time she welcomed joining a group of people: when they were professionals working a crime scene.

'Hey, Mikey.' She handed over a Macca's long black: Mike was not a hipster. 'Is it a coincidence that you always live closer to the murder scene than I do?'

'*Gracias.*' Mike stood the cup on a car bonnet and flipped back a sheet on his clipboard; he was first detective on scene but not lead detective, which was always confusing. Their boss, Bill Meeks, chose seemingly at random who would take charge of each case.

'Ah, maybe, but perhaps not.' He thought about making a crack about her living in a more upmarket part of town, but something deeper sparked his mind. 'I think you choose to live as far away as possible from any drama.'

'Wow, thanks, Sigmund.' She smiled. 'You might be right, though.'

She swept a three-sixty: fifteen people working, aware of what needed doing and how to do it. They didn't need managing, as such – that would insult their professionalism. It was more a question of making sure things were done in sequence, and done once. Plus, any little extras she noticed or needed on the way round.

The scene itself was soggy open ground with occasional clumps of conifers, away from prying eyes. The quarry was fifteen kilometres from Earlville: the whole district was isolated and mainly fetid marsh – swamps dominated between here and the golf course to the south. The last building she'd noticed on her way in had been a disused barn about two kilometres away, half-hearted graffiti on one wall. Now she spotted chimney smoke in the distance, apparently the nearest habitation. Any murderer would, she suspected, have used this road both in and out. Forensics ought to be well contained, well preserved, and significant.

'We have a single victim?'

'Absolutely. Walk with me.' Mike picked up the coffee and nodded to a tech as they passed the ute; she was taking tyre impressions from the verge. 'Forensics have swept the immediate area, so we're good here. No footprints, tyre tracks or drag marks close to the body, so we've currently no line on how it got here. Chucked it down last night, though, so plenty got washed away. Search team is –' he checked his watch – 'about fifteen minutes away. They'll grid a further four hundred metres.'

They stopped outside the tent. Mike squinted at the emerging sunlight and, instead of leading the way inside, turned towards an older man sitting on a log some yards away.

'This genius –' he tipped his cup at a small, wiry man in dungarees, who scowled back – 'found the body exactly as is, around 6.30 a.m. Willie Fitzgibbons.' Mike dropped his voice. 'I've known him vaguely for a few years. I'll do the intros later, but it's hard to pick him doing this kind of stuff.' Fitzgibbons bristled at the attention, then carried on scratching at dried soil on his braces.

'He swears he didn't touch it,' continued Mike, 'but we've taken DNA and fingerprints for comparison. We're doing his tyres now, for elimination. He saw it from the ute: got near enough to check the guy was dead, and shoo the crows from the eyeballs.'

Dana pulled a face. Mike wasn't the kind to hype up the grisly factor. If he said it was putrid, it was. 'Nice,' she replied. 'I won't be having the mixed grill for lunch, then.'

'Yup. Might want to lay off olives for a week or two, as well.'

Dana was generally immune to viewing gore: twelve months seconded to the medical examiner early in her career. She could swallow it down if there were interesting forensics, but generally wasn't fussed about seeing too much. Although, given the error she'd made on her last murder, she reminded herself to pay more attention this time.

'Dead body's a white male?'

They eased back towards the tent and Mike lifted a flap. Forensics and Pathology were still moving carefully around the corpse: two more people would have complicated that. Dana took in what she could from the periphery.

The ground looked hardened by frost, with a slightly melted surface. She recalled heavy rain off and on all night, but a run of dry, cold days before that. The restraints looked to be standard mountaineering rope. Dana looked closer at the bindings. Sometimes a giveaway knot told of fishermen, or truckies, or S&M devotees. There could be a lot of information in a knot.

The posts standing proud of the soil seemed to be treated pine; possibly fence posts from any hardware place in the country. The wooden surfaces looked old, but it was open country out here and they might weather quickly. All she could see at the base was mud. They'd presumably been driven in with plenty of force, given the hardened ground – so possibly men; or women with specialist equipment. There was no apparent need for the posts to be here, other than to stage a corpse. Dana was already thinking more than one perpetrator, purely because of the logistics. Pile drivers, rain, darkness, maybe a dead weight: tricky for any one person to negotiate. It was hard to say how long the posts had been there, though. She was about to request when she saw a tech lean down and take a detailed photo of how the uprights met the soil.

'Not dressed for a cold, wet night, was he?' she asked.

Mike had already logged the clothing and they'd taken casts from the soles of muddied training shoes. The dead man wore cheap-looking jeans and a rucked-up, blood-encrusted track top: he was unlikely to be an alumnus of UCLA. Low-priced clothes, from a street market or dollar-value store: easy to acquire, little thought. Generic, almost: as though the victim had no personality. Dana noticed a long scar along the victim's abdomen: he had no shirt underneath the track top and the scar had faded into a hard line of knotted skin.

'Victim's name is Curtis Mason Monroe. Had his wallet still on him, with cash in it. All of forty-one bucks. Driver's licence, Medicare, but no bank cards.' Mike flipped pages back and forth. 'Twenty-seven; local, from near Earlville. Released yesterday from prison. Fifteen-year sentence for rape; he's paroled after nine, because he's such a wonderful human being. Parole office is waiting for us to visit. When we woke up the designated liaison, they called Monroe "no great loss".'

Dana guessed the scar was possibly a prison shank, then, though it looked even older than that. 'Everyone's a charmer these days.'

She moved closer and reminded herself to ignore the victim's past. That would come later: it wasn't a dead rapist, it was a dead human being. Officers would go the extra mile without blinking for a child; but her team should avoid believing this victim was less dignified, innocent or needing justice than any other. She included herself in that admonishment.

She caught another glimpse as the techs moved around. Monroe had clearly pulled against restraints at some point. Though not necessarily these restraints, at this scene. The rope marks didn't look as fresh as she'd expect, although they'd been compromised in places by the crows. His injuries were mainly to his left abdomen; a major gouge that she would guess as an axe, or some other heavy implement with a large blade. A scythe would do equally well. She couldn't see a blood trail: presumably the heavy damage was done *in situ*.

'Any idea how long he's been here?'

The pathologist – a locum she didn't know – shook his head and returned to the body. She felt like she'd shouted in a library. Mike glared at him.

'My guess, as a dumb detective with no scientific qualifications –' he raised his voice for the pathologist, who visibly flinched without turning – 'is three to nine hours. He's wet from rain; the crows would have started around dawn; no other animals seem to have eaten; no bugs I could see; and rigor looks pretty early.'

Dana chewed her lip. She reckoned Mike was just about on the money. The timescale almost certainly meant no witnesses, and narrowed the range of suspects: a dark wet night on a road to nowhere.

'So between 10 p.m. and five this morning, say?'

''Tis the killing time.'

They both regarded the body. Murder was a monstrous, heinous act: something huge had to well up in a human mind to do such a thing. Unless they were a psychopath. But psychopaths rarely indulged in scene-setting: it didn't fit their sense of themselves as the centre of the world.

'No defensive wounds,' chipped in Mike. There was no evidence yet that Monroe had fought his attacker, or attackers. He might have known, or trusted, his assailants. Dana would need toxicology to tell if he'd been sedated.

They stepped back and leaned against a marked Commodore to allow extra lighting equipment to come in: large arc lamps to remove any shadows and get the strongest images.

'All yours, Dana.'

Mike juggled hands to preserve the coffee and handed her the clipboard, watching as she signed to take official control as lead detective. She felt a flutter of anxiety, instantly quelled by the comfort of familiarity. Structure, context and certainty always soothed: it was the ad-libbing that drained her.

'Thank you, Mikey. Thoughts?' she asked.

'Deliberate, targeted. Not necessarily brutal; almost quick and merciful. Someone who knows him; maybe pretty well. Probably more than one someone – he's a heavy guy, especially when he's dead, and those posts aren't there by accident. Killed here: moving him during a rainstorm would have been a pain. But possibly rendered immobile elsewhere and moved here for theatrics, which must hold meaning. There's easier ways to kill, and for sure better ways to avoid detection.'

'There *are* easier ways,' she corrected. 'Not "there is".'

'*Tak*, Saga.'

They smiled and Mike continued.

'Whoever did this could have buried the body a hundred metres off the road, and no one would ever have found it. Area's got nothing but swamps, especially to the north. Drop him in one of those and he's never seen again. Maybe they want him found, for some reason: send a message, perhaps? Anyway, killed for who he was or what he was, or maybe what he knew. No robbery, nothing random about it; and not a dire case of bad luck. Hard to see past revenge for what he did, I'd say.'

She looked around again. This place had been chosen for a reason, she sensed. 'One day released from Du Pont prison – why come here?'

'Ah, well, here's where it gets freaky.' He took a swig of bad coffee as though it was the nectar of the gods. 'I wasn't here when Monroe's original case happened: none of us were. I was going to look it up when Ali gave me a shout.'

Mike beckoned to a swarm of four people, and Constable Ali McMahon peeled away from them and approached. Tall, willowy, with the perfectly refined balance of an international-standard archer, she lifted a handful of papers to her face to shield herself from the sun, which was gaining the upper hand now the mist was dissipating. Her voice had a beguiling rough edge to it.

'Hey. So, I heard the ID of the body on the police radio and it rang bells. You remember I stuffed myself up doing that triathlon?' Dana didn't; it was the sort of personal detail that slid its frictionless way through her brain. She nodded anyway.

'I couldn't work Family Safety while my Achilles recovered, so I was prison liaison for a few months: all office, all the time. Monroe was one of the cases approaching parole. He was convicted of raping a trainee teacher over there. About, oh, a kilometre tops. So he had a connection to this area from that.'

The thick band of trees Ali identified followed a ragged line as it descended towards a brook, which eventually fed into the quarry. In early August it all looked stark and inert, and every inch the place where life was snuffed out. Dana never liked offenders returning to the scene of the crime. Gloating, re-living; or fuelling someone's anger, frustration and need to lash out. No good ever came of it.

'But here's the kicker.' Ali had a fresh-scrubbed, good-at-all-sports vitality. 'Monroe had no family here – they disowned him entirely and moved across country – so the parole board were nervous because he had no place to go. I just checked the prisoner release records for this month. Turns out he found some assistance. See the run of pines over there? Beyond that, there's a cottage owned by two sisters: Suzanne and Marika Doyle. He was due to stay there.'

Ali pointed to a dead-straight line of conifers perpendicular to the road. Dana hadn't noticed a driveway back there. Now she saw again the top of a chimney, yielding a hint of smoke.

'Renting it? From them?'

Ali glanced nervously at Mike before replying.

'Nuh-uh. *With* them. At their request. They've been writing to him for the past two years.' Ali puffed her cheeks in disbelief. 'The Doyle sisters were good friends with a rapist.'

Chapter 3

Dana stood as Ali wandered off, organizing all the relevant prisoner material to be sent through. Lucy would collate it for a briefing. Seeing Monroe's parole officer was less urgent now, Dana decided; he'd be backfilling gaps in the data they'd already uncovered.

'Weird, right?' Mike's voice slid through her reverie.

'Unusual, for certain.'

Dana collected herself. It was tempting to go at this revelation in a rush, or make judgements about the two women. 'So are these sisters some kind of benevolent agency, or habitual campaigners, or something? Any overt reason they'd be working with ex-offenders at all, let alone this one?'

Mike spread his arms. 'Dunno, never heard of them before.'

Dana knew Mike wanted to do something. *She* thought the best thing to do right now was nothing. Let the information come to her at this stage; process it, piece it together. It was surely wasted effort to take action from fragmented impressions. But she was now leading a team that generally did it a different way: Mike was getting fidgety.

'Let's sort out this Willie guy, then, Mikey.'

They walked towards Willie, who sat cleaning one fingernail with another. He was shivering noticeably, and it occurred to Dana that he was in shock.

'Good morning, Mr Fitzgibbons. I'm Detective Dana Russo, I'm in charge of this investigation.' She offered a hand, but it hung in mid-air. Willie grunted and wouldn't look at her.

'Cold and damp if you're not moving, isn't it?' she said. 'Could you please tell me what you were doing up here this morning?'

Willie spluttered and wiped his mouth. 'Out for a drive.'

Mike snorted, and his shadow loomed over Willie. 'Do you want me to take a look inside the big eskie there, Willie? C'mon, don't waste our time. This is a murder investigation. We aren't interested in your lower-league hobbies.'

Mike did looming better than Dana; they both knew it. Willie let out a long sigh and gave in.

'Been out all night. I tent up on the other side of the quarry; there's a space in the trees there. Didn't hear nothing but rain all night. No noises, nothing funny. Driving back through here at six, saw what you're seeing now. Didn't touch him. Just kept the birds off the . . . you know.'

'Yes, I saw,' replied Dana. 'Thank you for doing that. Are you up here regularly, Mr Fitzgibbons?'

'Nope.' Willie looked up at a glowering Mike, and relented. 'Well. Not . . . no. Every couple of months.'

'Have you ever seen anything odd, unusual? Especially here, or over there where the pines run out?'

'Unusual?'

'People hanging around, any farm equipment, signs of movement; parked cars?'

'Nope.'

'What about the posts there? Were they in place the last time you occasionally visited?'

'Maybe. Don't remember.'

He avoided eye contact and his answers were minimal. Yet she got no vibe from him. Sometimes, she had to go with her instinct. They had an initial statement that uniform had taken. Mike clearly knew what had brought Willie up here and didn't link it to this death. She had wondered if the dead man had disturbed Willie doing whatever, but the scenario didn't fit. Willie did know what was out of place or unusual, even if he was currently holding back: they might want to follow up.

'Okay, Mr Fitzgibbons, that's all for now, thank you. We might need to get back to you. Where do you work?'

'Refinery. Maintenance crew.'

'Well, whether you feel it or not, you've had a shock today. I'd like you to stay at home, or near it. And keep your phone handy. We'll call your boss and explain.'

Willie wiped his hands on his front. 'I can't. Wait, I shouldn't . . . they won't like it.'

'Don't worry,' replied Dana, thinking of Lucy. 'The person who's ringing them will make sure they understand. She's extremely good at that sort of thing. Thank you for your time.'

Dana and Mike turned away. 'Mikey, I want you to go to the parole office, please, get what you can from the caring genius who looked after Monroe. We're getting the basic bio fed through to Luce, so what I want from Parole is the intangible stuff, especially anything that indicates motive. Thank you.'

She checked through the paperwork again, to make sure she hadn't missed anything. She could hear Mike speak to Fitzgibbons as he passed him.

'Willie, you and I get along fine when you don't annoy me. I know what's in those eskies. And who buys them. I do not accept that behaviour: it isn't "traditional hunting law" if you're not indigenous – and you're not. You've got cousins interstate: practise your bloody hobby there. Now get lost.'

*

Mike set off for the parole office to interview Monroe's assigned officer and Dana prowled a ten-metre stretch of verge, head bowed in
thought and finger and thumb tapping together. Her kneecap was
fizzing – she'd rushed here this morning and hadn't had time to do her
daily physio. Clusters of officers worked away but watched her, wondering why she didn't chat until the search team arrived. After
receiving crucial information she liked to take a minute to evaluate
what assumptions she was making, and whether they'd send her in a
bad direction.

Monroe's past was unavoidably linked to his present state. Now
she'd stepped away and was in investigation mode, she could concede
that he was not a person who was dead, nor a man who'd been killed.
He was a convicted rapist: one day out of prison, he'd been murdered.
The assumption that he was murdered because of his crime was not,
she concluded, unreasonable. It was the likeliest – but not the only –
option. She'd need the search team to focus on the original crime scene
from nine years ago, and any pathway to the dead body. If there'd been
any re-enactment, any homage, or any sense of forcing him to confront his previous crime, there ought to be a trail between the two
points.

That being so, she would need to know about the original crime.
Dana put in a call to Lucy, who should have arrived at work by now:
she was punctual beyond belief.

'Hey, Dana. You'll want to know about Curtis Monroe, yeah?'

Lucy's voice made Dana smile; she turned away from the crime
scene, as if she weren't allowed to enjoy anything near it.

'You're too spooky, Luce. Yes, please. Ali's sending you some links
and trails to follow; she used to be prisoner liaison. I've got Mikey
visiting the parole office. I'd like a bio for an 0900 briefing, please.
Scan all the transcripts from the trial: we'll probably need them. Uh,

any newspaper coverage about the reactions to the trial and the sentence – who thought it wasn't enough, who vowed vengeance, that sort of thing. Also, what Monroe might have said: contrition, arrogance, anything that might stick in the craw or fuel the flames. Thank you.'

The background information would build a picture. Now she needed paperwork in case they found anything useful nearby.

'Please pre-prepare several applications for Close Proximity: I think we'll be using that new legislation. And a search warrant: I'll need one for –' she double-checked an online map on her iPad – 'Weaver's Cottage, about a kilometre from this location. Please include the surrounding area beyond the cottage. Thanks, Luce.'

Lucy's fingers clattered at speed across the keyboard, sounding like bats emerging from a cave. 'Prison visitor lists, too?'

'You are so far ahead of me all I can see is a distant figure on the horizon.'

'Waving, not drowning, chick. I'm all over it.'

At the crime scene the hearse glided to a halt as the corpse was brought from the tent and placed on the sliders. It was slick: the body bag exposed for two seconds. They'd recently had a seminar about the danger of civilian drones filming crime scenes; Dana scanned the skies but couldn't see anything.

As the hearse did a three-pointer, Dana caught Ali's eye.

'Ali, are you able to stay and direct the search team for me, please?'

'Sure.'

Dana never quite knew how to take Ali. She was bright and perky and Dana was sure she was popular. But she seemed to Dana over-literal and devoid of any angles. Dana preferred people with sarcasm, or impatience, or irony; anything to knock off the smooth edges and serve up a little imperfection.

'Thank you. We've already covered the crime scene and surrounding area. I want the search team to split in half so they can focus on two areas, and the pathways between those two areas and here.' Dana turned them both to the east. 'Firstly, the old crime scene from nine years ago. If you can't recall the exact location, ring Lucy – she'll find the precise co-ordinates from the trial paperwork. Then, the main ways of getting from there to here. It was dark and wet, so path of least resistance: any reasonably clear line of access needs covering. I'm looking for signs of disturbance or recent activity. Also, evidence of a shrine to the original victim; anything that might have kicked things off.'

For some reason, it annoyed Dana that Ali wasn't taking notes. Although the instructions weren't complicated, so maybe writing it down would be more to show Dana she was taking it seriously. Which would mean this was Dana's issue, not Ali's.

'Also, we'll be doing a full assessment of the cottage belonging to these Doyle sisters. Please get the search team to that part of the road, and tell Stu to wait until I arrive. I'll have a warrant by the time he gets there. It's the most recent place Monroe might have been. So, again, cover the ground between the cottage and here. Any indication that anyone's travelled between the two points in the past twenty-four hours. Thank you.'

Ali turned away to dial the search coordinator. Dana decided to walk to the cottage – it gave her a viable excuse to be alone for a few minutes, and she always took those.

The case seemed to have a number of advantages already, and Dana was always wary when that happened. They knew who the victim was, and where he'd been for every minute of nine years: bar the last twenty-four hours. No problems with identification or tracing, then. The location had, effectively, one way in or out, so the forensics ought to be strong. And the killing was clearly deliberate and, on some level, pre-meditated. That meant no confusion about possible 'accidents' or 'things getting out of control'. They were looking for a cold-blooded killer, or killers. Finally, the body was displayed – overt, deliberate and sending a message.

So perhaps the question was, who would want to send that message? And why pick Curtis Monroe to send it?

Chapter 4

The sun ought to have lifted her spirits. But Dana kept glancing around her, as though something was about to snap from the mist. Trees dripped fingers of moss and seemed half-liquid. The air felt rotten and trapped.

Too far from the crime scene to hear her colleagues, Dana stopped and listened for the silence. But there was none. Instead, there were gurgles and hisses; water sluicing over ground and seething back again. The land – and the swamp that covered it – was in perpetual and disconcerting motion. Mike was right: throw a body into any of the dozens of marshes here and no one would ever know. Why, then, leave it to be found?

Dana stopped at the cottage's driveway, next to a mailbox that was askew more from age and damp than malicious intent. An ironic flyer for solar panels had dropped from its mouth onto sodden grass. The mailbox was part-hidden by a bush, and the driveway was simply tufty grass with sporadic pools of gravel: hence, she hadn't noticed it on her way to the crime scene. Across the road, several hectares of heathland and boggy peat stretched away, a miasma of fog drifting up from it and billowing lazily. According to Mike's comment as he left the crime scene, you could only cross much of this area in a boat.

The sun was stronger here, the coat that had been necessary an hour ago now redundant. Her phone rang and the digital image of a signed search warrant appeared. She zoomed in to check that the details covered all she'd requested from Bill Meeks. Fifteen minutes from request to signed copy – maybe new technology was useful after all. Bill also messaged that he was going to be in a training course all day and half the next. While she texted thanks, the two search-team SUVs rolled up.

Stu was in the second vehicle. He let a heavily tinted window glide down.

'Good morrow.' He grinned and looked off to the left. 'This place is, uh, rank.'

'Do I put you down as *neither satisfied nor dissatisfied*, Stu?'

'Deeply troubled, in capital letters. Can think of two accidental deaths around here in the last few years. Almost anywhere more than fifty metres off the road is lethal – swamp everywhere. That's the hazards we know about. You could hide a bus in most of this stuff. Uh, you want half of us up at the crime scene, half waiting here for your signal?'

'Yes, please. Ali's co-ordinating up there.' She waved her phone. 'I've got the warrant from Bill, so assuming someone's home, I'll need a few minutes to serve it and be polite, and then we're a go. Oh, hold on. You've got a printer in there now, haven't you?'

A rear window rolled down as Stu said, 'Yeah, see Milo in the back.'

Milo had a small printer plugged into a socket by his foot.

'We use this to print out stuff on memory sticks, sometimes,' he explained.

'Interesting second name: in-the-back.'

'Yeah, took my wife's name when we married. Her first name is "Knife".'

Dana laughed. 'Ex-wife now, I imagine?'

'As fast as I could fill out the forms. There you go; not top-quality, but readable.' He handed back three sheets still warm from the printer. There was a flaw on the roller that meant each had blotches of ink, but it was legible enough.

'Thank you, Mr in-the-back.'

'Okay.' Stu raised a hand to the front vehicle, which was easing away towards the sunlight. 'Home owners staying in to watch, or not?'

Dana looked off to the cottage, its left flank barely visible around a large bush. Render was blushed with rust stains from the gutters, and mould from decades of rain-soaked westerlies.

'I don't know yet. Probably not; it's possibly the victim's last-known location so we'll be looking for trace, blood, whatever. I don't think the residents will be happy about that.'

'They rarely are,' muttered Stu. She knew he believed search areas should be fundamentally human-free; anything else was a colossal pain. 'All right. My legions stand ready to serve.'

Dana's face brightened. 'Five minutes, please, Stu. Then arrive if I haven't signalled.'

She turned and headed up the driveway, which stayed a loose affiliation of gravel and grass. She wondered how the residents got about: it was miles from the nearest store – not counting a petrol station – and she couldn't see any vehicle parked nearby. There was no sign of recent activity, be it tyres or footprints. There was, however, enough standing water to remind her that such traces might have been there yesterday. The forensics weren't quite as clear cut as she'd hoped an hour ago. Her kneecap was starting to ping with the exercise and the damp; she limped slightly.

The cottage was tall and slender: she could tell that it lacked depth. It was almost the façade of a cottage: two storeys high but barely six metres across, and seemingly one room from front to back. The steep roof pitch hinted at early century; the single-glazed windows were coated with blooms of condensation. It stood proud of the land by at least a metre – there were cracked stone steps up to the door – because this area regularly flooded. Several tiles hung precariously over the guttering, which sprouted curls of yellowing grass. It was small, unkempt, exhausted and, from the outside, it looked cold inside. Dana was imagining chaotic, musty, smelling of wet dog somehow; dodgy electrics and plumbing, and spongy walls of time-dulled anaglypta. She was already longing for the neat streets and mud-free entrances of her own neighbourhood in Carlton.

She'd reached a clearing near the front door when an upstairs window screeched open. A young woman held on to a curled metal latch, her cardigan flapping in a breeze that wasn't apparent at ground level. Her brown hair nuzzled the sill and long, thin fingers pointed to Dana.

'What do you want?' An accent-free but exasperated voice, as if Dana were the tenth visitor that morning.

Dana flipped her ID and held it up. 'I'm Detective Dana Russo. Are you Suzanne or Marika Doyle?'

The woman stared, her face blank. 'Suzanne. What's this about?'

'I have a warrant to search your house and the surrounding area. Would you open the door, please?'

Suzanne spoke with a surprise she failed to show on her face. 'Warrant? What? You haven't answered the question.'

'I'm here to execute a lawful search warrant, Ms Doyle. That is definitely the answer to your question. Open the door now, please.'

Suzanne glanced into the room, as if someone was there. Marika, maybe. 'It's pretty early. You woke me up. Give me a few minutes.'

Dana was surprised to feel irritated. Suzanne had become annoying very quickly: perhaps not by stalling but because of who she'd seemingly allowed into her home recently.

'Ms Doyle. This is not a chat over a coffee. This is a lawfully obtained search warrant for all your property. You must open the door right now. If not –' she pointed back down the driveway – 'I have a team with a door opener that has three tonnes of force. They can smash it off the hinges, with no compensation. I'm sure you prefer your house with the door attached. I don't care how you're dressed, but I do care if you don't cooperate. Now. Thank you.'

Suzanne sighed theatrically and closed the window. Dana walked slowly up to the scuffed front door and saw Suzanne's frame gradually fill the semi-opaque glass panel above the knocker. There were several clunks, as if items were being kicked aside, then the door opened. Suzanne walked past the threshold without acknowledging Dana and headed for another room. As Dana stepped in, the tyres from the SUV crunched to a halt behind her. Without looking back, Dana gave it a thumbs-up that said so far, so good. Then a raised palm, to indicate they should hold.

She'd been right about the cottage. Piles of gear hogged each horizontal surface as though clinging to life. Junk, mainly: disembowelled clocks and radios that clearly didn't work, mounds of yellowing magazines, desiccated sets of encyclopaedias, old and torn clothes. One of the two bookcases was a trapezoid of lurching timber and loosened bolts, held up by the edge of the chimney. Dana was standing on the kind of swirl-patterned carpet they had in old-fashioned saloon bars, complete with ash stains and aroma of dried something. A couch that was too low – the legs had been sawn down – sat along one wall, three saucers of cigarette butts at its feet like obedient pups. Near the window was a pristine flat-screen: not a speck of dust. She looked instinctively for other technology – a laptop, for example – but could see none.

Beyond the living room was a kitchen: a cheap lean-to conservatory filled with stand-alone cabinets, an off-white stove-top laced with specks of splattered food, and an overburdened sink area. Suzanne sat at a kitchen table, visible from the living room through a set of French windows that had been pinned back by archive boxes of photo albums. She fiddled with some mushrooms, ostensibly peeling them into a blue ceramic bowl, but taking surreptitious glances as Dana picked her way through the debris. Suzanne spoke to the bowl.

'If we'd known you were coming, Officer, we'd have tidied up.'

'No need,' Dana deadpanned. 'We like the authentic, distressed look.'

Suzanne was now fussing with a folded newspaper. Maybe she had a short attention span. 'I should probably see that warrant.'

They often felt that: not that they could tell a real warrant from a fake one. Dana watched Suzanne skim each sheet. Technically, the new legislation meant it was up to the recipient to challenge the detail. Suzanne's eyes swam lazily after the text, constantly seeking focus. Dana decided that the woman would need a tox screen later.

'Do you have any questions about this warrant, Suzanne?' she asked, securing the legal double-lock. She waved a pen.

'Mmkay,' Suzanne mumbled, seemingly satisfied. She scribbled something-or-other on the final sheet. It might have been a signature.

The kitchen was no more orderly. The splattering on the hob looked like soup. Pans tiered with careless disregard, opened boxes of cereal encouraging a trail of tiny ants, a small volcano of used teabags next to the kettle. To one side, a tower of wire baskets held potatoes, onions, half a cauliflower and what looked like part of a squash. Tea-coloured splashes leapt up the tiles, past some pegs that held large mugs in primary colours; a cress plant splayed itself on the sill above the sink. Through the glass was a drab and barren patch of grass, a concrete and asbestos shed in one corner. From it, a washing line eased to and fro in the freshening wind, various black items waving balletically. The half-drawn curtains in the living room gave the kitchen a sepia tinge.

The place was a mess. Stu was going to be thrilled.

Close up, she could see that Suzanne looked not so much stoned, as

exhausted. The kind of exhaustion that came from regular sleep depriv-
ation. The type of deep-rooted fatigue that made people deadly drivers,
or malleable fools.

'Is Marika here?'

Suzanne shrugged. 'Out running. Back in . . . maybe an hour.'

'An hour?'

Suzanne's hand flitted back towards the mushrooms, then changed
its mind. Maybe it wasn't weariness that was making Suzanne nervy.
Perhaps it was merely conscience. Maybe it was Dana's presence, or the
thought of the search. Or the absence of Marika.

'She's a cross-country-running freak. Fifteen clicks, most days.'

Damn, thought Dana. It would give Marika a chance to see them
here, and hide. Or at least decide what story to tell. No doubt she would
know the surrounding countryside like the back of her hand. Dana had
wanted them both available instantly, but life often disappointed.

'What is she wearing?'

'What? Why do you care?' When she looked up, Suzanne's impatience faded immediately, as if she couldn't hold an emotion long
enough to express it fully.

'We need to speak to her. It's urgent.' Dana waited a beat. 'For her
own protection.'

It was technically correct. They had no current suspect for the murder: it was possible that the killer would come after the two people
who'd perhaps shielded Monroe after his release. Dana thought it
unlikely for now, but it was leverage nonetheless.

'Her own . . .?' Suzanne looked startled, before seeming to regain
the script. 'Wow, aren't you a drama queen? Marika can look after
herself.'

'No doubt she can. What is she wearing, please?'

'Ugh.' Suzanne looked up like a bored teenager. 'She has this black
ninja thing. Black running gear, including the shoes.'

'Did she take a phone with her?'

Suzanne pointed at an amateurish pottery effort of a fruit bowl that held a banana on the turn, two greying satsumas and a Samsung.

'Phones interfere with her concentration, apparently.' She propped her head with one hand, letting the elbow slide along the table, like a child.

Dana looked around for a photo of the two of them. There was only one, hidden behind a pile of books. Dana noticed for the first time – and now she felt stupid for not seeing it earlier – that the surface of the sideboard consisted wholly of history books. She saw another stack of the same near an armchair.

She reached past *The Fifth French Republic* and *Castro's Early Years* to a silver-framed photo. Like the television, this was dust-free and cared for. Suzanne was maybe fourteen here; Dana guessed about a decade ago. Suzanne was a shiny-faced beauty with a curly, dimpled smile, resplendent in full riding gear. She stood, beaming, next to a chestnut horse with a noble head and white fetlocks, and a silver trophy on the grass that it nuzzled as though it knew what it was. On the other side of the horse a skinny whelp of perhaps nine stood gawky and uninterested, occupying a flimsy black dress swept to one side by a sudden gust, looking past the camera with a studied indifference. Thin white legs crossed awkwardly; a pout; dark eyes under an uneven fringe.

Marika.

Dana's internal radar pinged. Suzanne hadn't asked what the search warrant was for; nor had she asked where Monroe was, nor even mentioned him. There was something skittish about her. Not simply the pale skin and tendency towards juvenile gesture; there was something else that made Dana think Suzanne had many problems, and no idea how to solve any of them.

'Suzanne, we're going to take you to the police station. We have a number of questions.'

Suzanne fussed under the table and found a pair of training shoes, slipping in to them without bothering with the laces. All her movements had a sense of lazy stoicism about them.

Dana held out her hand. 'Your keys, please. The search team will lock up when they're done.'

It was rare to get them without an argument, in Dana's experience. People were either angling to stay – which they were legally allowed to do, although they rarely realized it – or they wanted the police out. Occasionally, they left lavish instructions on exactly what the cat liked to eat. But Suzanne simply dropped the keys into Dana's palm. She rose languidly and shuffled out, pausing to grab a coat from the rack by the door. Dana's elbow swept Marika's phone into an evidence bag.

They stepped outside. Dana gave Milo a description of Marika, and suggested there might be a more recent photo of her elsewhere in the cottage. Next, she passed the house keys and phone to Stu, who disappeared around the back of the SUV to suit up with the rest of the team.

She indicated to Suzanne to begin walking towards the road. As she rang for a uniform to bring a patrol car, Dana watched the loping gait of the woman in front of her. It was girlishly slanted, stunted; immature. Suzanne's face said thirty-five and tiring; some of her behaviour said eighteen and petulant. Dana was unnerved by how submissive Suzanne appeared to be, underneath her initial defiance. She gave every indication that – if Dana told her to – she'd walk into the bush, kneel down, and wait for the bullet. As if that would be inevitable.

Once Suzanne had been taken away to the station, Dana walked back to her car. The cottage was a mess, but nothing on the ground floor immediately implied Monroe had ever been there. Except maybe the cigarettes – she hadn't been close enough to spot any other indications, but she suspected at least one of the sisters smoked. Suzanne, probably:

Dana couldn't imagine Marika puffing twenty a day and still running fifteen kilometres. Assuming she did.

Lucy was kicking in the necessary paperwork. They could now go before a judge and argue for Close Proximity: for Suzanne to be treated almost as a super-witness. They had to justify to a judge why they needed to use the extra powers, which in Dana's view simply sharpened up their own act. Based originally on anti-terrorism statutes, each sentence had to be inch-perfect. Dana and Mike wouldn't allow anyone but Lucy to prepare those applications.

Dana began to wonder if the host address and support letters from the sisters had simply been to get Monroe parole, and he'd never taken up the offer. Perhaps something solely to satisfy the authorities and tip the balance of the parole decision. Why the Doyles would take part in that, she couldn't imagine. Maybe Monroe intended to visit the scene of his old crime, and the two sisters were a way of achieving that.

But she didn't think so. All her instincts told her the cottage held some implications for the murder, one way or another. Suzanne's cooperation might yield plenty of information: she didn't strike Dana as having the mental strength to be a hold-out. By the time she got back to the station, Dana would have some feedback from Mike about Monroe, some background details on both the victim and the sisters, and maybe Stu's initial search from within the cottage.

That might be enough to prise open Suzanne.

Chapter 5

The regional parole office had been shunted, in the modern way of things, well away from anyone they might wish to speak to. The private sector idolized physical proximity and its imagined agglomeration of ideas and creativity; the public sector got pushed into cheap lodgings. As part of the criminal justice system, Parole might have wanted to be near a court or a police station. However, according to the management consultants who'd oozed through the government department the previous year, *efficiency dividends could be liberated* by sending them to a business park on the outskirts of Earlville. Ironically squashed between two companies whose business names both promised 'solutions', Parole sat as the epitome of problems. People that society wanted to ignore came here, as did those charged with helping them with their reintegration into that same society. Parolees would need a car to get here – just at the time they were least likely to have one.

When those valuable clients arrived, they saw the same identikit office building as the other five in the business park: clinker brick below a flat roof, crude louvre shutters across west-facing windows, air-conditioners wheeling away next to storm drains and car parks. Parole's workforce clearly earned less than their neighbours: there was more trade for South Korea than Germany in their parking spaces.

Mike was surprised to find the parole office so busy when he arrived. A chilly 0800 hrs was sometimes when he stood outside a public service admin block, blowing warmth into his hands while he waited for one of the few already working inside to let him in. This office had at least a dozen workers diligently tapping out emails.

Likewise, he'd anticipated Vernon Harper would be a shirt-sleeved, harassed-looking middle-aged man, pulled to and fro by a rip current of files and audit trails, bemoaning his lot in an airless office where conversation required prairie-dogging a colleague over a divider. In reality, Vernon radiated the affable confidence of the never-in-trouble and occupied a corner suite with a view towards the park. If Vernon had presented himself as the unfeasibly young CEO of a multimedia start-up, Mike could hardly have argued.

'Coffee, Detective? It's single origin, Costa Rican.'

Vernon hovered hopefully by his Italian machine, which swooped and swirled in a handsome series of tasteful pastel shades. A convex reflection of his immaculate hands loomed in the chrome.

'Bit early for me, thanks. You were telephoned about Curtis Monroe.'

'Sure, sure.'

Vernon reached into a surprisingly small collection of neat files and took out a blue one. Mike assumed colour coding, and blue meant recently released. Perhaps, recently deceased.

'I had a copy made for you of all our information. It's there in date order, but I did an executive summary for the first page.'

Vernon perched on the corner of his own desk, relaxed and eager but strangely distant.

The opening page outlined the sketch of a life badly lived. Curtis Monroe had started okay, but gone downhill. School had produced little but an inability to choose acquaintances wisely. In between bouts of working in tyre shops was low-grade theft, sliding into burglary, and then credit fraud. These were seasoned by two drug possessions, for marijuana. No violence, though; not until the night nearly ten years ago. In a wooded area near the current murder scene, Curtis had been with trainee teacher Louise Montgomery on a summer night. Curtis was arrested the next day, convicted inside two months, and went to prison. Louise eventually finished her teacher training, and moved across the state border.

'What did you think of Monroe?'

Vernon seemed both vexed and affronted by the question: the very notion that he, a refined single-origin drinker, might have to mix with the hoi-polloi. Mike immediately thought *professional manager*: melting from one 'leadership and mentoring opportunity' to another, never alighting long enough to leave a real mark, or be associated with a real mess. Good networker; great at faking passion at interviews; assiduous user of the correct jargon; politically astute for his own purposes; unfailingly polite. No use at all.

'I never met him, I'm afraid.' Vernon's voice lubricated each word with insincerity. 'The system is that we only become involved when a prisoner applies for parole and makes it through a paper test: that's done in-house by the prison staff. Then a parole officer meets the prisoner prior to the parole board, and again prior to release. The notes of those appointments are in the green section.'

In other words, thought Mike, he was talking to the wrong person. As Vernon should have guessed and understood right from the start.

'So who did that? Who actually met him?'

'Patterson. He was the case officer.'

Mike waited, but Vernon smiled back at him vacantly.

'And Patterson is here . . .?'

'In the Caribbean, with his girlfriend. Cuba, to be exact.' Vernon frowned, as though he'd personally recommended somewhere superior.

'And when might Patterson be coming back?'

'Oh, he's still got eight or nine days there. Maybe ten. Certainly eight.' Vernon nodded to himself, as if the exact timing of the delay would please Mike greatly.

They could, thought Mike, talk to the prison officers who dealt with Monroe; maybe a cell-mate if he had one. But Parole apparently knew little or nothing about how Monroe was feeling, how he'd been acting, or what he planned to do after release. More and more, the use of the Doyles' address was feeling like a concoction. Mike was sure Lucy was getting further into Monroe's life than he was, and she was sitting at a keyboard.

He was still interested in the correspondence from the sisters, and the arrangements they had suggested for Curtis's release. This appeared to be missing from the file.

'We've been told Monroe was corresponding with two people on a regular basis, but there isn't anything in here.'

Vernon now appeared less sure, more eager for this to finish.

'We, uh, don't usually record anything about prisoner correspondence. We're notified if the prisoner contacts anyone with a criminal record, or anyone to do with the victim. That's relevant to the parole decision, of course. I assume neither of those was the case here?'

Mike felt Vernon was definitely the person to know that, seeing as it was his job. All of Mike's remaining fellow-public-servant bonhomie fizzled away.

'You don't take notice of prisoner correspondence? Seriously?'

Vernon sensed the change of tone and decided he'd be safer behind the desk. His manicured fingers traced the edge as he moved, as if he were testing his underlings on the quality of their dusting.

'Until their release it's a security matter, Detective. For the prison, I mean: he's their responsibility.' Vernon folded his hands on one knee primly. 'When parole is being considered, we ask the prison whether the inmate has been in contact with anyone who'd present a problem.

In this case, quite the reverse. As you'll see from the orange section, their view was that corresponding with civilians was helping Curtis rehabilitate. Normalizing. It scored in his favour.'

'Did you run any checks on these, uh, civilians?'

'No need, Detective. The prison checks for criminal records. They also read each letter and verify that it contains nothing untoward. We have a Memorandum of Understanding.'

Vernon was starting to reach for protocols to hide behind, and that got on Mike's nerves. He was beginning to wish he could talk to a harassed prairie dog.

'Let me make sure I have this, Vernon.' Mike's expression was one of disdain. Vernon swallowed cartoonishly. 'A convicted rapist starts correspondence to, and from, two women. You're unconcerned for their safety, and view a rapist writing to women as a positive thing. You rely on the prison to check the letters, even though they're only checking for things relevant to them, such as escape plans. Also, you make no checks on whether the people he's writing to have any political affiliations, criminal intelligence against them, links to gangs or organized crime, or somesuch. Just assume that, if they have no actual criminal record, they're genuine and lovely people. Is that accurate?'

Vernon blanched and reflexively flicked a small Newton's cradle. They both listened to the clacking of ball bearings, as though tapping out the declining rhythm of Vernon's future career path.

'The M of U is quite specific, Detective. Prison is responsible until release. We have an input into the parole decision process but, like you, I imagine, we're recipients, not creators.' Vernon had passed from healthy to ashen in no time at all.

'Vernon, is there anything in here about what's in the letters, how often they're written, or when they're sent?'

Vernon looked down like a sports mascot during a stadium's one-minute silence.

'Anything other than the contact details; about where Curtis was going to live, and who already lives there? Anything about the women's safety, for example?'

More sombre mascot.

Mike stood silently and walked to the door. Vernon made one last plea for clemency.

'My team have heavy workloads. It's not possible to verify every-thing. I'm sure you sympathize with that difficulty, hmm?' One glance at Mike told him that he didn't. 'Detective, we . . . it's not our role, is it? I'm sure you understand.'

Mike opened the door a little. 'Oh yeah,' he said. 'I totally get how this all works, Vern.'

Sometimes parole officers were mines of unofficial but crucial infor-mation. But occasionally, as he suspected Vernon preferred, they behaved like an arm's-length excuse factory, hiding behind minimum standards and service-level agreements.

As he was nearing reception he was ambushed by a woman in a blood-red blouse and black pencil skirt.

'Detective? Do you have a sec?'

It was delivered in a hoarse whisper, and she beckoned him around the corner to a deep alcove. Down one side were rows of hanging files; on the other, a long kitchen counter with several guillotines, piles of plastic bindings and flat boxes of laminates.

'You asked Harper about Curtis Monroe, yes?'

Mike nodded warily.

'Sorry, you don't know me from Adam. I'm Aline Hanscombe. I work with Pete Patterson: he was Monroe's case officer. I did up that file you're holding, such as it is. I'm guessing Harper told you nothing?'

'Pretty much zero. Though I learned Vern likes high-quality coffee.'

She smiled, and settled back against the counter. 'Yeah, I think he brought that machine in because he thought if we made it for him, we'd spit in it.'

'I physically cannot imagine that. You heard something about Monroe?'

'Only what I cadged from overhearing Pete. We don't share clients, but we do share whinges. Pete's informal view – which can't be in that file – was that Monroe wasn't ready. Not that he hadn't tried to rehabilitate: he had. Monroe did all the courses going, kept himself tidy, all you could ask. No, it was more . . . Pete felt he literally wasn't ready. For the world. Hadn't been a responsible adult before he went in. Pete thought he'd backslide, sooner or later. Lack of the basic skills, Detective: gets most of them in the end.'

'I see. And where Monroe was going? The sisters?'

'Yeah, another issue. It was the one address presented to the parole board. But the sisters had provided a letter stating they'd give him a roof and food in the short term. Always a weird situation, I thought. The prison have photocopies of all the letters – you'd be able to get them. Apparently, nothing weird or crazy from either side: sports chatter, weather, this and that. Anyway, ask for the prison officer that covers the mail – Ben Appleby. The kind that likes to know everyone's secrets, you know?'

'Will do. Thanks, Aline. And by the way, your boss? Don't worry about him. Guy like Vern will move on to "fresh challenges" in months. You can mop up the debris then.'

She rolled her eyes, clearly praying for the day.

Chapter 6

Dana dropped her car at home and walked the five minutes to her office. It gave her another island in the day: she grabbed at solo time, as though she could haul herself to safer ground by clinging to it.

The footpath took her past the playing fields. Two swarms of girls were chasing a hockey ball with varying degrees of enthusiasm. At each end, a goalkeeper stood with sleeves pulled down to protect their fingers against the wind: an easterly was pouring in and it was now colder than it had been last night. Dana felt a sting of sympathy; crap at sports, picked anyway and banished, with the expectation that the goal was where they'd annoy the team least. An early lesson in group dynamics. Her kneecap fizzed in empathy.

Already, a couple of hours into the investigation, she could feel the pull of others' momentum wrenching her out of her rhythm: the fundamental difference between her true speed, and police speed, was starkly apparent. The case, and the culture, wanted her to skim like a windsurfer: carving out her own direction and ignoring the depths. But she wanted to dive long and stay submerged until she could surface on her own terms, sure of her line of reasoning.

Two reporters were waiting at the station reception. One was an old hand in a duffel coat who stayed seated, feet on a plastic stool, fixated on his crossword. A bright blue Thermos sat beside him, and she caught the faint aroma of tomato soup. The other reporter was a pretty young thing who'd look good in front of camera, but fluttered around Dana as she walked. A steely stare usually sufficed, but this newbie clearly thought that hanging about talking noisily was an impressive display of tenacity.

'Reese. Reese McCartney. Two c's. Do you have a statement about the murder?'

The woman had vivid blue eyes and smartened surfer-chick hair, and was surely destined for a Nightly Eyewitness Action News somewhere, alongside a silver-and-mahogany male newsreader thirty years older than her.

'Hmm. Reese. You'll notice that your fellow journalist there stayed seated.' She smiled back to the old man, who grinned into his newspaper. 'Randall knows me well and he didn't bother getting up, let alone invading my personal space and talking loud enough to wake the dead. You can learn from Randall, and save yourself some stress. Feel free to get a coffee, or have a cupcake, or play with your telephone. I'll make a statement at noon, and you'll get nothing before. Good morning.'

She turned and scanned her ID card. As she passed through the doorway she looked back. 'Hey, Randy.'

The old man lifted a hand. 'Hey, Dana.' He dropped it and moved on to 4 down – *Shakespeare's hero can't see wood for trees.*

Randall, she knew, had his sources. He could probably circumvent her, but he was wise enough to know that would work once: after that, he'd get the death stare from her each time. He was a wily old bird who could have retired a decade ago; he kept going because he didn't know what else to do. His beloved wife had died a month before he was intending to quit. Each time Dana met him she wondered what would become of him if, or rather when, his boss told him to pack it in.

Dana made a note that she'd have to stay on top of the media. Willie Fitzgibbon would likely blab to a journalist. Lots of civilians wanted to tell someone, as if they needed validation. Journalists were good at that, and Dana could tell from Willie's panicked response to having a day off that he needed the money. Lucy's text had confirmed she'd already gone full attack-mode at the Human Resources person at the refinery, who'd dared to suggest the police were overreacting a tad.

Usually, Bill Meeks would tackle the media and run interference for her – the perils of being the boss. But he was away today on a training course. What was it? Had a stupid name, she recalled. Leadership . . . Leadership . . . *Leadership – beyond the manager.* That was it. Bill had sworn you didn't get a certificate at the end of it; you got a printout of how high it sent your blood pressure.

There was another, more pressing aspect to the media: the Doyle sisters and their lawyers would have access to it. Dana liked to hold back details – especially crime scene details – in case it was an advantage. Whatever she gave to the reporters, or they discovered by other means, would probably be in play when she interviewed the Doyles.

She currently had a team of six, including her. Ali McMahon had been seconded for a day or two, for her understanding of Monroe's release. She would have some experience of family chemistry from her day job, which might help if the Doyle sisters continued to loom large. Lucy was admin/everything; Mike was second in command. They still had Rainer Holt on attachment from uniform for six months, and there was a part-time civilian investigator, Richard Wallace. Mike had worked with Wallace recently on a nasty homophobic assault, and rated him. It was a small enough group for her to feel a semblance of control. As ever, she hated doing the briefing.

They all filed into the incident room and spread around the room. Only one whiteboard filled – Lucy's writing was little more than the bare bones. Rainer still hadn't remembered to slouch while on duty.

Dana noticed Lucy and Ali picking opposite sides of the room. Richard went past Mike.

'Jeez, Rich,' whispered Mike. 'Those wheels were about an inch from my toe.'

Richard spun around, grinned and looked down. 'Take it from me, Mikey, toes are overrated.'

'Okay. This body –' she waved at several blown-up crime scene photos on a whiteboard – 'was found at 0630 today by a crusty old guy called Willie Fitzgibbons. He's a maintenance supervisor at the refinery; no record. He's also a part-time hunter, trapper, pelt collector. Not a suspect at this time. The body was, as you can see, staged.'

Dana took a deep breath, moving closer to the whiteboard to hide an emerging flush around her neck.

'The knot used on all the limbs is a single-column tie. It's a common knot in bondage situations, but especially for beginners to that scene. If you don't know what you're doing, but you don't want it to go wrong, that's the knot you'd use. It means anyone could and probably would tie it that way. So no particular insight: except that the perpetrator, or perpetrators, are not old hands at it.'

She'd been talking to the board to stem a tremor in her voice. She pointed to the crime scene photos and felt able to turn around. 'That location is on the way to the old quarry, out near Maritime. The nearest home is about a kilometre away – we'll come back to that – but generally, there's a whole lot of marsh, some trees and the quarry itself. It's about seven kilometres to the main road, around twenty minutes to Earlville.'

Ali lifted an arm. 'Boss?'

'You just need "Dana". Yes, Ali?'

'For reference – it's seven clicks by road to the main road, but there is an old trail that crosses a corner of the golf course: that's to the south. Possible way in and out on foot, if you know about it and you're gutsy enough to take on the swamp. I told the search team – they had it on their list.'

'Excellent. Thanks, Ali. Yes, we aren't familiar with this terrain, so have a look at the e-pack Lucy's sent you and get to know the basic markers, please. Whoever did this seemingly understood where they were, why it mattered.'

Dana pointed to a close-up of the victim's face, marvelling again at the apparent serenity.

'Victim's name is Curtis Mason Monroe. Only child; parents moved across the nation eight years ago. Age twenty-seven, released yesterday from Du Pont prison after serving nine of fifteen for the rape of Louise Montgomery. The rape occurred near where his body was found, so there's possibly a connection to the original crime. No sign of robbery – his wallet was still in his pocket – so the motive would appear to be personal.

'Death is believed to have been caused by a blow with a sharp, wide blade to the victim's left side, slicing the heart in two. More or less instantaneous. No post-mortem until this afternoon: my gut says probably axe, cleaver, scythe; something with that scale of blade, maybe a curve to it. There were more blows after the fatal one, so it's hard to be absolutely sure. However, someone might have played with him for a while.'

Rainer piped up. 'Sorry, any sign of other wounds? Bruises? Cuts?'

'No. A few minor scratches, but no evidence of defensive wounds.' Dana flicked through paperwork, before she found the medical records Lucy had conjured from somewhere. 'He had an old abdomen injury which I thought would be a prison shank. Not for the first time, I was wrong. He got it aged fourteen: tried to climb a fence and impaled himself on it. The good news was, it was the fence surrounding Earlville Mercy Hospital: that saved his life. The wound was about an inch from slicing his liver open, and that would have been *adios*.'

'Sliding doors, right?' interjected Mike. 'Three centimetres lower and there would have been no rape, and therefore no murder.'

Dana decided not to challenge the *therefore* at this stage.

'True, Mikey. For our purposes, that scar is way too old to be relevant here. There was some blood spatter around the fatal wound, though. Forensics should come through about that soon; for now, we should expect the assailant, or assailants, to have needed to clean themselves up.'

Rainer made notes, licking his lip as he concentrated, like a small child learning to write. Dana continued.

'Time of death is probably between 2200 and 0500. The state of rigor, the degree of decomposition, the amount of scavenging, all suggest one end of that window, but the ME won't commit further until after autopsy. Luce, you've retro-fitted the weather data?'

Lucy flicked back a page in her file.

'I absolutely have. Last night was a series of "rain events", each with a short dry period between them. The rainfall went west to east in a series of waves, so we use the radar and backtrack from known weather stations to guess trajectory and timings. It was raining at the crime scene from 2215 to 0115, then again from 0330 to 0500, which was the last of the rain. From the window on time of death the locum gave, whenever the fatal blow was delivered, there's a one in two chance it happened during the rain.'

Lucy looked back at Dana and beamed. It was the type of work no one else would have thought to do.

'Thanks, Luce. Willie Fitzgibbon heard the rain but didn't note the times, so we needed Luce to calculate it. The information yields three issues, as I see it. Firstly, it's needed by the ME for an accurate time of death: that might become important if we need to pin down alibis, travelling times, and so on.

'Secondly, that amount of rain compromises the forensics: there are no footprints, no drag marks or obvious tyre tracks that demonstrate how or when the victim was placed at the scene. He might have been there for hours, or put there and finished off a few minutes later: we have no way of telling. He has rope marks against his wrists and ankles, so he definitely pushed against *some* ropes in the last twenty-four hours. Not necessarily those ropes. Forensics are looking for skin tissue in the fibres, and fibres in the skin: that might also tell us if he was conscious when he was tied.

'Thirdly, I think killing in the rain may also speak to the degree of resolve in the actual event – it wasn't put off until the heavy rain finished. So whether it was planned for months or spur-of-the-moment, my thinking for now is that when the time came, it had a sense of urgency about it.'

It nagged at Dana that she didn't have much clue about motive and therefore found it hard to picture the perpetrator in the act – the degree of improvisation, or planning, or clear-up; the rush or calm; whether they lingered with the body after death.

'Now, in the last two years of his prison time, Monroe was corresponding with two local women: Marika and Suzanne Doyle. They share a cottage which is the closest human habitation to the crime scene. Stuart is currently there executing the search warrant. We have Suzanne in station; Marika was supposedly cross-country running, but she hasn't reappeared yet. Luce, you were working on background for them as well?'

Lucy spoke without referring to her notes.

'Absolutely. Suzanne is twenty-five, Marika nineteen. Sisters. Father – Orson – died in military uniform, but not like you'd think. A soldier went postal in training camp and wiped out three; the dad was among them. Mother – Mary – died four years ago, after a lot of mental health issues. She was found in swamp near the cottage. The sisters inherited the property, and some limited life insurance, which they spent in the first year. The cottage is just a one-bedder; practically worthless, given the state it's in. Suzanne works nights shelf-filling at the local supermarket; no idea what Marika does with her time. No priors; no links to intelligence, or other problems. As far as our records go, they're a low-income, low-noise duo. Oh, Suzanne used to be a top-class junior showjumper. I feel sure that's important to this case.'

'Yes, it is,' agreed Dana. 'Equestrian skill is always the first thing we look for, Luce.'

Lucy grinned. 'For reference, while the sisters were writing about once every two weeks, there's no computer record they ever visited Monroe in prison.'

'Good to know.' Dana's optimism at the crime scene had now dissipated: a reasonable start now felt thin. When she laid it out like that in the briefing, all they had was a vague sense of who died and where; no idea why he was dead, or who might have motive. 'So, I'll go around the room, and I want questions, please. No speculation, no answers: let's run with what we don't know, then start eliminating. Rainer?'

'I've been working with you guys too long, because I barely saw the dead body. The thing that stood out for me first in those photos was the shape of the framework. Does the cross signify something ritualistic? Was Monroe a born-again Christian in prison? Is it some kind of eye-for-an-eye, or paying for sins past?'

'Ali?'

'How did Monroe know his attacker, or attackers? Why did he seem to trust them? Why no defensive wounds? Did he meet them out there, or somewhere else? Was he blindsided? How long was that cross frame there?'

'Mikey?'

'Who has a motive? Who has a motive for *seeming* to have a motive? Is someone throwing us off with this cross? Why leave him somewhere that can be seen? Why not hide him, drop him in a swamp?'

'Richard?'

'Who else but the sisters knew where Monroe would be that night? Did Monroe go to that spot of his own accord, or did someone force him there?'

'Luce?'

'Where did Monroe go after release? Who picked him up from the prison? What was his route? What had he been doing in the hours between release and death? Where did he go?'

Dana looked at the whiteboard while she assimilated all the questions. She would need to be able to answer them all, in time. 'Okay, good. Thank you. From that, I get several strands of thought, so I'll apportion accordingly. Firstly, Luce points out that we don't yet know what happened to Monroe after release. If we can accurately track the time from the prison, we'll possibly stumble across the killer. This clearly isn't random or opportunistic. Who picked him up, where he went, did he spend money, did he get a mobile phone, where's he been sleeping? As comprehensive a timeline as possible. Rich and Luce – yours, please.'

'The letters?'

'Good catch, Mikey. What did Parole know?'

'Ah, Parole generally knew the thick end of nothing. No monitoring of the letters – they left that to the prison, and seemed pretty complacent both about what was in the letters, and that two women were corresponding with a convicted rapist. Monroe's parole officer is away in Cuba for another week or so. I did speak to someone else. Monroe comes off as trying to rebuild, but lacking the life skills and likely to reoffend. Not a repeat of his previous offence: more that he'd do something else illegal and slide backwards.'

'Ali, can you please go to Du Pont prison first and get any letters they've saved? Speak to . . .' Dana looked to Mike.

'Ben Appleby.'

'. . . about them. Also, anything you can get on Monroe's record inside – friends who were recently released, enemies. Check for the three D's: drugs, debts, disrespect. Who did visit him, if not the sisters? Also, if he found religion, or anything that plays into the staging, there should be a chaplain who might be useful. Use your judgement about who might have the inside view. Thank you.'

'Second, there's the iconography of the cross. As you say, Mikey, it's potentially a distraction. But that would be interesting in itself: who needs to bluff us? There are also the logistics: who built it, and when? That gives us a window not simply into who, but the degree of planning and therefore motive. Richard – that'll be you, please.'

'Third, there's the obvious link to Monroe's former crime. I think we all thought *family or friend takes revenge* as soon as we found out what Monroe had done nine years ago. We have to follow through with that, but I want an experienced eye and ear for Louise Montgomery. So that's you, please, Mikey.'

'Fourth, there are ongoing forensics and the post-mortem. Rainer, I need you on top of that, please. In particular, any evidence about where Monroe might have been, anything to indicate drugs or drink, any reason for the lack of defensive wounds, or any detail on the weapon or who might wield it. Those things will feed into what the rest of the team will uncover. Also, can you prepare whatever comes through from Stuart's cottage search, please? We'll all need to be on top of that.

'Personally, I'll be interviewing Suzanne Doyle. Luce and Rainer, can you keep trying to trace Marika, please? There's something about those sisters that doesn't sit right. As far as we know, their cottage is definitely where Monroe was supposed to head after release, but we have nothing yet to confirm that he got there. Okay, it's 0915 now. Reconvene at 1200 or before. Thanks, everyone.'

*

Mike looked across as they all dispersed.

'Ali, can I pick your brains?'

She seemed surprised, and wary. 'Sure.'

They parked on two edges of a desk, facing the whiteboard. Mike often found the positioning of the details on the board told a tale: what was currently most likely or unlikely. This whiteboard was random papers and photos. Not even Lucy had a take on where this was heading.

'I'm going to interview Louise Montgomery. You did Family Safety until your Achilles. I know you've never met her but, generally, what kind of thing should I do, or avoid?'

'Well, Mikey, you're an experienced detective: I don't want to patronize you or anything.'

Mike held up both palms. 'I have two teenage girls: I get patronized while my key's still in the door. I'm asking because I need to get this right, so treat me like I know nothing. Best way to learn.' He dropped his voice. 'I've interviewed victims of serious crime, of course, including a number of rapes. But not years later; not when it's settled in their minds and the attitudes have hardened. Usually when I see them it's all fluid and confusing: they don't know which way is up. All I have to do is guide them; they're soothed by someone knowing what they're doing. I'm sensing Louise will be different.'

Ali pursed her lips.

'Okay. Well, number one, don't walk on eggshells. She'll have had insensitive people around her in the past, sure. But she'll also have had people back off, try to avoid saying the wrong thing, unsure of the terminology. There comes a point where victims feel they're being treated like rare china and simply want a normal conversation with someone who doesn't pussyfoot around. She'll want you to treat her like an adult.' She chopped her hands for emphasis. 'At the same time, it's nine years ago. So while generally it's not as raw as it was, there'll be glimpses:

the trauma's still there. It might feel part of her now. So, don't be cruel; but no kid gloves, either. She stood in court and faced down Monroe from the witness box. That's as tough as they come. Don't baby her.'

Plus, thought Mike, her family had moved away years ago. Presumably, they thought she was sufficiently recovered that they could be physically apart.

'Number two,' continued Ali. 'When you tell her about Monroe being dead? Don't react to her reaction. People are often surprised by their own responses. I've seen relatives who appear untroubled by someone's death; people who confuse themselves by not crying or falling apart. She'll look for validation from your reaction to her. Don't give it. She needs to find her own path, not have it implied by your face. See?'

It wasn't something Mike had consciously thought about. As a detective, he was used to responses that were visceral, instant; half formed. They were interesting and relevant to the investigation. Louise had deep-rooted feelings that this news would jolt, but not create. Ali was right: he shouldn't set any moral tone at all.

'Anything else?'

Ali shrugged. 'Third, don't be her friend. You can assist in some practical terms – tea, coffee, tissues – but you're not her bestie. It's tricky when someone's vulnerable and hurting, but that distance would matter as much with a nine-year-old crime as a fresh one.' She looked slyly at the board. 'Fourth, well, I guess she's a suspect, isn't she? Motive, for sure. In the middle of the night, she might have no alibi. She lives an hour from the crime scene; would certainly know the terrain. That would be opportunity. So I suppose that's a reason for the distance thing as well.'

Mike had considered the same issue. On the other hand, nothing in the parole file suggested she'd even been told about Curtis's release: more likely was a bureaucratic *snafu* that she hadn't been informed. All the same, someone else might have tipped her off informally.

'You know the rest of the drill yourself. At least you're definitely the detective; your role is clear cut not simply for you, but for Louise. When I've dealt with someone like that, none of us were totally sure what my part was: I had a foot in Victim Support, and a foot in investigative mode. For all the training, there was a large grey area for me that you won't have.' She smiled. 'Can I ask one in return?'

'Of course.'

'I, uh, that is, I'm not quite sure how to take Lucy. I mean, she's been fine and all, but I kind of get the impression she doesn't need me at all to get this stuff done.'

Mike looked serious. 'Are you now, or have you ever been, a lawyer?'

She looked perplexed. 'No.'

'That's good. She really hates, and I mean hates, lawyers. I have no idea why. But if you're not a lawyer, she's fine. Look, Luce is extremely, ludicrously capable. She is pretty much omnipotent, but she's also generous. What she needs is your operational experience, your case expertise; she can't replace those herself and she's fully aware of that. Stick to the operational input and she'll start bouncing ideas off you. Don't hold back when she does – you've probably noticed that there's – *there are* – six of us, so all the ideas count. Some crimes just give off a vibe: I think we have a long way to go on this one.'

Chapter 7

Thursday, 1 August 2019. 0940 hrs

Suzanne Doyle was in Interview One, with her lawyer. Sally Dupree was a silky-haired local celebrity: she'd risen off a famously collapsed murder trial of a TV presenter some years ago, and had been coasting ever since. Sally wore kitten heels and had contact lenses to make her brown eyes blue. She lived behind electric gates with her third husband and seventh maid; the past three mayors of Carlton called her 'invaluable'; she was a trustee of several philanthropic organizations. Sally had appeared in the regional newspaper's Sunday magazine last month, parading two unnervingly formal children and a distracted shih tzu.

Dana was surprised; the hourly fee was surely way out of Suzanne's reach. But Sally was not, despite her website-acclaimed pedigree, a criminal lawyer in the main. Her speciality was tax: offshore trusts, vehicles and shells, *minimization, not evasion*. It bothered Dana that Sally was here because she was clearly doing someone a favour, but Dana couldn't yet decide who that was: it was unlikely to be Suzanne herself. Dana comforted herself that Lucy would be watching the video feed of the interview, drawing the same conclusion about the Dupree Paradox and doing some digging.

The first interview would be awkward; Dana feeling her way into how Suzanne was placed. Had Curtis even turned up at Suzanne's home? If so, did she know where he'd ended up? If so, what role did she play, if any?

Those answers were the ultimate destination, but she'd start elsewhere. From Suzanne's perspective, the investigation was currently a closed book and it suited Dana to keep her in the dark as long as possible. It was tempting to rush in and ask about alibis, motives, whereabouts and actions. But then Dana might blow it early on. Better, given the current lack of information, to gradually build by working around the margins. Until they had more forensics, detailed background on the sisters' lives was the most useful data interviews could provide.

Dana dealt with handshakes and introductions, and waited as the recorder began. Close Proximity allowed the taking of some clothing for forensics. Suzanne looked smaller and thinner in the standard-issue jumpsuit than she had at home; there, a long T-shirt under the cardigan had hidden exposed collar bones, and swamped milky arms. The jumpsuit took a decade off the twenty-five-year-old, but Suzanne looked more tired than ever. Now they knew she worked nights at the supermarket, they had a potential reason for that. But Dana remained of the view that Suzanne's was a marrow-deep fatigue: less to do with shifts, more with constantly fighting something that couldn't be beaten.

Dana took her time setting out her papers, while Sally Dupree checked her dazzling watch.

'How long have you and your sister lived in the cottage, Suzanne?'

Before Suzanne could draw breath, Sally dived in with a brassy, declarative voice unsuited to the room. It bounced around itself like an excitable puppy.

'My client is here as a courtesy, Detective. Perhaps we should establish *why* she's here, before she decides whether to assist you.'

Sally had a fox-that-beat-the-tripwire smirk. Suzanne gave it all a zombified thousand-yard stare. Her flinches said that, despite the façade, she was listening to each word. Dana looked calmly at Sally before resuming.

'I'd like to know when you and Marika began living in that house, please.'

Sally dropped a manicured hand onto Suzanne's arm to stay her. Dana knew a flinch when she saw one. 'Detective, we expect you to outline the nature of this conversation. It's my client's legal right,' she brayed.

Dana focused on steady breathing. 'Is that so, Ms Dupree? I've been a detective for five years, and I'm unaware of that statute. Please state it for me.'

'Don't you know your statutes, Detective? Huh. I would think that would be your bread and butter.'

Dana gave an amiable smile. 'Yes, it should be. I'm clearly ignorant on the subject. It would be a slam dunk for you to best me right now by giving the act, section and paragraph. Wouldn't it?'

Sally glowered. 'Keep it by the book, Detective.'

'Always.' Dana looked to Suzanne, who flinched again under her direct gaze. 'So, Suzanne, how long have you lived in that cottage?'

'Since I was ten or so.'

'It was you, your sister, Marika, and your mother, at that point?'

Suzanne scratched her palm. She had acne on one temple and freckles on each cheek. 'Yeah, we were living on the base before that. Then Dad died. Marika was little then.'

Dana saw Sally itching to dive in again, and wanted her to do so. Sally needed to be put firmly back into her box; her shenanigans were disrupting the rhythm.

'Three of you. It's a one-bedroomed cottage, Suzanne.'

'Oh, really. What are you asking her that for?'

Sally's voice pitched up at the end in faux indignation. Dana noted that her eyebrow had twitched in salacious interest. *One for the dinner party chatter* had been Sally's initial take, before her lawyer instincts kicked in.

'Ms Dupree.' Dana's finger and thumb tapped below the table. 'I'm guessing that since your famous case, you haven't troubled the law enforcement community with your expertise.'

Sally's outrage started to fade, demonstrating its own flimsiness.

'So let me bring you, and your client here, up to speed.' Dana opened a file purely for the silent pause it allowed. 'Suzanne is here because we have questions regarding a prisoner recently released for a violent crime. *That* makes her a key witness. The prisoner has some connection to Suzanne and her sister. *That* makes her a key witness. So in case I haven't made the point: Suzanne is a key witness.'

Sally glared like a child caught stealing from a purse. Suzanne gulped and started looking to the mirror for consolation.

'Now,' Dana continued, 'under current law in this state, I can treat Suzanne as simply helping us with the investigation; or I can treat her as something more. We call this distinction Close Proximity. We can divide witnesses into those we believe have information but no role; and those who may have both information *and* a role. The latter is Close Proximity: it changes the rules on what I can and cannot do with Suzanne. It means I can keep her here longer, and ask different questions, than if she were an ordinary witness. It also, as I'm sure you're aware, gives us immediate and automatic access to some forensic material and certain information, as of right. That includes bank data, details of property ownership, mobile phone and internet data, and information from public utilities and services.'

The laundry list was formidable: it was why the legislation had been challenged all the way, for several years. Dana glanced at Suzanne to make sure the implications were sinking in. They were.

'The distinction was first laid out in draft legislation four years ago. All appeals against it concluded last month, when it passed into statute. Suzanne is – as a judge has allowed and until a judge deems otherwise – a witness with Close Proximity. I will treat her, and question her, as such.'

The mere fact that Dana had received judicial consent for Close Proximity told Sally there was a lot more to the case, and Suzanne's relationship to it, that was being withheld. Not just by Dana: Suzanne was presumably holding back as well. Sally's mouth twitched but the Botox stopped too much change in her expression, which curled at the edges like warm paper.

'Now,' continued Dana, 'let's settle how I will behave towards your client. If you'd contacted your colleagues before beginning this case, as I'm sure you have, they would have told you this about me: I don't intimidate. I don't shout or scream or bang the table. I don't sneer, swear or insult. So let's dispense with the most likely scenario: you, attempting to impress your client by making some show of trying to slap me down. I'm not going to break the rules, and you know it. What your client needs from you is concern for her welfare, and legal advice when required. What your client will not need is protecting from my questions, or how I present them. Are we clear, Ms Dupree?'

'I fail to see what—'

'Ms Dupree. What you believe my motive might be is irrelevant to me, and to your client, and to this interview. It has no jurisdiction.' Dana's voice was calm and quiet. 'If you believe that I'm infringing Suzanne's rights in any way, you will definitely need to come at me with chapter and verse, section and paragraph, fire and brimstone. If you have that now, please, let's hear it. If not,' Dana drew back and turned a page in the file, 'perhaps we should continue with the interview and conclude as soon as possible, so that Suzanne can get some much-needed sleep.'

Sally sank back in her chair, beyond Suzanne's peripheral vision. Dana would have sworn Suzanne looked a little glad.

'Suzanne. A one-bedroomed cottage?'

Suzanne stared at the table. 'We all piled in together, Detective.'

Dana was about to add another question when there was a rap on the two-way mirror. One long, two short: Lucy.

'Excuse me, please. Interview stopped 0949 hrs.'

As Dana walked to the door Sally tried a consoling pat on her client's shoulder, met with a squirming recoil from Suzanne.

Lucy was waiting outside. 'Lawyer trouble. David Rowe's arrived. Says Little Miss Tax-a-doodle here was filling for him, because he was interstate overnight. He'll be representing Suzanne, and he wants a word with his client. Sorry, chick.'

'Damn.'

Suzanne was seemingly ready to talk. But the tape in the interview room had recorded the interruption, and nothing Suzanne said alongside Sally would now be admissible. A change of lawyers meant a required hiatus: Dana had to suck it up. David Rowe was good. Fair, but good. Dana needed to turn a drawback into some kind of benefit.

'Thanks, Luce. I'll be with you in a few minutes.'

She stepped back into the room and sat down, turning the recorder back on.

'Suzanne, another lawyer has arrived and will be taking up your case. I'm afraid Ms Dupree will no longer be representing you. Interview suspended, 0950 hrs.' She shut off both recorders. 'I'm sorry about that.'

Both Dana and Suzanne looked at Sally. Dana could feel the disdain billowing off Suzanne.

'David's here at last, is he?' Sally could barely clear up her papers fast enough.

'Suzanne, your lawyer will be David Rowe. He wants to speak to

you before we resume. I suggest we all break for some food and coffee
and when you and David are ready we'll speak again.'

Dana held the door open for Sally and inhaled a nauseating wave
of perfume as the woman passed. 'Goodbye, Ms Dupree. Always a
pleasure.'

Sally spun on her heel and nearly collided with David Rowe, who
gave her an over-chivalrous bow.

'Thanks for standing in, Duper,' he grinned.

Sally bustled down the corridor, feigning dignity. David watched
with an amused detachment and a quiet shake of the head, as though
Sally were a palomino who'd just screwed up in the dressage section.

'Hello, David.'

'Dana. That charming woman likes colleagues to call her *Super
Duper*. Imagine my working day.'

They shook hands. David was maybe ten years older than her, and
ageing well. He was sleek without being oily, and always gave an air of
being both controlled and highly competent. Dana would want a lawyer like him, and a friend like Lucy, if she was ever in trouble.

'To bring you up to speed, Counsellor: we're talking to Suzanne
under the Close Proximity rule, which began at . . . here it is, 0829 this
morning. We're looking for her sister, Marika, and we'll want to talk to
her as well, under the same rule. I'll ask for some refreshments to be
sent in. I'm looking to resume in around two hours, if that suits.'

'Absolutely. Thank you, Dana.' His client was tugging at her sleeves
and seeking solace in the floor. 'Better provide plenty of sugar if you
want her to stay awake.'

Chapter 8

Louise Montgomery lived in a medium-rise apartment block a few kilometres over the state border in the small town of Gerson. The town had lifted recently with the expansion of a nearby RAAF base, which now held a number of warehouses full of emergency aid. The runway had been extended to take heavy aircraft capable of airlifting supplies to any beleaguered part of Australia within hours. Floods, droughts, cyclones and bushfires were now the stock in trade: Team Gerson didn't think they'd run out of customers.

It was a modern apartment complex for second-time-buying professionals, with a gym that was never used after 7 a.m. The building curved around the three eucalypts that survived its construction. Across the street was a small strip of shops: an IGA that sold everything, a Thai takeaway, a physio's office, a hair salon and a petrol station. Mike guessed that Louise would live on the top floor: her past trauma would have made security the crucial purchase factor. There would be only one door into her home. This way she could see some humanity without having to touch it: a common pathology for serious depression, and survivors of major trauma.

Mike had phoned the management company of the complex; CCTV from the main exit and underground garage would be emailed to Lucy. He noted as he approached that a determined person might be able to leave and return without showing up on camera.

He buzzed the apartment.

'Who are you?'

'Louise Montgomery? My name is Detective Mike Francis, Carlton Police. I'd like a few minutes of your time, please, if I may.' He raised his ID close to the camera.

The pause was so long Mike wondered if she'd walked off, or was on her way down.

'Sixth floor, on the left.'

The scratchy intercom made it difficult to judge her mood. The lift held tenacious aromas of cleaning fluid and the vinegar used on the mirrored wall.

When he knocked on the apartment door it opened a few centimetres on the chain. He couldn't see her but heard a disembodied voice. 'Show me your ID again. I'll need to ring and check.'

'Of course.'

He passed it through the gap and the door closed for a minute. Mike glanced around the corridor. Paintings from attached-to-the-motel restaurants; each carpet tile was forty centimetres square.

A scrape of chain against metal, then three clacks, told him the door was opening.

Louise was a thirty-two-year-old in black jeans and blue sweatshirt, hair swept back by a yellow clasp, and deep-set eyes that looked more at the air around him than his face. She stepped back and he walked in, turning himself away from her as he passed close to minimize any sense of threat. To the right was an open-plan kitchen, leading to a living room where the TV was tuned to a jazz radio station. One armchair full of files and papers. A desk with a computer, a headset hanging from one corner of the monitor. To the left, closed doors suggested a bedroom and bathroom.

Louise didn't ask what this was about. After muting Beiderbecke, she returned his ID without glancing up. She indicated a lone dining chair that flattened itself against the wall like a spy, and she curled up on one end of the sofa opposite. As she sat, she shifted something in her hand and he caught a glimpse of a knife's ivory handle.

Mike looked at a stack of files. 'Sorry, interrupting some work?'

She glanced at the pile, as if it was likely to turn on her. 'I, I work from home these days. Online tutoring. Doesn't stop the paperwork, though.'

Mike waited for anything further, but she seemingly had nothing to give. As he'd expected, he found himself nervous having the conversation: being here felt monstrously intrusive.

'Louise, I'll come straight to the point. Curtis Mason Monroe was found dead this morning.'

Her eyes widened, then the hint of a smile was caught and withdrawn. She looked down. 'Someone killed him in prison?'

Mike watched. Was that a rehearsed response, to imply she had no idea Monroe was out? He tried to carry out Ali's advice: moral neutrality.

'Has anyone contacted you about him recently?'

'No.'

She picked up her phone and flipped it. 'I mean, that's not . . . I had a call a few days ago from someone claiming to be from Parole. They left a voicemail. I . . . check people out before I reply.' She waved at the files. 'But I was busy marking and, well, I never followed up. Perhaps I didn't want to. So maybe, yeah. But not . . . you know, I didn't get round to talking to anyone.'

'I understand. Did the person calling you give a name?'

Louise searched on the phone. She held it at arm's length as the message played.

'*Hello, Ms Montgomery. My name is Pete Patterson. I'm a parole officer in Earlville covering the case of Curtis Monroe. I have some information for you, but I need you to call me so that we can arrange to meet. I'd appreciate it if you could contact me at the parole office: the reception number is 555 2246. They can verify who I am and put you through. Thank you.'*

Her hand was shaking as she put it down. She shrank back a touch, as though Monroe's name on a message was poison enough.

'Did you know what Patterson wanted?'

'Nope. Couldn't be good, right? Nothing about Curtis Monroe was good.'

'Louise, you'll understand that we need to find out what happened to Monroe. So I have to ask you a few questions.'

'How did he die?' She couldn't look at him when she asked.

'We don't know much yet. We're trying to find out more. I know you moved interstate from Carlton a few years ago, and your family went west. Could you fill that out for me, please?'

She looked to her hands: her skin was sallow and dry, her movements skittish. 'We stayed in Carlton for a couple of years, until I'd finished teacher training. Then we all moved. My parents wanted to go out west. It's where the grandchildren are. I never provided any.'

She wanted affirmation, or at least acknowledgement, that her estrangement from the family wasn't her fault. Mike deadpanned it and saw the disappointment he engendered.

'I'm an hour from the airport here, so we're a few hours apart. Theoretically.' She rubbed her hand across her face. 'Anyway, after college I taught at the local school here in Gerson for years, but it got . . . I had some health problems.'

Mike waited patiently for her to continue. Birds swarmed across the view of a blustery sky, flicking a shadow across the room that grabbed her attention momentarily. She looked down as she resumed.

'I, uh, I struggled. After. They said I would. They weren't wrong.'

She gave a watery smile and grabbed the hem of her long sweatshirt like a childhood teddy bear. 'It was going okay for a couple of years. Five or six, I suppose. Delayed reaction – that's what you get for burying it. I tried, but I reached a point a few years ago where I wasn't improving, and then I started going backwards. Small things, but they added up. I created little rituals, obsessions. Work suffered. Workers suffered. My behaviour became increasingly . . . difficult for others. I know it did. *Hard to accommodate*, they said, in the final letter. They recommended me for a website. Government thing – online teaching of kids in remote areas and overseas. It's better that way. It's . . . doable.'

Mike took a punt. 'And your family – they don't know about this change?'

'No, they don't. After they moved, we drifted apart. Or I fell away. One of those. Both. They'd started to . . . started to tell me I should be over it by now. That I was letting it keep a hold of my life. They meant well, I know. But, uh, eventually, I got angry. And then the calls were less frequent. And they couldn't come at Christmas, because of the grandkids. Or any other time. But I was welcome to go there, whenever.' She drifted, as if he weren't there at all. 'But I didn't feel it. Welcome, I mean. So no, I didn't let them have my news.'

The confession hung in the air a while. Mike looked around with fresh eyes. A polystyrene box by the sink from a food delivery company. A hefty sag at one end of the sofa. The carpet showed no signs of fading from sunlight streaming in. The place didn't smell, as such, but it felt heavily lived in; the air was brackish, somehow. This woman never left her apartment.

'Is there no one you can contact? Or I could contact for you? There are people, experts, who specialize—'

'No.' Her cry echoed. She swept her hair with her hand. 'Sorry, I didn't mean to snap.'

No, he thought, *and you tried for years not to.*

She stood suddenly without seeming to quite know why, squinted at the front door, then sat again. The knife beside the cushion blinked at him.

'No, I don't want anyone . . . done all that. Done the *prescribed* thing.' She shoved her hands underneath her thighs, as if she didn't trust herself. 'This is my way of doing it. Sort of works. I've made my life smaller. Better that way. Once again, Detective, it's doable. And right now, that's enough for me.'

'Louise, I have to ask you about the last twenty-four hours. Where you've been, anyone you've seen, that kind of thing.'

She looked up, surprised. 'Alibi?'

He shrugged. 'Call it box-ticking.'

She looked around the apartment, almost as though she were seeing it for the first time. The closeness of the walls, the sense of everything being – *needing to be* – within reach of a person sitting down, rarely moving.

'I was here. I'm always here. I, uh, don't know how to prove that, if that's what you mean. Oh.'

She rose again, gathering the knife and pocketing it, and went over to the polystyrene box. She tugged a receipt from under some potatoes and passed it to him warily. 'The guy, he brought the box to the door. He'd have a time, I guess.'

Mike took the receipt and studied it carefully. Delivery was early evening: not an alibi for the murder. 'Did you speak to him?'

'No, he knows to leave it outside. We have an understanding: I only order if he's the one on shift. But I think he might've still been waiting for the lift when I brought it inside. Maybe.'

Mike waved the receipt. 'Thank you, we'll check it out. Anything else that might help us? You say you teach kids online? Maybe some records of that?'

'Oh, yeah. Um. Let me think.'

He realized that this kind of back-and-forth was becoming too quick for her; she wasn't used to it. Teaching kids didn't count. It held no personal emotional charge for her; it was a task. Whenever she cared, she lacked the skills for conversational speed. He made a conscious decision to slow down.

Louise reached to a wire in-tray by her monitor and passed a card, using the same wary body language. As he reached out to take it Mike noticed that, in this room at least, there were no photographs. Nothing personal at all, in fact.

'They're the agency,' explained Louise. 'They can tell you when I was teaching, and who. You could follow that up, I suppose.'

Mike took his time putting it in his pocket. 'Thank you. Anything else? Ever pop across the street, there?' He motioned to the string of shops and the traffic around it.

'No, never. Well, once a week to the ATM, Sundays. But not the shops. No. Sorry.'

'That's okay.' He made another note on his pad, again to slow the interaction. 'And you've no information that any of your family have been in this part of the country lately? Say, the last few weeks?' He knew it was a forlorn question, but he felt he needed to have asked it.

She snorted. 'They'd never come he— no, I have no information about that.'

'Do you own a car, Louise?'

'Yup. Honda. In the dealer in Gerson for the past two weeks. Gearbox problem. They say the part's got to come from Japan. I don't really believe— wait, you don't care. Uh, anyway, car's getting fixed.'

'Okay, well that's everything for now. Thank you, Louise.'

Mike stood and stepped towards the front door, and she followed, several metres behind.

'It might be possible we have to contact you again at some point. But I promise you, if that's the case, it will be me, and in person.'

She turned away: his promise tugged at her somehow. Her hand patted the knife pocket reflexively.

'Okay.'

He'd opened the front door before he half-turned and placed a shred of the notebook page on the chest of drawers. He spoke softly to the wall. 'If you ever want a . . . slightly bigger life. She helped someone close to me. She's good.'

Louise nodded silently and closed the door behind him. *Scrape. Clack. Clack. Clack.*

The corridor felt antiseptic and rootless, and a world away from the space behind the door.

Chapter 9

Rainer pulled up outside the Belmont residence. Marika was still elusive and so he'd decided to follow a hunch for a while. In the photo he'd printed out the home was forty years younger and immaculate in every way, gleaming on a summer's day with trees in full leaf. What he saw now was faded grandeur: an atrophied garden, dulled and peeling paintwork, smeared upstairs windows, a general air of neglect. The quoins at each corner were crumbling. Detritus lay where it fell, and nature slowly claimed it. Weeds infiltrated the gravel drive unhindered, colonizing a furrow down the middle. The chilly metallic sky, bare branches and standing water near the gate – they all added to a sense of accumulating distress.

The house was isolated, as though no one dared build near it. A century old, it had been constructed when labour was cheap, but craft was valued: it told in the details. Stone detailing, barley-sugar pillars at the entrance, and lions topping the gate posts. It was not the home of a landowner – that would have had a nod to farming or rural tropes; some form of Australiana. Instead, the feel was more old-school European – established, solid, virtuous. It was a house built on riches from things that couldn't be eaten or dug from the ground: a twentieth-century affluence. The Belmonts had been big in aircraft engineering.

The doorbell was an old-fashioned rope contraption, but he could hear the clang inside the house. He didn't realize there was an intercom until he heard a voice. 'Who the hell are you?'

The voice sounded older, ratty; impatient. Clara Belmont, he was sure. The newspaper article yielding the photo had said she'd be eighty-two years old.

'Carlton Police.' He announced it to the porch in general, unsure where to direct his voice. 'Is that Clara? Clara Belmont? My name's Rainer Holt. I have ID.'

He couldn't see any movement behind the door. But it was only glazed above eye level; perhaps she was there, but shorter than him.

The door opened with a squeal of complaint. Clara was in a motorized wheelchair, an oxygen masked clamped across her face. The plastic line ran to a cylinder held to the chair by a metal bracket. A red shawl was tucked across her lap like a blanket. She took a big puff and removed the mask; it made a sucking sound as it let go of her skin.

'Show me.'

He opened the ID and held it in front of him. It was, he realized, a test of how sharp her eyesight was. Most of the writing on the ID was tiny.

'Officer 7115 Holt . . . you're really police? You look about fourteen to me. Come on in, then. Take off your shoes. I pay that silly cow to clean, but she's hopeless. If you get mud in here, it'll never leave.'

She didn't wait for him, but instead hummed back into another room. While he removed his shoes he looked around the entrance hall. Walnut panels to dado height trundled up a half-turn staircase. A chandelier light had a third of its bulbs missing. Next to some hanging coats and discarded boots was a grandfather clock. Its mechanism was broken, light glinting off the tarnished metal façade.

He followed her wheel marks into a parlour of dark carpet, more panelling and a sandstone fireplace with a grate filled by artificial flowers. A large window at one end drew in a muted light, and held it from the far reaches of the room. The air felt musty and dead – old books, closed doors, silent hours and forgotten coffee. Clara had resumed a position by the window, feet nuzzling a cast-iron radiator; the threadbare tracks in the rug announced this was her usual eyrie. To her right a second cylinder lay waiting, already linked to a mask. To her left, a half-done jigsaw was scattered across a slanted table, bespoke for the hobby. The New York subway map. He pointed. 'Tricky to do?'

'Not that bad. The stations are the easy bit: I lived there for thirty years. The white gaps in between are a bitch.'

He settled into a winged chair that also looked out through the large window. She had a perfect view of the corner: high enough to see over a low hedge and looking down the long straight to the lights of the petrol station. A narrow road snaked to the left, down towards the Doyles' and then on to the quarry. Rain was falling to the east in diagonal cascades, but moving away.

'Beautiful house, Ms Belmont.'

'Ah, don't give me that "muzz" crap. It's Clara.' She fussed wistfully at the shawl. 'And yes, it was lovely. Once. God knows what upstairs is like now.'

'It's from about 1900, or so?'

'Very good, young man. 1905. Either you know your architecture, or you looked it up on the internet?'

He blushed, caught. It seemed to warm her.

'Busted,' he said. 'You owned the place long?'

'Well, it's always been in my family. I'm the last one left. Forgotten Queen of the Belmonts. I was born upstairs, and I damn well intend to die here.' She rapped her knuckle on the arm of the chair for emphasis. Her fingers were wiry and vein-strewn, but still had suppleness and strength.

Rainer gave her a sidelong glance as she fumed. One of the things

Dana had taught him was to listen to the gaps. 'Intend to die generally, or intend to be specifically here when it happens?'

She looked at him for a second. Her voice softened. 'Oh, both. Definitely both. And bless you for asking direct. Too many people tiptoe around it.'

They sat in amiable silence while she harvested another puff. Rainer wanted to burst into the questions. But he was sure Clara didn't get much conversation.

'Please eat that, young man.' She pointed to a slice of something on the table between them; maybe carrot cake, wrapped in unfurling butcher's paper. 'My cleaner means well, but I'll gag on the gluten. Choking to death on crumbs is a bit undignified for a family of our achievement.'

Rainer felt obliged and scooped it up, holding the paper under his chin as he ate. 'The oxygen?' He indicated the spare tank.

'Emphysema.'

She noted his attempt at an empathic look. She waved her hand dismissively. 'Oh, forty a day since I was sixteen; don't go feeling sorry for me. Not now, of course – none of these idiots will bring me a pack.' She slurped from the type of water bottle he normally saw in hospitals. 'It'll get me in the end, but no one can tell me when, or exactly how. Damn oxygen and modern science: I'm sick enough to hate it all, but just healthy enough to carry on living.'

Rainer swallowed a lump of the greasy cake and looked around. The double doors opposite the window were ajar; he could see the end of a bed. She'd clearly abandoned a large part of her home.

'What if there's an emergency when your help isn't around?'

'With any luck I'll croak out, and my grabby little nephew inherits the house. Then he'll find out it's mortgaged to the hilt, and a touch beyond. I may have forgotten to mention that to him.' She leaned towards him, conspiratorially. 'You know, he rings me every month, exactly the same time. He calls me because his telephone reminds him. Little bastard.'

Rainer smiled. 'No, but seriously, Clara?'

She pointed to what looked like a fat biro hanging from a thin chain around her neck.

'I hit this button, they're supposed to come running. Being a profit-chasing bunch of hyenas, it's more of a light jog.' She held it in her hand, dubious. 'I used to push it accidentally, bending over. So then we agreed I'd have to press it three times – one, two, three – for them to know I meant it. Like a bat signal, but for old women. A batty signal, in fact. Ha.'

He grinned. There was a gold carriage clock on a shelf above the spare oxygen: it had a twisting mechanism that drew his attention momentarily.

'Clara, we're looking into a death that took place last night, down towards the quarry. Have you heard anything about it?'

She scuffed some lint from her lap to the floor. 'Absolutely. Little Miss Fusspot comes in here each morning to change the bottles and get on my nerves. So yes, I heard. Some of you stupidly refuelled their cars at gossip central down there.' She jabbed a finger towards the petrol station. 'Not surprising old Barney got the basics out of them. What I heard is some man with his guts hanging out, lying on the ground like he was stapled there, yes?'

'You don't seem too startled by it.'

Clara sniffed and stared out of the window. 'Well, I didn't know him, so he's nothing to me. I know four people. Five, now you've turned up.' She scowled momentarily. 'Besides, I was a nurse for *Médecins sans Frontières*.' Her French accent was impeccable. 'Saw all kinds of injuries – machete attacks, torture, landmines; all of it. People can be animals, young man. I'm not afraid of a little gore. But I sense you are.'

She turned a sharp look towards him, and he found both her

directness and her accuracy unnerving. But it was, he reminded himself, good for the investigation that she was so precise.

'Did you see anything at all yesterday? Movements along the road?'

'Hmm. Yesterday? There's a milk truck that goes past here about eleven, but he must have been late because I was eating lunch when he passed. He toots, even if he has no idea whether I'm here or not. Or, I suppose, because he always knows I am. Anyway, he was late.'

She ran a finger through the dust on the windowsill, tutting.

'Now, afternoon, I saw Marika Doyle on her little motorbike thingy again.'

Rainer raised an eyebrow. 'Marika has a motorbike?'

'Not a motorbike. I don't know what those stupid machines are called. You sit like you're on a horse, but it has four wheels. She got it after Mary died.'

'A quad bike?'

'Yes, yes, that's it. Slow as hell; might as well be a horse. Makes an infernal racket when it goes past; I can hear it from the kitchen. She'd been out early morning, but only as far as the petrol station – I could see her fill up and come back. No friendly toot from that girl, I can assure you. I also heard the engine after dark, but it wasn't going past: it was pootling around in the distance somewhere. Maybe nine, or ten? Not long after ten, definitely, because I was still up listening to the radio.'

'Maybe the sound of your heavy-metal music drowned it out later?'

She looked out of the corner of her eye and twitched a smile. 'More of a Sibelius girl, myself. No, I still hear the engine if she isn't going past the house: it's a bit of a bowl down there, and the wind's usually from that direction.'

'No other movements apart from that?'

'Well, Marika went out lunchtime. Then I didn't hear her come back until mid-afternoon. Here's the odd thing: going out, she was the only one on the machine, but on the way back she had company. I've never seen anyone but her on that thing. Suzanne always walks past here – dark, rain, whatever. Must take her an hour to get to that supermarket. But yesterday, Suzanne and a big chap were sitting on the back. They looked cold as hell, too. None too comfortable, I'd imagine.'

'Could you see much, if they were all wearing crash helmets?'

Clara smiled. 'Ever the police officer, eh? *She* was wearing one: Princess Marika. God forbid anything happen to her precious little mind. The other two? Nothing. She would regard them as disposable, I shouldn't wonder.'

Rainer adjusted himself in the chair. 'We have to be exact about the timings, Clara. Definitely when?'

'Hmm. Yes. That was a few minutes after four. The news had finished, and they'd just started the weather forecast. I watched them coming up the road there – ridiculously slow, with three people on it. The thing sagged at the back and I wasn't sure they'd make it.' Clara narrowed her eyes, as if re-seeing the incident. 'She took the corner too ragged, as always, nearly toppled it. Ballast at the back probably kept it on the road. By the time they'd gone past, I'd missed the damn forecast. So yes, a few minutes after four.'

'And can you describe the man on the back?'

'Well, he's your dead man, isn't he? So you'd know what he looks like. The only other person who went down that road yesterday was the scraggy old one with the ute. I've seen him a few times. He came back this morning, same time as some of your lot. So one of the two men is accounted for: the other one must be the dead man.'

Rainer thought back to the maps he'd seen this morning, and Dana's briefing. 'Unless someone came through the golf course: you wouldn't see them then.'

'Yes, that's true. Although that area – between the quarry and the golf course – is full of bogs; total quagmire. They move, too: rise and fall across the seasons. If you knew what you were doing, you might possibly make it. Possibly. No doubt Marika could do it with her eyes shut. But a stranger would misjudge it, and die.'

'All the same . . . the man on the quad bike?'

'Uurrgghh, if you insist.' She lifted her hands and held them in front of her, as if framing the memory with her fingertips. 'Maybe thirty, scruffy, white. He was wearing jeans, one of those tracksuit tops with the hood. Really short hair, almost bald. He looked cold, and pretty unsure where he was going.'

'What about the women? How did they seem?'

She fixed him with a sardonic look, as if he needed to play catch-up if he wanted to ask her serious questions.

'Seem? Oh, I know those two of old. They *seemed* exactly the same as always. Marika had a smarmy, know-it-all look on her face, but probably none too excited about finally having to share her precious machine. Suzanne looked startled, like someone had prodded her with a knitting needle.'

'You've known the sisters a while, then?'

'Oh, yes. They've lived down there for, oh, well over a decade: fifteen years, maybe? Mad Mary brought them, crazy old coot that she was. Before all this –' she flapped the oxygen cord – 'I used to be quite mobile. In years gone by I babysat Marika, while Mummy took Suzanne to her bloody horsey events.'

She stopped, and he was about to ask another question when she suddenly resumed.

'Awful, awful child, that Marika. Hateful. Something . . . *off* about her. I refused to babysit, after a while. I'd have killed the little brat, I swear.'

'A handful?'

'Oh, young man, you don't know the half of it. Malice in every pore. Always a fight with her, always. What to eat, what toy to play with, bedtime; all of it. I mean, it all had to be a scrap, all the time, and she had to win. I was sympathetic at first, given Mary's problems, but, well, I came to despise it. Despise Marika.'

The recollection shortened her breath and made it audible; a scratchy wheeze that sounded painful. She took a big gulp of oxygen, and he waited for her to settle down and nod that she was able to continue.

'And Suzanne?'

'Hmm, well, I saw less of her, of course. Her being away show-jumping was why I was babysitting. But generally? Pretty and mousy; apologetic. But both were, uh, very much conditioned by their mother. To say the least.'

'Oh?'

'Hmm. Good with the little prompts, aren't we? Well, I was a nurse, not a psychiatrist. But if I say loony tunes, you'll get the meaning. Mary never got over her husband dying, I'd say.' Her voice lost some of its abrasive confidence. The recollection clearly made her emotional, for all the tough-love brusqueness. She clasped the edge of the shawl tightly. 'Mary channelled both the girls into tight little corridors of being: she seemed terrified that if they broadened their horizons in any way, she'd lose them. Fear of loss, generally, I suppose. That's why she always went to horse events with Suzanne – didn't want the girl evolving or maturing, oh no. As a mother, she was either/or. I mean, she either loved them and suffocated them, or they were pretty much dead to her. No in-between.'

A shallow rumble turned out to be the milk lorry hustling past. When it tooted, Clara squealed with delight like a six-year-old.

They shared a smile.

Chapter 10

Ali sat in a corridor that doubled as the reception for the prison admin block. It was outside the walls of the prison itself and so required no special security measures, but they were clearly not used to visitors there, even from law enforcement. A water cooler bubbled every couple of minutes, but no one used it. She heard raised chatter and then a smattering of applause from a meeting room nearby; several people passed her and offered a tight smile.

The journey to Du Pont prison had taken her down the thirteen-kilometre causeway from the highway, across a wide lagoon of putrid water and sucking mud. It was the sole way in or out of the area: the prison allegedly deliberately emptied its waste into the broiling swamp surrounds to make them even less appetizing. The causeway was barely wide enough for a road: so narrow that drivers inching past each other could shake hands. When there was an escape alert, teams of dog handlers fanned out across the tarmac: Dobermans straining and reaching in a scene that appeared to wind back the decades. For that reason, the causeway had been named Eaglehawk Neck Road.

Du Pont seemed to revel in its brutal Victorian splendour, a historic monument still serving its original purpose. The brickwork – especially the double wall surrounding the entire complex – had to be sprayed twice a year to stop mould from simply eating it. Fog slithered across it daily, drizzle fell on it constantly; what gnawed at the prisoners was not merely the fact of incarceration but the double insult and psychological damage of incarceration *here*. Du Pont had by far the worst record in the state for suicide and depression among inmates, and many put it down to the building itself.

She'd emailed Ben Appleby before leaving, with requests for various data. When she'd checked her phone, she'd seen his reply and promise it would all be ready for her. He was now tied up with a meeting and she had twenty minutes to kill. She preferred activity to deliberation: twenty minutes gave her an unwelcome chance to consider the impending divorce, the sale of what she'd laughably called 'the forever home', and the likely vista of the dating disasters she'd married to avoid.

Before leaving the station she'd bumped into a colleague from Family Safety, and told her about working under Dana Russo for a few days. Amid the general acceptance that Dana was clever, several choice phrases came up: *loner, straight edge . . . not a real detective.*

Ali could see the first – Dana appeared to take every opportunity to stand apart from others, even when a clump of them were working ten metres away at the crime scene. It didn't feel to her like Dana was being rude, though it looked it.

The second seemed more implied than demonstrated. Dana was unfailingly polite – Ali had never heard 'please' and 'thank you' so often – and spoke softly. Apparently, Dana was some kind of whiz at interrogating suspects, though Ali felt that claim unconvincing. But there was no doubt Dana was by-the-book. Ali found it reassuring – her current boss habitually massaged performance figures and skirted workplace rules on secondary incomes. He regularly appeared late in the office, carrying stock for a one-man company selling sports memorabilia. It was a change for Ali not to be taking a sly check of whatever the boss was doing in case she got sliced by the resulting shrapnel.

The third was more problematic. Someone couldn't, surely, lead a murder investigation if they weren't a proper detective? Ali's colleague suggested that, while Dana had been a detective for five years, she still lacked some of the basics. Nearly four years in Fraud, largely tracking criminals from her office, had left Dana with no feel for what was happening in the criminal community. Each case, her friend said, was a one-off for Dana: solvable by staying in the station while others worked the angles. Dana had no well of basic knowledge of crime in her area. She seemingly swooped from on high, left the legwork to others, and got the glory when the confessions came. It was heavily implied that Mike Francis was a saint for working alongside her, apparently not rated higher than her by the current hierarchy.

'Ali, is it?'

She stood to shake hands with a tall man whose forearms were a sea of tats; a sleeve on both arms extended above the elbow. Ben was wiry, had thinning hair and droopy eyelids, as though he'd just woken and would be fully with her in a minute. The starched and clipped movements said ex-military.

'Come on through.' The door squealed as rubber draught excluders fought for grip. 'We've had the decorators in, so I can't offer you a seat in our offices. Mine reeks of paint – I get a migraine in about ten minutes.' He carried on speaking over his shoulder as she scurried to keep a pace he would probably term *brisk*. 'Prison service paint: they buy in bulk and we get the same crap they use in the cells. At least when we go crazy and start licking the walls, we won't get lead poisoning. Here, we can use this while the boss is out.'

He motioned her into a large office that had a circular meeting table at one end. With the door closed, it had a quiet, contemplative appeal.

Ali opened a notebook. 'Sorry this is short notice. We're looking for everything we can on Curtis Monroe; especially his release.'

Ben held open both palms. 'Ah, not surprised to get some kind of call, to be honest. I'd thought he was destined to come back. I was Curtis's case worker in here for a couple of years. I stopped around 2015, when I took on some other stuff. Got fed up with dealing with prisoners' lazy bitching. Once you're incarcerated, you get incredibly agitated about someone taking your toothpaste, or whether someone else got more dessert than you. It's like dealing with tall children, and I ran out of patience with it.'

'Curtis was a pain in the butt, then?'

He smiled and passed over a file of photocopied material. There was even a contents page. 'To be fair, he was one of the better ones. We try not to set too much store on what they came in for, but you know: how positive can you feel about the potential behaviour of a rapist? But no, Curtis was quiet and pretty easy-going; found his place in the unit fairly quickly and wasn't any trouble. Considering his lack of education, he was a pretty good reader, so we were able to tap into that and get him into some programmes.'

The answer surprised Ali, who'd assumed any sexual offence meant the prisoner was some kind of problem: either their behaviour, or the attitude and intent of other inmates.

'Model prisoner?'

Ben shrugged. She was liking him more now they were talking. He'd been a bit stiff and stand-offish at first, but she could sense he enjoyed interacting with the prisoners.

'Inasmuch as they can be. Sex offenders are sectioned off a lot from the mainstream prisoners, naturally, so that helps. Curtis muled drugs around the complex, but they all do that. In fact, it's solidly not in their best interests to refuse. But there's those that do it for obligation and their own safety, and those that join the club, as it were. Curtis wasn't interested in drugs, or gangs, or a lot of that. So yeah, we couldn't fault his stay with us; and we couldn't oppose his parole even if we'd wanted to.'

It tallied with what little Mike had gleaned from Parole, and what she'd seen of Lucy's research so far. She felt frustrated that there wasn't a clear line of sight from Curtis's prison life. It was the obvious place to look but there were no fight reports, no reprimands in the contents sheet of the file. Nothing to indicate Curtis would have a serious problem less than twenty-four hours after release.

'No problems with other prisoners?'

'Look –' he flicked the edge of the file nearest him with a fingernail – 'no prisoner here is exempt from hassle, okay? I mean, even the quiet ones: they get picked on, that kind of thing. It isn't possible to sail through unhindered. But Curtis never started anything; never caused friction; never represented a threat to a prisoner or the staff.' He spread his hands. 'What can I tell you? Low maintenance, did his time.'

Ali got the feeling there was something beyond these responses, but her reach was flimsy. Prisons were one-offs: the data was partial and loaded. The supplier of the information always had an angle or preference, and verification was all but impossible.

'Did Curtis discover religion in here, in any way?'

Ben raised an eyebrow, as though it was an odd question. Ali didn't think so; plenty of prisoners did find religion, or pretended to. 'Religion? Curtis? Nope. I mean, he went to Christmas events and suchlike, but they all do that. Free food, a few chocolates, in return for miming to some carols. But no, never joined a Bible-reading group or anything like that.'

'Hmm. Who were his friends in here? Anyone released recently?'

Ben's tone had turned a little patronizing, she believed; it left Ali not quite trusting him. She felt as though she'd met people like him before, and it hadn't ended well.

'Look, in prison, you don't have friends. You have a bunch of people you must stay on good terms with because you're locked away with them twenty-three hours plus. It's . . . strategic, in your interests. You don't have to like 'em, just get on. Curtis got on. I wouldn't say he had anyone he confided in, nor did he have anyone out to get him. He was bland, to be honest.'

'I see.'

She reached for something Mike had mentioned as she was heading for the door. 'Was Curtis ever mixed up in any gangs here?'

Ben narrowed his eyes. It was clear he didn't welcome the question. 'Gangs are for outside, Ali. It's not like the movies. You'd be amazed how well prisoners and prison officers get on. I mean, we're both in here together; we have to get on in some ways or there'd be carnage. So no; no gangs. *Cliques.*'

It was evasive, but Ali knew she had no real way of proving him wrong.

'Cliques, then?'

'Yeah, he milled around with a few. Don't forget, he was in here for nine years: longer than most. But nothing major; low-level stuff. Curtis was never a worry, Ali. Never in our sights for anything significant.'

It was perfectly possible that Curtis Monroe was exactly as he was being described; a time-server who created no waves and left no impression. But to test that, they would have to use other means. Ben Appleby was stonewalling; she felt rather than knew it. But he was sure of his ground and controlled the flow of information. Probably better to come at that another way, than antagonize him.

'Could you explain the policies on letter-writing? We were a bit confused.'

'Ah, yeah, I sensed that.' He rested on his elbows again. She assumed that this was less threatening ground for him.

'Look, each prison is different. Last place I worked at they were strict, but it's down to each governor. This one, he encourages all kinds of letters as long as they aren't –' he air-quoted – ' *"related to escape or criminal activity, or uttering profanities or obscenities"*. I had to memorize that bit. Basically, prisoners who can write without swearing or begging for nude photos can carry on, as long as it's fairly vanilla. We read each letter in and out, and photocopy a dip sample. If there's nothing untoward, we have nothing we can mention to the parole board either way: it's simply noted that the prisoner wrote so many letters, and received so many letters.'

Again, she was annoyed that nothing solid was coming out of this. She'd expected some revelation about Curtis's state of mind, or plans.

'You don't check the bona-fides of the people they write to?'

'We run criminal records checks, but that's about it. If the letters aren't telling us to look further, we don't have the time for fishing expeditions. Of all the things we need to give attention to, innocuous letters aren't a priority.'

She raised an eyebrow. 'Okay, but if a rapist is writing to women?'

Ben smiled and raised his hands. 'Yeah, of course I looked into that, when I saw who Curtis was writing to. For that reason, this file has a photocopy of each letter in either direction.'

Outside, a bell rang briefly, but Ben didn't seem to flinch. 'But you'd be surprised,' he continued. 'Most rapists get letters, and many are from women. Lots of abuse, but not always. Same with murderers. Some people have a hobby, almost; they write to lots of prisoners, and they see it as some kind of humanizing thing. Often works, too: prisoners respond in kind, and it's a way of reminding them they're actually people and not animals.'

It made sense intellectually, but she couldn't shake an internal shiver at the mere thought of it. She usually dealt with family offences all day: the idea of any convicted sex offender getting succour from the kindness of strangers appalled her.

'Others get a bit of a thrill out of it, maybe –' he shrugged – 'or have some interest in crime generally. It's like people who watch true crime – being interested isn't the same as wanting to do it, or condoning it. But if the prisoner is here for sexual offences, yeah, we look closer. And we did.'

Ben turned the file and flipped to the third document – a report for the governor on the letter-writing. 'It was the women who wrote first, so Curtis didn't start the conversation. That matters, in relation to our policy. I rang the two women concerned and spoke to a . . . yeah, here, Marika Doyle. We chatted about why they were writing to Curtis in particular, and what they expected, and where the limits were.'

Ali made a note. She felt Dana would be interested to hear that Marika, despite being the youngest and seventeen when the letters began, seemed to have made the first move in the communication. Also, it struck her that, several years ago, the Doyles had a landline that they didn't have now. 'So why were they writing to Curtis?' she asked.

'I noted everything: you always need half an eye to something coming back to haunt you.' He flicked until he found a handwritten page. 'Ah, here we are. Marika said that the crime had taken place a short walk from their house, so they'd always wondered about it, and felt affected by it. They'd watched the news at the time, and decided eventually to find out more about the person: not the crime, the person. They understood the rules; they knew I'd snap the whole thing if either end stepped out of line. But I have to say, they were both faultless.'

'Nothing ever . . . how do I want to say it . . . escalated? No hint of anger on either side, for example?'

'Nope. Not at all. Curtis wanted to know about life outside generally. His family cut him off after the trial, and he didn't seem to have any friends beyond the walls, or inside them. I think he felt he'd lose touch with reality. So they told him all about new technology, sports news, general life stuff. Personally, I found it tedious to read, but Curtis genuinely got something from it. I asked him about it from time to time, and he thought the sisters were great. I got the impression he hadn't felt helped often, and I had to admit those women had done that.'

'He was worried about being released?'

Ben smiled. 'Good catch. Yeah, a lot of them are, especially if they've been in a while. Institutionalized. They don't know how the modern world works, and they feel they stand out a mile. That leads to conflict, which they aren't good enough at side-stepping or defusing. So they end up back here. That's what I expected with Curtis: he'd get tied up in some kind of low-grade problem. He wasn't experienced enough at being an adult in the outside world – never lived alone, for example. One transgression would break parole; he comes back to complete the final six.'

It still wasn't making sense to Ali. Two sisters; one was ten when there was a horrendous crime near their home. Seven years later, they befriend the man who did it.

'What about the sisters? What did they want to know?'

'Oh, they were the opposite. They knew little about prison life. They wanted to know what it was like in here. A couple of times they got personal, wondering what Curtis felt about the crime. But mostly, it was chitchat about how prisoners stayed fit, did they watch movies, was it noisy, or cold. Just general curiosity.'

'Were the sisters contacting anyone else in the prison? Ever try to visit?'

'Not that I'm aware. They were on a watchlist that we keep on file. If they'd tried to visit, or contacted staff, we'd have matched their names. And I've checked the visitor logs again: no visits, or applications to visit. In fact, apart from a couple of journalists who tried and failed in the early days, Curtis had no visitors at all.'

'Wow, that must have hurt.'

Ben's voice, which had softened over the interview, sharpened up. 'Yeah, well, he should have tried not being a rapist, then. Look, we try to treat prisoners with respect, but we can't be surprised that no one wanted to come see Curtis, after what he did.'

Ali realized she didn't know much about the crime itself; merely the bare bones. Perhaps she should have read up more before leaving the station; Curtis was the subject matter, after all.

'Can you tell me anything about the lead-up to Curtis's release?'

'Sure. All the paperwork is in there, along with a pre-hearing file, and anything else I could think to throw in.' Ben scratched at his forearm, where she could see a couple of fresh mosquito bites. 'Bottom line: he got to the point where he was entitled to a parole hearing, and the sisters volunteered to take him in. All his communication with them was by letter, as far as I know – he usually sold his phone credit in return for protection – so I'm fairly sure he didn't ask or expect. No log of any call to their home number from this complex, except the one I made to Marika back when. They said they could take him in for a couple of weeks; no more, because they didn't have a lot of space.'

'You can say that again,' she murmured.

'Oh?' Ben's interest flicked upward sharply.

'One bedroom. Three people, including Curtis.'

Ben was wide-eyed, before puffing out his cheeks. 'Jesus. Parole should have been all over that. How did they miss it?'

'Don't know yet. They're pushing all the responsibility back on you guys. We're caught in the middle of the dogfight.' She put down her notebook. 'Off the top of my head: the address was Weaver's Cottage, so possibly they assumed it had enough bedrooms? Or maybe they never dreamt two women would offer a place to a rapist in a one-bedroom home.'

'Christ. I mean, I never saw Curtis raise a hand in here, but, Christ. You know what happened to him?'

'We know he's dead. But we don't know if he even went to the sisters' place.' She leaned forward. 'I don't suppose . . .'

Ben folded his arms, smiling. 'What, that we have CCTV of him leaving here, and whose car he got into?'

She laughed. 'Yeah, and next week's lotto numbers.'

'If I knew those, I'd have a ticket and I wouldn't be sharing. But yes, as it happens, we do have footage.'

Her turn to be amazed. 'No way.'

'Yes way. The new governor arrived about six weeks ago. He has this thing about filming prisoners as they walk away. His last place, they'd caught some armed robbers picking up a buddy, and simply driving straight to the next bank job. After that, he decided to make it standard operating procedure there, and now here. We had the cameras put in ten days before Curtis left.'

He reached into his shirt pocket and dropped a memory stick onto the table. 'We have weird protocols about emailing footage from any of our cameras. Some of it ended up on YouTube last year so, you know . . .'

She grinned. 'You've already looked, right?'

'Couldn't resist. White Nissan, probably a rental. Two women in the front. Clear enough to identify them, if you know who you're looking for.'

He spread his hands.

'Are we good, or are we good?'

The prison chaplain, Father Peters – 'call me Terry'– was waiting when Ben Appleby dropped Ali back at the main office reception. The handover was, she thought, noticeably cool.

With the sun out, they found a couple of white plastic chairs in a sheltered outdoor corner that wasn't blasted too hard by belching air conditioners. A metal bucket was filled with sand and cigarette stubs. A butcher bird twirled its vocals in the distance. Without a breeze, it was almost too warm.

'You wanted to know about Curtis Monroe?' His voice sounded blunted, somehow; it still carried the soft rain of Nova Scotia, despite thirty years in Australia.

'Yeah, we do. He spent the last nine years here; there's a limit to what we can discover about him outside these walls.'

Terry stared thoughtfully at the ground and clasped his hands together. 'I often think this, with long-termers. That, you know, they almost cease to have a self beyond these fences. As though they were only born when they arrived.'

Terry seemed very reflective, thought Ali. There was a melancholy that moulded itself around him like an aura. She noticed the blood vessels in his cheeks: a drinker.

'Did you spend much time with him? Ben seemed to think he didn't discover religion in here.'

Terry smiled and sat back into a diagonal slash of shadow. 'Like Appleby would have a clue. I've been in this prison for twenty-two years, Ali.' Ali caught a breath: *been in this prison*, not *worked in this prison*. 'I can count the number of prisoners who've *actually* found religion in here on the fingers of one hand. My job isn't to convert, or even preach: it's to listen, offer solace. More than anything, it's to be a non-judgemental, quiet sort of presence in their lives. A lot of them come from chaotic backgrounds, of course; then they get here, and it all seems to be noise. Mainly because they aren't used to the sounds themselves – they jar, they take getting used to. Then, they keep meeting people who are bristling, putting on a front. It's all – whether they admit it or not – intimidating. Talking quietly to someone who can't cause them problems: that's the main thing I can offer. Actual religion is a bit of a bolt-on for these men.'

'I see. But you had discussions with Curtis? Got a sense of who he was?'

'Oh yes. Got a real sense of that.'

Terry's eyes misted. He squinted, apparently in the hope that Ali would think his blurring vision was due to the sun. Ali wasn't deflected: Curtis meant more to him than just another prisoner.

'And that sense was . . .?'

'Ah, well. Curtis was in here for rape. I don't think he ever came to terms with it: what he'd done. What he knew he'd done. It pitched him in with some very clever, very dangerous people. Those who knew how to manipulate, unravel a person. It took him a while to find his own space, to avoid getting into complicated arrangements, preventable relationships.'

'You helped him to find his feet?'

'Yes, yes. I suppose so, in a way. Curtis didn't really know who he was when he came in; and he felt very defined by his crime. More so than others, really. I mean, someone in here for burglary doesn't define themselves only as a burglar: that's just their occupation. Not so with Curtis; the crime was him and he was the crime. Most other sex offenders had various aspects to their lives already – the crimes are their dark corner but there are other facets, other faces, presented to the world. Curtis was . . . hmm, raw; immature in the true sense of the word. Half formed: frightened that sex offenders would shape the other half. He didn't want to go out as more troubled than when he came in.'

Oot, not *out*; his Canadian accent got stronger as he became more emotional.

'Did he find a way to do that?'

'Yes, yes. In the end. And through a strange route. You know about the letters?'

'Suzanne and Marika Doyle? Yeah, that was the main reason I spoke to Ben Appleby. What was your take on that?'

'Oh, I wasn't a fan, not at first. Of course, I wasn't there to tell Curtis what to do, but all the same. He'd made progress in the first seven years; found if not his tribe or direction, then at least his . . . orientation. I thought writing to the two women would set him back. But it didn't. No, it gave him a sense of purpose. Those letters felt like a veneer of civilization, I think: a veneer that talking in a cell to a prison chaplain couldn't supply.'

She let him look away towards the main gate, which glinted sunlight as it slid open and a black van entered the complex. Ali noted that Terry hadn't mentioned Suzanne or Marika by name: possibly he saw them somehow as enemies, or at least rivals for Curtis's time and attention. She didn't need to embarrass Terry by confirming what he meant about *orientation*: the implication was clear enough.

'What about his early life? We're trawling here, Terry, to be honest.'

'Ah, yeah. Everyone thinks all our lives are on the net, but that isn't true, is it? Before Facebook, which was what, 2007? Yeah, before then, surprisingly difficult to trace.'

She wondered if he had, in his private moments, attempted to scout Curtis's earlier life.

'It wasn't a silver spoon and private school, that's for sure. But materially? Not bad. A long way from the worst I've seen. Two brothers, both became tradies: I think they all thought he'd follow suit. But he was into the weed by fifteen; just did shifts at the tyre place to make ends meet. Nothing to indicate what he'd end up doing, for sure. But then, who knows what goes on in people's heads? I get paid to have a clue: haven't got any idea, really. It's unknowable.'

Again, a slide towards melancholy that Ali had to prevent. 'Did Curtis have any enemies in here, anyone who'd want to do him harm?'

He frowned. 'Oh, Lord, no. No, no. He wasn't that type of person. Popular enough, without being anyone's favourite. He dabbled in moving drugs around; but they all do. It's clear who's a regular courier and who isn't. I think he was trusted to move some around; that usually indicates that the dealers see him as no threat, but unlikely to be a joiner, either. Look, each inmate has to do their share; it's like their version of national service. By making each prisoner do at least some runs, the dealers make everyone complicit. Keeps them if not loyal, then at least reluctant to blow the whistle: they have skin in the game, whether they like it or not. Curtis didn't like doing it, but eventually he recognized that it gave him a relatively quiet life, by our standards. No, there were no major spats; no grudges. I took him around the unit on the last day – I usually do that for leavers – and everyone shook hands, hugged. It was nice: I think he appreciated the gesture. He was nervous about stepping outside, eh. There was one minor problem, right at the end, though.'

'Oh?' Ali lifted herself from a picture of Curtis Monroe begrudging handing off drugs to another prisoner, as though that was morally worse than his original crime.

'Yeah, odd thing. Doesn't happen often. They get their parole release date a few weeks before – gives them time to mentally adjust and make some practical arrangements; the same for the various authorities. But Curtis was in the front office, right by the door, when a lawyer says he can't leave yet. Apparently, some last-minute screw-up: certain people hadn't been told yet, protocols haven't been completed. Took about an hour to sort out. Curtis looked happy with it when it was all done, though, so I can't imagine that . . . affected what happened.'

Ali felt drawn into Terry's silences. Each one had a downward trajectory: they oozed regret. He apparently had taken this role expecting that it would be good for him; that he would relish it and be good at it. Part of his sadness seemed a sense that he wasn't as effective as he'd once hoped; he was a time-filler when he thought he would turn lives around. In addition, he endured the daily sweet agony of being so close, yet so far away: that was exquisite torture. But he lacked the will-power to break away from it all.

'Who do you think would want him dead, Terry?'

'Don't know. Can't think of anyone. He was – beneath what he'd done, of course – quite sweet. Last few years, he had a real sense that he wanted to make amends in some way for his crime, beyond doing his sentence, but he couldn't seem to work out how. We discussed it a number of times. No religious penance; I couldn't coax him into that. Confession didn't do much for him; he'd confessed that very night. No; penance had to be something active, and we couldn't find something that suited.'

'And the Doyle sisters?'

'Well, I couldn't compete.' He coughed. 'Not with that. I mean outsiders, civilians, treating him like a normal person? Well, that would be gold to Curtis, wouldn't it? Better than nattering to some old priest, eh. They seemed harmless enough. I never questioned that side of it, to be honest. Why, you think they're involved?'

There was a frisson behind the question: he was hoping the sisters would be implicated and this might, in some way, tarnish their living image in the eyes of a dead man. He was floundering in grief he had to cloak.

'Well, they live near where Curtis was found, and he'd written to them; we have to follow that.'

Terry shook his head and stood. 'Ah, well, he was headed for their place. So, you know, chances are it would happen near theirs, no matter who did it. Yeah. What a waste. What a waste of a human life.'

Chapter 11

Dana took a thought-walk while Lucy collated some more information. Pieces were coming in slowly, but it was difficult to form a coherent whole. Dana felt each rag of information had to be wrung out of somewhere, given grudgingly by the universe. She needed some tangible sign that they were getting a hold on the case. They were all working diligently but lacked the pulse of motivation that would come from a major break.

There was still no sign of Marika – she hadn't returned to the house, nor had she been seen elsewhere. Details had been circulated, but so far not even a hoax call had surfaced. Dana found it unsettling: Marika had had enough time to leave the country by now. They'd sent out warnings to stop that, but maybe too late. Lucy was working back through airline passenger lists from this morning.

Nothing about Marika's recent behaviour, or her current state, could be ruled out. There was a lot of swamp near that house: awkward to navigate, near impossible for humans to search and be sure nothing had been missed. Dana had authorized the use of the drone with infra red: it was currently up doing grid sweeps of the area. The next step might be dogs, taking a signal from some of Marika's clothes in the cottage and fanning outward. That may find her if she was still

anywhere near the cottage. But east of the quarry lay swathes of woodland and marsh, stretching towards national park and then state
forest. Marika had a lot of cover. Dana was sure Suzanne knew where
her sister was.

Ali had rung from the prison, and Mike had emailed in some basic
notes from his meeting with Louise Montgomery: he was now stuck
on the highway after a trailer rolled its load. Lucy was collating the
incoming so Dana could do another briefing. Rainer had gone out
briefly somewhere 'on a hunch'. Lucy suggested that Rainer was absolutely thrilled to have had a hunch in the first place, telling her that he
was 'beaming like a kid who'd mastered "*Frère Jacques*" on the recorder'.

The trees lining the main street were about to bloom, despite the
threatened frost. Carlton had a reputation for producing chocolate-box
cuteness each spring for about three weeks, when the lack of biodiversity
paid off and every tree in town flourished at the same time. Eager snap-
pers descended from the city to a place that otherwise held its charms
solidly within. They mused about downsizing and tree-changing: until
they looked closer and saw that Carlton was merely a small town near
nowhere and three hours from the city on a good day; glorying in a clear
view of an oil refinery; and still with crappy broadband. Dana liked
that – it was a place to live in, more than a place to visit.

She stepped down an alleyway that used to house large wheelie bins,
sweat-mottled restaurant hands grabbing a cigarette break and, at night,
the odd rat or two. Now it was a 'laneway'. The change in title apparently decreed that it was now a bohemian and sophisticated urban
destination, showcasing the best in fusion cuisine and wannabe singer-
songwriters. Four tables and eight chairs promised *al fresco* coffee and
gluten-free treats. Carlton's nascent gentrification was feeble, yet bother-
some. Posters for poetry slams and tapas nights told her to avoid the
place after dark. It was a relief to turn back onto a proper street.

She was disappointed, and surprised, that nothing was showing up as possible revenge for Curtis's original crime. That kind of motivation would narrow the suspects considerably, and give a clear line of sight for the investigation. Retribution was the first and most obvious strand of thought: Curtis perished barely a day after release, with the cross formation suggesting punishment and vengeance. But Louise Montgomery seemed unlikely; the rest of her family had been confirmed as sixteen hundred kilometres away, videoed taking part in a choral competition in a Baptist church until 11 p.m. There appeared no other person who might intervene in that way: no partner for Louise, no group or individual taking undue interest in the case. There wasn't, in the original trial and media coverage she'd managed to read, any threat to Curtis at the time. The overall tone in court seemed to be crushing sadness and lives hollowed out.

Which left, in lieu of anything else, the Doyle sisters. Dana was wary of going too far down that track too early. It was tempting to simply view their entire behaviour as bizarre, and draw rapid assumptions from it. They'd had a fractured childhood; they may have shared a bed from an early age; they wrote to a known rapist and invited him to their home; they were evasive now. She knew it would be easy to run a line from oddball to guilty, without collecting enough solid evidence along the way. Dana had seen it before – done it before, in fact – and she wanted the others to overtly act as a bulwark against it. She made a mental note to remind Mike to do exactly that: whisper in the emperor's ear about mortality.

A text came in from Lucy. She read it, stopped in the middle of the pavement, then apologized to a harassed mother shepherding two kids and a pushchair. She read it again, and realized the heat she was feeling was coming from her own skin.

Dinner at mine tonight? 7pm? I say dinner, it's ping food. No biggie if you're too wrapped up in the case, or whatever. Talking too much, even in a text. Sorry. L.

Dana hand-searched the edge of a nearby bench, without taking her eyes off the text. She bit her lip. Something she'd waited for, considered offering, held back from, thought was gone, pushed to the back of her mind: it was now swimming in front of her.

She replied with a shaky hand. *Cool. I'll bring dessert. D.*

Work. She must get back to work. The phone felt larger in her hand – more important – as she tucked it back into her pocket.

She could interview Suzanne again soon but didn't currently have a plan for doing so. She could push Suzanne about her early life, about writing to Curtis; about what happened in those hours after his release. But she felt it was too early to be tipping her hand on what they had uncovered so far. The crime scene should remain their preserve, and Suzanne – and David Rowe – should keep guessing about what they were facing. Knowing the crime scene details would give Suzanne a way of shaping the narrative. Armed with that knowledge, whatever Suzanne said couldn't be adequately countered; not without Marika's version of events. It would be the gaps, differences and variations between the two sisters that would be key to opening up their defences. Assuming, Dana admonished herself, they had anything beyond their own privacy to be defensive about. Dana was reminded of a previous case and the potential for what she termed the *prurience of incredulity*: probing private aspects not because they were germane to the case, but because her own disbelief about them made the details fascinating to her.

They needed more around the crime scene, the cottage, and Marika, to get much further. Despite what he'd done with his life, Curtis deserved more; she felt she was letting him down.

Back in the office, Lucy was going through some details on a screen with Richard Wallace. Rainer arrived a few seconds behind Dana, red-faced, as if he'd jogged some distance. She considered the whiteboard and, like

Mike before her, drew some conclusions about their progress from the haphazard layout of current evidence. Black writing – known facts – was basic. Blue writing – speculation yet to be proven – was flimsy and repetitive. Red writing – unanswered questions – dominated. Files were too thin, desks too neat: an air of gearing up, not forging ahead. She felt a sting of *not good enough* about her leadership.

'Okay,' she began. All three turned to face her.

'Mikey is on his way back from interviewing Louise Montgomery. More of his notes are on the shared drive, but the gist is that he doesn't see her as a suspect at this point. Her family are all verified as being too far away, at a religious meeting. Louise herself seems to be a virtual recluse. There are details to be checked on the CCTV in the apartment building where she lives, and the roads around it. Mikey identified no obvious alibi; but his feeling for now is that she's a low priority unless something significant rings an alarm.'

'Damn,' said Rainer. 'What about a boyfriend, an ex, something like that?'

'Nope, not that we're aware of: Luce is checking the reports and transcripts from the trial time. Nothing on there, Luce?'

She turned to face Lucy for the first time since the text and tried not to show what had passed between them. Lucy checked her notes, presumably feeling the same.

'Zero. Zip. Nada. I'm about three quarters through the information, but no one seems that way inclined. No threats, no overt displays of anger or bitterness. Only devastation, to be honest. It's all really . . . I don't know how to describe it. Louise is all shock; as you'd expect. But steely on the stand – very controlled and focused giving evidence. The defence got a bit sleazy but it seems they soon realized they were on to a loser: she didn't embellish, backtrack or waver.'

'I don't get something,' said Richard. 'He admitted it; so why a trial?'

'Ah, yes.' Dana nodded. 'Good question, Rich. Luce?'

'He got talked into it by his lawyer. The argument was going to be that Curtis was a decent bloke who'd gone too far in the moment, so just agreed with whatever the cops put forward. Then, later, realized the charge was a reach, so pleaded "not guilty".'

'Speaks to him being suggestible; maybe weak.'

'Yup. It's undoubtedly true he confessed almost as soon as he was arrested. Very cooperative, after that. If I hadn't read all the details and I was just going on the interview room I might think he'd confessed for someone else. His not guilty plea was a surprise. But no; he did it – DNA, everything, all lined up. There's a constant sense that he wanted to unwind time and make it unhappen, if you see what I mean.'

Dana understood Louise's need to swallow down bile and try to move forward or, at least, she comprehended the theory. But part of her would have been tempted to swipe back at Curtis, even if it meant waiting nine years for the opportunity.

'Any other way of checking the alibi for Louise?'

'Already done it. So Louise works for a company called Tutorus Inc. She teaches young people in isolated areas around the world: lots of army brats, kids with parents in charities and international agencies, and so on. Taxes are paid – or not – through the Cayman Islands, but all the heavy lifting comes through a call centre in Bangalore. I spoke to the impeccably polite Rajesh. You'd have loved him.'

Dana smiled. 'He sounds my kind of guy. Is he her supervisor?'

'Ah, in the loose sense of the word. Team leader and mentor; so, a supervisor she's never met. But yeah, he's responsible for her workload and support. He pulled the logs for the night in question. Seems Louise tutored four different students between 7 p.m. and 3 a.m., never more than twenty-five minutes between sessions. Plus, Rajesh video-conferenced with her and another tutor twice that night.'

It took an hour to get to the crime scene from Louise's apartment,

Dana recalled. Maybe forty-five minutes in the dead of night, with the fear of God in you. The whole murder, plus the travel, would be near two hours, minimum. In addition, they had no evidence Louise knew Curtis was out; let alone that he was at, or near, the Doyle sisters' place.

'So never enough time to even reach here, let alone carry out a murder and get back?'

'None that I can see.'

'What about,' interjected Richard, 'her using a mobile device? She could do the tutorials without being in her apartment.'

Dana was pleased to see people challenging evidence.

'I asked Rajesh about that,' replied Lucy. 'He said that used to be a risk, but they got wise to it. Too many tutors phoning in their performance, literally. It was *undermining curriculum quality and the student experience*. So now their software tracks the IP address, and they keep video of the tutorials. He's asking his boss if they can email the tutorial footage to us, but he speed-searched each one while I waited, and said there's nothing hinky about the background behind Louise. Actually, he said *untoward*. Which I liked.'

'Okay.' Dana's finger and thumb tapped. 'But it doesn't entirely rule out Louise; maybe she got someone else to do the dirty work. She could maintain her alibi while a paid killer is wiping out Curtis in a manner of her choosing. Conspiracy's still a long-shot option we need to work through. Can you keep on the CCTV footage from the apartment block and around it, and get Louise's mobile phone logs and banking, please? Check them for anything . . .'

'Untoward,' they both said together, and smiled.

Dana was loath to let go of Louise Montgomery entirely, simply because revenge seemed so obvious that it felt foolish to downgrade it.

'All right. We have Ali on her way back from Du Pont prison.' She picked up a briefing sheet Lucy had compiled from Ali's phone call.

'Bullet points are –' she counted them off on her fingers – 'that the sisters instigated the communication with Curtis; the letters were all above board with no hint of anything to come; the sisters never visited prison or tried to do so; and Curtis was pretty much a model prisoner – no evidence of problems that might bite him.'

It seemed every aspect of the case was partial, lacking enough strength to punch through the fog and reveal itself as important.

'Now, there might be more in the detail, or some subtleties we haven't got to yet, but for now my feeling is there's precious little there that points to motive. It's clearly unusual for women to be offering a place to someone like Curtis, but until a motive presents itself, we have to assume that they had a legitimate reason for doing so. We might get that out of Suzanne, or maybe Marika, in interviews. But that'll take time. In the meantime, we need to build up evidence: give me leverage to get that out of them.'

They all looked downbeat. Like her, she surmised, they'd presumed that there would be something from the prison they could get their teeth into; some semblance of why the crime was committed, if it wasn't simple revenge for Louise.

'However, the more relevant news is a CCTV camera that, thank God, someone thought to place near the prison gates. It's picked up footage of Curtis getting into a car driven by two women. Once Ali gets back with the memory stick, Lucy will start following the car. Luce?'

'Absolutely. The prison refused to email the video, by the way. Something about data ownership and security: they mumbled a feeble reason. Hence, the stick. The prison officer Ali met thought it was probably a hire car. If so, it might well have a black box and we can access the data there. Otherwise, it's trying to pick them up from other cameras, or other data like financials, phone.'

It would be a start if they could begin tracing where everyone went in those hours. Currently, they had no timeline, and therefore no way to spot anomalies or overlaps. Dana was sure there were pieces of data that would place the trio somewhere for most of the day. She tried to think where Curtis might want to go, immediately after release. Maybe something prosaic, like getting comfort food or a beer.

'Richard, you've been following those trails already, yes?'

'I have. The sisters' financials will arrive in under an hour; bank had a security breach and had to reset, otherwise it would already be here. There's no current evidence that Suzanne has a mobile phone, but we have a request out for data on whether Marika has a second phone. That'll take another couple of hours, I've been told.' He held his hands open as if apologizing.

'Oh,' interjected Lucy. 'Ali said that the prison officer phoned the sisters when they started writing to Curtis – the girls had a landline number at that time. Two years ago.'

She passed Richard a note of the number.

'Good catch, Ali. Hmm.' Dana tapped finger and thumb again. 'Why would they quit a landline? Any thoughts?'

'Maybe it was too expensive to justify,' said Rainer. 'They don't seem too flush, nor have many friends, so perhaps it felt like a luxury to them.'

'True,' replied Dana. 'But I don't know . . . internet? Streaming programs, films? The mobile coverage out there must suck: without a landline they might have no internet in the house.'

No one had a reply. Being online now seemed a modern basic – like running water and windows that close – so they had no idea why the sisters would seem to make a conscious decision to do without.

Dana re-calculated. She found herself wondering again what Curtis would have thought when he stepped out of the gates and found the sisters waiting for him. Maybe he was relieved they'd shown up, as promised. Or did he think their offer of help was weird? Or didn't he care, given that he had no friends, no other place to go, and only the loose change from nine years before?

'All right. Seemingly only Marika has a mobile; Suzanne doesn't.

I'm always uneasy these days when we find someone with no mobile phone: it doesn't feel right.' She eye-rolled. 'Welcome to the new normal. And I'm suspicious that Marika would go out without hers. I mean, a nineteen-year-old who leaves her phone at home? I'm even less convinced about that one.'

Richard tapped a pen against his leg. 'I agree. Forensics are compiling from the Samsung you found at the cottage. I just spoke to Dennis Markos and he says it's a brand-new phone, pay-as-you-go: it has some credit on it, but no calls in or out. It's an empty shell, basically, unless we find something hidden deep within. The sisters might have bought it for Curtis to use? Like, a head start on a new life?'

'Yes, that's good thinking,' said Dana.

He grinned. 'Lucy and I are trawling to see if we can uncover any other phone use out there: we're trying to get triangulation data for the area around the cottage, in case there's a regular signal from another number.' Richard paused, for the drama. 'But I did make some progress on the cross thing.'

'Excellent. Go ahead.'

Richard re-settled himself and pointed towards his screen. Rainer shuffled along the desk to get a better view.

'Okay, well, you asked us to acquaint ourselves with the area from Lucy's e-pack, and I started with the satellite photos of the area by the crime scene: I've never been there. I wanted to understand the ways in and out; especially that route through the golf course that Ali mentioned. But I thought I saw something, so I looked on some older photos.'

He clicked and brought up the satellite image they'd all had from Lucy as a starting point. It was a morass of different greys, showing primarily the road and the wooded sections. Then he clicked to another image; a small area by the roadside was highlighted.

'The area where the body was found is this bit, here. That's where the boom gate used to be, to enter the quarry's property. Back when the quarry operated, you had to stop there and be signed in: some bored guy who stayed in his hut when it rained, you know the type of thing. Here's what it used to look like.'

He clicked again to show part of a page from a corporate brochure. The scene looked staged in its cheery matiness between driver and bored guy, but Dana recognized the background from this morning.

'So, at the spot where the gate lifted was a metal contraption to hold the barrier, and the hinge that raised it. Take away the barrier itself, and you see four wooden posts. From the top, in this next photo, they form a cross shape. I figured they couldn't be bothered to take the posts out when they closed down the quarry: that is, the posts have been there for years.'

Dana hadn't foreseen that use for the posts – they'd seemed to be simply wedged into the ground specifically to form a cross.

'Would those posts hold the weight of the boom gate?' she asked. 'I mean, they're only rammed into the earth.'

'Ah, no, not so,' replied Richard. 'I thought that, too. No, we were fooled by about twelve years' neglect: nature took over a bit. In fact, they're set in concrete – the forensics team moved away the vegetation after you'd gone to the cottage. Photos are here – see?'

Sure enough, the new forensics photos showed dirt and scrubby grass peeled back from the edge of the post. Tarnished concrete, stained by the tannins in the soil, lay beneath.

'I tracked down a . . . Stacey Watkins, who used to work at the quarry. He has some of the old equipment and maps; wants to put up an exhibition at Earlville Museum, but they keep turning him down.' Richard grinned at Lucy. 'I like people who're angry and frustrated: they talk more. Stacey said they cleared every possible bit of metal scrap from the site. They were told by Highways to take the posts out, but they left them where the barrier had been. It seems to be total coincidence that they create your cross: it's simply how the posts were set up to contain the gate mechanism.' He hesitated so they could take that in. 'If so, that means no deliberate set-up of the scene – they were simply using posts that were already there. It also widens the time-frame for the murderer to think about all this.'

That was true, thought Dana. It didn't narrow down who might have used the posts, nor did it require a certain type of person to have done so. Or a certain number of people. There was no need for phys-ical strength, or construction skills, or specialist equipment – it was simply opportunism. Also, anyone aware that the posts existed could have thought to use them in this way. It ruled nothing in or out; it merely demonstrated how far the team had to go.

'Good,' she said. 'Thank you. Good creativity to find it. I think we're going to need plenty of that before the case is over: it's not giving us anything for free.' Dana caught herself in an assumption. 'Although, we should hang fire, here. Just because the posts might have been *in situ* doesn't necessarily mean the cruciform held no meaning for the perpetrators: it could still have been why they chose to leave the body there. Good work, Rich, thank you.'

She gave him a thumbs-up and turned. 'Rainer, you ran away, but you came back to us.'

Before he could answer, Lucy chimed in. 'Whatever we said to upset you, we're sorry. We do know how to pronounce your name, even if some of us don't always show it.' She winked at Dana, who mimed a *mea culpa* with her hands.

Rainer patted his chest. 'I appreciate that more than I can ever say, people. I did some mining on Curtis; got hold of one of his brothers on the phone. So when he's little, Curtis is really cute. I mean, ser-iously, he's like a human Labrador pup: I'll put the photos up. As he gets into his teens, he doesn't really go for moody; more . . . floppy. Bright enough at school, but he doesn't really try. Gets into weed about age fifteen, apparently, but he seems to have been behaving like a stoner for a few years before. I spoke to a friend of mine who was at school with him. She says: a kind soul, really. Laid back, nothing ever got him riled; popular enough without being anyone's real focus. The paying for the weed got a little tricky; so, a couple of burglaries. Each time, he was too incompetent to get away with it. He seemed disappointed in himself, but not to the extent that he gave it up. The burglary, or the weed. She was shocked, when Louise's case was on the news. Out of character, she thought.'

Dana wasn't sure what to make of the information. There was a consistency there, across time, that surely spoke to a reasonably accurate assessment of who Curtis had been: a relatively gentle, somewhat suggestible but amiable teenager. All the same, he'd then gone and done something monstrous. It was hard to think that genuinely came out of the blue.

'Luce – in the trial. Your view, please: does Curtis seem angry to be caught, thinking the prosecution are twisting evidence, or appalled at what he did?'

'In my capacity as an untrained but highly gifted psychiatrist? Definitely the third. He wasn't really fighting any of the evidence presented: the lawyer had a go for him, but in the witness box Curtis basically caved. He seemed as if he thought the trial was just confirming what he already knew deep down; though maybe not why he'd done it.'

'Thank you. Sorry, Rainer, I interrupted your flow.'

'No probs. Secondly, the search team. Stu is filing on the shared drive as we speak. There's nothing they've found at the original rape location in the woods that indicates anyone's been there for years. In fact, they found a falcon's nest above it, and apparently those things don't nest anywhere humans frequent. So he thinks no one's even visited. No shrine, nothing. Likewise, nothing on the route between there and the site of our homicide.' Rainer rose and moved across to the whiteboard. While he'd been chirpy enough when he first joined the unit, Dana was pleased with how much his confidence had grown. She had to admit, that was more down to Mike and Lucy than to her. 'The one fresh thing they uncovered at the homicide location was a partial tyre print, about forty metres from the posts. I'll come back to that. You'll want the highlights from the cottage?'

They all nodded.

'Stu's found hairs from Curtis Monroe at the cottage. We won this month's *getting DNA results quickly* lottery. Lab confirmed the DNA a few minutes ago – that's where I was rushing from. Hairs on the couch in the living room, a couple on the sink in the upstairs bathroom, and on a pillow in the bed. Curtis's fingerprints are on the bathroom sink and toilet flush, a mug by the sofa, and the door handles for the living room, bathroom and bedroom.'

Dana felt a little flush of triumph. They could at least place Curtis in the cottage during those missing hours between lunchtime yesterday, and dawn today.

'Type of hair?'

'Mainly from the head. Some body. But arms; not any others. I assume that's what you were asking?'

'It was. Blood?'

'Absolutely none. Not even in the drains, nor the ground surrounding the cottage. Nor any bleached clean-up of blood. And no, uh, bodily fluids from Curtis that they could find either.'

Dana was surprised. A man released from prison usually sought release: early and quickly and more than once. Even if he had to do it himself. She'd been sure there would be traces, even if they didn't link Curtis to either of the sisters.

'Seriously?' It was Lucy who said out loud what everyone was thinking.

'Absolutely. Stu said they couldn't believe it either. Checked everywhere twice, including the shed in the back yard. Nothing, not even spit.'

Dana thought about it. Again, she wondered what expectations Curtis would have had when he climbed into the car at the prison gates. Did they go somewhere before arriving at the cottage? She snapped out of the speculation and focused on the facts. Curtis had been in the cottage, but was apparently not killed there. It was some leverage for another crack at Suzanne; a legitimate starting point if Dana wanted to dive into questions about last night.

Except she didn't. Right now, she didn't want to begin probing Suzanne: she wanted Marika in custody so she could play one off against the other.

'Okay. So, we have something. Curtis was in there, at some point. That's a big first step. Anything else?'

Rainer scanned the report.

'The cigarettes in those ashtrays on the floor are Curtis's own; no other DNA on them. He also had fingerprints on an empty bottle of vodka in the rubbish bin, but we'll have to wait for the autopsy to see how much he consumed.'

If anything, thought Dana. The vodka could be a peace offering bought by him; a thank-you. They shouldn't assume Curtis was a drinker at all. On the other hand, there was nothing currently to suggest either of the sisters drank – no alcohol visible at the cottage.

'You said "secondly", Rainer, like there's something else?'

'Yeah,' said Richard. 'Tell us your hunch, Rainer. Give.'

Rainer couldn't hide a slight stab of pride. 'Fine, fine. So, like Rich, I went back to the e-pack and the satellite photos from Luce. I noticed that where the sisters' road comes out to the main road, there's a house right on the corner. Had to trawl the internet for a while, but I managed to get a name. The old lady who lives there is Clara Belmont: that's where I've been for the last hour or so.'

Lucy pointed. 'I can see a couple of cake crumbs. Nah, other side . . . got it. I reckon cake ladies are the best witnesses.'

'Hmm. It came out of a packet and it was horrible, but I was a good boy and didn't let on. So yeah, Clara was a bit of a goldmine. She has emphysema, bless her. So she sits by the window all day, doing a jigsaw when she has the puff. Nurse comes in each day and – I quote here – "fusses the pants off me with her stupid poking around". Other than that, it's Clara and her keen observation.'

Dana wondered about the old lady's eyesight, and whether her condition meant she took naps during the day, possibly without realizing.

'Good witness?' she asked.

'Oh yeah, really good. If I was ever murdered, I'd be happy for Clara to witness it. Twenty-twenty; doesn't miss a trick; good insight; clear as a bell.'

Dana was surprised: witnesses like that were rare.

'I asked her about the sisters,' continued Rainer. 'Oh, she knew them since they were kids. Not to speak to, these days, since she never leaves the house. But she used to babysit Marika back in the day, and she was not complimentary. Certainly, as a younger girl, Marika seems to have been a nightmare. Clara says the sisters don't have a car: Suzanne walks to and from the supermarket job, even when it's raining. Which is odd; because although they don't have a car, Clara says they have a vehicle.'

Dana was conscious that they were all leaning towards Rainer.

'According to Clara, shortly after the mother died – about four years ago – Marika started razzing around on one of those all-terrain vehicles. You know, like a chunky four-wheel motorbike? I think they mainly use them for farm work; they're maxed out at a fairly low speed. Of course, you can drive ATVs in this state when you're fifteen, because you only need a scooter licence. Imagine. Anyway, Clara's seen

Marika riding down the road on this thing many a time. Never gives her sister a lift anywhere: only Marika, on her own. Except, yesterday afternoon she saw Marika giving Suzanne and Curtis Monroe a ride; on their way back *towards* the cottage. Hasn't seen Marika since.'

It felt significant: at least one of the sisters had a means of transport. It had bothered Dana when she visited the cottage – so isolated, yet no sign of a car. Now she couldn't help reaching for an image of an unconscious or dead Curtis Monroe draped over the back of the ATV like a wrangled steer, bumping over rough ground on the way to the cross. Followed later by the empty ATV sliding silently into a marsh, the swamp lapping over it until it disappeared. It was, she knew, getting ahead of herself, but she could see from Lucy's face that the same footage had occurred to her.

'So,' continued Rainer, 'there's no sign of the vehicle anywhere near the cottage, and no outbuildings where it could be hidden. But back at the homicide scene, there was a partial tyre print they couldn't account for immediately. Haven't spoken to Stu yet, but I saw one of the other search guys just now . . . Milo, is it? He said the print could be from an ATV, but they'd have to double-check now they had the suggestion. They were lucky to spot it at all. The partial had been almost completely overlaid with the tracks of the ute when that man . . .'

'Willie Fitzgibbons,' prompted Lucy.

'. . . thanks, Luce, Willie, turned around for a better look at the body. If it is an ATV track, it places the vehicle near the crime scene some time between the first recent rain, and Willie finding the body this morning.'

Dana thought out loud. '*Potentially* places. There may be more than one ATV in the area: please check for other registrations, Rainer. So some time from yesterday afternoon to six this morning? That includes the killing zone, but a lot of time before and after. If Marika is used to zooming around the district, it's possible she went past the crime location. Although . . . if she had no reason to stop, why halt there? Maybe she saw the body – because Curtis was already dead. And why not park on the road? Chances are, nothing's coming in either direction, so why go off the tarmac?'

The questions were all rhetorical: she was relying on Lucy being able to recite them later, when they might form part of future briefings.

'Clara narrowed that window for us,' beamed Rainer.

'When did she say she saw the ATV with three of them?'

'Uh, four. Five minutes after four, in fact.'

'All right. Good. Yes, that closes the window a bit: Curtis died for certain after 4 p.m. but, according to body temp, probably before 3 a.m. Plus, we believe Curtis spent some time at the cottage but wasn't killed there. So we're down to a maximum of eleven hours for the window but, realistically, below ten hours. Right now, we can assume Curtis was dead by the cross at 0300 hours. Those ten hours before that are the current unknown.'

It felt like progress. It had come because Rainer and Richard had thought laterally.

'Rainer, please check with Stu about any ATV tyre tracks either near the cottage, or between there and the crime scene. And check if there's any way of knowing whether the ATV was loaded down when it stopped at the homicide scene. Maybe the depth of the imprint? I'm wondering if we can tell whether the ATV had only Marika on it when it stopped at the crime scene, or also had a passenger, or all three of them. It's theoretically possible she drove the three of them to that point at four o'clock yesterday afternoon and then took them all back to the cottage, though I can't think of a good reason why. Still, anything that places a vehicle there, let's chase it.'

Rainer made a note. 'If it's any help, I know the make and model. After I left Clara, I spoke to Barney – the guy who owns the service station down the road. He knew the model type; his brother used to have one exactly like it. But he didn't see the three of them go past yesterday afternoon, and his CCTV covers the pumps, not the road.'

'Crap. I was hoping they would have filled up.'

'Nah, Marika did that yesterday morning, around seven. On her own.'

'Still,' pondered Dana, 'make and model will give Forensics the kerb weight, so that might help them work out what extra weight might have been in the ATV when it made the print. It's a long shot. Pass what you know, and see what they can make of it.'

'Will do. One more thing? Clara heard the ATV on the move last night. Definitely after 7 p.m., but before ten thirty. It didn't go past her place, though; she could only hear it moving around in the distance.'

Dana knew it was time to prep, and begin asking more questions of Suzanne Doyle. Marika was out there somewhere, but tricky to find. In the meantime, the older sister was the only game in town and Dana needed to maintain momentum; it wasn't ideal, but perhaps more background through Suzanne would yield new avenues. Suzanne had the chance to lie to Dana and get ahead of what might be coming; Dana would need to bring some tricks to the next party.

Chapter 12

Dana was nearing Interview One when Lucy hollered. They met in the corridor under a buzzing fluorescent light that needed replacing.

Lucy waved a sheet of paper. 'The mystery of the disappearing lawyer? This morning?'

'Ah, yes,' replied Dana. 'The Dupree Paradox. Why was she there? And who paid for her time?'

'David Rowe. And David Rowe. Arranged for Dupree to run interference for an hour or so. He's the Doyles' attorney of record: handled the compensation claims for the father's death, the legal work on buying the cottage, and the will when the mother died. Because – get this – he's Mary Doyle's brother.'

'Oh?' Dana realized she shouldn't be surprised: there were wheels within wheels all over this region. 'So he's *Uncle Dave* for Suzanne and Marika?'

'Exactly. Which explains, detective chick, why the penniless Suzanne has a top-notch lawyer.'

It was useful, and interesting, and no doubt relevant. But straight off the bat, Dana couldn't think how she could use it for advantage. There was nothing illegal or unethical about it; nor did David have an obligation to disclose it to her. But Dana couldn't shake a feeling that the close family link would become influential, somehow. It also meant she might need to interview David as a witness – background on both Mary and the family atmosphere in the cottage. That might take some doing.

'Thanks, Luce – good sleuthing. Shouldn't keep them waiting.'

'Laters.'

Dana entered Interview One and shook hands with David, then with Suzanne, who seemed vaguely disturbed by the gesture.

'May I sit down, Suzanne?'

She looked quickly to David for a social cue. Seeing nothing, she shrugged. 'Your house, not mine.'

The room had a double recorder: one digital, one old-school. The latter made its familiar grinding sound initially then settled down. David looked calm and poised, as usual. Blessed with a permanent just-shaved look, he sat contentedly in front of a yellow legal pad. Dana wondered how much control he had over his client and, in particular, over her reticence or cooperation. Suzanne was the One True Source at present; Dana needed her talking, and needed David to at least yield to that.

Suzanne fiddled with the cuff of her jumpsuit. Now that skin forensics were completed they'd allowed her a shower: her skin still looked blotchy from the hot water. Like a fluffy cat, she looked thinner and more vulnerable when wet. Under David's counsel her attitude had changed. She'd lost some of her wide-eyed sadness and air of submission: now she looked bored and irritated.

It wasn't clear to Dana how much Suzanne knew about Curtis's fate. Discussions in this room about the last day or so would have to wait – preferably, until Marika was here. Dana wasn't dismissing the idea of a third-party involvement and would continue to direct part of the team's efforts down that road for now. But she felt Suzanne and Marika at least held important information.

'Suzanne, I'd like to talk more about your early life, if I may.'

Suzanne looked annoyed. 'Yeah, about that. What does it have to do with anything?'

Dana's vision passed to her notes via a brief look at David. He was sitting back, out of his client's field of vision, and he eye-rolled at Dana. She presumed that he'd been dealing with this attitude since he arrived. The victim act from earlier was no more the real Suzanne than the sulky young woman she was doing now: Suzanne was an actress wherever she went.

'You said previously that you first moved to the cottage fifteen years ago?'

Suzanne exhaled, in what Dana saw as a theatrical bluff. 'Look, are you going to explain what this is all about? I mean, I've been dragged in here, and you haven't said why.'

'No, I haven't.'

'Well, shouldn't you? Don't you have to, or something?'

There were two possibilities here. First: Suzanne was not involved in Curtis Monroe's death and had no knowledge of it. That was possible, though she lived very close to the crime scene and had met Curtis yesterday: a witness had identified them travelling together on the quad bike and Curtis's trace was in her cottage. Second: she knew both about Curtis's death and what the police had discovered that morning. In fact, she could even have sneaked from her cottage at the first sign of a police presence, and got close enough to view it for herself. But wait, there was a third alternative. That Suzanne was aware that Curtis was dead but had no idea what the police currently knew.

If it was the first option, Dana could accelerate future discussions and focus elsewhere. It wouldn't take long to prove Suzanne's lack of involvement, so there was no harm in building up gradually now. If it was the second option, then they'd begun a game of bluff and double-bluff and it was likely Suzanne hadn't yet shared with David Rowe what she knew. If it was the third, Dana would need to tread carefully to preserve the advantage she currently held.

'No, Suzanne, I don't have to. You're being detained under Close Proximity rules, as a witness. We're not obliged to tell you any details about what we're investigating, or what we've found. We can, however, ask you questions: you're a witness, so you may have information useful to our investigation.'

'Why does knowing about my childhood help?'

'I make the determination about what is relevant and why. I have to justify that to a judge tomorrow, to see if your detention continues. You have the right to sue me later if what I ask you is deemed irrelevant or prurient; your lawyer would be able to assist, if it came to that. But it won't. So, I'll ask again: you first moved to the cottage fifteen years ago?'

Something between a shrug and a whine moved Suzanne's shoulders. 'Yup.' Her posture was twenty degrees off-centre, skewed towards a corner.

'Why did you move there?'

Suzanne looked at David, as if imploring him to intervene with some television-lawyer complaint about *relevance, Your Honour.* 'I dunno for sure. I was a kid. Just turned ten. We got kicked off the base. Dad's death was an embarrassment to the service, I remember that much. Not good for recruitment when your own workmate shoots you. They couldn't ship us off fast enough: the whole family was negative publicity on legs. Plus, Mum couldn't be relied on in front of the cameras, so we had to go. We had some kind of, uh, compensation. But it wasn't much. Wasn't enough. Ended up in that dump of a cottage.'

Dana knew Suzanne was highly intelligent: a scholarship had her destined for a first-class honours in History, before fate intervened. Hence, Dana recalled, the battery of books in the cottage.

'It's certainly a long way from anywhere. Was that why your mother chose it?'

Suzanne turned to David again. 'Aren't you going to object, or stop her, or something?'

'Detective Russo understands the rules of the Close Proximity doctrine extremely well. As you'll recall, Suzanne, from the last time you were in this room. She knows I'll pull her up if she crosses the line. She hasn't crossed the line, Suzanne. She can't currently see the line from where she's sitting. We discussed this. We agreed what you would do. So answer the nice lady's question.'

Suzanne glared at him, as though he'd suddenly cower and buckle. He merely raised an eyebrow. Suzanne began speaking before completing the turn.

'I think mostly it was cheap to buy,' she said. 'Mum had this thing about owning where we lived, so we couldn't be kicked out at the whim of someone else. It became super-important to her that we owned it, free and clear. It was *liberating*, apparently. So we sacrificed everything else for that.'

'Everything else?'

'Oh, cash, convenience, space, people nearby. All the reasons most people have when they buy a house, she ignored.' Suzanne puffed her cheeks in exasperation. 'I think she preferred it, anyway; she knew her behaviour was odd, so she didn't like people around to point that out.'

'I see. Your father's death must have hit the family hard.'

'Hmm, I can see why you'd think so. It was a shock – I mean, the way it came; the shooting. But don't think we were a happy family until that point. Everyone does it, don't they? Says nice things about people when they die; all sins forgiven, everything under the carpet. The army wanted victims as flawless heroes: reputation of the regiment, and all. It suited everyone involved to go that way.'

'But it was more complicated than that?'

'God, yeah. Mum couldn't help it, I know: I got that, never forgot it. But I mean, she was a pain; screwed up and difficult to live with, for all of us.'

Suzanne swept her hair to one side. Dana recalled the photo she'd seen in the cottage, taken a decade ago: a pretty, assured girl in good health. If she'd seen that photo and nothing else, Dana doubted she'd have picked up on Suzanne's traumatized background. However, Dana could see that the last few years had exacted a toll. Suzanne was wan, her gestures pale imitations. Her apparent feistiness was exactly that: apparent. Most of her sentences tailed off, as though she weren't sure what the reaction of a human being should be.

'Mum had meds, didn't always take them. She got obsessed – insects on the wall, or underneath her skin; people watching her, government cameras in the cereal box. All kinds of paranoid, is what she was. Voices, apparitions – the full nine yards. But at the time of the shooting? We all had our way of dealing with her. Marika didn't get it – she was four. Dad and I had to have . . . what are they called? Coping mechanisms? Yeah, those.'

'And what were they?'

Suzanne picked at one ragged fingernail with another.

'Dad withdrew, got cold. Mum was too much effort, too much like hard work. He avoided. Cheated. Not as in another woman. He cheated at being a father: ducked out, left us to it. Orson was a coward. Mr Brave Soldier, credit to the flag? Couldn't even face up to his own family. To be fair, Mum wasn't exactly listening by then. Her world didn't include us: we were visitors. Dad stayed at the office a lot, and he wasn't at home when he *was* at home, if you see what I mean. Ironic: he was shot when he was doing overtime he didn't need to do. His stupid coping mechanism got him killed.'

Dana decided to let that lie for a while. She was starting to build a picture of the household and didn't want Suzanne drifting down an old track about her father. Dana wanted more about Mary, and what she'd wrought on the two sisters.

'And your way of coping with your mother, Suzanne? What was that?'

Suzanne started, as if Dana's question was naive. Dana noted that Suzanne liked it when the questions implied she was the decision-maker, the analyser; a person with agency.

'Well, I had the little brat to look after whenever Mum was in La-La-Land.'

'Marika was what, four or five, when you moved here?'

'I was nearly ten, so yeah. She was a kid. Still is.' The light suddenly disappeared from Suzanne's eyes, replaced by smoky anger.

Dana cut the volume further. Her next statement was a drop of dye, cast into a bowl of water. 'Marika's nineteen now, though. An adult.'

Suzanne's voice was cold. 'She is still . . . a child.'

Dana let the silence that followed linger. She wasn't sure if Suzanne was building up some kind of defence here: the laying of foundations for excuses focusing on Marika – what Marika might have done; what motivated Marika; how Marika was to blame. Sisters or no, Suzanne was here and her sibling wasn't: she had opportunity, and reason, to protect herself.

Suzanne turned again to David and spoke as if only they were in the room. 'How long do I have to answer this crap? I want to go home.'

David had the same ability to remain unflappable as the most effect-ive police officers – the capacity to button down gestures, modulate the voice, ooze calm. He placed his pen quietly on the pad.

'Suzanne, we've discussed this. Under the Close Proximity doctrine, you're here for either seventy-two hours, or until the detective says you can leave; whichever comes sooner. Until then, as we've agreed, you'll cooperate with the investigation, because you're a decent citizen with nothing to hide.'

Suzanne fumed. The dial seemed to be turned up whenever Marika was mentioned. Being an only child, Dana felt unqualified to think through sibling love. Or hate. But there was certainly a fuse there.

Strategically, Dana had hit a crossroads. There were still ground rules to be established here; the balance and boundaries of discussions to come. Dana's practical authority in this room was flimsy, since Suzanne didn't appear to care less. That apparent insouciance was, Dana knew, a front. But Suzanne was good at it, practised. Dana needed a verbal bomb exploding: to reset the parameters, get to a new balance.

Dana disliked it when interviewees kept whining to their lawyer. She needed David to hold full authority over his client. So far Suzanne had proven intelligent, aware and eloquent but also eager to regress into sulky adolescence. Especially with Marika still in the wind, Dana needed to keep the investigation moving forward.

She shot a subliminal glance at David. 'Your mother wanted the three of you in the same bed, always?'

Suzanne's pupils widened, and she slapped the table with one palm. Before she could reply, David rolled in with the objection.

'We will not be going down that line of questioning, Detective.' The voice was calm, but firm, as Dana knew it would be. His face, however, glowed with indignation.

'Quite right, Counsellor. Apologies, Suzanne.'

Suzanne stared and then looked gratefully at her lawyer.

Dana watched the comprehension of what she'd done – and why – sweep across his features like a tropical storm front. It was, as he knew, totally out of character for her to do such a thing; it took a couple of heartbeats for him to work it out. He was now aware that her previous question had been carefully calibrated.

Dana had allowed David to demonstrate that he was guarding Suzanne's best interests. This meant Suzanne was now reassured by

David's willingness to intervene, and how effective it was, satisfied that she'd purely be answering the questions she had to answer. David was now happy that his client would settle down and cooperate. And all these things suited Dana.

'Suzanne, do you have any idea where Marika has gone?'

Suzanne shook her head slowly – uncertainly, in fact – but a flush rose around her throat. She was, Dana surmised, worried about her sister. For her sister. About what her sister might do. Might have done. Might allege. Might know.

'I thought she'd gone out for a run.' Her voice was distant; Dana noted the subtle change. In the cottage, Suzanne had said Marika *had* gone for a run, as though she'd witnessed the leaving. Now it seemed in doubt, somehow: perhaps a foundation for claiming that Marika had left while Suzanne was sleeping.

'Frankly, I'm worried, Suzanne. Marika might be caught in a swamp somewhere, might have fallen. There's a lot of bog out there. People perish. It'll be dark in a few hours. Does Marika have any survival gear?'

Suzanne frowned, perplexed. 'Survival gear?'

'There'll be a frost tonight. Marika might be out of doors some-where; no warm clothes, no shelter, nothing.' Dana needed Suzanne to think the police were out of ideas and evidence: it would make Suzanne feel superior, and therefore bolder. 'Besides, there may be someone out there looking to do her harm.'

Suzanne clasped her hands behind her head, but her fingers trem-bled before she hid them. 'Ha. Bless you. I mean, you don't know her; so I get it, I do. The abstract concept of Marika – fools people who've never had to deal with her.' She smiled thinly and adopted a simpering tone. 'Little waif and stray? Tiny little bird of a thing? What will she do? However will she cope?'

Suzanne snorted and flicked a look at David, as though he already knew this.

She dropped her hands to her lap. 'Don't worry about Marika, Detective. She'll be fine. After the apocalypse, the first three things out of the rubble will be cockroaches, Iggy Pop and Marika Doyle.'

'But two minutes ago, Suzanne, you said she was a child.'

Suzanne stalled, her mouth open. There was a glimpse of what she was like when things went wrong: frozen, incapacitated. She rocked forward and folded her arms on the table. 'She is. Emotionally, mentally, she refused to grow up. But don't think she's weak, Detective. My little sister's a survivor. She knows how to, uh . . . pray.'

Dana tilted her head to acknowledge the homonym. Suzanne was evidencing a forensic, sharp mind and wouldn't be able to hide behind her churlish persona again.

'So, where would she have gone, in your opinion?'

'Oh, not far. Into the swamp, someplace. Knows that whole zone forwards, back and upside down. She has her little hidey-holes. She started going off into the marshes when she was nine or ten. I used to freak out about it, but Mum was, uh, chemically relaxed about the whole thing.'

'That doesn't sound very maternal.'

Suzanne grimaced. 'Well, she wasn't. I think a piece of her wanted Marika to perish out there. It would've been a tragic but understandable accident: Mum would get some sympathy and more meds, and there'd be one less mouth to feed. I think Marika picked up on that pretty early.'

'It has to leave a mark.'

'Oh yeah. In all kinds of ways. Things you couldn't possibly imagine, Detective.'

I seriously doubt that, thought Dana. She scribbled in Pitman while Suzanne looked at her fingernails again, as though planning a manicure.

'So, unlikely that she's left the swamp? No friends in town, or anything like that?'

'She – we – literally have no friends.'

'But you have each other, right, Suzanne?'

The reply was flat, metallic. 'I think we both regard that as a poor bargain. You have no idea.'

Suzanne seemed to want that to sink in. Once again Dana wondered if this was the true sibling dynamic, or if Suzanne was laying out blame, and her own escape route.

'After you moved here, I understand that your mother took you to equestrian events and Marika was looked after by a neighbour. Is that accurate?'

'Once or twice a week, yeah. For a while. The old lady from down the lane. She was old then; ancient now.'

'Hmm. Her name is Clara. Clara Belmont. You know who she is, Suzanne. I think it best you stop any further pretence at simple-minded ignorance. We can see through the *I don't notice much* shtick: you, me and your . . . lawyer.'

David blinked slowly, to signify assent. He now realized that Dana knew about the family connection.

'So,' continued Dana, 'you must have been good at horse-riding early?'

'Yes, I was.' Dana's placid silence had drawn her forward again. 'Not boasting – I just was. It's pretty rare to find you're seriously good at something straight off the bat. Yeah, natural affinity: getting a horse to do what I wanted was as simple as breathing. Besides, I like horses.'

'Because?'

'Because they don't lie to you, and you can't lie to them. Dealing with a horse strips away the . . . the artifice, Detective. The fakery. The walls we put up. Horses can sense your mood, but they don't respond to crap. Nor do they dish it out. Horses are easier and more honest than people. I liked them. Besides, they worked for Mum. Horses, I mean: something about them was . . . centred, soothing for her. She liked being around them, and she was an easier and more pleasant human being for those few hours. It was worth it, if only for that. Of course, as soon as I wasn't chasing a rosette, all those bets were off. When I wasn't competing, I became the focus for a different reason.'

Dana gave her time to elaborate, but Suzanne didn't want it.

'Hmm. Was it tricky, financing your hobby? I understand horses aren't cheap.'

'I had a . . . we had help. Financially. Got me off the ground.'

Something in the air between the two told Dana that Suzanne's benefactor had been Uncle David. Perhaps it was the one kind of support his sister would accept – Dana was getting the impression that Mary had been too volatile, or too proud, or too broken, to permit direct help for herself.

Dana felt a need to pace the questions about the family's past: it was clearly raw for Suzanne, and she would need time for the inflammation to die back. Jumping around the timescales also kept Suzanne off-balance. 'You work at the supermarket, Suzanne?'

'Yeah, three nights a week. Shelf-filler. It's a dream come true.'

'No other type of work you could find? Smart girl like you?'

'Oh, there's a wide variety of jobs for the just-shy-of-graduating around here. Especially with no transport. As you know, I'm sure, it's the local council, the refinery, or move away. There was nothing in the first two, and I . . . I can't move.'

Dana nodded, to let her know she understood the cause of paralysis. 'Shift-working must be a killer.'

Suzanne wound an errant thread around her finger until the tip turned white. 'Mostly, it's not too bad. Night before last was my third in a row – it hits you when you stop. But generally, it's okay. I kinda like it.'

'Because?'

'Because it's brain donor work. I already know how it all goes – you can do it on autopilot. When I get there the stuff's been offloaded, the pallets are waiting and all we have to do is put it on the shelves the right way around. Plug in your headphones, off you go. I don't have to think or deal with anyone but Fubsy.'

Dana frowned. 'Sorry, Fubsy?'

'Ah, I mean Brian. We do the same shifts. Brian Aroona. He's a . . . an *indigenous person*. Perfect workmate: super-quiet, reliable, almost no conversation. We understand each other perfectly.'

'I don't get to Fubsy from Brian Aroona.'

'No, you wouldn't. Apparently, at school, his teachers called him Fubsy – Fat Useless Bastard. They said he'd end up in a dead-end job if he didn't try harder, and here he is. With a . . . smart girl like me.'

'But they didn't tell *you* that, Suzanne. Straight-A record. Scholarship for your degree. Top grades.'

Suzanne regarded her hands yet again, as though they'd caused every difficulty in her life. 'Well, Detective, there you go. Let that be a lesson to us all: being clever gets you nowhere in this world. It's gilding the lily; it's counterproductive. You rarely need the smarts you so carefully nurtured. Employers are scared of it – they want *good enough* instead of *too good*. I'm a walking example of why you should spend less time with books, more time building networks of useful idiots.'

The concept hit home harder than Suzanne could have known.

'What about Marika? Has she ever worked?'

'No, she's my house husband. Has been since I moved back. She looks after the cottage.'

Dana deadpanned it. 'She's done a stand-out job, I could tell.'

'Ha. Yeah. Well, Marika keeps the things clean that she considers important.'

'The television?'

'For one.'

'The photo of the two of you.'

'Very observant, Detective. Yeah, the one without our mother in it. Just me, Marika and good ol' Tax Break.'

'Seriously?'

'Unfortunately, yeah. The owner let me ride the horse, but he named the poor thing. He thought it was hilarious, but I'm sure Tax Break knew everyone was laughing at him. He always seemed a little humiliated, I always thought.' Suzanne glared straight at Dana. 'I recognize the look when I see it.'

Dana allowed her what she clearly felt was a win. There was a gauche need for victory in Suzanne, and it suited Dana for the woman to think she was ahead on points.

'I am genuinely worried about Marika, Suzanne. Even if she knows the swamp well, there's no accounting for accidents. Marika has no contacts? No one she might reach out to? I read that she saw a psychiatrist at some point.'

'All three of us saw shrinks, at some point. Useless, aren't they, Detective?'

Dana held a determined stare, as though simply waiting Suzanne out and not crackling inside. 'You don't approve of modern psychotherapy, Suzanne?'

'It didn't help Mum. And it didn't help Marika or me with Mum. Especially after she died. Bereavement counselling: what a joke. No, I don't approve, Detective. It's for the shallow and callow. Empty words that don't work: except the reason they don't work is allegedly because *you* didn't take them to heart. Waste of money. Sorry, Unc.'

She turned to David for the last word. Clearly, he'd covered a lot more than some horse-riding costs; it was increasingly important to Dana that she could speak to him. So she was grateful when David looked to her.

'I think that's enough probing for now, Detective. Suzanne's done three night shifts in a row; I can see she needs some rest.'

Dana looked back to Suzanne, who seemed very pleased with how it had gone. 'Of course. May we resume in a couple of hours? We can bring some food and drink in the meantime.'

Chapter 13

As Suzanne was taken to a holding cell, Dana turned to David Rowe. 'Do you have a few minutes, please? Now we've established that you're family, I was hoping I could get some details from you. It would obviate the need to bother Suzanne about them. In particular, about Mary.'

David tucked his pen into an inside pocket and patted his tie. 'Always happy to oblige someone who uses the word "obviate", Dana.' They shared a smile. 'Perhaps you can outline your case and we can save you a lot of time. I'm sure Suzanne, or Marika for that matter, isn't involved.'

David would not make a good angler: he lacked patience and his casting was haphazard.

'I'll be discussing salient points with your nieces as and when, Counsellor, as you'd expect. But I would like to minimize traumatic conversations if I can.' It was only partly true: Dana was quite prepared to go to the darkest places. It was often where she found the most light.

David shifted his briefcase from hand to hand. 'Look, I have to square some of the paperwork with your custody officer, then I need to go back to the office for an hour or two. Meet you at the rear door, and you can walk me home.'

'Excellent, thank you. I won't carry your schoolbooks for you, though.'

'Ah, that remains the male prerogative. See you in ten or fifteen.'

Dana thought about returning to the incident room. She wasn't sure what stage her team was at, though she expected Mike to have beaten the traffic incident and made it back to base. He and Lucy could hold the fort for now. She needed this chat with David Rowe to set the background and tactics for her next run at Suzanne. Marika was still out there somewhere, no doubt shivering as the temperature began to fall away in the growling easterly. Until Marika was found, Suzanne was all Dana had to go at.

It wasn't yet clear whether Suzanne knew they'd found Curtis's body, or just some lingering forensics that kick-started an investigation; or simply thought Curtis was missing. Clearly, David knew even less than Suzanne, and Dana intended to keep it that way. As, she thought, did Suzanne at this point.

Dana realized she still had to deal with the two reporters in reception, who'd been cooling their heels for some time, expecting an update. She was an hour later than she'd promised, and cursed herself for the error. It was always better to feed them morsels: it kept them from obtaining snacks from other sources. Randall Crawley was no problem – trustworthy, consistent, with little personal ambition: she saw a kindred spirit. Reece the aspiring autocutie was another matter.

At reception, Miriam pointed surreptitiously to show the two journalists were waiting. Dana took a gulp of oxygen and wished Bill Meeks were here to deal with this crap. Randall folded his newspaper along the same creases he'd created this morning, and placed his Thermos carefully into his rucksack. Reece Two Cs came from the window to Dana's personal space in three impatient strides.

'You have a statement for us now?'

Dana motioned to the chairs near Randall – she knew he had sciatica and would appreciate not having to move quickly.

'Firstly, I apologize for being late. I was held up in interview, unfortunately.' Randall inclined his head in acceptance, but the etiquette whistled over Reece's head.

'I can give you some details but, as I'm sure you appreciate, the autopsy hasn't been conducted yet and we're in the first few hours of the investigation. For now, I can tell you that the body of a man was found at 0630 today by a passer-by. The location remains a crime scene, and I do not expect to see journalists or photographers near it, nor drones above it. Next of kin have been informed: they currently live interstate, and they've made clear to my fellow officers that they don't have a statement for the media at this difficult and painful time.'

Reece's telephone was thrust too close for Dana's liking. She glared at it until Reece realized and moved it back. Randall sat rigidly against the wall, a foldaway step under his feet to ease his posture, and relied on Pitman.

'The next steps will be to hold an autopsy to officially determine cause of death and continue our investigations at or near the scene. Thank you.'

Reece blanched. 'What? That's it? Who is it? What about suspects? What about how he died?'

'Ms McCartney. As I just said, the autopsy will look to determine cause of death. That will be carried out by the medical examiner this afternoon. We're keeping an open mind on how the person died; also on the involvement of anyone else. We're a few hours into the investigation. There will be an update at six o'clock; if there are any developments, they'll be passed to you at that time.'

'Have you charged anyone?'

The scattergun pot-shots made Dana feel something akin to sympathy. Or maybe, it was pity. Perhaps Reece's tactic worked one time in fifty; someone felt bullied, or goaded, or plain angry. The other times were wasted ammunition.

'No one has been charged at this time, Ms McCartney.'

Reece's shoulders slumped. Several hours' waiting, off and on; away from the office, and no one even charged. She'd felt hung out to dry as soon as she was told to cover a half-story in Earlville, and now there was no pay-off. It wasn't, she thought as she scowled, a waste of time for the old man: it *was* his time. She was on the point of turning away when Randall spoke.

'Detective, has anyone been detained under Close Proximity?'

Dana demurred. It would be unlikely Randall had tapped a source for that question: he had them, but he probably wouldn't be using them at this stage. More likely, he was clever enough to know about the new law and had taken a punt.

'One person, Randy. But I'm sure you won't read too much into that.' Randall smiled, but Reece was back in the game.

'I've heard of that. Isn't that pretty much the same as charging them?'

Dana fixed a glare that made Reece buckle before she bristled. 'No, Ms McCartney. It's completely different. That's why it needed a totally new piece of legislation. Close Proximity means exactly that: nothing more.'

Reece had the blank stare of someone who didn't get nuance, or didn't care for it. 'My readers might imply it's the same thing.'

'The readers of the newspaper you work for . . . won't *imply* anything, Ms McCartney. They might *infer*; but they'd be wrong to do so. Close Proximity is not the same as a charge.'

Something in Dana's head said she should stop now; she was getting drawn in by Reece's ignorance, but she felt the point was worth making.

'I'm aware that some people think allegation means guilty, or accusation means proof, but we don't operate like that here. The person detained has not been charged with anything. They are cooperating, and all we are seeking is the truth. I'll provide another statement at six o'clock. Thank you, and apologies again for the delay.'

Randall smoothly folded the little step, lifted his rucksack and began packing up. Reece thought she could squeeze some blood from the stone.

'But . . . we have questions, Detective. You won't answer our questions?'

'*Our* questions, Ms McCartney? I hear one person asking questions now. The other person is moving on. Thank you both. Good afternoon.'

She managed to smile at them as Randall raised his hat. Before she could even reach the door back into the station she could hear Reece's irritable screech.

'We're not getting anywhere here. You're local – why do you put up with this crap?'

Randall sighed as he watched Dana disappear into the building. It was a bad sign when he'd rather drink some soup than talk to a fellow journalist. It was either an indication he was too old for this game or that this woman was extremely, egregiously annoying.

'Look, at the risk of being called – what's the thing? – oh yeah, a *mansplainer* or whatever, let me give you some advice from an old guy who's been doing this for fifty years. Take it for what it is, Reece, do what you like.' He waited, but she looked as though she was itching to use her phone. He decided to plough on. 'As a journalist, there are three types of detective, okay? First type wants you to like him; wants a friend. He'll talk and talk and spill all kinds of stuff, as long as you suck up to him. So yuk it up, laugh when he laughs, smile, nod a lot, keep pouring the drinks. He – and it's nearly always a he – has a big ego and a big mouth. After he's told you more than he should, make

sure the report has some garbage about him being a sharp media operator: "shrewd", or something like that. Reason is: he'll do the same
next time, even if he gets chewed out over the leak. He'll take your
schmoozing about him being "media savvy" over his boss telling him
to rein it in.'

He stopped to see if she was taking it in or tuning it out. She'd per-
fected a flat, emotion-free face like a dinner plate that told him nothing.
Or everything.

'Second type is the old-school, who doesn't give anything to the
media. Thinks we're maggots on a corpse. Can't see the point of our
tiny human existence and won't give up a thing. Circumvent that person. It's likely they aren't popular in-house, because they're probably
too inflexible about all kinds of things and rub people up the wrong
way with petty rules. But the best way around them is anyone who isn't
a police officer – because the badge still brings a certain loyalty, no
matter how begrudging it is. So instead: nurses, doctors, tow-truck
operators, cleaners, witnesses, relatives. You have to go to them because
the police won't play ball.

'Third type is like Dana here. Clever enough to know they have to
give you something, so you don't go harassing grieving widows and
busy medics. But smart enough not to be drawn in by your ego-
massaging, so they won't go overboard. Be nice to them. Be respectful.
Be courteous. As they learn you can be trusted, you'll get more. But go
around them? You'll lose big-time. They'll cut you off in ways you don't
want. They'll go after you.'

Reece harrumphed and walked in a tight little circle. Clearly, to her,
it all smacked of the long term. She ignored her phone when it buzzed,
and Randall took that as a sign of her exasperation.

'So my advice with Dana is go with the flow – she'll make sure you
have enough to report, and in a timescale for your deadlines. She gets
it. In return, we don't try to dig under her foundations. Don't try to

outsmart her – you won't. And don't mistake her being polite for being weak.' Randall leaned in. 'I mean, your predecessor is now working part-time, filing one-paragraphs on road repairs. Isn't he?'

Reece stopped moving and Randall thought he'd made progress. Then she shrugged her shoulders and answered the vibrating phone as she moved outdoors. She gave a finger-wave through the glass, as though Randall were a family dog waiting loyally by the window.

Miriam's voice sparked from the other side of reception.

'Need a cab, Randy?'

Randall put away the notepad and hoisted his rucksack. 'No, thanks. Parked around the corner. Say thanks to Dana for me.'

Miriam pointed a biro at Reece's back, now fending off the stiff breeze. 'Got your hands full with her.'

Randall grinned. 'The media. Don't you love us?'

Chapter 14

Thursday, 1 August 2019. 1325 hrs

David half skipped the last few metres to the doorway, to indicate his apologies at the delay. Two visiting officers from city divisions, still addicted to nicotine, had given Dana a determinedly wide berth while she'd waited. Surreptitious and watery nods of greeting: it felt like they knew something she soon would, or ought to already.

Dana tried to read David. She knew he was, in essence, a steady and solid lawyer. This case seemed a little outside his wheelhouse: he usually spent much of his time dealing with probate cases. But he was conscientious and systematic, and that would play well here. She could use that: David wouldn't get ahead of himself or make leaps of judgement. No, she concluded, his natural inclination would be to let things play out as they may, knowing any trial was months away and he didn't have to fight the battle right now. Police and prosecutors had to win every skirmish, every time; the defence just had to win once, anytime.

Unless, she thought, there was some compelling reason why he might be more proactive in defending his nieces.

'You want to know about Mary?' he asked.

They began walking across the car park, towards the civic centre and the main square. A garbage bin overflowed with last night's fast-food;

a waterfall of polystyrene. The breeze was cold, but the sunshine felt unseasonably warm in the lee of the buildings.

'Please. The more I can get a picture from you, the less I'll need from Suzanne. Or Marika, when the opportunity arrives.'

He grunted. 'Assuming it arrives.' She looked at him, but he stared pointedly ahead. 'Mary started to go wrong about age sixteen, seventeen. I'm four years older; at law studies by then. Nearly the same age gap as Suze and Rika.' He seemed to regret lapsing into shortened names, and re-gathered. 'Ironically, I noticed it more easily than my parents – seeing Mary each day softened her decline for them. Not that any of us could spot anything initially. The change was glacial, and deeply private. She started to develop little rituals that we thought were quirky at first. But over time they became . . .'

'Intrusive?' Dana sensed the truth of the description before she spoke it, then felt the familiarity of its resonance.

'Exactly. Borderline obsessive. They began to influence the course of her life.' Their pace slowed as David started to choose his words more forensically. 'She dropped out of veterinary training, had a few run-ins with the police, and with people who weren't the friends she'd supposed. Some of it might have been a young woman finding her way in the world, but not all of it. There was a sense it was too . . . embedded. Too dominant.'

Dana got a picture of someone whose life had unravelled gently; a thread in the wind, a series of unwise or illogical steps that aggregated. That was, she thought, how the steepest falls came: gradually.

They passed a cart selling paper cones of heated macadamia nuts; the aroma saturated the path.

'She received some medical help, then?'

'Oh, a battery of doctors, yeah. Then psychologists and psychiatrists.' David jerked his head back towards the station. 'I'm sure some of Suzanne's attitudes back there were learned at her mother's knee.

Mary had a habit of telling her eldest precisely what she'd gone through with the medics. Marika was spared – or, at least, I thought she was.'

Dana could see that David's eyes were beginning to moisten. She slowed their walking pace still further, until they came to a halt in the plaza. Shoppers and office workers hustled by; they were an island.

'After Suzanne got the scholarship for university, in those final years, Marika was alone with Mary – teenage carer, lackey, victim. I was stupid not to push things and help her more. After Mary died, I found out a bit more about how she'd been: how she'd behaved and what that caused. Hard not to blame yourself for that kind of spiral when you can't denounce Marika for her role, and won't put it on Mary because she's sick.'

That was true, thought Dana as they resumed, climbing some steps and strolling into the cool shade set by City Hall. *Sick people can't help it.* Or can they? She felt that line of forgiveness could only run so far. Her own life told her that the line would become tense, then fray, then break. It would snap with visible force and flail around with unexpected consequences. All from giving a sick person too much leeway. In the final analysis, Dana believed, it could actually be *their* fault, and it could actually be *their* shame. Medical diagnosis only granted so much absolution. Especially if their worst instincts had been indulged by others.

When she shivered, it was surely because of the temperature of the shadows.

'Was Mary ever officially diagnosed?'

'No, not officially. Well, many times, but never quite the same diagnosis twice. Some form of schizophrenia, maybe. Elements of psychosis – her world made sense to her, but not to others. We never got to the bottom of it; just tried meds and combinations of meds, hoping something would work for her. Each expert had a different take. Their ideas bled into each other, crossed over and under, cancelled out. They're never definitive, these people: I learned that much.'

They sat on a bench and squinted at the fountain as it sparkled. A skinny busker with a carefully curated barista beard was packing away his saxophone, counting his rewards as they slipped through his fingers.

'The weird thing was, she seemed to stabilize in her early twenties. That was when she married and had Suzanne. For a while, it looked like it might work out. I don't think Orson was the passion of her life, but she had enough surplus emotion for the two of them: steady was exactly what she needed. Then Marika came along. Difficult time from a breech birth, emergency C-section; Mary was traumatized. The schizo – sorry, whatever it ultimately was – returned with a vengeance. There comes a day when post-partum depression isn't post-partum any more, it's joined forces with other problems, and it's now your life. Orson's shooting at the barracks was the final straw.'

He sat forward, elbows on knees, and gently knocked the handle of his briefcase to and fro. Tradies began erecting fencing at the far end of the plaza; a parade tonight for local youngsters who'd won a soccer tournament in Canberra.

'I had to step in a bit then, when they moved to the cottage. I tried not to dominate Mary's life, you know? Big brother clomping around oblivious, making things worse. We never know when to offer and when to step back, do we? So whatever we do is some degree of wrong.'

He turned to face her, disarmingly open.

'I feel like I misjudged it, Dana. I got there too late. Far too late. Meds kept the ragged edges away, when she took them. In those final years, alone with Marika, Mary had this idea that true life *was* rapid swings and highs and lows; that vivid was the only light there should be. She thought the meds shut off her life, by smoothing it out. With Suzanne escaping as quickly as she could, Marika was left with the scraps of her mother. Days got . . . dark. Mary was impossible to live with, but Marika wouldn't leave. Hated her, but clung to her. They got, what's the expression? Co-dependent. They started to mirror each other, link arms against the world. In those last two years with Mary, I wasn't even allowed to visit.'

As she listened, Dana flipped her perspective to that of the girls: specifically, Marika. At some point, Suzanne – already the golden girl with the dimples and the ponies – had escaped to a different and better life at university. Marika was left alone with an increasingly unstable mother. It would become a battle of wills, Dana suspected: blow and counterblow, tactics, survival mode, desperation. Marika would start to believe that every relationship was a battle with one exhausted victor and one bloodied loser. Once embedded, it was a hard attitude to shift, Dana knew.

'The night Mary died, I got a phone call around eleven at night. They had a landline back then. I knew, if Marika called, that Mary would be gone. Suzanne was home for a visit – I guess that was part of the escalation of the night. When I got there Marika was hysterical, Suzanne was a curled-up ball. I scoured the area near the cottage as best I could, called Mary's name in the darkness. That place – the swamps – terrifies me, Dana. It's wicked, pitiless. One step out of line and you're gone. Mary was under the surface in a marsh.' He lifted one hand as though holding a goblet. 'Only her hand showing: white fingers in black water. Long, long gone. Even at that moment, I thought, *thank God.* Shameful to think that way, but some people's lives are better when they're extinguished. You know?'

Dana knew. She squeezed his forearm. 'David, I'm so sorry. That sounds like a fricking nightmare.'

It sounded familiar, too. The past had a way of rushing at Dana sometimes – barrelling with increasing speed then, as she braced for the impact, sliding through her and beyond, as if she was nothing. She had that sensation now: Mary Doyle was disconcertingly close to Dana's mother, right down to the pathology of her cruelty.

'Thank you. Thanks. So those girls – I blame myself, inasmuch as I blame anyone. They're good kids, both of them. But they have a harsh little shell; I don't know what breaks through it, but if it cracks, they'll disintegrate.' He turned to face her; ruddy, full of regret. 'So you'll understand that I . . . I mean, I . . . I will watch over them. This time. I will guard them.'

In other words, Dana now realized, he intended to be as ferocious a defender as he could and Dana should prepare for that.

'I'd expect nothing less, David. Nothing less.'

Chapter 15

Mike tried to throw his jacket the last two metres to the peg, James Bond-style. He failed badly; the coat fell with a gentle sigh onto the edge of his desk, before slipping to the floor in a further act of mute defiance. Lucy gave him a Roman emperor's thumbs-down.

'No Russian-supermodel sex for you, Mikey Bond. You're as ordinary as the rest of us.'

Mike picked up the jacket. 'As if I didn't know, Luce. Still, Barb would never have gone for it. So no loss, really.'

Lucy smiled. 'Don't you guys have a cheat list?'

Mike sat and clicked on emails. 'Nah, we were never into that kind of thing. Celebs: who has the time? And they're so needy. Neither of us could deal with that kind of heavy-duty maintenance. My own wife thinks I'm hard work because I don't like cushions.'

Lucy tapped her pen against her teeth, knowing it would make Mike wince. Anything to do with teeth or eyes. 'What do you have against cushions?'

'They're unnecessary and intrusive. They're the parsley sprig of furniture.'

At the top of the email list was one marked urgent from Peter

Kasparov, the kingpin of the Intelligence Unit at Central. The phone rang as he reached for it, making him jump. Lucy laughed.

'Detective Mike Francis, can I help you?'

The voice on the other end coughed, then lifted. 'Ooh, yes, please, Mikey.' There was a pause, and a shift towards pantomime-villain. 'You know, deep down, what I crave.'

'Kaspar, that was spooky and worrying. I lack the courage, protective equipment and bleach to explore what you crave. Anyway, I was literally about to call you.'

'Yeah, they all say that, Mikey. Yet they never call. They take out a restraining order and use lawyers for all contact. And then claim, bizarrely, that "the crawlspace under your house" is somehow *not a valid address.*'

'Sometimes I forget how difficult it is to be a stalker, Kaspar. People like me see the glamorous side.'

Kasparov chuckled. 'Ain't that the truth.'

'Right, I'll take you off conference call now. Luce says hi. Your email had a red exclamation mark.'

'Lucy is too smart to be outraged by my rigmarole. Yes, red flag: it did, it did. I was flicking through the daily diatribe just now and I saw you have an unexplained death. Curtis Mason Monroe?'

Incidents such as unexplained deaths made it to a rolling log of information available via Intranet. Usually, it was light on the details.

'We do indeed. Working full time on it. He show up on your side?'

Kasparov became more circumspect. 'Hmm. In a manner of speaking. Hold on.' There was a pause, a click of a closing door, the radio being switched on to a music station and a squeak as Kasparov resumed his seat. Cher tried to *turn back time* in the background, without a hint of irony.

'All right. All hush-hush, on the QT. I hear the wannabe spies in C4 have had an operation going for the past few days, in Du Pont prison. Neo-Nazi gangs prosper, as they are wont to do, and currently control most of the drugs going in and out of the place. Top of the pops is the absurdly named Aryan Force. Where do they get these people? Anyway, usually this is run-of-the-mill stuff and we don't get involved. But it's starting to create waves in an election year – three overdoses from super-strength hits. Which is a sign of a lack of discipline, or a surfeit of competition. Or both. The Chief was persuaded by the state minister to take down a few: *pour décourager les autres*, as it were.'

Mike scribbled notes frantically, wishing once again that he had Dana's ability to use Pitman. Or Dana's discipline, to learn it in the first place. 'Your French accent is strangely seductive to me. I imagine your nail polish today is less black, more *noir*. Don't stop, Kaspar.'

'Once again, they all say that. So, the operation culminated yesterday, when the Aryans' three top bigots at Du Pont were blown out of business in one fell swoop. Courtesy of crucial intelligence from . . .'

'Curtis Mason Monroe.'

'Game, set, bingo. He wouldn't give out the vital details until he was literally a metre from the prison door. They moved in on the Nazi dickheads an hour later. All done and dusted in minutes; but someone, somewhere, would have been trying to work out where the leak came from. They might have figured out it was Monroe and shown their displeasure.'

'Hmmm. That's a fair chance.' Mike had always thought there would be another angle to this; one that didn't involve the sisters. The degree of violence in the killing suggested it; as did the failure to drop the body into the swamp. The prison, however, had been adamant that Monroe was pretty much a clean-skin: that's what they'd told Ali. She was due back any minute from a quick lunch.

'Although,' he countered, 'the prison service claim no knowledge of Curtis Monroe running drugs to a significant degree, or being heavily involved. In fact, they say he was a reluctant and occasional mule and kept his distance from all that.'

Kasparov grunted. 'Yes, that's what C4 thought as well. Until it was untrue. *When the facts change, sir, I change my mind,* and all that.' Kasparov assumed, correctly, that quoting an economist would sail over Mike's head; Dana would have been a different matter. 'Monroe was barely on their radar, yet he was right in the middle of it – his evidence was spot on and couldn't have come from a marginal figure.'

Mike wondered. Ali had been sent to the prison largely to focus on the letters between Curtis Monroe and the sisters. A lesser aim was Curtis's general behaviour in Du Pont and any well-documented blues or breaches of discipline. She'd had no reason to travel down this specific route: they hadn't known it existed. All the same, someone with good instincts might have suspected something awry.

'We missed all that, Kaspar. Or any hint of that.'

'Don't beat yourself up. The operation was restricted to seven people at our end, including the Big Chief. Even I, with my magnificent empire here, wasn't party to it. All my knowledge is retrospective, which isn't like me at all. And that caution reflects a view that these dipsticks will have all manner of networks: we can't rule out some of our own keeping the Nazis stocked with tip-offs, to be honest. As far as the dealing in prison goes? Two options: one, that some of the guards must have been in on this and getting paid off. Maybe you spoke to one of those and he tried to head you off at the pass. This scale of drug-pushing – and the inside/outside passing it entailed – required a degree of collusion from people who should have known better. Second possibility: maybe Monroe was fairly innocent, but was wrong place and wrong time. Saw something major he shouldn't.'

Mike scanned the notes from Ali on one side of the screen and the data from Lucy on the other side. 'Yeah, he was in there for nine years. We knew he was exposed to it, even out there on the sex offenders' wing.'

'Oh, they're the worst, apparently. Nothing to do, all day to do it, and the guards try to have as little to do with them as possible. They pass through like lepers in the Middle Ages; all they're missing is a bell and a cloak. They're perfect for moving stock, it seems.'

Mike hadn't thought of it that way. He'd assumed that sex offenders were isolated from the main prison population and as such lacked the mobility to be of much use for drug movements. On the other hand, as Kasparov pointed out, they were pariahs who might be given a wide berth.

'I take it, Kaspar, I've heard nothing from you at all about this?'

'No,' replied Kasparov cheerily. 'I'm completely ignorant on the subject and have never discussed it in any way. But we have had a chat in the last ten minutes about your upcoming birthday. Oh, and I suppose sports, and other manly stuff.'

'You forgot motorbikes. And craft beers.'

'Ah yeah, we'd have guffawed and shoulder-shucked; a pretend-choke and a grapple. Look, since we haven't spoken on this, I haven't had any reason to tell you to contact Wickham Watts, in C4. He won't be able to talk to you about this, either. And he certainly won't be able to take you to a quiet meeting with anyone at Aryan Force who might know more about Curtis Monroe. He won't be able to do that.'

'Marvellous. I won't reach out to him straight away, and we won't fix a time or place for that.'

'No problem.' Kasparov turned down the radio. Cher had gone, presumably lamenting her failure; Rupert Holmes was now cheating on his wife, with his wife. 'Oh, wait, can you tell Dana from me that her suggestion was awesome?'

'What suggestion?'

'Ah, us minions in Intelligence never let slip any confidential data. I've just demonstrated that. Dana suggested something, and it proved most appropriate. Bye, Mikey.'

'So long, Kaspar. Appreciate it.'

Lucy's hands hovered over the keyboard, where they'd remained as she tuned in to Mike's half of the conversation.

'Another avenue, Mikey?'

'Possibly, Luce, possibly.'

Mike could see Ali approaching down the corridor – another reason for liking this office was the warning he had of approaches, good or bad. It struck him that Ali's evidence from Du Pont was now to be considered partial, possibly useless. He couldn't tell if she'd been too credulous and not pushed hard enough at this Ben Appleby. Possibly, Appleby was part of the ring and had been directing her away from such a notion, as Kasparov suggested. Or maybe he was one of the *don't-ask-don't-tell* types that Mike had previously encountered in prisons. Some units tolerated certain drugs, and porn, because they kept the inmates relatively content and docile: perhaps Appleby was one of those. Whichever; Mike had to mull over whether they should send Ali back to the same place. It might feel like a punishment for poor work. Or, equally, it might simply look that way to others. Alternatively, not sending her might suggest she wasn't to be trusted.

Mike was saved by the bell: Dana appeared in the corridor behind Ali, right on cue. He breathed a sigh of relief.

Mike's raised eyebrow diverted Dana into another office. She stood against a whiteboard while Ali fidgeted with a ring binder and Mike updated them both. As he spoke, Dana was changing tack. She'd been intending to simply push the previous agendas forward. Above all, find Marika. But also more on the rental car, and another search for what she regarded as extant but missing mobile phones. Mike had thrown a spanner into the works.

Ali went pale. 'So Curtis was up to his eyes in drug-running?'

The implication was clear. 'Hmm. Maybe. Probably. But we don't know yet.' Mike caught Ali's disappointment, then Dana's permission to mollify. 'Since the operation to take out the dealer hierarchy was highly secretive, we only have any idea about it from unofficial sources. So we can't say exactly what Curtis had done, or how much, or for how long.'

That was all true, thought Dana, but the news opened up a channel, even if it merely needed pursuing to cover the bases. Dana was glad; she disliked a unidirectional investigation, because it usually smacked of complacency. She always believed there were other options that had to – at the least – be tied down. For her, this was an opportunity; for Ali, it would feel like a rebuke.

Mike concluded: 'Maybe Curtis lucked into the info without getting his hands dirty. Or he might have been involved, or committed, or whatever.'

'Eggs and bacon, Mikey: the chicken's involved, but the pig is committed,' offered Dana. 'At minimum, Curtis knew enough to drop a major bomb into the mix as he was running away. It seemingly created a whole lot of blast and plenty of collateral damage. I doubt all those nice Aryans intended to take exposure as simply life's rich tapestry.'

'I missed all of it.' Ali's voice sounded far away and her eyes were rooted on the carpet in front of her.

'Ah, don't go down that trail, Ali,' said Dana. 'A handful of people knew about this operation; that tells me that Curtis's evidence came as a lightning bolt to all kinds of people. You wouldn't have known; you wouldn't have had any reason to delve at this stage. I'm happy with your interview.'

Mike took up the cudgels. 'Agreed. The word is, the whole drug thing had flown under various security processes. Remains to be seen why that was. None of us would have got more, unless we'd gone armed with new facts we're not supposed to have. The question is, what do we do with them?'

'Hmm.' Dana moved away from the wall and grabbed a whiteboard pen, simply to shift the room: everyone had figuratively and literally come to a grinding halt.

'It certainly throws a new angle in there: an alternative to the sisters. For which I'm grateful, as you know, Mikey. Without getting ahead of ourselves, there's an option that Curtis was killed by someone who knew – or worked out – that he'd spilled the beans as he was walking. Which would explain the failure, or refusal, to cover up the body: it was left exposed as either a warning, or as proof the contract had been fulfilled.' She tapped the pen against her wrist. 'It's possible the information that Curtis provided could only have come from him. *Mosaic*: he might have damned himself that way, without fully realizing.'

It made sense to Dana that Curtis had supplied disparate little nuggets of information, each of which seemed impossible to trace back to him and him alone. But he'd spilled enough of them that, seen together, they could only come from someone who'd been in certain places at certain times. Mosaic responses: each was benign, but they built a picture that wasn't. The end result would be that he pointed the finger at himself.

Dana looked to Mike. 'Do we . . . can we get anything further from *that source*, Mikey?'

'I'm thinking not. *That source* went out on a limb for us there, and I don't think that's repeatable. Besides, I don't believe *that source* has anything further at this point. Maybe in a day or two?'

'Okay. Time isn't our friend, here. Sixtyish hours left on Suzanne's ticket. Any ideas, Ali?'

Ali appeared surprised to be asked. It jolted Dana: perhaps she and Mike came across as a self-sufficient team of two.

'Prisons are weird places to get information,' mused Ali. 'They hold it all: you can't cross-reference. I'm not sure going back to Appleby, or anyone else, would give us much right now.'

'Yes, there's no third party and no other context. I agree.' Dana started counting off her reasoning on her fingers. 'One, if we ask further at the prison it'll put backs up and probably undermine the new covert operation and its aftermath. Two, we aren't even supposed to know about it at this point; we'd be showing our hand and maybe putting others in trouble. Three, we run the risk of tipping off whoever's responsible – maybe – for the murder, to further cover their tracks. All the media have reported so far is a dead body, with one person detained under Close Proximity. The possible killer may think we're miles away from this angle, so their guard could be down.'

'If it's revenge for what Curtis did to the Nazis,' suggested Ali, 'won't the killer be long gone by now? I mean, wouldn't the Aryans have sent him interstate as soon as he did it? Or overseas?'

'Not necessarily,' replied Dana. 'Case in point: last year we convicted a wife who paid a neighbour to kill her husband. The neighbour still had most of the cash, with both sets of fingerprints on it; he also still had the weapon and a *written receipt* for the transaction.'

Ali slowly realized it wasn't a gag.

'No, seriously,' continued Dana. 'He kept it as insurance; to take her down with him if it came to it. So no: even if someone was contracted, they might well be local, and remain local. We don't have enough yet to start going state-wide, let alone interstate.'

'Yeah, the McGinnis case: people can be surprisingly and blessedly thick,' said Mike. 'Plus, we don't know how far the tentacles of this network reach. *That source* thought it had hooks into a number of agencies, including ours. We have to proceed carefully, I reckon.'

'Agreed,' said Dana, nodding. She wanted alternative theories of the murder, to avoid fixating on the Doyle sisters without solid evidence. But the case had begun to take on additional and sensitive political dimensions that worried her. She disliked tiptoeing around departmental egos or highly sensitive data. It added extra angles and wrinkles;

further issues that distracted her. She'd be expected, as lead, to cover the politics on behalf of her team. She didn't believe herself best equipped for it; Mike, she thought, had better antenna and instincts on this. Her thinking was largely based on what she imagined Mike would do.

'We need anything we can find that moves us further down this particular road, but which we'd find anyway if we weren't on this road.'

She looked up and saw two bemused faces. It wasn't like her to communicate in such an opaque way; it told her that she was flustered, leading inadequately.

'Sorry, that was brainless. An example: we can keep trawling CCTV and other sources to track where this rented Nissan went. That might also, accidentally, show us if anyone was following Curtis and who they were, but the line of inquiry is expected of us. Anyone monitoring, or sticking an oar in, or looking for danger signs, they'll only see us diligently working the sisters' whereabouts. That way we're protecting ourselves and *that source*, furthering the investigation and putting off bringing in others and tipping our hand. As Mikey says, we need to be aware here; in case the Aryans' network runs deep, wide or high up. So let's stick to what we can do to further the lines around Suzanne and Marika, but also notice anything that points towards these Aryan dipsticks or their acolytes. Sound reasonable?'

Mike agreed, but Ali shrugged, as though – now she'd been exonerated from conducting a lax interview – all this was above her paygrade. Once again, she seemed to Dana not so much shallow, more limited; Dana would have to factor that into future decisions. Ali would do what was asked, but she might not think about it as carefully as, say, Rainer. Dana would need to give Ali clear and channelled tasks.

Mike raised a finger. 'How much of this do we tell the others? Do they need protecting?'

It was a good point. Rainer and Ali were constables. But Lucy and

Richard were civilians: their security clearances were lower, so they were even less entitled to be privy to this information than Dana and Mike. All the same, the other three in the team needed to know what to look for, at least, and Dana disliked asymmetric team knowledge on principle. It usually backfired.

'I think we tell them; but it needs reiterating that this cannot go beyond the team. Not to anyone. If *that source* is correct, there might be people in our own organization who have other loyalties, and few qualms about disclosure. Let's get the team up to speed.'

Chapter 16

The atmosphere in the office had changed since this morning. Mike's briefing to Dana about the possible involvement of Aryan Force had, she needed to admit, opened windows and let the air in. The previous hours had felt like a stifling tunnel, the team groping their way along the walls. Now, potentially, they had more than one path. Richard came in and deposited some sandwiches on Lucy's desk, along with her change. Mike stood by Ali. Rainer sidled in last-minute.

'All right. Let's get us all up to the same page, then we'll review where we're going next. We have some important information we need to share, which might alter our approach. But first, I want us all at the same point. Lucy?'

Lucy scooted her chair to the corner of her desk, able to see everyone but also reach the mouse. 'Okay. So Rich and I were down for . . .' – she checked her notes without needing to do so – '. . . timeline for the pick-up from Du Pont prison forwards, and finding Marika Doyle. Bad news – nothing on Marika. She's just plain gone. Stu's minions have been flying the drones in a grid around the cottage, presently out to an eight-kilometre radius, but nothing doing. We have infrared on two of the three and all we've found is a wild pig and some black swans.' Lucy shrugged. 'Stu says it isn't worth pursuing, in his view, but he'll keep at it if you want.'

'All right, I hear him, Luce. Can he please restrict his flights to infra-red sweeps nearer the house? Let's say one kilometre. I need to cover the possibility that she comes back there later, thinking we're gone. I'll play it by ear, once darkness falls. Thanks.' The last word was almost a whisper.

Marika. Marika. Dana wondered if she was starting to fetishize the appearance of Marika. Clearly, she could be as useful a witness as Suzanne – perhaps, more so – but Dana decided she had to avoid pin-ning all her hopes on finding the younger sister. It was starting to eat at her that Marika was seemingly so easily evading their attention.

'Shall do,' noted Lucy. 'Nothing cropping up about associates or places she might go. She has no phone, rarely leaves the house. You get the idea. Zero audit trail: quite a feat these days. Marika's offering no clues.'

Dana could only get so far by going at Suzanne. One sister could say what she liked, as long as it couldn't be contradicted by physical evidence. Two sisters opened fissures that Dana could exploit. Over and above that, Dana had experienced the marshland and held real fears for Marika's well-being. Marika's years of navigation and hiding didn't change the salient fact: the swamps *moved.* They rose and sub-sided; any mental map would be a guideline, not a guarantee.

Lucy sensed Dana's mood and tried to sound more upbeat. 'We've had better luck on tracing the three of them after they left Du Pont. We got Ali's footage of Curtis leaving the prison. The rented Nissan was waiting in the car park. He stumbles twice just getting to the car.'

'Yes,' said Dana, nodding. 'He would.'

'Why's that?' asked Richard.

'Because for nine years he's been on totally flat, smooth surfaces. Other than stairs, he's put his foot down flat every few seconds for nearly a decade. Plus, in prison, his horizons are really short: just to the end of a corridor, at best. So his balance is used to his eye-line being slightly lower. In the real world horizons are bigger, the natural eye-line is higher, and the ground is rutted, marked; not smooth.'

'Wow,' whispered Lucy. 'Anyway, as Ali found today, Du Pont is on a little raft of land with a long causeway through the swamp to get there: Eaglehawk Neck Road. There's a camera at the end of that, where it meets the main road. The rental Nissan goes through that checkpoint eleven minutes after leaving the prison; quite slow for thirteen kilometres, but you can see as the Nissan approaches that Suzanne is hardly pushing the speed limit.'

'Well, she's rarely driving, is she?' suggested Mike. 'So I suppose she's a bit cautious.'

Ali added, 'Plus, if her tyres hit the edge and she spins, she'll slide into the marsh: they'd all be dead in thirty seconds.'

'True,' agreed Lucy, turning to the spreadsheet. 'The car has no black box, and the satnav was switched off. It was hired on the day, by the way, at 1345. The sisters paid cash. The prison pick-up is 1502, and they pass the checkpoint at 1513, visible on cameras. As I say, from there, we have no way to trace their route using software. However, there's one obvious route from the checkpoint into town, and they use it: so we clock them at 1524 arriving in Earlville, down by the sports complex. There's a glimpse from the edge of an office block, then a firmer sighting as they turn off near the railway station. Rossmoyne Street, to be exact. That's 1529.'

She looked at Dana, who was still staring at the floor. It was clear to all of them that the failure to find Marika was like a dragging chain for Dana.

'The next sighting is the McDonald's, next door to the car hire place. Now they're on foot; Suzanne and Curtis. Marika's not in shot at any time here, so they must have offloaded her somewhere between the railway station and car rental place. 1537 at Macca's: this tallies with the computer entry for returning the car. They'd drop the keys into a box outside the office, but a laser inside the box screens each key fob as it passes and logs on to the computer. Then, six minutes inside Macca's, where we have them on screen all the time; out they come with, ironically, three Happy Meals: 1543. They walk back towards the railway station, but we lose track of them once they turn the corner from Macca's. Then, finally, a brief sighting of the three of them riding on the quad bike at 1554, at a set of temporary traffic lights, headed to Maritime and their cottage. The next sighting would be by Clara Belmont, a few minutes after 4 p.m. as they turn for the final road to the cottage.'

Dana tried to pull up her mood. 'So we've tracked their entire time from prison to home?'

'Yeah, we have. About an hour, all up. Apparently, all they did was drive from Du Pont to near the railway station, drop off Marika, ditch the car, buy some nutritious quality food, walk back to wherever Marika was waiting with the ATV and then *put-put* home at an annoyingly slow speed.'

Dana wandered over to the whiteboards. It had been eight hours since the body was discovered. Yet the pull of expectations made it feel as if they should have more. Much more. There was an awful lot of red writing – the speculation, the unknown, the questions; the as yet unverified. Unverifiable, without Marika or a third party.

'Crap. I was hoping there would be something significant, unusual. A confrontation, maybe, or them fighting among themselves. Something.'

'Well . . . we . . .' Lucy pointed to the screen with her biro.

'Spill, Luce.'

'It might be nothing, but anyway. When they drove to the prison, both the girls were wearing the same things – identical sweaters, yellow as it turns out. When Curtis got in the car he was in the clothes he'd worn in prison for his final day. But by the time they'd passed the initial checkpoint he'd thrown a top over himself; so had the girls.'

'Which was?' Mike beat Dana to the question.

'Fluoro. They were all wearing fluoro vests. Like tradies: miners, plumbers, construction workers. Orange, to be precise – Macca's has the fancy colour camera. Fluoro. God knows why.'

Rainer noted that Clara Belmont hadn't mentioned that, and he felt sure she would have done.

'They must have wanted to stand out,' said Dana. 'They wanted to be recognized. Or, at least, visible on camera. Tell me, Luce, if they'd chosen to, could they have done all that today without being on camera?'

Lucy clicked a map onscreen, the trio's journey a red squiggle across the district.

'Hmm. Well, they can't avoid the checkpoint near Du Pont, not without a submarine. Nor the camera on the edge of town: it's the main road between town and prison. I don't know if some of the tracks they'd use otherwise are viable in a standard car; they're not graded so they'd probably need four-wheel-drive.' More clicks, then a zoom on to Earlville proper. 'If they absolutely have to have a Macca's, they have no choice with the in-store camera. I know Curtis talked about them in some letters; that could have been a non-negotiable, I suppose. But they could have bought burgers and chips from a place with no cameras. And they could have taken a different route for most of the journey home – out past the airfield, for example. So . . . between first coming to the edge of Earlville and reaching home; yes, they could have stayed camera-free. But they didn't.'

This felt important: something that played to overt intent. Anything deliberate was useful. Somehow.

'No, they did not,' Dana murmured. 'I was wondering . . .'

'If the fluoro clothes were at the cottage?' Lucy grinned. 'Already checked the search inventory. Nothing at all, nothing even remotely like it.'

Dana looked around the room. Just because she felt this was significant, didn't mean it was.

'So what does all that tell us, people?'

Richard shrugged. 'Macca's wasn't busy. Normally takes ten minutes.'

Dana smiled. 'There speaks a frequent flyer, Rich.'

'It's literally how I roll. They give good ramp. Proper turning angles, non-slip surface: can't fault 'em.'

'But aside from good luck with fast-food service?'

Rainer piped up. 'They're laying down a trail. They want to be seen at various stages. It matters. For some reason, it matters that, later on, people like us will be able to trace them back in some way.'

Dana added *trail?* to the whiteboard. 'Which implies they were expecting something to happen to Curtis. Luce, what was their demeanour?'

Lucy tilted a pen at Richard before replying. 'Rich and I were discussing this, trawling the footage. In the car, I'd say stony-faced and silent. They don't look around, they don't speak, they don't face each other or wave their hands, or anything. Maybe they knew where the cameras were and they were more animated elsewhere. But I doubt it. If I didn't know better, I'd say it was an automatic pilot and they were mannequins. But once the car has been ditched, Suzanne and Curtis are talking. Not chatting, exactly, I'd say talking. Yeah, Rich?'

She turned for confirmation. Richard coughed and moved forward.

'Absolutely. It's the sole time we know they *are* talking, and it looks like a business meeting. Formal, distance between them, a few nods. Even waiting for the food in the "restaurant": stilted, two strangers.'

Which implied, thought Dana, that Marika had more to do with the letters than Suzanne. Possibly. Although, she wouldn't know that until she could get at Marika.

Rainer spoke up again. 'Uh, I have a question about the fluoro. I think Clara Belmont would have mentioned it. I mean, I can go back and ask her, or ring. But if that kind of clothing isn't something the sisters usually have, and then suddenly the three of them look like highlighter pens when they ride slowly past . . . well, Clara's going to spot it, and she's going to call it, surely?'

'Yeah, that's a good point,' agreed Mike. 'The time between the last camera and Clara's house is how long, Luce?'

'Urgh, closed the spreadsheet, sorry. Here, okay . . . nine minutes, assuming Clara's timing is precise.'

'It is,' said Rainer.

'All right,' continued Mike. 'So the service station that Clara can see from her house: the sisters know they can't be on camera if they're simply passing by on the road. You have to pull in, to be onscreen. They're locals; they'd understand that. They stopped and took off the fluoro before they drove past Clara's. Is that reasonable?'

Dana waited for any dissention, but Mike was right. The sisters – and, by extension, Curtis, who must surely have known and accepted why they were doing it – had lain a visible trail, expecting it to be followed. Once they felt that was no longer necessary, they removed that clothing and it hadn't been found anywhere.

'It's a reasonable assumption, Mikey, yes. But it's not reasonable behaviour, is it? In fact, it's weird. I don't see why they're doing that.'

No one did.

'Anything else, Rich?'

'There's no other mobile phone at the Doyle house: only that unused Samsung you found. We've tried all the companies and came up with zilch: no other contract for that property. Of course, they could have bought a pay-as-you-go with cash; we've checked some of the suppliers within the area, but we've got a few more to go. The landline was dropped eighteen months ago. No reason given, just a short letter from Suzanne asking for it to be disconnected.'

Dana still couldn't buy the concept of young women completely without telephones of any kind. She'd expected a landline; probably a mobile. Even though their finances were pushed, it was the kind of thing people now regarded as a necessity. That was without considering the security: two women alone in an isolated cottage. It bothered her that they couldn't trace any technology to the sisters – it limited the room for manoeuvre.

'Okay, can you put the date for that letter on the whiteboard, please? We might uncover some precipitating incident related to that: it could speak to how the sisters' lives were developing and why they contacted Curtis in the first place. Anything else?'

'CCTV from Louise's apartment building in Gerson: no evidence of her leaving or returning. Nothing from her financials except direct debits for bills, a couple of payments to a Honda dealer, and around forty dollars a week taken out in cash. So her alibi's strengthened. Oh.' Richard slapped his forehead. 'Financials from the Doyle sisters. They have one bank account: nominally in both their names, but in reality only Suzanne makes payments or withdrawals. Marika doesn't even have a bank card. They don't buy anything on credit: they take out cash and spend that. Old school. Their bills are paid by direct debit: electric, water, local rates, insurance and rego for the ATV, and that's it. No telephone company payments.'

'Any variation in the cash they're taking out? Especially recently?'

'It's unnervingly regular, and on a par with the same period last year. No significant one-off payments, either: no holiday, no car, no splurges of any kind. The one item that's out of synch with consistent cash withdrawals is three months ago, when they took out twice the usual weekly amount. Once, mind. No indication what that was for.'

The double-dip could have been the extra cash they splurged on hiring a car for half a day. That might suggest the planning for Curtis's release went back months. Possibly, the planning for murder went back as far, or further. But without other data, the financial records were another blind alley. Dana had suspected that the sisters would be a cash-only pairing. Perhaps one of them – Marika, possibly – couldn't be trusted with easy access. More likely, something about the isolation had made them nervous of things like owning a credit card, or online banking, or even tap-and-go. In her view it played into a wariness, recoiling from the world. They lived on a meagre and well-ordered budget: the house search suggested monotony in food choices and a plethora of second-hand clothes and books.

'So, no other phone of any kind that we can distinguish. What about triangulating any signals we can't account for in the area?'

'I've been trying that,' replied Lucy. 'Three service providers rent space on the two masts in the area: one by the service station, one near the entrance to the golf club. So it's bi-angulating, rather than triangulating. Assuming that's a word. But two masts explains why the signal comes and goes. Anyway, we haven't got much. See here.'

Lucy angled the screen to give Dana a general sense of what was on it; Mike and Ali were closer and picked up more detail. 'So, the way they send the data through: they divide our region into cute little hexagons. In urban areas, the hexagons are small and tightly packed because there are plenty of masts. In the area near the Doyle cottage, it's one giant hexagon that would take an hour to walk across. The data can confirm whether a phone was used within that hexagon – but not where in that area. *Not enough masts to granulate*, I was told. Any calls might have been on the road, for instance, or up a creek. There's been no mobile phone used in that hexagon for the past four weeks, until Willie called us about the body and we turned up. Prior to that, one used around once a week for about nine months. Not a regular pattern, but switched on for about ten to twenty minutes each time.'

'Not linked to a phone account?'

'Nah, out in the breeze. A pay-as-you-go burner?'

'Can we please cross-reference those times with the employment records for Suzanne Doyle?' asked Dana. 'It might eliminate her as the caller, if the calls were made while she was at work. Which, barring strangers inexplicably driving through from nowhere to nowhere, would bump Marika to the top of the list. I suspect Marika has a phone and hides it out in the swamp: it'll be in some waterproof container in a tree stump, or something.'

'Shall do.'

'No way of knowing the number that person called?'

'Nope. Only that the phone was on, and connecting to a tower.'

Ali spoke up, seemingly glad to have some input to offer. 'I checked with the prison while I was there, about calls to Curtis. None through the official channels since about six months after he entered prison – some journalists initially sniffed around for an interview but dropped it. But they did say that if someone rings the prisoner area from a burner, it's currently impossible to trace.' She held up both palms. 'Yup, I pulled that face, too. Their lawyers call them that way, so there's privacy issues with the authorities monitoring it. There's no records about who rang, who spoke, or when. There's some software that might help a bit, but no budget for it.'

Hmm, thought Dana. *If I was a prison governor, that would be a priority.*

'Okay, thank you, everyone, good work. I know it seems like cul-de-sacs all round, but often these little nuggets come together later in surprising ways.' Dana turned to Rainer. 'ATV tracks?'

'Yes, yes. I followed up the possibility of ATV tracks with the search team. As you'll remember, we found a partial near the crime scene that didn't match any vehicle there. Forensics took plaster impressions and the tyres fit the ATV version Marika has; so that's a plus. But they fit a number of other vehicles as well – there are four similar registered ATVs within a ten-kilometre radius, so I imagine a defence lawyer would raise that. Especially as we checked it, and they're entitled to see the files . . .'

'I know, I know,' agreed Dana. 'Disclosure's a pain. Let's comfort ourselves that we're helping human liberty and justice for all, and move on. Is there any way they can trace the partial to Marika's vehicle in particular?'

'*Nein*. Not without having the actual vehicle in their possession. Stuart suggested that the ATV was normally parked behind a rhododendron near the road, but it's entirely gravel there: we've got no comparison track that we definitely know is Marika's vehicle. There are a couple of distinct tread patterns to our mystery vehicle, which could be matched, but without having Marika's ATV in the hangar it's all speculation.'

The ATV was a strange one; on what they presently knew, Dana couldn't understand why it would have been bought for, or by, Marika. It was out of synch with their current lives and what Dana knew about their lives when Mary was around. It was just enough of a vehicle to transport people dead or alive, but seemingly ethereal and easy to hide.

'Crap. Could they at least indicate how many people might have been aboard the generic ATV they can't trace?'

'They estimated. And they made it extremely clear it was an estimate. They took the tyre impressions from Willie's pick-up as a comparison. They know how much that weighs, and how deep an impression it left on the self-same mud, in the same conditions, so they work backwards from that, knowing how much an empty ATV weighs. I told them Suzanne was around sixty kilos, Marika maybe sixty as well, Curtis possibly ninety-five. Does that sound about right?'

Dana pondered. It was certainly close for Suzanne; they'd get a definite weight for Curtis from the impending autopsy, but it sounded okay. Without seeing a contemporary Marika, Dana thought sixty was high for a potentially waif-like young woman.

'Exact enough at this stage. So they concluded all three were on the ATV when it left those tyre marks?'

'Yes, yes they did. Between two hundred and two-thirty kilos of additional weight. Estimated. Although getting them to commit fully to that will be a stretch. It's all conjecture and maybes at this point. And, of course, Curtis plus another similar-sized man would make a similar weight. Just saying.'

'Nicely done, Rainer, thank you. For me, it most likely places all three on the ATV, at the scene of the crime, on the evening or night of the crime. We also have no evidence of footprints from the crime scene to the scene of the rape; they weren't giving Curtis a lift so that he could wander off there. What we don't know, however, is whether Curtis ever left that spot after he got off the ATV.'

Dana rose. She needed time apart from this, in a different setting, to think it through more carefully. She resolved to visit the autopsy. It wasn't something she often did, given that she trusted the pair conducting it; the visit was more about her own need for small crumbs of solitude whenever she could grab them. She focused on the whiteboard.

'Okay. Thank you, everyone, for your efforts. I know it's frustrating so far. I'm going to summarize where we are now, before we share some new information. Stop me if I miss anything out, or misrepresent.

'Other than the letters, we have no way to currently link Curtis to the sisters, prior to their meeting yesterday. All the necessary details about picking Curtis up from the prison were clear and visible in the letters. I believe the sisters – or one of them – were in fact telephoning Curtis intermittently, using a burner phone that's hidden somewhere in the swamp. But I can't prove that, for now.

'We can track the sisters' route and their behaviour, from prison gate to their front door. I'm interested that Suzanne did nearly all the speaking to Curtis but appeared stilted and distanced. I'd have guessed

Marika might have had the closer connection, although given that part of their behaviour is deliberate, and they are aware that the cameras are running, that could be a double-bluff. What stands out is the use of fluoro. It's seemingly an overt attempt to ensure they are visible on various cameras. Once it's served its purpose, the clothing is hidden. I have no idea why.

'We now have a wider picture of Suzanne and Marika, an isolated pairing who choose to be on the periphery. Suzanne earns and controls the money, so, in a financial sense, the younger sister is very much the junior. Perhaps Marika has more sway in other ways – we won't know until we meet her. Regardless, they lead an unusual life that appears, from what we can prove, to have no electronic devices and no internet at all.

'At this point, we have no forensics that link the sisters directly to the murder, only to having picked up Curtis from prison, and transported him back to their house. And we can imply, not prove, that they visited the crime scene with Curtis prior to the murder. We still, crucially, have no motive for them wanting to hurt Curtis, let alone kill him. And no evidence that Suzanne or Marika committed any crime at all. So . . . we keep at the sisters' involvement, certainly, but we need other options as well.'

'Daft question from me?'

'Fire away, Luce.'

'What do they think we know? Suzanne and David Rowe?'

'No, actually, that's a very good question. I don't know for certain, and I couldn't find out without tipping them off. But for now, I think they're stuck. I'm sure they've realized that we're going to be talking about Curtis Monroe, but neither I nor they have mentioned him at this point. The media have reported a body found, but I don't believe Suzanne or David know precisely what we found at the crime scene. And I'm not sure what significance that holds. For example, if the sisters are nothing to do with the crime, they wouldn't know anything about the body. So, early days, but I'll be keeping my powder dry.

'Now, Mike has come across some information that opens out another branch of the investigation. The two branches need to go in parallel from here on in. They are currently equally important. I'd like them both pursued, please, and each to look at punching holes in the argument of the other. Anyone is free to do that at any time, okay? So, Mikey.'

Mike filled in the blanks on the Aryan connection, restricting his references to Kasparov as *that source*. Lucy bit her lip; Rainer made notes; Richard stroked his chin and raised his eyebrows occasionally. Dana tried not to be judgemental but felt the potential ramifications of Aryan involvement were still a little beyond Ali.

Dana went back to the whiteboard. 'Thank you, Mikey. As just intimated, we aren't supposed to know about this angle, so keep it held tight, please. We have to work on it subtly: others are out on a limb, here. Notwithstanding that, how does the new information compare with what we have on the sisters? Anyone?'

Rainer offered, 'I still like the sisters for it, though I can't say why because that Aryan angle looks more logical. But the fact that the Doyles contacted Curtis, built some kind of relationship and took him in when he was released: it bugs me. I can't say why they did it, but I can't see that contact turning out well. Something went wrong.'

'Anyone else?'

Lucy pitched in. 'Nah, I like the Aryans, now that we've uncovered that connection. They have motive, which the sisters don't. I've always felt that was the weakest link for the Doyles. Besides, this murder is too public to be the sisters, surely? They know about the swamps. The body was left that way as a signal and the Aryans had urgent need of a signal.'

'Mikey?'

'I veer towards the Aryans: as Luce said, they have motive and means, and opportunity isn't a stretch. What we have on the sisters is too flimsy to hang a murder charge on. In fact, I could make a case for the Aryans – and against the sisters – right here and now.'

Dana sat on the corner of the desk. 'You're the Doyles' new defence lawyer, Mikey. Fire.'

'Okay.' Mike grabbed his lapels and talked down his nose at the assembled. 'My clients the Doyles are basically nice people. They lost their mother and it made them re-think their lives. They wanted to do something good, to give back. So they started writing to Curtis Monroe. The letters were neutral – vaguely supportive and optimistic, but nothing untoward, according to the prison, parole team and, frankly, the police. Nothing to indicate any problem. They offered him a place to stay for a few days, maybe a new Samsung and hot food. By 10 p.m. Curtis is fed and watered, dozing on the couch and drunk. A nice, non-belligerent drunk, though. My clients weren't worried.

'Option A. At around 10 p.m. Curtis got a call on a phone of his own: not on the Samsung because we can see that's never been used. My clients have no idea who called Curtis. He stumbled out of the house towards the road. My clients didn't follow. They heard a car leaving, but Curtis didn't return. No idea where he went, or who the driver was. No idea there was anything wrong until the detective turned up waving a warrant. Oh, and Marika regularly goes off for a night or two: the sisters need a bit of time apart, cooped up in that house as they are.

'Option B. This negates the question Dana now has about the tower data showing no phone being used that night in that district. Sometime after 10 p.m. there's a knock on the door. Clara Belmont is already asleep and didn't hear a car pass her house. My clients don't get visitors, especially at night. They're worried. They send Curtis to see who it is. He steps outside, seems to know the visitor. There's a conversation, but my clients don't see who it is and can't hear what's said. Curtis leaves with the person. My clients hear a car shortly afterwards on the road, but see nothing. They presumed it was an old friend, and that Curtis went off on a now-you're-out-of-prison bender. Perhaps it turned out to be the Aryans taking him on a one-way trip. Who knows? They aren't his keeper – they don't own Curtis. If he didn't come back in a day or two, maybe they'd have tried to find him. Perhaps they'd figure he'd sorted out something else. Again, they know nothing until the detective comes knocking the next day.

'Now, aside from the telephone tower data for the first option, either version fits with what we have. They fit a neutral reading of the letters while Curtis was in prison; the camera footage of the sisters picking up Curtis from prison; their conduct whenever they're on camera; Clara Belmont's sighting in the late afternoon; the forensics placing Curtis in the living room, bedroom and bathroom; the rough time of death; the lack of forensic proof at the crime scene; the lack of apparent motive for the sisters; the potential motive from Aryan Force; the absence of Marika today.'

Mike's performance concluded, he spread his hands and asked, 'Do we have anything that drives a coach and horses through any of that?'

Jeez, thought Dana, *we do not*. There was nothing significant in either of those defences that they could demolish. Both were plausible, fitted with practically all they knew and would work with a jury. At best, they presented viable alternatives; so much so, Dana doubted they'd get as far as a trial with what they currently held. Still, she had to probe further.

'As you corrected yourself, Mikey: option A doesn't allow for the evidence from the phone masts. We have no evidence any phone was used in that area in the past few weeks. But I agree that's minor. The partial of the ATV tyre is another wrinkle but can be explained away without much problem. And we haven't had the tox screen back yet, so we can't be sure Curtis was drunk or drugged. But, like you, I suspect something like that will turn up in autopsy later: probably alcohol. And now we have this game with the fluoro: your options don't specifically address that. But those are all side issues: you've hit the highlights, Mikey – well played. For me, the crucial thing missing with the sisters is motive. Like Luce said.'

Lucy beamed and gave a thumbs-up.

'Yeah, I know,' replied Mike. 'Part of me wondered if there was something in Curtis's past where he crossed paths with one of the sisters. His rape conviction might not have been his first sexual assault: we know how often the conviction is the last, or latest, in a series of crimes. But it doesn't feel too likely: the need for revenge in that case would be less than the need to steer well clear of him, I reckon.'

That was true. They'd found no evidence linking Curtis with either sister at any time, though he'd lived in Earlville all his life, so was often within a few kilometres of them. The age gap between Curtis, at twenty-seven, and Suzanne, at twenty-five, had them at the same school in different years. But that felt insubstantial: they'd found no evidence they ever met. It seemed to Dana something to tick off, rather than something vital.

'I still think we're missing something crucial in the letters,' she said. 'They were the first point of contact, and the means of getting Curtis to that cottage, on that afternoon. He was dead, close to that cottage, that night. There has to be more in those letters that we're missing. Any ideas?'

Lucy offered. 'Word cloud?'

'Let's imagine I'm pretending to be ignorant of what that is, Luce.'

'Take each word in the letters, take out the obvious ones like *I*, *me*, *and*, *but*, *it* . . . then the remainder are shown graphically. The more frequent they are, the nearer they are to the centre of the graphic, and the larger they are. Helps you to see potential patterns or priorities.'

'Hmm. I like the sound of that; thanks, Luce. Ali, can you also take another swing at the correspondence, please? The first time we looked at the letters, we weren't as far down this road as we are now, so new things might jump out at you this time. I have a set of copies on my desk, if you want to go through them at home rather than here. You're up to nine hours on shift so far, so feel free to take the copies home if you wish.

'Mikey, you're on for this meeting with a source this afternoon, so please focus on that. But if you get a chance, please try to push *los Federales* on anything that might support this Aryan connection. I'm hoping we can tap them, without tipping off anyone local that we have this avenue to explore. Luce, please go at those letters and the cloud thingy; it'll be useful to have all that text on a searchable file, as well. Rainer and Richard, please go through the CCTV footage of Curtis and the sisters. This time, go thirty minutes before and after they appear on each camera. We're looking for any evidence that someone was following them, or taking an interest. Plus, Rainer, please interview the key people who may have interacted with the trio; specifically, the staff in Macca's and the car-rental agency who served them. Thank you.

'I'll be attending the autopsy, trying to get something else on who and why. Then, another shot at Suzanne – probably the last of the day before her lawyer insists she rests up. Thank you, everyone.'

Chapter 17

Thursday, 1 August 2019. 1500 hrs

Dana scanned her ID by the door of the medical examination unit. The building, five hundred metres from Carlton station, doubled as a regional centre for all sorts of scientific effort. Various staff worked to prevent food-safety mishaps, epidemics, water-safety issues, crop sabotage, as well as examining dead bodies. The glass frontage was intended to convey transparency and openness to public scrutiny, but each day every blackout blind was down.

Inside, it hadn't changed much in six years. Back then, Dana was barely out of her basic training. Colleagues at central training school had laughed and told her 'morgue duty' was for slow-trackers and slackers: especially sent to the backside of nowhere down at Carlton. Most police officers working with a MedEx were being parked, or seeing out time, or being punished for infractions or failures to launch. All the ambitious high-flyers, she was told, were not scaling the dizzying peaks by spending twelve months babysitting corpses in the 'dreary regions', followed by several years in Fraud. Dana took them at their word. She didn't want to be a high-flyer, with the attendant pressures and constant thrum of politicking, schmoozing, finding mentors and 'champions'. All the same, it wasn't the done thing to admit that she really liked working with the MedEx and would happily have stayed for ever if they hadn't held her to automatic rotation.

The unit still exhibited an uneasy combination of smells from laboratory and office: brutal bleach and placid, warm dust. The corridor floors were a shiny and tenacious vinyl, impervious to body fluids and spinning rubber wheels; the lights were still overbearing and migraine-inducing. In the rooms that skulked away from the main traffic zones, scientists preferred working in the dark; so had she. There remained the quiet, contemplative sincerity to the atmosphere that had resonated with her. Scientists held fast – beyond the usual petty human squabbles – to a purity of purpose she'd admired and wanted to share. It was a search for science's undeniable truth, instead of settling for the justice system's plausible blame. Although the sole police officer in the building, she'd often felt these were her kind of people.

Professor Bruce Keller was now returned from a six-month sabbatical and in his last three years as medical examiner. Younger doctors were pushing for the post, and only Bill Meeks's personal intervention had secured Keller this final fixed-term contract. If he hadn't been offered that, Keller would have walked. Dana had thought it was crazy: to throw away all that experience because of a lame and simplistic policy from Central. The next MedEx would be unlikely to put in such long and unsocial hours; wouldn't take the extra twenty minutes to explain to a raw police officer how blood flowed within the brain. Bill had bought them an extra three years, and as she opened the door to the examination suite Dana resolved to come down here regularly, merely to learn. She didn't do enough of that; was caught up too easily in the rush. It was another potential island in the day, and one that was legitimate enough to stand scrutiny.

Keller looked up from a clipboard and beamed. His hair totally silver now, he retained the skinny upper body of the gifted amateur cyclist; he regularly won events well outside his age group. His hands were, she felt, beautiful. Slim, tapered, almost line-free even now; they resembled a sketch of an artist's hand. They moved with subtlety and grace even when he was merely holding a pen; she recalled that, in her early months in the unit, she was often caught staring at them.

'Miss Russo! How marvellous.'

They each lifted a hand in a wave from several yards away: hugging would have compromised lab sterility. Besides, both preferred a warm but completely antiseptic display of fondness.

'Hello, Professor. I was thinking, walking down that corridor, that I should come here more often. I've missed the old place.'

He smiled. 'And it misses you. I think you might have been the last one to take all this seriously. Everyone since seems to view it as a punishment and can't wait for rotation. Lots of scowls, begrudging effort, half-hearted interest. Please say you'll quit the detecting bit and come back to us.'

The idea was more tempting than he probably realized, she thought. At least once a day her imposter syndrome would kick in and she'd wonder what the big cheeses would say if she asked for a transfer, and a *demotion*. Just to lose the pressure; the yawning gap between her introversion and the organization's relentless momentum.

'Never say never, Professor. I was hoping to be in time for Curtis Mason Monroe.'

'Spot on. I was about to scrub and begin. It's all still where it used to be, I think.'

He gestured at a pile of gowns and masks on a nearby shelf. They both suited up and prepped in companionable silence: Keller was not a small-talker and viewed quiet as a sign of good manners, serious thought and respect both for the work at hand and the victim. Nothing made him more impatient than empty gibbering.

Curtis Mason Monroe was laid out under a white sheet, illuminated by an impossibly strong light that virtually obliterated a sense of shape.

Above and to the left, a microphone hung like a stalactite from the ceiling. Keller eased it into position directly above Monroe's sternum and peeled back the sheet. Keller's medical assistant, Sarah, nodded at Dana, their smiles discernible under the masks.

Dana watched as Keller made the early observations. Part of the basics came from the locum at the scene, but that examination had been rudimentary and consisted mainly of context. It provided photos of the scene's staging, close-ups of wounds and bindings, general information about conditions, such as the soil under the body. The locum had been a collector; Keller would be the analyst. Lucy had sent Keller her work on the weather systems tracking the area that night. It affected the calculation of time of death: air temperature mattered, and each sweep of squally rain dropped the temperature five degrees until it passed.

'Please thank Miss Delaney for me. Excellent work, excellent.'

Curtis Mason Monroe had a doughy complexion and a lack of muscle tone. Too much sitting; too much cheap and poor food; too little effort. His hair was military-short: presumably through choice, Dana thought, because these days it wasn't compulsory in prison. She looked to his hands out of instinct: callouses on both index fingers, some healed nicks on several pads. Carpentry, she guessed, or maybe metalwork. Standard prison time-filler, but one that indicated he could be trusted with sharp objects: it wasn't true of all prisoners.

Sarah started filling in the forms. The corpse was 101 kilos, and 1.81 metres. Monroe was heftier than Dana had initially thought: she could now compare him to Suzanne and note the difference in potential power. It made Dana wonder how the sisters had controlled or moved Monroe – assuming they had. Alternatively, some Aryan muscle could move Monroe through threat, rather than manhandling. Monroe had some skin issues around the back of the neck: not a wound or abrasion, possibly an aversion to fabric or washing powder. The scar on his abdomen glinted in the powerful lamp, like a streak of quicksilver escaping his body. Keller looked up.

'Do you know the provenance of this, Miss Russo? We haven't read the documents from the prison yet.'

'Yes,' she said. 'It was on his medical records before entering prison, so it's over a decade old. He accidentally impaled himself on a fence post.'

'Hmm.' Keller and Sarah looked closer. 'Lucky boy,' he murmured. 'An inch to the side and it was bye-bye time.'

Sarah looked up at Dana with a gleam in her eye. 'Has Professor Keller always thought the people on his slab were fortunate?'

Dana smiled. 'To be examined by the best? Yes.'

There were a couple of minutes between initial inspection and first incision. Keller and Sarah washed the body. Closely, carefully. Their movements were smooth and practised; they were well used to negotiating each other's space without speaking. They treated Curtis Monroe as if he were still alive but suffering terrible burns; their touch was delicate and considered.

Dana watched silently; her reverence for their reverence. Whenever she saw a dead body, no matter where she saw it or how the person had died, at least a sliver of Dana always thought the same thing. *Lucky you.* The dead person had slipped the shackles. Never again would they suffer pain or endure their own sense of loss; be cheated or abused; struggle, yet fail. They'd slid into a land where they could no longer be reached. Dana was sure no more awaited them after this, and that was what she envied above all: the *nothing* in their future.

Keller pulled the temperature data Lucy had provided and tapped the keyboard thoughtfully.

'Time of death is between 11 p.m. and 3 a.m. I would veer towards the start of that window, if it's any help.'

Dana wasn't sure it was. If the sisters were involved, it didn't matter which part of the dead of night was relevant; they were each other's sole alibi and the crime took place near their home but a long way from anywhere else. If they weren't involved but the Aryans were, then presumably Curtis Monroe had left the cottage before midnight; the investigation currently had no one else to ask about alibis and timing.

Keller began to slice in smooth, certain arcs. He opened and peeled, removed each organ carefully and weighed it, pausing to examine colour and texture. Aside from being dead, Monroe wasn't in especially bad shape. The heart had been split in two by one of the blows he'd received; Keller laid each part in a separate steel bowl.

'The incision's smooth but efficient.' He pointed with the scalpel as Dana came closer. 'See here? There's a slight folding around the front edge of the wound. The blade went through quickly – although it was enough to do the damage, it wasn't as sharp as, say, this scalpel. So it's a wider blade than that. I'd say about seven or eight millimetres thick, but I'll get you a more definitive measurement soon.'

'Brutal, though, isn't it?' said Dana. 'Whoever did this put some heft behind it.' Away from the crime scene, Curtis's body – and the damage inflicted – seemed starker and more horrendous than it had beside the swamp.

'Yes, true,' agreed Keller. 'I don't know that it speaks to motive, though.' He stood back for a moment. 'Once someone decides to kill – decides *absolutely* – then the force involved might be opportunistic or accidental, not a measure of hatred. If a little old lady pushes you down the stairs, the damage comes from the stairs and from gravity, not the force of her push or the malice in her heart. Yes?'

That was true; but Dana realized she'd previously underestimated the brutality and horror of the killing. Seeing the body initially *in situ*, she'd focused on the processes to be followed. As, she felt, had everyone else: eager to do a professional job and cover all bases, they sometimes pushed aside the barbarism of taking a life. Curtis Mason

Monroe had had his heart ripped in two; had something sharp and heavy launched at him, more than once. And he was placed in a position that said *crucified*. Perhaps revenge for his previous crime, but it spoke to a callous attitude that was chilling when she stood back and absorbed it.

'Was there any foreign debris on the blade as it went in?' Dana was hoping for something that would help to define what weapon was used: grass shards because it was a scythe, for example.

'I can't see anything,' replied Keller.

Sarah waved her hand over the area. 'Methylated spirit. A tiny whiff. So perhaps an axe, or a sword, Professor?'

'I never doubt your olfactory skills, Sarah. Yes, more likely an axe, though. See this angle, Miss Russo? It's curved – convex, by the look. But we'll try some measuring.'

Sarah moved away to fetch a camera from the nearby bench. Again, Dana marvelled at the silence and the cool air, and the sense that this work was touching a void, sighting the impossible. She looked back down at Curtis Monroe, the lucky one. She wondered if he wanted her to find his killer, or if he didn't care now. Or if he'd ever cared. The more they found out, the more he seemed to have carried a stoic acceptance that his life was about to end. Nothing, yet, that suggested he'd struggled to stay alive. People assumed that everyone had a basic human instinct to fight for life, to cling to it. But some didn't. And knew they didn't.

'Each photo Sarah takes is the same distance from a fixed point,' explained Keller. 'That way, everything in the photo can be located – to within a fraction of an inch – by how it sits compared to that point. It means we can, or the computer can, instantly offer three-dimensional images. Better than an X-ray in some ways, because it's more solid.'

'Impressive.'

'Yes and no,' replied Sarah. 'It is extremely useful, but you'd find similar technology at your dentist if you went for a dental implant.'

Sarah had the three-dimensional view now. Monroe's anonymized image was spun and flipped on the screen, able to be sighted from any angle.

'What can this tell me about the wounds?' asked Dana.

Sarah zoomed the image as Keller spoke.

'As you can see, Miss Russo, three separate entries. Since it's probably an axe of some kind, it's unlikely they made a fourth effort that exactly overlays a previous one – they wouldn't be that accurate with the swing. All the same, it's overkill. Mr Monroe would have died after the first one: heart split in two. Each blow flew in from his left. Oh, look at the muscles: yes, his hands would have been at least level with the shoulder for each blow. The muscles were already stretched upwards when they were breached.'

As in, a cruciform position. Confirming, Dana thought, that Monroe was probably already tied up before the attack came. A hired killer – or two, with one holding a weapon – could sort that out easily. For the two sisters, it was trickier because of Curtis's weight and power.

'Any particular kind of skill or strength required for the blows?'

'I wouldn't say so, no. Especially if the body was immobile at that point. The axe isn't huge, so anyone could lift it. The kind an organization might keep in case of fire, for example. But sharp enough to cut through using its own weight and gravity: no need to be muscular. A man or woman, or adolescent; no special ability wielding it is required. Perhaps an ability to avoid hesitation on contact? They followed through without indecision, it seems to me.'

It floated into Dana's mind that Keller's analysis didn't rule out waif-life Marika, either. Her thoughts flicked back to what had been said about the muscles being stretched when assaulted: now she considered the way Monroe had been tied.

As though reading her mind, Sarah clicked to bring up photos of the bound hands at the crime scene.

'And what,' asked Keller, 'do we deduce from the binding?'

Dana peered closer. 'Standard domestic rope: too small for towing. We don't have the mountains near here for rock-climbing, though that remains a possibility. More likely: the kind of rope you'd buy if you wanted to strap down a tarpaulin, for example. Any hardware shop, probably impossible to trace. Scenes of Crime have tested it: since I haven't heard otherwise yet, I assume it had no usable fingerprints. So the perpetrator, or perpetrators, had gloves. Given the temperature at the time, they might have been in gloves anyway. But I'm inclined to believe that they were prepared, forensically aware, and intended all this.'

She knew Keller – and Sarah – expected her to follow on.

'The knot is a single-column tie. I noticed it at the scene: the same knot is used on both wrists and the feet. A single-column tie is a rookie knot. That might lead me to think the person or persons tying it weren't experienced in binding people. But I don't discount the option of it being a professional, or an experienced S&M enthusiast, trying to mislead me.' Dana failed to notice the blush around Sarah's nape. 'Since it's a beginner's knot, it doesn't draw the investigation towards particular groups or individual backgrounds: the perpetrator may have chosen it for that reason.

'There were signs,' she continued, 'that Monroe had pulled against rope recently: he had abrasions that matched the width of this rope. But I'm still awaiting evidence that proves it was against these ropes, or at this scene. However, each wrist was tied to a separate post. I'm minded that he was not bound before he got to the crime scene, only once he arrived. So either he complied, or he was sedated in some way. Which is your kingdom, Professor.'

Keller smiled. 'I'm glad you haven't forgotten everything, Miss Russo. And the shape he was tied in, the cruciform. Any views on that?'

'When I first arrived at the scene, I thought he'd been placed like that deliberately – that it was part of the murderer's staging. At that time, I was thinking ritualistic, possibly with a religious overtone. But we have some evidence that the posts were already there. Tying Monroe to those posts may have been simply a means of ensuring he was immobile, to allow the axe blows to be accurate and unhindered.'

'I concur. The rope marks on the wrists –' he turned back to the corpse and indicated with his pen – 'show one line. If Mr Monroe had his hands bound while he was being transported to the scene, other rope marks would be higher on the wrist; they'd be visibly different and you'd see two or three tracks around the wrist where the rope was looped and re-looped. Also, look back at the heart.'

Sarah was already handing him the bowl: these two danced sublimely through their work.

'This is the first blow, here. We can tell, because?'

'Because the other two blows overlap it; the edges of the trauma lines overlay each other a little.'

'Good, good. The first blow is not exactly perpendicular to the body: it's down slightly, towards the lower ribs. Assuming Mr Monroe was lying on the ground and was bound as shown in the photos, the likelihood is of a right-handed assailant, standing astride the victim's waist and striking from the right. Hence, the weight of the axe pulls the blade towards the assailant's feet. Whereas here the second and third strikes slant upwards, towards Mr Monroe's face. Conclusion?'

'Someone not especially used to using this tool. Possibly the same assailant switched positions, standing over the head and swinging backhand twice. Or, another assailant, left-handed, was standing in that position and took their turn for forehand blows two and three.'

'Or?'

Dana thought. Keller never pushed because he wished to embarrass; he knew her well enough to understand that she had the answer, somewhere.

'Or . . . exactly vice versa. First blow was a backhand from a left-hander; second and third were backhands from a right-hander. In which case, they were deliberately looking to create wounds that suggested one thing while another was taking place. Unlikely, since most people swing forehand, so chances are the first blow was forehand, and therefore right-handed.'

'Or,' chimed Sarah, 'one or two assailants who are ambidextrous and like to play with detectives' heads.'

Keller smiled. 'Sarah and her ambidextrous murderers.'

Dana smiled too, but she'd been thinking the same thing.

'No, I think in this case Sarah has a good point. There are professional sportsmen, and women, who play right-handed but are lefties in real life. It depends on your upbringing.'

'Precisely, Dana,' beamed Sarah. 'Someone who grew up in a tightly bound environment, with an overbearing parent, might end up an *ambi*. They're corralled into being right-handed, for example, but away from the family they use their left as a form of rebellion. They end up equally adept at both.'

A tightly bound environment with an overbearing parent.

'Regardless of the forehand/backhand issue, Professor, they'd have blood spatter on them?'

Keller grunted. 'Hmm. Yes. Substantial. On their feet and lower limbs simply from the spray as the axe went through flesh. But as the heart was struck, wider spray that would have gone higher.'

Dana bit her lip. 'But we found no spray at the scene; only a small pool and lividity under the victim's back and flank.'

Keller raised an eyebrow and took a fresh look at the crime scene photos from Scenes of Crime. Then he double-checked by lifting Curtis to look at his spine.

'Well, in that case, your killer, or killers, used sheets or tarpaulins. Miss Delaney's data demonstrates several significant storms; they would have washed much of the sprayed blood into the soil. Especially on the body itself. But some blood would remain on the soil below the body, unless the assailant had covers underneath Mr Monroe at the time of striking. I would also expect bloody footprints.'

'No, there aren't any with blood in them. Only scuff marks from shoes. We haven't got a match to those marks, either.'

'Then your perpetrators did this.'

Keller mimed pulling a tarpaulin away, folding it carefully so that none of the blood dripped out. Then sliding his feet around the general area, moving the dirt around and relying on subsequent rain to render it useless for forensics by soaking it in. It also meant, thought Dana, that the assailants took away their shoes and clothing. The degree of forensic awareness and care looked . . . professional.

'So the rain,' interjected Sarah, 'was a big stroke of luck.'

Dana leaned back against a counter. 'Yes and no. It was for the killer, or killers, in the sense that it came at precisely the right time. The storms were squally and, when it rained, it rained hard; they washed away significant forensics. It wasn't lucky for the victim in that perhaps the weather forecast helped to decide when Curtis Monroe was killed, or whether he was killed at all. Maybe the murderer was relying on rain to cover their actions – assuming they had reasons why the killing had to be carried out at that location. If it had been a clear night the murderer may have waited, and Curtis might have escaped all this.'

'Ah,' replied Keller, raising a finger. 'But Sarah and I – and you, Miss Russo – would simply have dropped Mr Monroe into the biggest bog we could find, wouldn't we? It's all fatal swamp out there. In which case, you'd never have found the body in the first place: the weather would have been moot, because you wouldn't know there was something to investigate.'

Dana kept coming back to that herself. It was a huge reason why the sisters were nothing to do with it; Marika especially knew that area backwards and would know how to lose something the size of a body. Dana suspected that if one of the women had successfully ditched the ATV, then secreting Monroe's corpse would be like shelling peas. If it *was* the sisters, why on earth would they leave the body on show, knowing they were the nearest people to it?

On the other hand, if it was an out-of-towner unfamiliar with the area, in the dead of night and a rainstorm, they might be unaware that they were surrounded by forensics-deadening swamp. Or they might want to leave the corpse visible so that the subsequent publicity served as a warning. Or proof that the task had been completed and final payment was due. Which would make Mike's view that Aryan Force were implicated much more likely.

'Any further questions at this juncture, Miss Russo?' Keller was already preparing a saw to open up the skull. Dana was never fond of the sound, nor of the smell.

'No, I don't think so, thank you. Oh, toxicology – any drugs or alcohol that might have made Monroe more pliant. That would be useful to know, please.'

Keller smiled. 'Already upstairs and being analysed. Sarah will drop off the report first thing tomorrow. Good to see you again, Miss Russo.'

As Dana got to the door, she turned. 'Thank you both very much. Three years, this week?'

Keller nodded again.

'Well, then,' said Dana. 'Happy anniversary.'

'Thank you,' they both replied.

Chapter 18

The café Wickham Watts had chosen for the meet was an improbably twee tea shop created to look like an Alpine chalet but placed next to a twenty-four-hour service station. Faux-Teutonic sat next to rumbling road trains, swapped-in gas bottles and neon-lit pump prices. White linen tablecloths, doilies, bone-china cups and the promise of a pyramid of Fondant Fancies if Mike ordered the Full Afternoon Tea. The juxtaposition of *ye olde* service and a discussion of large-scale drug-dealing hit Mike's sense of the absurd. C4 often had a po-faced attitude that their work was more important and edgy than anyone else's: Mike had a feeling he was going to like Wickham Watts.

They'd agreed to connect early, before a meeting with Lucas Baker. While Baker appeared to be a young management consultant with a burgeoning portfolio, Mike had been assured this was a smooth front for rough edges: Baker was the acceptable face of Aryan Force and one of its leading strategic lights. Apparently.

Mike picked the C4 officer as undercover while Wickham was still in his car. A dark jacket was hung from a hook behind the driver's seat; the sunroof was open on a chilly afternoon; the radio aerial hinted at more technology than average. Wickham wore Ray-bans that he took off in a melodramatic gesture before looking around the car park, like the opening credits of a TV show. Yes, Wickham had a sense of theatre, thought Mike.

'Hi, Mike,' he said, pumping their handshake energetically. Wickham was over six feet, toned and central-casting smooth: a squared-off jaw, short Action Man hair and expensive teeth. He would play himself, in any subsequent movie. He would make sure he played himself.

'Call me Mikey. Undercover today, Wickham?' asked Mike, *sotto voce*.

'Ha, practically a day off. But you never know who's keeping tabs. So never off duty, really.' He raised his voice as they sat. 'The scones here are great. Little old lady in the next village bakes them.'

'More an éclair man, myself.'

'Oh,' replied Wickham, as the waitress left them two coffees. 'Get you and your fancy Carlton ways.'

Mike grinned, and took a sip. An elderly couple shuffled off towards the door in a flurry of knitwear, almost knocking a display of walking sticks into the foyer. The waitress retreated through flapping saloon doors to the kitchen, to apathetically swipe left. It gave the pair plenty of space and no one to disturb them.

Wickham Watts sat forward and stared at his phone, waving it vaguely at the table. Mike realized he was checking for listening devices. Seemingly satisfied, Wickham pocketed the phone.

'Define the concept of *McMafia*, Mikey.'

'Sure. It's the idea that crime organizations don't always carry out the deeds themselves; they also farm it out like a franchise. That way, they cream off some of the profits, have little work and almost zero risk.'

Wickham blinked, clearly wanting more reassurance that Mike had some handle on this conversation. Mike continued.

'So, the franchisee pays the crime organization for the right to call themselves that umbrella name – *CrimeULike*, or whatever. The franchisee gets the occasional helping hand or logistic work; carries the implied threat of the parent organization; and avoids being in a local war.' Mike shrugged. 'Al-Qaeda is like the Mafia is like McDonald's.'

Christ, he thought, *I described that like Dana would.*

'Good explanation. Sub-contracting the grunt work, but keeping the name and the power: that's what happened in Du Pont prison. The fascist dickheads in Du Pont are a local wing of a much larger group.' Wickham's gaze swept the car park before he resumed. 'So, Aryan Force has been looking to control the drug trade in all the prisons in the country – that's their stated aim. Or, at least, that's what we now understand to be their stated aim. We pretty much had no idea on this until Curtis Monroe rolled. He was a flood of information, frankly.'

Mike frowned. 'He was that important?'

Wickham puffed his cheeks. It was an embarrassment to the C4 unit that they'd had no idea of Curtis's real involvement, nor of the extent of what he would reveal.

'As it turned out, yeah. He'd indicated a few days before release that he wanted to say something, so we'd set up a fake lawyer for the day. A state agent, recently transferred from across country: wouldn't be recognizable. The cover story was a last-minute screw-up on who'd been told about Curtis's release, which needed some extra paperwork. That got us alone in a room with the guy, a few minutes before he walked out of Du Pont. We expected a couple of names, and that would be it. What he produced was a blow-by-blow inside account.'

Mike pictured Curtis Monroe spilling his guts to a state agent then blithely climbing into a hired Nissan piloted by Suzanne Doyle, and riding around in a fluoro vest. The lack of precaution seemed recklessly naive.

'Didn't you want to keep hold of him after that, pump him for more?'

'Oh Christ, yeah. But we'd already signed an agreement with him.

It left him clear of any and all charges: full immunity. And it specifically stopped us following him, stopping him or getting anywhere near
him. He wanted to unload and then have nothing to do with us.'

'Is that common?'

'No, it's not.'

Wickham hesitated, deciding how to frame the next statement. He
looked odd, mused Mike, when he stopped. He was the sort of person
who should always be in motion; that kind of kinetic personality that
would sweep others along with him. But only while things were going
well. If it all turned to ratchet, the likes of Wickham Watts would
probably be beyond arm's length, watching the errors that would surely
be labelled yours.

Wickham splayed his hands, almost in apology. 'But we had no
choice, from our end. If that was how the source wanted to play it, we
had to tag along: we needed the information, and it turned out to be
gold. Usually, the source wants to disappear and get a new identity, or
wants money. None of that applied to Curtis Monroe. He didn't want
to be seen talking to the authorities at the prison, but he didn't appear
to care much what happened after that. He wanted to get out to see
"my girls", as he called them.'

'The Doyle sisters?'

'That would be correct. I think the term would be "besotted". He
seemed to believe it would end up fine, as long as he got to the sisters.
Idealization, I think they call it. Anyway, he set the rules and we were
legally obliged to play along, no matter how suicidal that appeared.'

That tagged with what Ali had discerned so far from the letters
between the Doyle sisters and Curtis. Wickham's view seemed to
chime with the idea that Curtis thought staying with the Doyles was
the next positive step in his rehabilitation. He'd been, it appeared, willing to bet his life on that.

'Hmm, okay. So how much of what he told you can you tell me?'

'I'll give you the basics, so you don't meet with Lucas Baker blind. Let me explain how their system works. Because, much as I despise the outcome, I have to admit it's smart, and it's innovative.'

Wickham sat forward again, leaning on his elbows and using carefully manicured hands for emphasis. Most gestures offered a glimpse of gold and black cufflinks. Wickham's expense forms, Mike decided, must be hilarious.

'So let's say you're in Du Pont. You already have an amphetamine habit: the prison doctors either ignore it or give you a lame substitute that doesn't do the job. You want what you want; you're willing to pay for it. You approach Aryan Force, or their representative, and say what you need. They then check you out – criminal records, references, links to law enforcement, social media: the whole thing, like you're applying to work in a bank. AF need to know that you're you; that you're who and what you say you are. They're tremendously careful – worried about infiltration – and they've built a solid network to guarantee they aren't compromised. Simply dismantling the network that checks you would take years we don't have: that's how far behind we are. That's why Curtis's evidence was so valuable, and surprising. Anyway, they come back to you and say they can cover your needs for a year, and it'll cost this much. Let's keep the numbers easy – say, ten thousand.

'Here's the clever bit. You don't pay those guys. No currency of any sort, or payment in kind, changes hands in the prison at all. Instead, one of your trusted friends on the outside finds the ten thousand. All paid up front – anything up to a year's fees. If you die, or move prison, it won't be repaid; if you move prisons, you're dealing with a new franchisee, of course. How you recompense your friend is between you and him. Payment to the Aryans goes through online systems and curtains, via VPNs and various backdoor routes. In fact, we believe it's largely processed by the Alvarez family – all this is Miguel Alvarez's brainwave – and naturally, they collect fat fees for organizing it. So, your buddy pays ten thousand-plus into somewhere or other, then it gets laundered, and *only then* Aryan Force get notified that you've paid. You're officially a *bronze*, as they term it. Bronze-level customer; a newbie. Now you have a contract. The AF bribe the guards, they move the product; you receive it in dribs and drabs over the period. That way, none of the chain is holding too much stock, too often. You're a happy customer, and the Nazis made a profit. But most of the heavy lifting was done outside Du Pont's gates, in cyberspace. By people who never meet, and never get remotely near the merchandise.'

It was a variation on a theme: in standard street buys there was often a separation between the person paid and the person who hands over the product. It made it more difficult to convict either of them of supply – the guy with the drugs handed them over for free; the guy who was paid had no drugs on him. This system made that once-removal a bigger gap, but the principle remained the same. What *was* new was the method of payment – upfront, via a third party, and laundered before you got the product. Safer because there was no easy trail between drug and money; plus, all the financial risk lay with the buyer. Miguel Alvarez, again, thought Mike: using a banker's brain for something even less ethical than banking.

'So the payment and delivery are done on trust?'

'Yeah, kind of. Not so much trust as contract. But yeah, trust enters into it. In fact, that's not so unusual. Terrorist groups move money internationally that way: informal networks that don't have an audit trail that connects the dots. It's low risk for the Aryans. It's helped them to take control of the trade in about a quarter of the country's prisons in the past three years.'

'And you had no idea?' Mike blurted before thinking. 'Sorry, that sounded bad.'

'Nah, fair comment. We asked ourselves the same thing; we can hardly complain if others come up with that. Frankly, Mikey, it was an acute embarrassment to the unit, and the force. Ah, look, we had some inkling but we missed most of it. They always seemed like petty thugs, with stupid racist crap tacked on. We knew Aryan Force were beefing up, but our mistake was taking that to be a political shift. Our analysts came up with lots of reasons why it fed into national politics – polarizing debates online, rising extremism, rabble-rousers everywhere, and so on. We focused on the Aryans' dickhead thinking when we should have paid more attention to the simple facts of money and power.'

Wickham shook his head, presumably annoyed at the analysts who'd led the likes of him down the wrong path. Mike bet that C4's corridors were blame-avoidance and finger-pointing frenzies.

'Plus,' Wickham sighed, 'we had no idea about how the payments were being made: we underestimated how big the trade was because we never had sight of the cash. It's part of Miguel's genius: not simply a smarter way of doing business, but one that was automatically out of plain sight.'

That all made sense to Mike. The temptation to see Aryan Force in political terms must have been great. The up-tops would want to view it that way: there was more funding in combating political extremism than disrupting drug-dealing among convicted criminals.

'And is it big business?' he asked.

'Oh yeah, it is. Look, prisoners are a small part of the national population, but it's a captive audience, and they're way heavier users than most people outside. Plus, it's not only the profits. It's the power, the leverage, that comes with the process. You get compromised staff all over the place; you get guards on a string; you get criminals who'll cooperate, or are plain grateful; you get a reputation. Fingers in pies, Mikey. It all strengthens Aryan Force's influence across the board.'

Yes, thought Mike, it would. And how would they react to Curtis setting off a landmine under them?

Wickham slurped his coffee while Mike thought. 'Go on, ask it,' he said.

'Sorry?'

'The obvious question. The one you've been dying to ask since I pulled into the car park, but thought was too rude. Look, Mikey, Lucas Baker is a shrewd one, so I need to know you have sufficient *cojones*, here.'

'Okaaay . . . It was obvious to me that you were undercover before I even spoke to you. Won't Baker have picked you already and, if not, won't he suss you now you're here with me?'

'Now we're getting somewhere. The short answer is yes. He picked me as an undercover operative the first time he clapped eyes on me, something he later had verified by his network.'

The two regarded each other warily, before the penny dropped.

'Ah,' said Mike. 'And he was supposed to, right?'

'There you go. We had a psychological profile of Baker done by a federal asset, early in the game. I don't set a lot of store by those things generally, but this was top notch. So Baker is a high-achiever: super-student, excellent business record and quickly established as a rising star in the state. His business went from one person to twenty-four, in two years. He's on some influential boards in the community; one of those people whose name keeps cropping up. And, in all that time, he's kept his political affiliations and opinions completely under wraps. No one saw the Nazi coming. He can be the latte-sipping liberal with the best of them; or he can play the wide-eyed country boy; he does a mean line in green pseudo-activism; he can act the religious conservative. But the flipside is that because he's extremely clever, he constantly wants it acknowledged. Challenge makes him hinky.'

Mike played with a sugar sachet and noted the empty car park. 'So you pandered to his ego.'

'Exactly. While others were setting up deep undercover, with strong legends behind them and lots of online evidence, I was sent in to be the kind of blundering, think-I'm-smart regional cop he was expecting. Little things, but mistakes Baker would notice, and preen himself for noticing. He's a city boy at heart – can't wait to sneer at the *deplorable bogans* in the regions.'

'You're a decoy duck, Wickham.'

'Ha! I sure am. Hence the theatrical way I do stuff, as though I'm some idiot on his first assignment, thinking he's James Bond or something. Baker has eyes everywhere, so I have to do it all the time. The idea is that Baker becomes fascinated by what kind of rookie error I'll make next and takes his eye off the others setting up the serious infiltration. Misdirection, see? Then, after a suitable period, I screwed up in front of him and fessed that I'm a police officer. Three weeks ago, he thinks he saw me snort some cocaine after a drugs arrest. Since then, he believes he owns me and I'm in his pocket. I feed him nothing important, and he assumes he's added to his network. It makes him . . . complacent. We hope.'

They both turned at the sound of tyres on gravel. A slate-grey Camry drove into the car park and came to a halt. It was flecked with mud up the flanks, and Mike itched to test forensics against the mud around Curtis Monroe's corpse. He found himself wondering if a Camry's boot could easily accommodate a dead body. The lights of the café on the windscreen shielded the driver from Mike's sight. Wickham observed, interested in Mike's reaction.

Lucas Baker climbed out of the car and buttoned his jacket. A Pringle sweater that wouldn't look out of place on a golf course, a light tan jacket, chinos and brown shoes. Baker radiated middle-class mediocrity but held himself high, undermining the regular-guy façade. Mike had been prepared for the nondescript vehicle, a fifteen-dollar haircut, off-the-rack clothing. That would all be part of Baker's subterfuge: masking his intellect and intent, hiding him in plain sight.

'He navigated upwards in Aryan Force,' murmured Wickham, 'without anyone outside picking him. Good camouflage.'

Mike understood criminals – the desperation, or the ego, or the lack of empathy. That made sense to him, even while he worked to stop it. But he could never quite get a handle on how racists got that way. It seemed dumb, like flat-Earthers were dumb, or those who thought lizard-people ran things. He couldn't odds it. Now Baker was at the door, lifting a hand to acknowledge Wickham, then scowling slightly at Mike's presence.

'Lucas, welcome, welcome. Thanks for coming.'

Their handshake, Mike observed, was a mutual two-handed double pump: it was almost a battle of insincerity. The overlaid second paw – the Bill Clintonesque *trust me* gesture – seemed more natural from Wickham than Baker, who clearly held his cards closer to his chest.

'Lucas, meet Mike.'

This time, Lucas extended one hand in a lukewarm greeting. 'Nice to meet you, Detective Francis.'

Mike tried not to glow as they all sat. Mike had presumed that the waitress was simply spinning her wheels in the kitchen, but she had a latte with cinnamon ready on the table before Baker had scooted his chair. Mike picked her delicate signal to Baker: she finger-tipped the tall glass at three o'clock on the rim as she drew back. As Wickham had said: eyes everywhere. She retired through the saloon doors.

Wickham mediated in a breezy, gauche way. 'So, introductions over, and I think we all know where we stand. Mike has a particular problem, Lucas, which might overlap with one of your own.'

'I doubt it. But you have as long as this coffee stays warm, Detective.'

Baker's voice held the remnants of a lisp that he'd clearly tried hard to eradicate but which probably reappeared fully when he was angry.

Mike had re-appraised his options after Wickham's pep talk, but felt he had to go with the original plan. There seemed little point being coy about how much he knew of Baker's habits or acquaintances: better to treat him as an equal and see where that went. Other than Kaspar's identity, Mike could hardly give away confidential information, since he pretty much didn't have any.

'Thank you. We have a mutual acquaintance. Curtis Mason Monroe. Sometime involved in commercial arrangements in Du Pont. Now dead, carved up and left near the old quarry at Maritime.'

Baker neither flinched nor twitched. Although, thought Mike, you'd need a pretty good poker face to be a high-up in an Aryan gang: you'd only bluff unconvincingly once.

'Since he was found murdered this morning,' continued Mike, 'it makes him our problem. However, he had caused your associates considerable difficulties in the previous twenty-four hours. Which is your problem. I think you can see the Venn diagram, Mr Baker. We're obliged to treat your associates as serious players in this. Unless they can categorically prove otherwise.'

Nothing from Baker. Mike considered sitting there and waiting him out; detectives usually won waiting contests. But he believed this time it might be counterproductive.

'One of our theories would be that, while your organization was hurt by the arrests at Du Pont yesterday, they were hardly holed below the waterline. It's a temporary rupture: I'm willing to bet you have plenty of volunteers to step up in their place. But that theory would also go that someone – either to make a point to others, or to prove their worth – stepped out of line when they killed Monroe. Because that action, of course, brings considerable scrutiny where it isn't wanted and undermines your business model.'

Mike stared pointedly at Baker. 'People like me. Make people like Alvarez. Reluctant to do business. With people like you.'

Wickham watched carefully. Baker took a long sip of his coffee, wiping his mouth with a strangely effete gesture.

'Detective Michael Lewis Francis,' began Baker. 'Wife, Barbara – quite the stunner, well done. You honeymooned in Japan: Kyoto, mainly. Lovely home, now you've thinned out those trees near the creek. New Samsung television in the rumpus room. Two daughters, one son. Your son is at scout camp this week: he learned how to do a reef knot this morning. An hour ago, your girls won their netball game at the leisure centre. Do congratulate them all, won't you?'

The air sizzled.

'Lucas Owen Baker,' replied Mike quietly. 'Blood: rhesus negative. Fractured collar bone six years ago. Your Camry is overdue for a service. Your sister was turned down for a job by ASIO last week because she's related to you. As of now you have five phones, only one registered.'

Baker breathed slowly. The waitress made a noise as she needlessly fussed with cutlery by the door. Baker twitched, then waited until he could see her on her phone, outdoors. Baker, Mike realized, was beholden to her: not the other way around. Because she was reporting back to others.

'I assume, Detective, you're bothering me because of politics?'

'You share some interesting views with some interesting people.'

'Hmm. Aryan Force? They get taken way too seriously by people like you. It always helps the budget negotiations to have a confected major threat, doesn't it? Standard tactic: hype up an off-the-shelf bogeyman, claim they're about to change the course of society, then demand extra resources to stop them.'

'But you do share their politics, Lucas?'

'I'm interested in how society can be more harmonious. We all should care about that.'

'Hmm. But the Aryan Force view seems to major on us white folks, doesn't it?'

'Keeping opposing forces apart can be good for the community.' Baker posed it as an intellectual hypothesis.

'Nah. I mean, Athletic Bilbao.'

'What?'

'Athletic Bilbao. They're a soccer team in Spain. Not racists in any way, mind, but they have this little kink to them. You can only play for them if you're native Basque. Black or white isn't a factor, neither's religion, but always Basque. It's laudable in one way, I suppose: they're connected to their fans, their community. There's a clarity to it, in your argument. But the trouble is, they haven't won a trophy in forty years. In sporting terms – trying to win cups – they're a failure. They've sacrificed achievement for notional purity. So, no, thanks. Ethnic purity equals epic fail.'

'Very amusingly put. What is it you think I do, Detective Francis?'

Mike heard Wickham let out the breath he'd been holding. Baker had acquired all those personal details on Mike in maybe ninety minutes. Mike suspected there was a leak in C4 itself; his presence here was too tightly known for any other answer.

'Well, your business card and your website suggest management consultancy. I'm sure you do a bit, to generate some legitimate invoices. But, overall, it's a way to launder your personal fees. I think you spend most of your time working for Aryan Force. I think you act as point of contact for the Alvarez finance team, who connect to you through trusted third parties. I think you finesse some of the higher-level corruption of officials at regional and state level. I think you put up an acceptable veneer for a bunch of unacceptable people, in return for money. Although I also think you're a true believer, but you keep that cloaked, because it's bad for your slices of legitimate business. Is what I think.'

Another sip, another prissy pad of the napkin.

'If we were to make the Herculean leap that what you've said is true, how am I actually connected to this Mr Monroe? And why would I help you?'

Mike had a choice here. He could soft-pedal, hoping for an error from Baker. But he sensed that window wasn't open. Baker would walk in a few minutes, regardless. So any opening had to come from finding common ground quickly, or from holding the upper hand.

'Monroe had recently given up some details of your operation. It led to arrests, some with product in hand. Messy, sticky: for you and your friends. But given the size and power of the network, the favours you're owed, the people you influence? Not a game-changer. More a chance to reset. Maybe some of those under the wheels were oxygen thieves anyway; maybe you wanted to clean house. Whatever. The outcome is that your lucrative business is temporarily inconvenienced. No big deal: more of an enforced day off. Like an extra ANZAC day.

'Then Monroe turns up murdered. This is different. Now all kinds of cops are involved; the public's aware and the media are interested. You don't want or need that kind of spotlight. Going under the radar has worked so far, but killing in public sends up a flare that we can't ignore. Plus, the killer didn't want to hide the body: the corpse was visible for a reason. So it must have been some kind of message. One that we can track back to Aryan Force, since they're the party Monroe hurt the day before.'

Baker stroked the side of his coffee glass with one finger, almost erotically, and listened absent-mindedly.

'So your motive for helping me, Mr Baker, is to have your own problem resolved by someone else. In a way that encourages others to believe that stepping out of line is bad for them. Perhaps you have a discipline problem, with someone who believed they'd ingratiate themselves by doing what they assumed was a favour. Possibly, someone needs reminding who they work for, and why the organization succeeds when it's low key. In which case, ensuring their arrest and conviction works for you, and washes your hands of their actions. Otherwise, we have to go poking around where you don't want us. We have to take you apart, on- and offline; pick out some key individuals; move some prisoners interstate. Might not be successful, of course. But it would scupper profits for a while, and make you look vulnerable to rivals. You have competitors, and they like wounded animals.'

Baker grunted. Despite being a high-up, it was likely Baker would have to consult others: the waitress had demonstrated there were strata beyond Baker's. Everyone in the world has a boss, thought Mike. This meeting was more a way of laying out a roadmap for Baker. The pay-off might come later, and indirectly, but only if Mike made a statement by leaving now. As Wickham had said, challenge made Baker edgy. Maybe Mike could needle him into subsequent action.

'Have a think about it. Oh, and that latte? It's a blend of black coffee and white milk. That's how it works: all mixed in together. Better than separating the individual parts.'

The chair screeched as Mike rose.

'Mr Baker. Wickham.'

Fresh air tasted good.

Chapter 19

Dana. David Rowe, Suzanne Doyle.

Interview Room One.

A packet of Tim Tams sweating on the table. A hint of cleaning fluid in the air. David's pen glinting in the brightness of the solitary light. The meek grinding of the physical tape and the liar's blink from the digital recorder.

The third interview was, Dana frequently found, the seminal one: the tipping point. The first two interviews often established the lines and the boundaries; set the tone and basic balance of power. By the third, each party had accepted their fundamental roles: the logic of being in a room with one person asking questions and another now feeling obliged to answer them.

Suzanne looked fully awake and apprised now. Freed of the urge to fake indolence, she resembled what she was – a smart young woman in a tight situation.

Dana reminded herself that Suzanne still had full agency regarding her sister at this point. She could get her retaliation in first – if that was what she sought – while Marika was playing hide-and-seek in the swamp. Dana's goal was to finesse Suzanne into being recklessly proactive.

'Suzanne, I'd like to talk about you leaving for university. Please tell me about the background to that.'

Suzanne squinted then glanced at David, seemingly less for guidance, more that she was about to spill something the rest of the family didn't know. 'Is this another thing you just fancy knowing about, Detective?'

Dana levelled her gaze. 'I get paid to discover the truth, Suzanne. It's my job. I ask anything I believe will help me to get to that place. Let's not insult each other with a game about what you'll answer, and what you won't. All three of us are well beyond it. University, please.'

Suzanne mulled that over. She could feel bounced by Dana's insistence, or she might feel she should embrace it. She did the latter. 'It was all a bit . . . *secret squirrel*. In the year before my exams, I was working part-time at the supermarket. I kept maybe a quarter of what I earned, but the rest had to go on them.' Suzanne stared – glared – at the table. Dana sensed a bubbling resentment there: long borne, never dissipated. 'Some of Mum's drugs weren't on the Medicare list. I had to pay full, big-pharma price and it was eating into what money I had. I was subsidizing her, basically. The pair of them were bludging off my effort. They assumed I would go full-time at the supermarket, so I could afford the meds and all the other bills. The idea suited them.'

Dana noted how Suzanne saw Mary and Marika as one. Two against one: she was propping up the two. Suzanne continued. 'Especially . . . especially when I finished exams and went full-time over the summer. It bought a bit of peace for a few weeks; Mum knew where her next pill was coming from.'

'But that was all misdirection?'

'Yeah. Well, not entirely, but, you know. I let them assume I'd do that long term, forget uni; and they did. I didn't try to change their minds or tell them what I was doing.' Suzanne looked up sharply. 'But they could have asked, or guessed, Detective, couldn't they? I was a smart eighteen-year-old: what would a reasonable person think a girl like that would want, eh? I mean, they assumed I was somehow happy to pay for them until we all died; they thought that was the limit of my ambition, for God's sake. They could have considered what I might want. Never did. It was all about them, always. So, you know, partly their fault.'

It was the logic of the con artist, thought Dana. She'd experienced herself being hoisted – *harmed* – by that fake construct. By the notion that people who were fooled or blind-sided had brought it on themselves; that they half wanted to believe the lies; that they were morally complicit when they didn't check adequately; that they indulged their greed or selfishness and had a price to pay; that the fraud was some kind of necessary ethical reckoning, a balancing of their sins. Wiping out a sense of guilt made a scam work better: Suzanne clearly knew her way around that landscape. Dana was all too familiar with the pathology; it clawed at her from the past.

She cleared her throat. 'But, by that point, you'd already secured your place at university?'

'Oh yeah, that was done. I'd gone to my History teacher, given him the full sob story. Which was true, by the way. *My mum didn't want me to leave home; she was dead against uni*, et cetera. We did all the forms at school; all the correspondence went there. By Christmas, I had it all sorted for February. Off to the city; new life.'

Dana considered her next question. She could comprehend how Suzanne's resentment flowed from a sense of feeling trapped and obligated.

'I can see that Mary might not have guessed. It seems as though her intuition was, hmm, somewhat blinkered. Would that be a correct reading?'

Both Suzanne and David nodded.

'And,' Dana continued, 'I can potentially understand why you wouldn't tell Mary until the last minute. But . . . Marika?'

'Yeah, well, she was twelve by then.' A quick look at David, seeking approval but fearing it wasn't there. 'I mean, Jesus, I wasn't her mother: I was her sister. I was leaving her . . . what?' She spread her arms, seeking absolution. 'In her own home, with her own mother? What more could I do at that point, eh? Tell me. Or I'll tell you. Nothing. You know what? There has to come a po– there has to be a day when you do things for yourself, doesn't there? Must be a time when your decision's about you, and not constantly about other people.'

Suzanne tried to control her breathing. She knew David was staring at her but refused to engage. She apparently couldn't afford, at this point, to have David's open disdain.

Dana understood that some of Suzanne's justification, and her vehemence, was for David's benefit: an explanation she needed him to swallow. Hence, Suzanne's questions: she wanted third-party affirmation by Dana, to show to David. But some of it was Suzanne telling herself that she did the right thing. By insisting on it, in this interview room – years after Mary had been buried – she demonstrated that the guilt was still swirling around in her mind. She hadn't found peace, even years later. Dana prodded the wound.

'Well, let's break that down, Suzanne. There were several implications to your leaving at that point, and to the fact that it was secret.'

Suzanne was paying full attention for once. For all the years brooding in her own mind, it clearly mattered to have another's view: someone with no skin in the game. If Dana could climb inside that scenario and provide fresh insight, she might be seen as less enemy, more confidante.

'For example, there's the economics: as you say, you were funding many of Mary's medications, and she was less likely to take them if you weren't there to pay for them. So she becomes less stable, harder to manage, at precisely the time you aren't helping Marika to deal with her.'

The first bullet didn't dent the armour. Suzanne shrugged.

'Secondly, you leaving creates a precedent: if you can go, then so, in time, can Marika. Then Mary would be alone with her problems. She would be scared of that – very much so – and inclined to refocus on stopping Marika going anywhere. That ratchets up the claustrophobia, the restrictions, for your sister. Those kinds of mental health problems are literally terrifying for the sufferer, as I'm sure you know. The fear is exhausting. Your precedent of walking away would add to that fear, I'm afraid.'

This bullet hit. There was clearly guilt there, driven by Suzanne's first-hand experience of Mary's anguish and panicked, aggressive demands. But not enough to buckle Suzanne, and not something she hadn't considered before.

'Thirdly, Marika no longer has you to help her deal with Mary: she's now had her responsibilities doubled, with no respite for weeks on end. She's not an adult at that time, not even a teenager.'

Closer. Nearly close enough. Suzanne may have considered that impact and now, perhaps, there was a feeling of regret; but also a belief that it was a sacrifice Marika would have needed to make. For the greater good. For the good of Suzanne. In the older sister's mind, one and the same. Dana was close to the mark, now.

'Fourthly, you demonstrated to Marika that you alone had the means and opportunity to leave, to start afresh. So your decision shouted that you had power, but Marika didn't. *Therefore*, Marika didn't: you win, so Marika must lose.'

Suzanne blanched. A new wound had been opened. This consequence held the greatest sting because it implied that Suzanne had taken something away, rather than refused to continue giving. Another nervous glance at David, who stared deliberately at his pad, then Suzanne recovered sufficiently to glare at Dana.

'You sound like Rika.'

Now Dana felt she was getting close to the atmosphere within the cottage. Two sisters in one bed, in a cottage surrounded by swamp, constantly rehashing decisions and consequences. Relentless sniping, skirmishes, squalls, yet clinging to each other every night.

'I'm not surprised. If she mentioned those things – even if she harped on about them – then she reacted in a rational way to the circumstances, wouldn't you say?'

It was deliberately provocative. Suzanne was too deeply into the conversation to measure her words.

'No, I would not say. No. Children aren't responsible for their parents, Detective. They aren't the adults, see? Not the parents' parent. Maybe me going would force them both to think more clearly about where all this was headed. Because we all knew where it would end up, but not when, and not exactly how.'

Dana checked the timer and scratched a Pitman note. Suzanne ploughed on.

'It could have been a . . . catalyst. Without good ol' Suzanne picking up the pieces, and the tab, maybe they'd start seeing it all differently.'

'And did they?'

Suzanne was blinking a lot. 'Apparently not. But I did give them that chance, didn't I? Going to uni wasn't all about me – it was about forcing something from them. Worth a try.'

'And Marika? She was twelve. Did you think you were being a catalyst for her emotional development when you left for university? Was it intended to be the making of her?'

'Like I said before, Detective, don't worry about Rika. Don't be fooled. Even when she was twelve she was bloody smart and manipulative. She was part of the toxic air I was escaping – not all the poison was in the swamp. Don't think she was an innocent little child, trying to help Mary. She had her own agenda.'

Dana found it hard to believe that assertion was totally true. Marika surely wasn't that monstrous – at least, not at that age. All the same, it tallied with the opinion of Clara Belmont.

'What *was* Marika's agenda at that point, Suzanne? When she was twelve?'

'Marika. Her agenda is always Marika. We are but chess pieces to her, Detective. You'll see. *What Rika wants, Rika gets.*'

'And what did she want, when you left?'

Light faded from Suzanne's face. 'She wanted me back. She wanted me never gone. She wanted me trapped. And she'd do anything to ensure that. Anything, Detective.'

Chapter 20

'Mikey, fancy a drive to the Doyles' cottage?'

Dana rested against the door frame. She suddenly felt tired; unbalanced by information that was not telling her enough. She needed to cleave herself from the moment, and she wanted a sharper line on the sisters' lives. Talking to Suzanne had yielded shrapnel from the girls' lives, but Dana couldn't get the pieces to coalesce around a sharp point.

'Sure.' Mike reached for his jacket. 'It's such pretty countryside out there. Come for the swamps and sucking quagmire; stay for the mosquitos and sense of death.'

Dana grinned. 'Never mind *Land of a Hundred Lakes* – which is technically untrue. You've just christened our new tourist slogan: I expect it on billboards soon. Seeing the Doyle cottage is a *life experience.*'

'Ah yeah,' said Mike, swinging his jacket over his shoulder, 'those things. What people buy you for birthdays, when you're so old they've run out of actual things to buy you.'

They made their way down to the underground garage, where the unmarked vehicles were kept.

'What's your bead on Baker, Mikey?' she asked.

Mike looked sceptical. 'My *bead*?'

'Bead's a real word.'

'I know, it's –' he shrugged – 'it's . . . quaint.'

'Ouchy. You know how to wound a girl.'

'Yeah, sometimes I lash out like that. Women love a bad boy.'

'I feel duly warned. So, Baker?'

'Very shrewd, well connected. The Feddies in Canberra came back with a big fat zero. I got the impression they have info but won't release it to a little ol' police station in the regions. Baker won't be giving up much that he thinks he can hide – most of it will be stuff he believes we'll uncover anyway. But . . . overall, I think we punctured a tyre or two. Regardless of who actually killed Curtis Monroe, fingers are being pointed towards Aryan Force, and they don't like it. Because it's bad for business, they might at least yield some alibi information.'

But, Dana took from that, most of what they learned would be their own hard slog. Probably without much help from the force on an official level – possibly, none. She would need to lean on Bill tomorrow; he might be able to pull some silent strings.

'You're not worried? Personal safety angle? They knew some very precise things about you; and the family.'

Mike signed the forms and fed his personal number into the keypad. The car keys slid out from the slot and he passed them to Dana.

'No. No, I'm not. I mean, it was unnerving. I wasn't expecting it, somehow: even though I'd essentially done the same to him. It suggested to me there's a leaky C4 in our midst, but that's not a huge surprise to me – there's always someone milling around who's made themselves vulnerable. No, it was more a flexing of muscles than an actual threat: proof that he had friends where he needed them. The point was made; I don't think he's the type to linger.'

'You're sure?'

'Yup. Thanks, though.'

'You can drive, Mikey.' She tossed the keys to Mike.

'Ooh, the keys to the executive Honda. I've made it, made it big. The family will be so proud.'

'I can see them, Mikey, waving you off in the morning. Barb and the kidlets; looking on in awe as you depart. *There goes Daddy. He drives an unmarked Honda when it's his turn. Brave Daddy.*'

'Little Danny might. But the girls are fifteen and seventeen. They quit calling me "Daddy" a decade ago.'

'I know, but the thing didn't work if it was "Dad".'

'Fair enough.'

The tyres squealed as they left the garage, and they headed west towards a hazy sun. Mike cut down a series of residential streets, nearly going past Dana's house. The century homes, eerily neat flower beds and gently blossoming trees settled her pulse. If you came from Earlville, you sneered that this district was *Stepford*, or *Desperate Housewives*. But order, restraint, symmetry: these things soothed her.

Mike took them through two roundabouts in quick succession. 'Remind me again why we're going out there, when Stu has finished the forensic sweeps?'

Dana indicated the outer lane as a set of roadworks came into view.

'You need a right here, Mikey. It's hard to put into words. I know Stu is diligent, and I'm not looking to uncover some killer fact. It won't be an object he missed, that's for sure. It might be a feeling, or some pieces of a puzzle that only fit if you've talked to one of the sisters. I don't want to face Suzanne tomorrow, and especially Marika when we find her, without some feel for the cottage, some idea of what it was like to live there.'

They passed the new Bunnings; the 'grand opening' of yet another hardware store was weeks away. At one stage of its construction it had faintly resembled an ocean liner. But the scaffolding had implied curves and sweeps that were not part of the building. Now it showcased the giant shed that it always was – a galvanized metal monument dem-onstrating the cheapest possible way to build an enclosed space.

Mike said nothing, and Dana felt compelled to elaborate. 'It's clear they regressed into nesting there: ditched the landline, seemingly no mobile, no visitors that we know of except their uncle, no friends. I'm getting a picture of the two of them with the walls closing in, so their environment, and how it shaped them, is crucial. Plus, how they lived when their mother was alive – I feel that's seriously important. It shaped their psyche.' Both their individual personalities, and their meshed one, she thought. 'There'll be some things that would never show up on a search team's assessment – and nor should they – that will be useful. Hopefully.'

The Honda had reached open country and cruised through heath-land and marsh that became more threadbare with each passing kilometre. This far from Carlton there was little traffic: the land was impossible to cultivate and was left to decay on its own.

'Would it be fair to file it under "F" for "Fishing"?' asked Mike.

Yes, she nodded, *it would*. But the kind of fishing where the angler will know where to cast. Fishing with insight: it could almost be her job description.

'You think the answer lies in the cottage, and with the sisters?'

'Yes, I do,' replied Dana, 'but on instinct; logic veers towards the Aryans. There's insufficient evidence to point to the Doyles in any way: all we have is circumstance. The original rape so close to the murder scene; two sisters who wrote to the victim; some DNA that suggests Monroe was in the cottage; an ATV tyre print. All manner of reasons why those things don't involve the sisters killing Monroe, as you dem-onstrated. But yes, I think the clues lie there somehow. Regardless of who killed Curtis, the Doyles and their cottage have more to give.' She frowned. 'So tell me I'm mortal.'

'Okay,' said Mike. 'Why now, and why Monroe? I mean, the initial rape was near their cottage, so that's a potential connection. But it was seven years between that crime and the sisters even writing to Monroe. Why then?'

'Good question. I've got Ali going through the letters again with a fine-toothed comb, trying to fathom the motive from that. In the letters, the sisters don't appear to mention why they started writing. When the prison rang Marika to make sure she knew the letter-writing rules – and comprehended who she was dealing with – Marika said she'd always wondered about the person behind the crime.'

Mike raised his finger. '*They'd* always wondered – not Marika.'

'Oh, good point. I'm inclined to see Marika speaking for both of them, maybe thinking for both of them. I shouldn't.'

'I don't believe their claim about starting the letters. It's not a good enough explanation for writing to a rapist, nor does it explain the seven-year gap.'

'I agree. Unless . . . unless one of the sisters was somehow witness to something involving that original crime. Maybe saw Monroe running away, that sort of thing. As far as I know, they weren't mentioned in the investigation. All the same, it would be a viable line. Could be anything; hearing the victim cry out, something like that.'

Mike didn't think that was convincing and neither, in truth, did Dana. The sisters' connection to the original crime surely couldn't lie dormant for seven years, take a further two years to ferment, then come through with enough force to make them kill. The trajectory of a merely tangential connection to the original rape wouldn't be enough.

'Lucy is going through the full investigation file from the rape,' replied Mike, 'but she'd have flagged up any Doyle in there. But again – why now? Or rather, why seven years after the event? Nothing seems to kick start that.'

'Good point. All I can think is that the letters started when Marika was seventeen. We haven't found any formative, life-changing fact from her seventeenth year that might be a catalyst. She was fourteen, fifteen when her mother died and Suzanne came home. Marika would have gone into care if Suzanne kept at her university course. Maybe at seventeen Marika's sprouting wings, throwing out nets in all directions to see what she catches.'

It was how Dana pictured adolescence: a series of half-planned experiments in a social realm. Pushing at boundaries; discovery, disappointment, emerging senses of who and why. She had to imagine it.

They slowed after the petrol station, both seeing the atrophying façade of Clara Belmont's home, and noting how good a vantage point it was. Now they were on the road to the cottage, not another soul in sight. Crows launched from a dead tree as they passed. Where the mist still clung, Dana presumed the swamp was deepest. The landscape seemed bleached; colours were muted if they were there at all, and an uneasy stillness pervaded. Dana had now called off the drones, except for hourly flights over the cottage itself. The road rose and Dana could see forest and swamp clear to the horizon. Marika had a lot of country to keep her hidden.

Mike continued. 'They simply have no reason for killing Monroe. Even if they brought him back to the cottage but things turned ugly: the state of the body, the crime scene, the apparently wiped forensics, the disappearance of the ATV? They all point to something more planned and, uh, *executed* than a panicked self-defence.'

'Ooh, good pun.'

'Been hangin' with you and Luce. So where's their motive?'

This was always the key for Dana: what would drive someone to kill? In her experience, murder motives were usually obvious. Victims often knew their killer; there was a prior relationship and a clear sense of that relationship deteriorating. The murder was simply the ultimate escalation, or degradation, of the relationship's trajectory. When the killer seemed to have no connection to the victim, motive became slippery.

'There isn't one. Not that I can fathom. But there is a motive if it's a prison argument about squealing on the Aryan Force.'

'Exactly. And they are a bunch of amoral dickheads, so I'd always be counting them in. Regardless of their stupid racist crap – which doesn't even make sense in their own terms – they want to own the prison trade, and Monroe screwed them over. That's motive. And they know people to get it done, no problem. Like I said in the briefing, maybe someone came to the cottage and took Monroe or coaxed him away. Then, the sisters are too scared of retribution to say anything. They might be victims here, too – they took in a guy down on his luck and perhaps they saw the murderer when he came to the cottage.'

Yes, thought Dana, that was still good thinking. It said that B followed A, so C resulted: it was clear and logical. She couldn't entirely understand why she didn't find it compelling; she simply didn't. Other things nagged at her.

'Good argument. I hadn't seen the sisters in exactly those terms, but I should. If they're innocent of the murder, they could be terrified of saying what they know. That might explain Marika hiding, too.'

'But you do think they know something?'

'Oh God, yes. Way more than they're telling, one way or another. The turn is just past those two trees. Hidden.'

They pulled off the road far enough to park; Mike was wary of driving further. He didn't trust this landscape, full stop. His background reading this afternoon had brought up four people taken by this area's swamps in the last five years, including Mary Doyle. When the landscape kills locals, he reflected, ignorant outsiders like him should take note.

The cottage looked as shabby as it had this morning. Then, the sun had been behind it. Now, in late afternoon, the milky light showed further cracks in the render from which plants peeked cautiously. The guttering looked even worse, clinging loosely like a withering vine.

Dana sought any signs that Marika might have returned, but the police tape was still intact.

The front door stuck; she had to give it an extra shove. Dust flew up in motes and a smell of damp carpet puffed from the floor. She and Mike knew instinctively how to split the search; he went upstairs, and she tried to decipher the lounge and kitchen. Her breath misted as it left her: without heating, the place quickly cooled. Warmth ran away from this cottage, any chance it got.

Once again it occurred to Dana that Marika only cleaned the television and the childhood photo of her and Suzanne. The next thing Dana noticed was that, except for the history books, there was little to indicate Suzanne lived there. Dana saw Marika's black clothes scattered, some shampoo for Marika's dark brown hair, Marika's tiny training shoes dropped behind the sofa. Maybe it was different upstairs; perhaps they'd split the domain that way. But Dana doubted it. This cottage felt like it was Marika's, but Suzanne also lived here. That way around.

In the kitchen, the oven door and the microwave door were littered with scratches. A deliberate, violent kind of obliterating act. Possibly the result of childhood tantrums by one of the girls. Below the counter top, the handles on the cupboards looked like they'd been scrappily taken off and remounted. There were extra screw holes and the handles were scratched and ragged.

Dana wondered why they hadn't filed down the scratches to avoid splinters. Another piece of basic maintenance that Marika didn't see as a priority? No, thought Dana. Something fell in her stomach. She held on to the counter for support, trying to stop childhood memories flooding back unhindered. They tore at her, made her eyes water. She stared at the kitchen cupboards, her internal radar fully primed.

She unlocked the back door with the keys Stuart had provided. The step beyond the door was lethal; split and rocky. Dana could see the shoe impressions where the sisters habitually jumped from the threshold to the turf, avoiding the step entirely. She couldn't risk it with her knee and stepped cautiously down. Like an old woman, she chided herself. To the left, she followed a large crack in the render that was turning green around the edges. It slithered under the kitchen window and disappeared behind a wooden pallet leaning against the wall. At that level, the render gave way to tired brickwork. Dana pulled the pallet away, saw what she now expected, and cursed. She was right, but hated being so.

The garden, if it could be called that, was a tatty collection of scrubby yet tenacious grass, concrete slabs of indeterminate purpose, and an asbestos-sided shed. Beyond the flimsy wire fence the turf looked firm right up to the distant trees. But tendrils were already coiling in the air between Dana and a distant clump of Casuarina; the 'grass' was floating on filthy water. The swamp lapped up right to the back fence: it was always at hand, always prowling. At night, thought Dana, the sisters would be able to hear the ground sucking and rolling.

She stepped gingerly back into the house. She could hear Mike moving around upstairs, not because he was especially heavy-footed, but because the building was so flimsy. It suited, she felt, a flimsy life. There was something shallow, hand to mouth about it. Dana wondered how much of this was simply a remnant from the years when Mary lived here and, presumably, dictated how things would be. Perhaps her swings of behaviour led to a sense that this place was never home; was always simply an address. There was an ennui in the air that suggested little had been altered since Mary died. The sisters had hidden here because, in some way, they feared the world and the judgements they would face. But, paradoxically, their home was careless, poorly maintained; sub-standard in many ways.

Mike came down the stairs and stood by the front door. 'Swapsies?'

'All yours, Mikey.'

She started up the stairs, hearing a muttered *look at this crap* from Mike as he saw the living room. At the top of the stairs was a small landing, where coats and sleeping bags had been chucked into a rudimentary pile.

She opened the bathroom door and stepped inside. As she'd expected, it felt cold and spartan – no discernible heat source, hard surfaces, and ingrained mould on the tile grouting. The ventilation brick was covered over with an old flannel, stained around the edges. As the outside temperature faded, condensation had migrated from the single-glazed window above the toilet, to the walls themselves. This bathroom would weep each day. She realized she was relieved to find two toothbrushes: everything else seemed shared. No cosmetics beyond simple skin creams and cotton pads: nothing that smelled nice, no luxuries and no adornments.

Back across the landing and into the one bedroom. This, Dana felt, might be key. While the sisters would have spent most of their time downstairs, she had some sense that the bedroom arrangements outweighed all else. Here, she was sure, Mary's legacy remained strongest.

The room was dominated by a large wooden sleigh bed – she estimated king-size. It looked like an heirloom; the kind of furniture Mary would have insisted on lugging around from home to home, cursed by each removal company who had to negotiate stairs. It had smooth walnut at each end and a nest of pillows flattened by time. The cover was thrown to one side and she could see from the indentation how the sisters slept. Together, coiled, interwoven – there was one furrow down the middle of the mattress.

And always had been.

Facing the bed was a large old wardrobe of three sections. One door hung drunkenly from a broken hinge, part of the general sense of atrophy. The other door simply wasn't there. The fixed middle section presumably once held a mirror, but there was a blank panel and a series of holes where the screws had been removed. Inside the wardrobe was a mass of crammed-together items: knits and heavy skirts, cheap jeans, oversized shirts, warm leggings. Simple, practical; dull colours and pragmatic fabrics. The shoes, scattered at the base of the wardrobe, were mainly boots and training shoes – nothing formal, let alone frivolous. Dana had a rough idea of the girls' sizes, but apart from shoes found it difficult to place many items with any particular sister. Presumably they shared and Marika wore them baggy. To one side, on a rudimentary shelf made from some bricks and the missing door of the wardrobe, more of Marika's running gear had been cast aside on top of a formidable collection of Stephen Kings. All the gear Marika ran in, as Suzanne had said that morning, was black.

Down in the kitchen, Mike was sitting on the back doorstep, watching the daylight die. There was barely enough space for her to squeeze in beside him. She leaned on his shoulder as she sat, as he knew she would, because her kneecap wouldn't play ball.

'You'll never get up again,' chuckled Mike. Above the meagre back garden and the landscape beyond, the sky faded to a chill night. 'So tell me, if this whole area is swamp, why doesn't this cottage cave in?'

'Good question, Mikey. Without knowing anything about it, my guess would be it's built on a tiny island of actual rock. I mean, there is a quarry down the road. So there's limestone there, for sure.'

'That's a good answer from someone who doesn't have the answer. Well played.'

They sat in companionable silence as the dusk settled. Mike strained to hear any birds: surely something was migrating, or settling down for the night, or beginning a hunt, or skimming the last few insects of the day? But no; they weren't.

Instead, the silence was undercut by a slow grinding. Like half-broken machinery in the distance; like the drowsy, gradual uncoiling of vast limbs. At various times the score was punctuated by other sounds – roiling, churning, heaving and subsiding. Dana let the signals from beyond the fence drift in to her, like sea mist.

'This place, Mikey – the land – never stops. It's always moving, always shifting. You can't rely on it: never presents the same twice. It turns on you. The girls lived most of their lives within this slippery thing.' She looked across to Mike. 'It's like the swamp toyed with both sisters but never quite took them. A cat with a near-dead mouse.'

'It took their mother,' Mike reminded her. 'It's unforgiving. Creepy. A crazy place to be, frankly.'

'And yet Marika seems to have conquered it. Understood it. Became a part of it. What did it do to her, to live in a place like this?'

Mike wondered that, too. Never would he live in a place like this. And he couldn't imagine how someone would inflict it on their kids, either. This wasn't isolation because it offered some pristine, back-to-nature ideal. This wasn't an opportunity. It was a mouldering, festering, collapsing mistake of a notion: one to be regretted and fixed.

Dana's phone rang. Randall. She should let the journalist go to voicemail, but something made her pick up.

'Good afternoon, Randy. What can I do for you?'

Randall laughed. 'You can owe me one, I reckon. I just found your missing Marika Doyle.'

Dana hadn't mentioned to Randall who they were looking for; the journalist had tapped some resource to find out. There was no point dwelling on that, or feigning ignorance now. It flitted through her mind that, to have spotted Marika, Randall must have found her in town somewhere. Which meant all their efforts out here with drones and thermal imaging had been a waste of time and money.

'How about I owe you two, Randy?'

'Because?'

'Because you'll also stand by and let our uniforms bring Marika in without sneaking a word with her first. That way, you get repaid before the day is out. Deal?'

Randall could get a minor scoop here, but all he'd get off Marika would be a simple phone photo and a few words, assuming she talked to him at all. If he held off, Dana would make sure he got something solid.

'Deal.'

Chapter 21

Dana sat on the cold stone stairs inside the police station, to stop herself pacing. She knew where Marika Doyle was; in a marked patrol car, slipping quietly through the Carlton traffic and now approaching the motor court behind the station. The young woman was secured: job done. Yet, Dana was on edge.

It was stupid, she thought, to invest so much in finding her. Marika might turn out to be a compulsive liar. Or David Rowe could tell her to shut up and she does just that. She could dissemble; wreck the investigation by throwing it off-track. Alternatively, she may have gone off into the swamp knowing nothing about Curtis Monroe's fate, in which case, she was little more than a source of background. If the Aryans were the killers, Marika might know nothing at all. There were myriad reasons to logically conclude that Marika Doyle would not be a particularly useful witness.

And yet.

Dana's instincts were firing and, this close to the surface, they were rarely wrong. In part, it was inference from her interviews with Suzanne. The elder sister seemed to hold all the reins: older, better qualified, the only driver's licence and the one wage-earner; the legal guardian after quitting university. But the younger sister seemingly held much of the power. That balance had a role to play, Dana felt, but she couldn't work out how.

Marika emerged from the patrol car: a slight young woman, dwarfed by two uniformed officers. She trailed one foot as she moved and Dana, watching from a landing between floors, thought she might be injured. But as Marika reached the steps she skipped them two at a time and Dana realized the reluctant movement was merely slouching.

Dark hair dragged across a pale, tight face; Marika was little taller than in her photo from a decade ago. A young woman still lingering in childhood. In other circumstances, she would be a loitering teen, shivering on a park bench or in a bus shelter, hunched into herself and eyeing the world shrewdly. The type who looked permanently chilly and hungry. The kind who might sneer at gushing charity but respond to a take-it-or-leave-it gesture of indifferent generosity. Dana's take was of a young woman fizzing with pent-up energy. It was hard to crystallize, but easy to sense.

By the time Dana reached the custody suite, Marika was in the medical room, receiving an appraisal. It would have helped Dana to get the doctor's assessment of Marika's state of mind. But Dana knew better than to ask him for any more than the minimum: was Marika fit to be detained, did she need any treatment or medication, and would she be fit to interview? The doctor was paid through the police but didn't work for them: he worked for the person he was treating, and for the public good. Patient confidentiality still reigned, though some officers tried to push the envelope.

Doc Butler emerged from the medical room, removing his glasses and scratching the end of his nose. Marika remained a half-shadow behind the door. He always seemed to Dana wilier than he liked to make out; acting the bumbling rural doc was an effective front, but she was long wise to it.

'How's she doing, Doctor?'

'Hmmm. All things considered, not bad. She was found in a railway carriage, someone said?'

'I believe so, yes. I haven't spoken to the arresting officers yet. I understand she was in one of the disused carriages down by the old cement factory in Earlville.'

'Yes, yeah, I know it.' Doc Butler paused to sign the form. 'Well, that explains the slight exposure: she's been cold and wet for some considerable time. Hours; maybe last night as well. She was a bit vague about time and place. She also hasn't slept much, if at all.'

The rail carriages were an established refuge for the homeless who lacked a car to sleep in, though they were mainly used on wet nights. In drier weather, there were other favourite spots: the carriages offered shelter, not insulation. Marika might have been worried about trespassing on a carriage that was someone else's regular haunt. Dana made a note to ask the team to follow up tomorrow morning: see if Marika was known down there, or a newbie.

'Emotionally and mentally speaking,' continued Butler, 'she's cogent and coherent for now, but exhausted. I can't consider her fit for interview at this time.'

'I understand,' replied Dana. 'In truth, I wasn't looking to interview Marika until morning, around 8 a.m. Do you believe she would be fit at that time?'

'Yeah, probably. But don't hold me to that: I'll have to see her again in the morning. Depends how the night goes, how much sleep she gets in the cell.'

Dana wanted to control that. 'I'm presuming the Lecter Theatre for tonight, at least?'

'Yeah, I think so. Although I've heard that the camera is on the blink, so you'll need to do something about that. Can't have her sitting on suicide watch if the custody officer can't see all she's doing. Defeats the object.'

'Quite so. I have the custody officer making arrangements for that. Are there any other requirements at this point?'

'Just hot food tonight, and in the morning. Plenty of hot, sugary fluids, too; whether she wants 'em or not.'

'Of course. Thank you, Doctor Butler.' In her peripheral vision Dana could see the door opening, and the Custody officer backing into the room, dragging a piece of furniture.

Thursday, 01 August 2019. 1800 hrs

Dana glanced at the clock in the corridor, determined to be on time for Randall and the next press update. Miriam hadn't phoned to tell her anyone else had arrived, and Reece Two Cs was not, apparently, in the reception area. All the same, Dana would be glad when Bill Meeks returned and relieved her of the media role.

Randall was right where he'd started this morning: his back rigid against the wall, feet propped up on the little step that made him resemble a garden gnome. Outside, the light was beginning to fade, reminding Dana of how long it had been since Willie Fitzgibbons had found the dead body.

'How's your sciatica, Randy?'

Randall stirred, harrumphing as he roused. 'Mmm? Oh, hey. Might have been having a power nap, there.'

'It's a habit of highly successful people,' said Dana, joining him on the bench. 'Sciatica the same?'

'Oh, it comes and goes; depends when I can afford the physio. This step helps, believe it or not. But everyone keeps telling me I look like that old guy in *Up*.'

Dana could imagine that; she could imagine Lucy openly saying so. 'Nice old Carl? I'd dearly love to tell you they're inaccurate, but . . .'

'I know, I know. So, what can you tell me, Dana?'

Dana had considered what she needed to, or should, tell Randall. When all was said and done, he was media; at minimum, what he wrote would be picked up by other agencies. And David Rowe. On the other hand, he deserved a reward for his virtue.

'Firstly, thank you for finding Marika Doyle and bringing her to our attention in that way. I do appreciate it, and therefore I won't ask how you came to know who we were searching for.'

'Or who tipped me off?'

'Yes, that too. As long as the tips don't get out of hand, as I'm sure they won't. Finding her wasn't only important for our investigation; Marika was suffering from exposure, and needed medical support. So thank you.'

Randall inclined his head graciously and nodded at his hovering pen.

'Further to our discussion at lunchtime,' continued Dana, 'the autopsy has been conducted on the body of one Curtis Mason Monroe. We are definitely looking at a homicide. The death occurred last night, on the old quarry road near Maritime. At this point, two people are being detained in station, both under the Close Proximity doctrine. We believe it to be an isolated incident, and therefore do not believe the public are in direct danger. However, anyone connected to the incident should be approached with caution. Better yet, anyone with information or suspicion should contact the station, using CrimeLine.'

Randall's shorthand was slower than Dana's and less precise. She could see several ambiguous strokes and hooks, simply by reading it from an angle.

'Hmm. That's all a bit *diluted rusk* for my editor's taste. Do you have anything more like solid food?'

Dana smiled. 'Why, Randy, you make it sound like your boss is a big baby.'

'Yeah, well, he doesn't look old enough to drive, to be honest. But he does like something more to chew on. Can we release the names of the detained?'

Because, thought Dana, *you have them, don't you?* She wondered who was leaking. Dana normally disliked revealing names at any point shy of the trial itself; *innocent until proven guilty*, and all that. But the modern world didn't seem to work in that way. Almost everyone appeared dismayed – not to say offended – if all details weren't gleefully given on request. Personal privacy had gone the way of wooden tennis racquets and cassette tapes.

'Okay, here's the situation. Clearly, you know the identities, Randy. On the one hand, the two detained people have no living parents or siblings. Only an uncle, who is next of kin and apprised of the situation. That would suggest revealing the names publicly. On the other hand, their detention is one of several lines of inquiry, and I'm loath to reveal their names because of the public tendency to assume guilt. So, at this time, I'm going to say no. That may change tomorrow, and you'll be the first to know if so.'

Randall looked disappointed, as she knew he would. His editor would be itching to release and would be aware that Randall had the information. Maybe the editor would overrule – it wasn't all in Randall's gift.

'However, I promised you something extra. So: Curtis Mason Monroe had been recently released from Du Pont prison. He was looking to remain in the local area after release. He was killed with an axe, or other large-bladed weapon. Curtis's family have been informed of these aspects, so you could release those.'

'I think that'll keep the tiny infant fed, at least for tonight.'

'Good.' Both sides had received satisfaction, and honour had been maintained. 'What happened to your new bestie, Reece?'

'She seemed so relentlessly old-school, didn't she? Quite put me to shame. Nah, gone about three minutes after you left, lunchtime. She's now covering a fashion shoot at some country club near the city. We're all going to be in religious gowns next summer, apparently.'

'Sort of a chic *Handmaid's Tale*? Urgh. Still, if it comes with a vow of silence, count me in. So you're the sole journalist actively covering this?'

'Yeah, I'm kind of the ambassador for us all. Not out of choice, mind. I reckon Reece probably has a note in her phone to check my paper's website late tonight, and first thing tomorrow. If it looks juicy enough, she'll copy and paste, then use Word Thesaurus to change a few of the phrases. That, in turn, will also be stolen – sorry, *uploaded and shared* – by a bunch of other people piggy-backing off my efforts. That's my job these days: to prepare copy to be stolen by six hundred people around the country who can't be bothered to do the legwork themselves. I'm carrying dozens of media graduates. Me, with the sciatica.'

'I hear you. Some things weren't better in the good old days, but I think journalism might have been.'

'You got that right.' The step scraped on the floor as he removed his feet. 'I'll get on with filing this. Thanks for those extra details. Nine a.m. tomorrow?'

'Please make it ten. Drive safely, Randy.'

Thursday, 01 August 2019. 1815 hrs

Dana's phone made her jump. She'd been sitting in her darkened office, blinds down, drifting through the case details like an untethered balloon. Sometimes, staring hard at a problem made it less visible: it swam before her eyes. Occasionally, settling back and letting it waft past her yielded dividends. Not this time.

'Howdy, Dana.' Bill Meeks sounded remarkably upbeat for someone who'd spent all day in a training course.

'Boss. Are you *beyond the manager* yet? Waving at the manager as they recede into the distance?'

'Urgh, it's a frickin' nightmare. I should have sent you. Or Mikey. Or the office cat. Anyone but me. Apparently, I've completed modules and I'm "on track". Although . . . I have three hours on gender identity tomorrow. But anyway, your murder. Monroe, isn't it?'

'It is.' Dana brought him up to speed as quickly as possible, figuring that Bill had a steak somewhere in his near future. At this point, she omitted anything to with Aryan Force – she was starting to worry about who knew what and wanted to protect Kaspar. She felt bad leaving Bill out of the loop, but there was little he could do until tomorrow, and it kept the discussion for a suitable environment. She finished with the news that Marika Doyle had been found, and was currently in station.

'Uh-huh. Who's her lawyer?'

'David Rowe. Same as Suzanne's.'

'Ah, crap. Seriously?'

'Unfortunately, yes. He's their uncle, so . . . not much to be done about it. I've decided to interview Marika tomorrow morning, rather than tonight. Apparently, she slept rough last night, and was probably cold and wet, so physically she's weak and I don't want David Rowe – or Doc Butler – calling a halt once we start: momentum will matter. Doc recommended it, and I want to stay on David Rowe's good side. I expect him to back the sisters all the way – expect nothing less – but there are ways and means, here. Since he's the lawyer for both he can be either extremely awkward, or basically cooperative. I prefer the latter, and letting his other client have some sleep is a way to secure that. Also, I have other forensics, some work on the letters between the Doyles and Monroe, and a further indicator of the tox screen, still to come back. Each of those might be a way in.'

'Ah, you might have a silver bullet?' ventured Bill.

'Actually, a silver bullet is for werewolves. You mean "magic bullet":

like antibiotics that home in on the problem and nowhere else. But people have started to use the –'

She could hear Bill's chuckle. 'Ah, is that what they taught you today, boss? Undermine your team's keen sense of vocabulary? Jeez, when's the ethics module?'

'Ha, sorry 'bout that, I couldn't resist. Heard that one today and I knew you'd bite. Okay, that all sounds good to me. You have Marika under Close Proximity?'

Dana nodded, even as she realized she was on the phone and so . . . she was getting exhausted. 'Yes. Lucy wrote the warrant application before she went home; it was passed by Judge Moretti thirty minutes ago. So yes, we have up to seventy-two hours. I don't think we should rush Marika; maybe a night in a cell will get her thinking.'

'I agree. Okay. Park the Doyles overnight. Get some rest, and then get your ducks in a row tomorrow morning before you go at Marika. Anything else?'

Dana puffed her cheeks. 'I'm glad I'm not interested in professional or personal growth of any kind. It sounds awful.'

'It's mind-bendingly dull. Think of this course like dry waterboarding – the same panic, same willingness to say anything to get out of the room. But, hey, the hotel suite has a TV that rises out of the foot of the bed. So really, I come out evens.'

Dana laughed. 'Night-night, boss. And thank you.'

'*De nada*. Say hi to the team.'

Chapter 22

Thursday, 1 August 2019. 1900 hrs

Dana pulled up outside a tall apartment block. Thirteen storeys high and one of three, it sat in a dell of light woodland that Dana had always thought was a park, but now wasn't sure. It was much closer to the refinery than Earlville or Carlton; vapour billowed behind the tower as if pouring from the building itself. Sodium lighting gave an orange glow to the area and glinted off windscreens that were becoming opaque with an impending frost. Around half the apartments were occupied, creating a haphazard mosaic of muted light across the façade of the building.

To the left was a low run of single-storey buildings, designed to be a group of local shops and offices for support services; all she could see was chipboard, graffiti and mesh shutters. The original local plan had been to construct eleven towers in an arc facing west, embracing a park. 1960s optimism faded after three towers, multiple acts of vandalism and the failure to get federal funding for a nearby road. Word was, the outside cladding would go up like a Roman candle and no resident could get insurance. Dana winced on Lucy's behalf.

Dana fumbled in her pocket for a nebulizer and took a hit as the car's condensation gradually cloaked the view of the apartments. She checked her face in the rear-view mirror and grimaced. Too rushed by the case to go home and fully prepare, she'd come straight from work. She thought Lucy would assume she would; all the same, she'd hurried. In part, it was her habitual 'crowding out' mechanism – filling the preceding hour reading investigation notes to avoid thinking how significant this was. Right now, they stood between friendship and something far deeper, far richer: this evening might be a bridge to a next level, or it might define a boundary. Deep breaths didn't seem to help: she could sense her body temperature rise and her hands were shaky.

Her steps echoed in the courtyard between car park and building and she felt her trick knee twinge. It wasn't the chilly air: it was her sliding composure. She pressed for apartment 122 and Lucy's voice sounded distant, like a recording reaching through the ether.

'Hey, chick. Level twelve, then turn right.'

Buzzed in, Dana walked across the tiled foyer. A noticeboard announced that recycling day was now Tuesday; a hastily written note below it snapped that not all plastics were recyclable, and residents should *Look at the label first, for Christ's sake*. Bolshie, yet caring and perfectly punctuated: Dana saw Lucy's hand.

In the spacious lift, the light made her look pallid and susceptible. She dabbed at a few beads of sweat with her handkerchief and took a deep breath. She couldn't delude herself into thinking this was simply some food with a friend.

When the lift door opened, she could see through a panoramic window to the west. The last glow of daylight was sinking behind one of the refinery stacks; a final silhouette until tomorrow. The freeway oozed around the industrial zone; a chicane of lights reaching towards the city and away to the coast.

Turning to the right, the zigzagged carpet arrowed the way to the apartment. Lucy already stood by the door, leaning against it; little more than a darkened shape against the light from within. Dana's finger and thumb snapped together incessantly. As she got nearer, a motion detector clicked and the hallway light came on. Lucy grinned and flipped her hair back; Dana hadn't noticed that Lucy was wearing it longer today. She couldn't understand why she wouldn't have noticed.

Dana raised a bag as she drew nearer. 'Hey. I brought dessert.'

Lucy retreated into the apartment and they both hesitated. Kiss? Hug? Neither quite knew; this felt like new ground. They both stuttered until Lucy indicated Dana should enter.

'Cool.' Lucy took a peek into the bag. 'Awesome. I'll put them in the freezer.'

The hall opened out into a living room with a bank of windows at one end. A large and well-padded sofa hugged one wall, next to an old armchair that looked much loved. Blue curtains were drawn, with a sliver opened to allow a light breeze to filter through. A flat-screen TV wedged itself between bookshelves. The kitchen lay off the living room, and away to the right was a closed door, a pure white light seeping from below it. To the left from the hallway an open door revealed a bed and a chest of drawers with a folded blanket on top. The place felt odd in some way; Dana couldn't figure it out.

Her nerves tingled; not just from being close to Lucy but because she felt the presence of something else.

Lucy kicked the freezer drawer closed and pointed to the bedroom. 'I get the view that doesn't include the refinery. In this tower, that's the luxury.'

Dana smiled. 'How long have you been here?'

'Oh, about three years. Moved here a few months before I started at the station.'

Dana herself had moved a year ago, joining the station after several years in the city working Fraud. Being a fraud, she felt. She couldn't kick the sense that something was off kilter.

'All this space to yourself?'

Lucy didn't reply straight away, and in the silence Dana thought she heard a low-level sound that wasn't refrigerator, or oven, or heating system.

'Not quite. I wanted you to . . .' Lucy bit her lip: her reluctance caught Dana off guard. Dana was used to a confident, assertive friend; the kind who'd tell you how bad it really was and then help you solve it. This was a different Lucy.

Dana's mind flipped through options like tumblers in a slot machine. A partner? A child? Lucy's home life was strictly partitioned from work – like Dana's – and Lucy's fumbling reticence made Dana edgy, as though she wasn't going to like this new information.

Lucy motioned Dana over to the closed door. The light under the door seemed more vivid, now she was close. 'I wanted you to meet my dad.'

Lucy pushed open the door. A smell of mild disinfectant hit Dana, closely followed by the sound of a ventilator pushing and subsiding and the beep of a monitor like an electronic metronome. The room was dominated by a hospital bed; iron rails along all four sides. Under it, a series of cables and black boxes. Above it, pure light spread in an arc that extended to the corner of the room.

Lucy's father was connected, held and cocooned by a plethora of wires, cannulas, plastic pipes and a face mask. His face looked palsied, though that may have been a visual trick from the mask. His skin was papery, his hair thin to the point of transparency.

'Dana Russo, meet William Delaney. His friends call him Tubs.'

She looked at Lucy. Something about parents always drove adults back to teenage years and beyond, she felt; so with Lucy now. Dana couldn't see Lucy's regular bravado of taking on the recalcitrant and the arrogant, nor her piecing together of disparate evidence. This Lucy wouldn't push detectives who knew she was as smart as they were.

Here was another little girl with a father who couldn't be saved.

But Lucy had saved her father anyway.

'Hello, Tubs, I'm Dana. Pleased to meet you. I'm hoping Luce will tell me about your nickname.'

Lucy seemed to exhale, as though she'd been holding her breath since opening the front door.

'He worked in factories all his life, but Dad's real joy was blues music. He was the drummer. Lots of drummers get called Tubs.'

'*Tubs Delaney*. Wow.' She looked back to the bed. 'Props to you, Tubs; that's a proper musician name. Assuming you don't go with *Clean Head*, or *Howling Wolf*, or whatever.'

Lucy smiled, her posture visibly relaxing. 'Hence my full name – Lucille.'

'Ah, you're named after BB King's guitar? Sweet.'

'I used to think so; until I heard he replaced his guitar every couple of years and named each one *Lucille*. Kinda took the gloss off it, to be named after a disposable and freshly purchased consumer item. So I went with Lucy.'

'Wise choice, I'd say.'

They both stood in the doorway, reluctant to step away, but not wishing to crowd the bed by moving into the room. Lucy broke the silence. 'I owe you an explanation, I guess.'

Dana touched Lucy's arm. 'You owe me nothing, Luce. But yes, I'd like to hear what happened to Tubs.'

Lucy moved towards the dining table, throwing a comment over her shoulder in a raised voice. 'In here, Dad, telling your life story. You've heard all this crap before. Feel free to tune us out.' The door stayed open of its own accord.

The dining table already held a jug of orange juice and two glasses. Lucy poured as she explained, her breath hesitant as emotion cut in. 'Dad worked in a plastics factory in Earlville. Used to do mouldings for those inserts in boxes of toys, that kind of thing? He was the union rep, too; frankly, he was a pain. Pretty hot on health and safety – self-taught, but really sharp. Several times a day, he had to wheel over what he'd done to a different part of the building for the next step in the process. It involved crossing an open part of the factory, a big space they left empty so the trucks and the forklifts had room to unload and turn. Above it, the roof was these old asbestos sheets and some clear corrugated plastic; the usual cheap crap to keep the rain off, and not much else.'

She set one juice in front of Dana and took a sip of her own. 'He told them constantly the roof was dangerous: it lifted in high wind, you could see it. They said it was fine, and anyway, it was expensive to change, inaccessible. Would have meant cranes, extra steel supports, closing that part of the factory for days. They wouldn't do it.' She scratched at the tablecloth and didn't look up. 'One day, four years ago, the roof broke as he was walking under it. He was pushing a trolley and a truck was reversing, so he never saw or heard anything. Big sheet of asbestos hit him here, right on the temple. Out like a light.'

Dana swallowed. Four months ago, she'd given Lucy her own revelation, about her own father. A heart attack on a blazing day, collapsed among the scarlet blossom of a poinciana tree; a young girl running for heart tablets; the screaming anger of her mother when it all proved too late; the birth of hatred, fear and abuse.

But, she thought now, she'd cheated. She'd done it on the telephone. She'd lacked the courage to tell Lucy about it face to face, with all the raw emotion that entailed. Dana had ducked the crucial, dangerous, life-repairing exposure of that.

Lucy continued, head down. 'I flew back from interstate and he was already in hospital. The company tried to cover it up, then deny responsibility; then deny he'd ever told them about the roof. I knew my dad, knew he'd have records. The ones he kept at work "mysteriously" disappeared, but I was certain he'd be smarter than that. I found the copies, got the other union reps behind me. I fought that company for over a year.'

Dana sat quietly, knowing how to listen to confessions.

'The company had this set of lawyers: big retainers, expensive suits, arrogance. They tried to weasel out of it each step of the way. Everything they could think of, to avoid paying for his care. I had nursing care for him constantly; they tried to argue he didn't need it. Bastards wanted me to turn the machines off. They were waiting for him to die.'

Both were survivors, Dana thought, in their own ways. But Dana survived her life and her past by watching, learning; hiding and sliding through quietly. Lucy took life's difficulties head on: she fought, usually won. But Lucy risked losing – that was the difference. Dana felt she knew which approach held more virtue, and it wasn't her own.

Lucy's hand quivered as she spoke. 'I mean, that was their preferred outcome. That he dies. I saw their brief from the company – one of the interns had a fit of conscience – and that's essentially what it said. *String it out, wait it out, until the lights go out.* While they were waiting, any excuse to save money. Why Tubs needed two meals a day not three; why they could use second-hand medical equipment, for Christ's sake; why any old nursing student would do, instead of a skilled and experienced specialist.'

Lucy shook her head, exhausted. Dana couldn't fathom the depths of energy the relentless struggle demanded. 'Eventually, we reached a deal. They pay for fifty hours a week of nursing care here, while I'm at work. That's why I'm so punctual – the nurse costs way more than I make, so if I'm late, her overtime means I'm losing money. Every six months a specialist team come and do some remedial work for him; they replenish the medical supplies, run some tests, keep him from deteriorating. The company insurance pays for that. It's less than he needs, less than he deserves, but more than he'd get from the goodwill and humanity of lawyers.'

Dana's hands were fidgeting at the injustice. 'What's his prognosis?'

'Well, he's never woken up. It's some form of persistent vegetative state. He never will wake up. I know it; we all know it.' She gestured to the bedroom. 'If he can hear me, Tubs knows it. Those machines can do it for him, and I can feed him liquid through a tube and clean up the other end. As for anything else? I don't know. Might never know. It's possible he can hear me, so I keep going with that. Keep talking to him, including him. Hoping he can hear. Might give him some comfort. Hope so. That's all I can do for him.'

Dana reached across and simply held Lucy's forearm. Her touch seemed to quell the shaking. 'Jesus, Luce. I mean . . . don't know what to say. Your mum?'

'A depressingly similar story. Died when I was three – septicaemia, leading to liver failure. Doctors didn't sew her up properly after a routine op. Medical negligence, but they got away with it. Lawyers got them off the hook. So . . . you know . . .'

'Hence your, uh, energetic response to lawyers generally. Christ, if I'd gone through all that, I'd be picking them off with a high-powered rifle.'

Lucy grinned at the table and finally looked up. 'Don't think I haven't considered it. Logistically awkward, difficult to maintain long term. Someone like you would catch me.'

Dana gave a watery smile in return. 'I'd never catch you, Luce, you're too smart. Even if I did, I'd . . .'

'Chuck me back in the water?'

'Tell you to throw in a distraction murder – upset the pattern . . . maybe do a politician; someone the public wouldn't miss.'

'After Mum died, Tubs took me to gigs to save on babysitting.'

'Seriously? When you were three? On a tour bus?'

'Ah, not quite. Four, by then. And they never got famous enough for a bus. Tubs used to arrive separately with the drum kit – he'd take up all the space if he travelled with the band. So I'd ride with him in the van, and once he was all set up I'd find a corner behind the stage – the speakers face forwards, of course – whack in some earplugs, and read. Probably classed as child abuse, or improper parenting, these days.'

'I can so picture you, too.'

'I loved it. Loved it. Each slap on the drum went through the floor and into me. I could feel it, physically feel it through my bones, when my dad was at work. Not many kids could say that. I thought he was deeply cool.'

Dana inclined her head. 'Sounds like he is, Luce.'

They stared at each other until the microwave's ping saved them both.

'Ah,' said Lucy, rising. 'The sound of cordon bleu cuisine. It needs ten minutes in the oven to brown. Would you . . . would you read to Tubs?'

'Sure. I have a bank statement in my bag . . .'

Lucy laughed. 'No, I read to him each evening. This month it's *Anna Karenina.*'

They both stood; while Dana moved to the bedroom door, Lucy edged towards the kitchen.

'Exactly ten pages, mind,' she warned over her shoulder. 'Don't let him smooth-talk you into any more than that.'

The tubes and mask, and the way they hid Tubs's features, were more intimidating than Tubs. She wondered if he could hear anything, comprehend anything. Probably not, she concluded, but that wasn't the point. Lucy was attempting to make up for an omission she hadn't actually made. She was trying to compensate for not being there at the factory: not swiping away the asbestos sheet, not rescuing Tubs. Dana knew all about false atonement: how it reached through the decades, ran deep in the marrow. The power of conscience – it surged beyond all logic and reason, right into the soul. Especially when that soul was one of the good ones.

Dana sat in the armchair next to the bed. Her nostrils filled with the impersonal scent of antibacterial wipes. The medical equipment was jarringly close and intrusive. She picked up the book and opened it at the marked page.

'Hello, Tubs. Sorry, but I'll be doing the reading today; Luce is creating wonders in the kitchen.' She stopped, as if he was going to react in some way. All she got was the thump-hiss of the machinery. 'But I should say upfront I'm not a silly-voice kind of girl. So if Luce has been doing all the Russian accents, this is going to be sub-optimal.'

Another pause. Crockery sounds from the other room.

'So, Chapter Eleven.'

'This lasagne's good, Luce.'

The radio muttered in the background: a ring-in debate about the freeway extension and how it would transform the local economy. The push-suck sound from the ventilator was something Dana had already habituated. She was free to focus on three freckles on Lucy's nose, just below the bridge.

Lucy grinned and waved her fork. 'I was certainly involved in preparation and delivery, of course. And I plated up like a pro. But, obviously, all the credit goes to the kindly bearded man on the box cover, who undoubtedly makes each of these by hand.'

Dana nearly spat a swig of orange juice. 'Oh, certainly. You can tell it has his personal touch.'

Dana looked behind her at the living room. The curtain billowed with what felt like a final breeze before the frost gripped for the night. Dana noticed a complete absence of photos of any kind. Lucy's computer was presumably in her bedroom.

'You've got a record player and a tape player in the corner, there. But you don't seem to have any records or tapes. Which, especially given Tubs's musical career, is an anomaly.'

Lucy's eyes sparkled. 'Yeah, that's very true.' She tidied her knife and fork so they were facing north/south, like Dana's. 'No, we never really kept any.' She tilted her head. 'Thing was, Tubs was a bit of a purist when it came to music. He thought it was . . . a living thing, and should be consumed that way.'

'So he hated recorded music?'

'Not so much hated as, I dunno, didn't think it was authentic. He thought that a tape should be simply a direct recording of what was played. He thought you should hear the scratches, the errors, the lumps and bumps; they were part of the humanity of it. Digital drove him crazy; so did autotune. He had no time for production, or echoes or fades – anything that made the recording less faithful. I used to argue with him all the time – that producing and engineering were skills in themselves, could add to the music; could make it something extra. He used to scoff: *music is what comes out of instruments and voices*.'

It made sense to Dana; an old-school attitude that focused on purity, a sense that something had to be experienced in a certain way to be appreciated, to count.

They both fell silent: not quite uncomfortable, but not quite fully relaxed. It all mattered too much, thought Dana. This; them. Almost too much. Part of her wanted to run. Lucy rescued them.

'Dessert. You brought dessert.' She rose and headed for the freezer.

Dana flushed warm again. She had what she saw as a gauche, almost childish taste in food. She viewed embellishments, side orders and garnishes as simply clutter. She couldn't tell veal from pork and thought people would silently sneer at her if they knew. Everywhere she looked, people professed themselves 'foodies': every holiday programme or magazine article seemed solely concerned with cooking in or eating out. She wondered what Lucy would think of her choice.

'Cool.' Lucy handed over a Sky Rocket lollipop and a piece of kitchen roll. 'Top-down, or bottom-up, chick?'

Dana regarded the three tiers of flavour. 'It's a personality test. One direction is civilized, one is an abomination. So make that a psychopath test. But no pressure; eat it however you like.'

'I used to love these as a kid. There was an ice-cream van that came round the district.' She inclined the lolly to the north. 'I grew up in the next block along. Now known as Aung San Suu Kyi House, for God's sake.'

Dana laughed. 'Bit ironic – naming people's homes after the most famous house arrest in the world.' This tower was called Cicely Saunders House. She'd have to google who that was, later.

Lucy began peeling the wrapper. 'It's not like Aung San's going to pitch up in Earlville to complain; she has bigger fish to fry over there. Anyway, the ice-cream van would arrive below and start its song, and each kid would rush out of their apartment at the same time and all try to catch the same lift. Which, of course, made it agonizingly slow, and stupidly crowded. It stopped on each floor – we'd nod at whoever got on, cram up a bit, all getting more agitated. When it got to the ground floor, maybe twenty kids burst out like a champagne cork: all of us convinced the guy would drive off before we got there.'

Dana struggled to tear the wrapper as elegantly and effectively as Lucy; it split into a number of ungainly slivers. 'Which would have been economic madness on his part.'

'Oh, totally – he was on to a guaranteed winner. When I was older, I realized that's the last thing he'd do. But when you're little, you can't see what's rational, can you?'

It came out almost before Dana realized it. 'Generally, that's true. But now and then there's some kid that has a rational, analytical view when they're, oh, seven or eight. Spooky little kid. They're a screaming success socially, take my word for it.'

A tilt of the head from Lucy. 'More screaming than success, though, right?'

'*Touché*, Luce.' Dana fluttered at the accuracy. Sometimes, a suspect hit a nerve during an interview, often without realizing. But it didn't make her shimmer inside like this. Lucy had a habit of cutting to the chase without seeming to wield a blade. Or an agenda.

'Anyhoo, chick: David Rowe. I got an email from Mikey about it. Rowe is lawyer for Marika, too?'

'Yes, he is,' replied Dana. 'I should have suspected David would stand for Suzanne *and* Marika. In fact, he told me as much, out on the plaza this afternoon. I sort of rationalized it and kidded myself at the same time; that he meant he'd find someone top-notch for Marika, and represent Suzanne himself. Which was dumb: it would smack of favourites. I think David's desperate to have some control of this thing, in exactly the way he didn't when Mary Doyle died.'

The symmetry struck her. Lucy trying to repair a mistake she never made in failing to protect her father; David doing the same because he couldn't protect the sisters from Mary Doyle. And Dana herself, forever trying to compensate for what happened on a blazing day when she was eight years old. Something unforgiveable. Unforgiven.

'You strike me as off balance about it, too,' suggested Lucy.

'Well, yes, that's fair comment. I'd been banking on being able to interview each sister separately, but quickly. I could get one version from one sister, then immediately go into the next room and see if that tallied. That's where the progress would be – in the gaps in each story, which the other sister would highlight without realizing it. Gaps are good.'

'Ah, David can make sure that doesn't happen?'

'*Précisément, chérie*. Firstly, I can't simply flit between the two, because David must be the lawyer present in each case. There'll be a hiatus each time, which kills rhythm. Secondly, he can brief each sister on what the other said – it's pretty much his obligation to do that. It's going to be extremely difficult to drive a wedge between the Doyles, or catch them out in a lie or a faked alibi. It makes it about ten times harder.'

'So how do you break them open?'

'Assuming there's something there we need? Luce, I have absolutely no idea. Focus on any gaps, definitely. I suppose, either by getting one to flip on the other, or by simply driving holes in each individual story. Mainly, by drilling for the truth all the time, until something gives. I suppose it ultimately hinges on me being able to get inside one of them: look out at the world from inside their head.'

Lucy grimaced.

'Unfortunately,' Dana said, 'Suzanne's got a messy, slippery personality, which doesn't help. Maybe Marika's easier to pick.'

Lucy rocked her hand to indicate her doubt. 'Not from what I've heard. Look what everyone's said about her: if half of that's accurate, she's a real slice.'

'True, true.' Dana had one tier of Sky Rocket left, and waved it. 'But I bet even Marika Doyle leaves the strawberry till last. She's not a monster, Luce . . .'

Dessert had turned to a lingering coffee; Lucy had gone the extra mile with some mints, which she'd presented with her trademark hand-sweep. The evening now felt pleasantly warm, tingly.

'Luce, there's something you should know.'

Lucy put down her cup. 'Okay.'

How to explain it? She'd rehearsed a hundred times, but that all disappeared.

'I, uh. Okay. So, tomorrow, I'm interviewing Marika. I need to get inside her head, as we said, and I think I have a way. You know something about Mary Doyle, now?'

'Some form of schizophrenia; two girls and her in one bed; ever-decreasing circles?'

'Right. Well, David Rowe filled me in on more of the details and I think I can use Marika's . . . I think I can connect . . . sorry.'

Dana could feel her arm tremble; a spasm that wouldn't subside. Part of her wanted to reach for her nebulizer.

Lucy reached across now and touched Dana's forearm. Dana took a deep breath. 'Okay, I'll just say it and maybe get it wrong: you'll piece it together.' A deeper, needy breath. 'The reason I think I can connect with Marika is that my mother seemed . . . well, she blamed me for my father's death, you remember that?'

Lucy nodded again. A few months earlier, Dana had pulled Nathan Whittler to pieces in an interview room. The shattering case had needed Dana to share traumas, to get Nathan to open up after fifteen years of silence. Lucy recalled Dana's telephoned confession that evening about her childhood. Dana's recollections of blinding heat, a little girl with a glass of water, a mother's blistering rage: impossible for Lucy to forget.

'Well, she certainly followed through. My mother took promises seriously. She started with some sort of . . . I dunno, like an exorcism. Not quite, but almost. A ritualistic thing with the connivance of half the church: I was an evil little girl to have allowed my father to die, to have caused it. People who should have known better – did know better – indulged her unhinged ideas.

'When that had no effect except to traumatize me, she would have little jags of cruelty at odd times. She would sometimes grab me in the night, tie me up, then go to work. She was forensic, took a lot of time with . . . she concentrated very hard. Like it was an engineering task, something that rewarded precision. Got more and more elaborate with the knots, too: almost a point of pride. After that it got . . . well, darker in various ways.' She closed her eyes. 'Anyway, I'm still alive, and still sentient, so I must have won, somehow.'

She looked to Lucy for a reaction: disgust, horror, something. Lucy remained implacable – concerned, upset for Dana; still there. Dana struggled to breathe.

'It all started the day after my father died – I told you she blamed me. Someone at the church heard her version of events: that I'd deliberately been too slow with the pills. They thought I'd only have done such a thing if something inside made me do it. So my mother started driving that something out of me. She had help. Had . . . *tacit approval.*'

Lucy held an image of young Dana: tiny, persecuted, helpless and alone. 'And this went on . . . for years? Didn't anyone see? Raise the alarm?'

'Ah, people see what they want to see. All they need is some vaguely benign interpretation of what they're witnessing. My first scars, for example; along the arms and the shoulder blades. My mother took me to hospital and said I'd fallen into a tangle of undergrowth; a careless tomboy. She rang the school with the same story. They didn't look closely; they wanted to believe.'

Dana looked away and talked to the window. 'If you know how to plan, Luce, and you have no ethics, it's surprisingly easy to get away with that kind of thing. Everyone around you wants their own path of least resistance.'

'God almighty. And you were eight when all that started?'

'Uh-huh.' Dana managed to turn back. 'Mummy's little demon. Carrying something within that must be cast out. She told herself she was rescuing me in some way. But I always believed, even when I was eight, that she knew exactly what she was doing and why. Now, I think she wanted to lash out and hurt something; purely to see a manifestation of how she felt inside – broken, obliterated.'

Lucy wanted to grab Dana and just hold, just protect her. 'Christ. How did you . . .?'

'Escape?' Dana's voice quivered; she fought to regain it. 'Well, it took years. A long time. I was twelve before I got up the courage, and before I found a way. I stole a video camera from my neighbour one day, and hid it on the bookshelf. Little thief, see? Just like Mother always said – *thief, liar, evil seed*. When my mother had another crack at my supposed evil, it was on tape. I ran to Child Services when I should have been at school.'

She could still feel her rubbery, weak legs as she ran, her view smeared by tears. She'd stumbled each time she'd looked back, certain that her mother could see through her soul and knew exactly where she was headed. Little Dana ran two kilometres, convinced with each step that a blow was about to smash her skull.

'I remember; still felt guilty for stealing, for missing classes, even then. I'd told two priests when I was nine; they just went to my mother and I got punished for more wickedness. I told a teacher when I was ten, but they did nothing. I had no access to the real machinery, you see; the social workers or the psychologists. I was hospitalized eleven times in four years, so Health had a file and an asterisk; I was mentioned in risk meetings, but it was a *watching brief*. For years. All my supposed protectors hadn't taken me seriously before that point, despite the evidence on my body. Scars, rope burns, bruises: all Child Services had when I was twelve was a thin file and *concerns*.'

One hand gripped another, ferociously. 'They were cowards. No one wanted to risk a false accusation: they preferred that I either suffered quietly or proved it totally. But even Child Services couldn't argue with the film.'

'They protected you in the end?'

'They moved me. A long way away.' Deep breath. 'And changed my name, and my age and gave me a whole new back story. Birth certificate, passport, medical records – the lot.' She blurted, as if the speed of the words would make them easier for Lucy to swallow. 'I . . . I wasn't Dana Russo until then.'

'You were . . .?'

'A different girl, with a different name, life, everything. I lived with foster parents until I was eighteen. I was lucky, in a way. This was before lots of things were computerized, or on the Web; no social media back then, either. The case never made the newspapers; Child Services buried paperwork; everything under the table. So it's surprisingly untraceable. A whole new me.'

'Jesus, Dana. And no one here recognizes you, from back then?'

'Not so far. You never know; the human mind is hard-wired that way. But I think anyone vaguely recognizing me now would think they'd seen the adult me somewhere recently: I don't think they'd automatically reach back that far. Plus, I look different: very much so, in many ways. Perhaps if someone had left town when I did and saw me now for the first time? Possibly. But no; nothing like that so far.'

'Wow. You're a box of surprises, chick.'

'Sorry, sorry, Luce. I know – a lot to take in. I had to be fostered, and I had to have a new identity. She would have found me. I had to hide every piece of who I'd been and start over. Sorry, Luce. Feel like I've been lying to you.'

'No, no. God, you have every right to keep that personal. Christ, Dana. Am I right to think she was batshit crazy?'

The phrase forced a weak smile. 'Jeez, Doc, stop with the medical jargon. Yes, she was. Driven to it by my father dying, I suppose. But she supplemented that; surrounded herself with people who didn't help. So much was self-inflicted. But she . . . yes.'

'And now? Your mother?'

Dana waved her hand. 'Uh, out of sight and out of mind. Kind of.'

'Well, you're Dana Russo to me. The right person, right here: that's all that matters.'

Dana blinked and swallowed hard. 'I can prove I'm Dana, but I can't prove that I was anyone else. The old me got obliterated completely. Had to be. I lost who I was, Luce; still building the new one. Plenty of bricks still missing.'

'Well, I've always said you're a legend. And it turns out you're literally that.'

Dana grinned and blinked back a tear. 'Puns. Puns make everything okay again.'

They lingered at the doorway while Dana fumbled with her coat. Lucy pretended to be testing the door handle on the cupboard, to avoid simply standing and staring. Finally in her coat, Dana flapped her arms once, like a child stepping onto an ice rink. It felt ludicrous.

'So, uh, see you tomorrow,' she mumbled.

'Bright and early, on the dot. Now you know why.'

'I do. Thank you so much for letting me meet Tubs. I really appreciate it. And thanks for this evening, and suggesting it and . . . well, just thanks.'

'I'm so glad you came. Truly.'

They leaned in for a hug and, for the first time she could ever remember, Dana clung. She reached and folded, glad to be in someone's arms. She felt Lucy's cheek burrow against her neck for a heartbeat. Then they separated; both grinned foolishly, and Dana stepped out.

At the end of the corridor Dana turned, knowing that Lucy would be framed against the hallway light. Wanting to see her one more time.

Chapter 23

Thursday, 1 August 2019. 2150 hrs

Ali waggled the bottle. If she could, she'd have wrung it out, but even in her state she knew that wasn't possible. It made an impossibly loud clunk when she dropped it into the bin, clattering against the other two.

Usually there would be a radio, or a playlist, echoing through the apartment. A shuffle from the year they'd met, maybe: songs she'd hated at the time, but now enjoyed because she knew the words. But she'd arrived home drained, listless. She'd drifted through the place in telling silence; starting things she didn't then finish, thinking of eating but not cooking. Opening wine was the one completed task of the evening. She didn't want company; she didn't want noise. *God*, she realized, *I'm turning into Dana Russo.* But without the composure that she saw in her temporary boss.

All around her were the exhibits of four visits to Ikea – the Disneyland of the coupled-up. The whole thing had smacked of being grown up; of having made a confident choice about the direction of her life. Four trips: crawling through the traffic, strolling around the store's control-freak one-way system. It all said life was going to be all right, because she was doing what adults did. And now look.

Jeez, she thought, *toughen up, girl.* Life mends: that's what her sister had said to her. Life mends itself, and you with it. Her sister was smart, but then, she'd married Steady Eddie and didn't have to worry about crap like this. Maybe that was the problem: if you married drama like Doug, you got what it said on the tin. Or in their case, the bottle.

She flicked a hand at the letter from her lawyer as she sat; it flowed into the air like a swan before drifting gently to the floor. There would be no problem, it assured her, getting the divorce through. Doug's well-documented womanizing, including the online evidence he'd – in her view, deliberately – left lying around, would see to that. A process was in motion; the system was locked in and would provide.

In truth, she'd made a poor choice, and this was the inevitable result: better to take the medicine. But her pride still insisted it was a good choice made bad by events – by chance twists of two careers; by the susceptibility to booze that they shared; by temptation appearing in the right place at the right time. Ali wanted it to be luck – even if it was bad luck. But it was her, always her: Doug was the outcome, not the catalyst. She should have known better, and always had. She'd lied to herself that he was somehow fixable – a relationship alchemy that, like all forms of alchemy, didn't exist.

Without the cover of the lawyer's letterhead, the stack of correspondence between Curtis Monroe and the Doyle sisters now took her bleary attention. She had genuinely intended to look at it closely this evening, until she'd opened the mail and been side-swiped by legal reality. Now it came back into whatever focus she could muster. A pile maybe two centimetres thick, in date sequence, each sheet with that characteristic grey haze that hallmarked a cheap photocopier.

Maybe she'd go through a few before switching on the late news. She half-planned to get up early tomorrow and do what she should have done tonight. It eased her conscience, took the imperative away. Which, paradoxically, made it easier to stay with it.

After maybe eight or nine letters, the sapling of an idea took shape in the back of her mind. By halfway through the pile, she had the idea firmly established. She had to rein it in. It was an effort to force herself to read what was there, not merely the parts she thought confirmed her view. Ali sobered up somewhat as she went, because it was a sobering idea.

When she'd finished the pile, she settled back. Her thighs ached from sitting uncomfortably and, she now realized, from tension. Those last few letters, as the parole date closed in and freedom began to shimmer in front of Curtis, had genuine drama – if you were skilled in looking. Even though she knew the outcome, Ali had read with the expectation that the Doyle sisters would suddenly switch track. She had, she contemplated, been hoping that they would.

If she'd known Dana better, or if Dana was that kind of person, Ali would have had her mobile number and would have called her there and then. As it was, she stumbled cotton-mouthed to the bathroom, drank a glass of water and flopped onto the bed. She sleepily promised herself she'd read the letters again in the morning.

Because she couldn't believe she was right. It was monstrous.

Chapter 24

Lucy tweaked the shoulder of her jacket as it sat on the back of the dining chair. She was humming quietly to herself. Sunlight flashed from a hundred windscreens out on the freeway. 'Mambo Number Five' was sliding and popping on the kitchen radio. The agency nurse would arrive shortly, and then Lucy could head to work. Dana, and the chance to work a murder, were waiting for her. The day couldn't get much better.

Last night had been beyond her expectations. Until Dana arrived, it had felt like a leap in the dark: not only regarding their relationship, but opening up about Tubs. Lucy hadn't been sure how Dana would react. No, wait; she *had* been sure. Absolutely certain, in fact.

Dana's own revelations had settled surprisingly quickly. Perhaps they would haunt Lucy well into the future but, last night, they hadn't. Dana was the person she knew, no matter what name she'd been born with. Lucy had felt trusted, wanted: that was always what Dana evoked. The intimacy from sharing secrets outweighed the burden of hearing them.

All the same, this morning she was flooded with thoughts about the holes in Dana's rebuilt life. Dana could explain who she was now, but that was a person with gaps, fault lines, fissures; spaces where a person should be. Dana could not explain who she'd been; couldn't even prove it. That girl had been erased, for ever: the price paid to flee her mother's cruelty.

It explained a lot of things.

She checked the clipboard at the end of Tubs's bed: a list she'd devised herself so that she could complete tasks like an automaton on the days when all types of fatigue overtook her. Today, however, she felt on her game.

This new nurse, Rita del Rey, impressed Lucy much more than the previous couple of offerings from the agency. Rita wasn't interested in going through the motions or taking time out to flick through celebrity gossip articles. Rita had a number of processes she insisted Tubs be party to; she'd carefully talked Lucy through them by staying – on her own time – one evening last month. The extra physio, the extra movement and stimulation options: these might all be absolutely useless for Tubs, but Lucy was pleased that Rita wanted to try them. Rita gave a damn, and Lucy liked people who did.

'So . . . Tubs . . . what did you make of Dana?'

Thump. Hiss. Thump. Hiss.

'My thoughts exactly. I'll keep you up to date on all future gossip, I swear.'

When the doorbell rang, Lucy frowned. Rita had her own key and, while she knocked and announced herself when she came in, she didn't need to wait for permission. Maybe it was one of the neighbours. The old bloke in number 121 sometimes fell over and his wife needed a hand hefting him back into his wheelchair. They all had to help each other here.

Lucy looked through the spyhole. Immediately in front of her was Dennis the Tech, acting sheepish. Behind him and looking away was a thin-faced, hard-looking man in a dark suit. He stared implacably at the elevator, features curled in the convex lens, seemingly knowing he was being watched. Military-short hair, tired eyes and clipped movements.

She opened the door. The man came forward, as though expecting her to step aside so that he could sweep in like a centurion. She held her ground, but looked to Dennis.

'*What it's pertaining?*' She put on the ludicrous accent, and Dennis sniggered behind a fist.

The other man looked quizzically at her. 'Sorry?'

He hadn't seen the movie. She repeated it for his benefit. '*What it's pertaining? Meaning? Regarding?*' She switched to her usual voice. 'Regarding?'

He flipped a badge then began putting it back in his pocket. 'Detective Ryan Butcher, Ethical Standards. This is Dennis Markos, IT Unit.'

She ran cold and clutched the door tighter. Now it made sense, Dennis turning up at her place when he'd never had reason to . . . Ethical Standards: Lord, this wasn't going to be pretty. Her mind raced.

'Dennis, I know. Morning, D.' Dennis inclined his head, now uncomfortable and wanting to curl into a ball. Lucy held out her hand. 'But you, sir, I do not. So I'll take a long and proper look at your ID, thank you.'

Butcher sighed and gave her the card.

Lucy read it slowly and silently, not taking it in. Was there anything she could do here, any way to stem the tide? She scratched with her mind at possibilities to stall, but couldn't think of one. There was a mutual plan, in case this arose. All she could do right now was play her part. She handed back the ID, scrabbling feverishly for something that might give her the edge when she didn't have it.

She'd agreed a plan with Bill Meeks, if this ever happened. All she had to do was follow through: ride it out, then hit back with the evidence she knew was on the cloud, and in Bill's office safe. If she could keep this Butcher character near the apartment door, so much the better. The plan was simple. But her mind was careening, pinballing . . . suddenly and disconcertingly unreliable. She was a smart woman who used her brain all day, every day: it frightened her to find that she couldn't rely on it now.

Butcher had a sour expression, as if the in-joke between two colleagues were a heinous crime. In truth, he disliked using a tech who knew the accused, but he had no option in a one-horse town like this. He didn't think Markos was stupid enough to stiff him on the computer side. But Butcher felt he was less intimidating if the tech and the accused were mates who shared dumb jokes.

'I have instructions to close down police software which is currently in use on your home computer and seize any records generated using that software. I have a warrant to do so.'

Dennis couldn't hide his embarrassment. Lucy wasn't surprised by the implied accusation, but still felt thrown by the timing of it.

'Does the warrant cover anything else?'

Butcher regarded her. He'd heard she was smart – maybe too smart for her own good. Possibly, the leeway she was seemingly granted had made her cocky, or she was used to getting her own way with police officers.

'All your emails, any phones. Markos – all of them. Oh, and it's at my discretion to search the rest of the apartment, if I deem it necessary.' He handed her the warrant and she took a ninety-second minute to stare at the words.

Lucy shivered. The email access was standard: she'd typed a hundred such warrant applications for Mike and Dana. Though when she was on the receiving end, the chilling thought of someone barrelling through her private life made her nauseous.

But she had bigger, more immediate issues: the prospect of Butcher seeing every room in the apartment. The main strand of the emergency plan was predicated on Ethical Standards simply going into the bed-room and doing their stuff on the computer. That, in itself, was awkward, but survivable. But if they searched the rest of the place, she'd be emotionally holed below the waterline.

Butcher decided he could make the running now. He raised an eyebrow and Lucy stood back, pointing to the open door of the bedroom.

'Computer's in there. Password-protected, D.' Dennis sloped past.

Butcher took a grim look around from the hallway. He could see a bathroom that appeared to be a jumble of railings and soft edges. Now that he looked twice, the place appeared odd, somehow. His eyes narrowed.

'Yeah, well,' he said. 'Go ahead and do your tech thing, Markos. All the relevant records, no mistakes.'

Dennis blinked at him. 'I'll need Luce to open up each part with her passwords. I don't know them; she's pretty good on IT security.'

Butcher frowned. 'Yeah, okay. Miss Delaney will kindly open the system up, as per the warrant.' He waved the folded paper officiously and looked again at the closed internal door in front of him.

Lucy didn't move.

'Go ahead, Miss Delaney.'

Lucy looked up at the ceiling, then down again. Then fixed Butcher with a glare. 'I won't start doing that until I have your solemn oath that you'll stand right there, in the hallway, until we're done. I won't have you roaming around my apartment.'

Butcher snorted. 'You don't have a choice. Warrant, remember? You don't get to make ultimatums. Searching this place is at my discretion, as I've already told you. With a witness to that.'

He waved a finger at Dennis, who looked even less comfortable now.

'Fine,' said Lucy, folding her arms. 'I'll stand here, in your way. If you try to come past, I'll drop you. Meanwhile, Dennis can start the fifty hours minimum he'll need to crack my security. No offence, D, I know you're good, but I was super-careful.'

Dennis looked back at Butcher. Forty–thirty to Lucy; Butcher's turn.

Butcher considered his options. All those conflict-resolution modules he'd taken had not included this kind of scenario. There was something else in this apartment that she was trying to hide. It would be better to secure the files, and then decide how to see the rest of the home. Break it down into bite-sized pieces, he told himself.

'Whatever. I swear by almighty God I'll stand in your hallway. Now give him the passwords.'

Lucy glared at him. She couldn't, she understood, stop Butcher walking around at any point. She could only make it embarrassing. She crouched down next to Dennis, who whispered, 'Sorry, Luce,' when he thought Butcher wasn't paying attention. Lucy managed a thin smile.

'Will this take long, Markos?' Butcher was bored. He was itching to search the place: Delaney was presumably hoping he would take pity on her. Probably hiding something: photos of Bill Meeks, maybe. Or perhaps some 'recreational use' she hadn't bothered to hide. All grist to the mill, as far as he was concerned.

'About four minutes, maybe five,' replied Dennis, muttering something unintelligible.

The time dragged. Butcher stared at his watch; Dennis kept making typing errors because he was shaking. Lucy put a hand on his forearm, to steady his nerves. She was feverishly trying to work out how to keep Butcher away from the other rooms. There was no viable reason, without revealing the actual reason; she couldn't see any legal right to stop him. She watched as Dennis unwound the systems and deleted them. The emails, data and audit trails were secured onto a memory stick. At last, Dennis eased the chair back and scowled at Butcher.

'All done. Sorry again, Luce.'

Butcher eye-rolled. Civilians and their little sensibilities. This was potentially serious stuff, yet Markos was mooning around like Delaney had watched her dog fall under a bus. Maybe she had him under her spell as well; when all was said and done, they were only here at all because she'd set up something confidentially with Bill Meeks.

Lucy stood. 'As Dennis is finished, you can leave now, Detective Butcher.'

'How long have you had those software packages on your home computer?'

'Dennis can tell you when they were added. I assume you aren't tech-savvy enough to understand that?'

She felt bad, goading and deriding a detective. But she had her back to the wall here.

'How long?'

She folded her arms again. The longer they were talking here, the longer they weren't wandering around the apartment.

'Hmm, that sounds like an interview question. As far as I know, I'm entitled to have a lawyer, or a union rep, sitting alongside me for an interview. So no, Detective: you don't get to ask me official questions that could hang me out to dry while you're taking up the oxygen here. Save it for an actual interview under lawful conditions. And stop treating me like an idiot.'

Butcher smirked. 'It's a perfectly simple question. Why would it hang you out to dry?'

Lucy glared. 'Seriously. Stop treating me like an idiot.'

They stared at each other, while Dennis tried to melt through the wall. Butcher glanced at the door to the next room, as though it led to a secret kingdom in a kids' book. *There be dragons.* He wanted in; there was something she didn't want him to see and it made him want it even more.

He held out a hand. 'Mobile, please.'

'What?'

'I need your mobile. Can't have you contacting other, uh, *potentially interested* parties. It's in the warrant – under "all other devices". Please don't use that home computer to try to contact anyone: frankly, I'm doing you a favour not taking it with us. We'll interview you straight after this, at the station. After that, you can have the mobile back. Which is, I'm sure you've noticed, another incentive to answer our questions quickly and cooperatively. Do you have a telephone land-line? Laptop? Tablet?'

She shook her head and reluctantly handed the phone across. He bagged it as a victory.

Butcher eyed up the door again. It clearly made her agitated. A strange type of apprehension: he couldn't quite place it. Because it didn't feel like full-on guilt; not like she had a gun in there, or what-ever. He stepped towards it.

'No, please don't. Please—'

He stopped and looked directly at Lucy. 'What? I'm entitled to search your entire property, Miss Delaney. And that's what I'll be doing. *Where are you going, Markos?*'

Dennis had almost reached the front door; his fingers were on the handle. His face was puce and Lucy could see drops of sweat on his temples.

'I did the tech bit. You don't need me any more. I can wait in the car. I don't want any part—'

'You'll stay right there, Markos. You're the witness.' He softened his voice. 'You know, for Miss Delaney's benefit: in case I'm a nasty bully. You want to help your good friend, right? So if you care about her wel-fare, you'll stick around. After you, Miss Delaney.'

She wasn't going to crumble in front of Butcher, she'd decided. But she might snap. She might well do that.

Lucy opened the door into the living room and stepped through. Butcher came in, a reluctant Dennis behind him. The room was immaculate – as the bedroom had been. Butcher pivoted but stayed silent. The warrant potentially allowed for a finger search, taking up floorboards, breaking Gyprock: whatever was necessary. Butcher couldn't see anything out of kilter, but he wasn't looking for something connecting her to Meeks unless it was in plain sight. The mobile was more likely to have the right kind of evidence. Or the emails.

A muted thump-hiss drew his eye to the light below the door. He motioned towards it and watched her flinch. Did it again, purely to observe the reaction.

'Please.' Lucy was agitated, but trying to stay civil. She could feel herself buckling. 'This isn't necessary. You've got the tech stuff. Just leave. This is . . . personal.'

Butcher raised an eyebrow as he thwacked the folded warrant against his thigh. 'Well, this whole case is about the personal, Miss Delaney. *Personal* access to confidential police systems, held on your *personal* computer. All off the books, huh? Ad lib, against the rules. Integrity and conduct matters are always *personal.*'

He moved towards the door and she tried to squeeze out a shout, but nothing would come. The door hinges squealed and Butcher looked in.

'Oh crap. Who's . . . who's that?'

Lucy kept her voice as low as she could. 'My father. My father is in a coma. He's here twenty-four seven.'

Butcher looked troubled, but she couldn't be sure why. Compassion was the least likely option.

'Jesus. There was nothing . . . your name . . . it said . . .'

Lucy lost it. Butcher looked troubled because he thought he'd been fed poor data, that was all. She looked at Butcher and saw lawyer – the same ones who fought to keep Tubs away from here in the first place. She screamed.

'Happy now? Happy? Got what you came for? Taken apart my privacy enough, have you? Get out. *Get out*. Leave him alone. Leave us alone. Get *out*, Butcher.'

Dennis was already gone: slapping the button by the lift. Butcher scuttled to the front door but made the mistake of turning to face Lucy. She'd gone from screaming to unnervingly quiet.

'Four people in the force know my father is here. Four. Dennis is the third, and I trust him not to say a word to anyone.' Dennis nodded from the end of the corridor. 'You are the fourth. If anyone, anywhere, indicates they know anything about this, I'll know it's you. I'll know. And I will take your life apart. Bank account, career, relationships, everything. Little pieces at your feet. I can do that.'

Butcher didn't even bother with the fake bristle. He simply left. Lucy closed the door and collapsed behind it. She was still on the floor when Rita tried to open the door and found her sobbing against the umbrella stand.

Chapter 25

Dana was surprised that Miriam scuttled over to her as she stepped through the main door. Miriam thrust an envelope into Dana's hand – the overnight forensics, courtesy of Sarah Keller – and then grabbed her arm.

'Oh my God, have you heard?'

Dana's eyes narrowed. Sometimes she took an interest in Miriam's shocked tones, only to find it was about dog pedicures, or a TV soapie being cancelled. 'Good morning. Heard what, Miriam?'

'Bill, Bill Meeks. He's gone.'

Dana put down her briefcase. Miriam must be confused: Dana certainly was. 'What do you mean, gone? He's on a two-day course, not missing. I spoke to him last night.'

'No, no; *gone*. Suspended. Not working here. They got in some City guy . . . uh, McCullough, I think he's called.'

'What? Why? What's . . . what reason did they give?'

Miriam shrugged, heading back to her desk. 'I dunno. Don't think they gave one. Bill's suspended until further notice, so they say. We have this guy McCullough now. My friend Katherine, works in Human Resources, says he's here for at least a year. It's a big thing, apparently.'

A year? Dana couldn't fathom it. They didn't do such things lightly;

it must be serious. Yet she couldn't imagine what it would be. She couldn't see Bill getting outside the regulations; he wasn't particularly a risk-taker and she valued his integrity. It was hard to picture him ever knowingly slipping the wrong side of the line. And yet . . .

She could only imagine how blind-sided Bill must feel; how betrayed by an institution that had demanded his loyalty. What would Bill do for twelve months, while all this blew itself out? What could Dana do, without him?

Dana picked up her briefcase. As the news sank deeper, she could feel a tremor in her hands. Bill was her backstop, her prop. He knew how to handle introversion, how to blend it with the rest of the team; how to nurture, but not let her off the hook. Dana needed that. She needed the nebulizer. She needed to be alone.

'Oh, Dana? Nearly forgot, all the excitement. He wants a briefing on your murder. The new guy. Like, right away.'

Dana knocked, and heard nothing. Her watch said eight o'clock: she wanted to prep further before her first crack at Marika Doyle. Eventually, a noise was barked through the door.

'In.'

She entered to find Anton McCullough in Bill's place, a near-empty desk in front of him. The symbolism was deliberate: a break from the recent past. He looked like an interloper; he looked like he knew he was an interloper. Bill's photos and certificates no longer lined the bookcase; he'd been swept away and crunched into three cardboard boxes near the door.

Given he was nicknamed *Mac the Knife*, she was surprised that McCullough turned out to be a small, wiry, weasel-featured man of fifty or so. The new chair almost swamped him; his slightly arthritic fingers barely reached the end of the arms. His suit crumpled around him, as though he'd lost a lot of weight recently. He declined to look at her, choosing instead to stare at a dusty corner. She closed the door and stood in the middle of the room.

'You requested an update on the Monroe case, sir?'

Now he seemed to regard her from an angle. His eyes met hers, but his face pointed past her to the window, almost as if he weren't paying attention.

'I ordered one. Sit down, Russo.' The voice was soft and brutal, like the leather on a cat o' nine tails.

Dana sat and waited for some indication that she was supposed to speak. It made her realize how much, in her communication with Bill, had been assumed and understood: they'd been naturally at ease with each other. She pegged McCullough as someone who tried to control matters by making others work him out.

'Russo, who are the three biggest drug-dealers in this district?'

The question came from nowhere. 'Sir?'

'Simple question.' He harrumphed, as though she'd annoyed him already. 'Who are the three biggest drug-dealers in this police district?'

Dana could feel her finger and thumb snapping together. The file of a current murder investigation sat fallow on her lap while she attended to what felt like a whim of a question. Who had she overheard from Mike, or the occasional visits from drugs officers?

'Alvarez, Richteau . . .'

He sighed quietly. 'Three, Russo. Try Carpenter.'

'Yes, sir. Carpenter.' She could feel the blush rise and felt off kilter, toppling.

'So you can't name them. Duly noted.' He stared at the fingers of blossom visible through the window. Dana waited for the next mortar shell to land.

'Tell me, Russo, how many CIs are you currently running?'

Once more, Dana tumbled through the air. 'Sir?'

'CIs, Russo. Covert Intelligence. Informants. Snitches. How many assets are *you personally* currently running?'

'None, sir.'

'None. You're a senior detective in this district, currently running a murder investigation, and yet you have no ear to the ground whatsoever. Can't even name the main drug-dealers around here, who have a hand in most crime.'

Dana got a sliver of insight: a bully who wanted everyone off balance. The kind of leader who thought making an example of one or two – a carefully chosen one or two – was the way to gain wider respect. She could feel the crosshairs.

'I, uh . . .'

'What?' Again, his eyes turned to her but his head stayed still, as though he were glancing at something putrid in the fridge. Swallowing her anger was both necessary and awkward.

'I don't believe most crime around here *is* drug-related, sir.'

This time there was a tilt of the head.

'Oh, don't you? The detective who doesn't know who the dealers are, and has no informants, knows this? It's all drug-related in City East, Russo. Not that you've spent any time in a city unit. So, why not here as well?'

It was tempting to back down. Dana was not a political animal: didn't thrive on it, ran away from it. Maybe she should acquiesce. But no; something in her welled up.

'In this region, sir, drug-dealing is a pyramid within itself. The top level mainly sells amphetamine, heroin and cocaine to the next level, who mostly sell ecstasy and crystal meth to the next, who sell dope to the next. The biggest dealers don't even touch the drugs: they merely launder the money into legitimate businesses and assets, or get the Alvarez family to do it for them. The people at the base – who buy most of the various drugs – are ordinary working people; they mainly finance their habits from lawful income. They're customers, not players.'

McCullough might have been listening to the garbage being emptied. It made no more impact on him than that.

'So,' she continued, 'the pyramid stays intact, and there's little need for acquisitive crime like burglary to finance any of it. Each level funds what it buys from above, using the income of selling to the level below; the base customers have legitimate income. The dealers like it that way: they know who they're working with and the whole model is stable and low maintenance. The big three have carved up the bulk of the regional market between them, and none seems inclined to break ranks; so there are no turf wars, either. The market's too small to attract any new players from outside: they can make much more money operating unhindered in City East. Sir.'

He gave no indication of having heard. Or whether he found her analysis convincing.

'Hmm. Precious few drug arrests around here.'

Dana knew what he was doing, and that she shouldn't bite. In an interview room, she'd never bite. This somehow felt more personal. She could imagine Mike's hissed warnings – *don't let him in, don't let him win.*

'As you say, sir, things must be much more sophisticated and complex in the city. Perhaps we're a simple bunch out here in the bush. Sir.'

He turned this time: they each stood their ground until McCullough looked away slowly and went back to his window stare.

'They suspended your boss at 6 a.m. Do you know why Billy Win-Win got bumped at dawn, Russo?'

He spat out the name. Bill had never mentioned McCullough to her: either a mutual animosity had been hidden, or the spite was one way. She suspected the latter. Her working life revolved around cases and the small team it took to deal with them. Organizational politics bored, annoyed and worried her. It was a game where she didn't know the rules, or the players; or often, the aims.

'No, sir.'

'You should.' McCullough turned to face her. He had a nuggety, unpleasant face, with the hint of a sneer loitering around the top lip. 'It's directly related to you, Russo. Or at least to your . . . uh, close colleagues.'

'Sir?'

'The secretary? Delaney?'

Dana shuddered: couldn't hide it quickly enough. McCullough noted the arrow hitting home.

'Admin officer, sir. Yes?'

In crisis, go pedantic.

'She and little Billy Win-Win had a relationship beyond this building. She had special access to police computer systems at home, courtesy of Billy. It's an Ethical Standards matter now.'

It didn't make sense; yet he'd said it as a matter of course and would surely know that she'd check. If he wasn't lying, then . . .

'What that says to me, Russo,' he continued, 'is that this is a pretty lazy ship. Inappropriate relationships, detectives who don't know the basics. The kind of bumbling around I should expect from regional, but won't tolerate. I'll be sorting it out. Monroe.'

She nearly dropped the file. She swallowed sharply, determined not to let him see it.

'Sir. Curtis Mason Monroe was released the day before yesterday on parole from Du Pont. He'd served nine of fifteen for rape. His body was found on Thursday morning near a quarry on a deserted road; it's close to the location of the original rape. He'd been tied to wooden posts in a cruciform; his left abdomen was gouged out. There are no witnesses; no fingerprints or DNA at the scene – there were several rainstorms on the night he died.'

McCullough closed his eyes. All his body language was carefully tuned. It made her skin crawl. And they were all stuck with him, for God knew how long.

'TOD?'

'The autopsy was yesterday afternoon. We were originally looking at a window for time of death of eleven hours up to 0600 yesterday morning. The medical examiner says it was likely between 11 p.m. and 3 a.m., probably nearer eleven.'

'Weapon?'

'There were three blows to the same area, so hard to pin it down for certain. The ME suggests a wide-blade axe. Something with a slight curve and some heft behind it.'

'Revenge killing?'

'We thought it likely, but there's currently no evidence of that. The original rape victim, Louise Montgomery, lives an hour away in a little town called Gerson, and was unaware of Monroe's release. Her alibi is firm, but we're still verifying. Her family is across the country and has a full alibi for time of death. She has no partner now, and didn't back then. No one made threats at the original trial or afterwards.'

A handful of people knew about the Aryan connection in Du Pont prison: Dana and Mike weren't supposed to be in that number. She'd held it back from Bill for good reasons. She kept it from McCullough now for other reasons: not least, she had to protect Peter Kasparov from this kind of person. 'Monroe might have upset someone while he was inside Du Pont; we're checking with intelligence sources for a possible motive from his prison life.'

The air seemed to crackle at her final statement. Nothing tangible: more, a subtle change in the chemistry. It was possible, she thought, that McCullough knew about the Aryan Force connection. He'd been high up in Criminal Investigation at Central in the past; whether he knew might depend on timing, or the extent of his connections.

'So who did it, Russo? You're Billy's golden girl: haven't you got any suspects?'

Dana paused for two beats to show her disdain: schoolyard descriptors.

'There's a cottage half a mile from the crime scene: the nearest habitation. Two sisters live there – Marika and Suzanne Doyle. They'd been writing to Monroe for the previous two years, and offered him a place to stay when he was released. An ATV tyre print near the crime scene may be linked to them. We've tracked some – but not all – of the hours after his release. Forensics prove he's been in that cottage; but there's no blood there, or evidence of a struggle.'

McCullough grunted. 'You've arrested them, though?'

'We brought in Suzanne yesterday morning under Close Proximity: I've interviewed her three times. Their private life is complicated, and we needed to speak to Marika as well. She hid out all day and was found late in the afternoon, in a pretty sorry state. The doctor insisted she recover from some exposure, so we're due to conduct the first interview with her this morning, also under Close Proximity.'

'Hmmph. Someone told me about this. Your speciality, eh, Russo? The reason they keep you around, indulge you: the off-chance you might get someone to confess. They aren't keeping you for your networking skills, are they? What was that case a few months ago? The nut in the cave?'

'I believe you're referring to Nathan Whittler, sir.'

'Yeah, him.' The eyes half opened; a facsimile of shrewd suspicion. 'You had him for *twelve hours*. When he was the one convincing suspect and had the victim's blood on him. And Billy thought you were some kind of hero for getting a confession.' McCullough puffed his cheeks. 'The bar's pretty low around here, isn't it? Hmm. So, you have the two sisters, and one of them did it.'

No, she thought, *I have two people in station who probably know a lot more than they're telling. Only a fool would consider them the sole game in town.*

'May or may not have done it; may or may not know who did. Sir. If Monroe made enemies inside prison, they're quite capable of sorting it out beyond the walls. We're at the early stages with that angle. Also, the sisters both have the same lawyer. So playing one sister's version off against the other's won't be so simple.'

McCullough's mobile phone rattled on the desk. He lifted it enough to see the caller ID, pulled a sour face and dropped it. Dana had good skills at reading upside down: the caller was named *wife*.

'Charge them both right now, and let the courts decide.'

'Sir?'

'You heard, Russo. Charge them both. Murder of.'

Dana didn't move a muscle, and that seemed to displease him.

'Jesus, Russo. One of them did it, surely? Once they both realize they're going down for murder, the one who didn't do it will roll on the one that did. Let the courts work out who's lying. Or maybe you want to be some warrior of the truth? Some holier-than-thou little know-it-all who has to work everything out. Grow up, Russo. The world's messy. One sister did it, the other is covering up. The courts can decide.'

Wouldn't work, thought Dana. She'd followed through precisely that potential chain of events. She'd considered the option of charging both and hoping it created leverage but discarded the notion. The court system would sever the cases and have separate lawyers at two trials. Each sister would constitute a viable alternative version of events – each would personify reasonable doubt in the case against the other. It happened sometimes with married couples who'd abused a child but refused to speak, and it would happen with the sisters. Each jury would be unlikely to convict – particularly for *murder* – when each sister had demonstrable doubt against their guilt: especially without strong forensics, obvious motive, or an eyewitness. Besides, sibling loyalty could run very deep. And she felt it did so in this case.

She had her composure in hand, now. She had found her way to polite but icy contempt.

'What if they both did it? Or neither did it? Sir.'

'Unlikely, in my experience. Which is seven times longer than yours. But so what? That'll come out in the fullness of time. Look, Russo, you're pretty raw about real crime, aren't you? Second murder of your career, no? Came up through Fraud? Those mean streets?' He flung a hand in her direction; it looked more withered when it was in motion. 'You got promoted because you can read a bank statement.'

She lined herself up. 'Yes, sir. It was that skill and only that skill that got me through.'

He wasn't tone deaf; she knew that much. He'd slithered through the politics at Central, so while his antenna was always for his own benefit, it clearly worked.

'Don't.' He dropped the volume. 'Don't, Russo. You can't win that fight. I can snap you.' He looked down and had a sly look when he glanced up again. 'Better yet, I can review the necessity of employing your little friend Delaney. Maybe there's some efficiency gains to be had there. Central would be pleased: lower overheads from day one. She's . . . *culpable* for Billy Win-Win's misdemeanours. Must have sweet-talked him somewhere along the line.'

He let that sink in. Dana frantically tried to keep her expression neutral. Felt herself fail.

'So don't, Russo. You don't have nearly enough leverage, and never will. Your solve rate is eighty-eight; my last year as a detective was ninety-three. Show some respect for that.'

Hmm, thought Dana. But in his last year, she bet he'd palmed off unsolvable cases to minions and jumped in on a few that were about to close. Plus, she felt, McCullough's solve rate might have been high, but his conviction rate wouldn't be: she'd bet her life on it. Lots of back-slapping at first; when the case went south he'd blame it on the lawyers, the jury, the victim – anyone but himself.

McCullough rose and strolled over to the window, hands in his pockets. When he spoke it was to the glass, as if she should already be out of the building.

'I'm off down to my coast home this morning. Got to get settled in, get the wife down here. So I won't be around the rest of the day. That's all you have for your petty little crusade. You have twenty-four hours. If you haven't wrapped it up with a bow by this time tomorrow, I'll charge the two sisters myself.'

When he turned around he gave a start, as if Dana were an unex-plained guest at dinner.

'Time's a-ticking, Russo.'

It felt as if the corridor was on fire. Heat shimmered across her; shock, anxiety, shame. It was like each morning of her life, except that this was out in the open: raw, exposed and seen by someone else. Wit-nessed by a person who'd noted it, filed it and would use it when he wanted. She felt vulnerable, for both Lucy and herself.

Dana opened the door to an empty training room off the main cor-ridor. Her hand was shaking. The instinct was to switch on the light, but instead she simply shut the door and sat in the darkness. *Think, Dana, think.* The nebulizer hissed as she used it. Her pulse refused to settle, feeling skittish rather than fast; like an animal on ice, scrambling for grip.

The removal of Bill was the kind of organizational coup that seemed to happen once in a while, but she couldn't see the reasoning. She knew the district's figures were decent – not outstanding, but decent. Bill had been at Carlton for eighteen months, and the usual rollover was around three to four years, so it was unlikely to be simply an accelerated swap-about of senior officers. McCullough hadn't given any indication that he wanted to be in this district; he clearly saw it as a Hicksville demotion of some kind, a pain to be endured. Perhaps the coup was more about shifting him than Bill, and her old boss was incidental damage. The organization was notorious for promoting those it wished to get rid of, irrespective of the impact on those it should retain.

But the thing with Lucy: that had been the true shaker. According to McCullough, Bill was specifically removed because of his relationship with Lucy, and he'd given her access to police computer systems from home as a result of their connection. As Dana fished out her phone from a pocket, amazed she'd remembered to charge it, she wondered about that. At no point did it cross her mind that Lucy and Bill were . . . McCullough had sneered that the relationship was deemed 'inappropriate' by the higher-ups, but Dana could see that insinuation even more clearly now. McCullough was a snide little bully who would max out the innuendo in a circumstance like this. Implication, she reminded herself, was not proof. Besides, she trusted Lucy and Bill and, more importantly, trusted their integrity. She would literally bet her life on it. There had to be another reason.

But the fact remained that Bill was suspended and Lucy was in the frame, somehow. A year, Miriam had claimed. Suspending such a senior officer wasn't done lightly: the taint remained, even if he was cleared. Dana came back to some vague notion that other factors were at play in the political cat-sack of Central and they were simply getting the backwash. She could imagine someone wanting McCullough out of sight and mind; she could also picture Bill being well meaning, but without heavyweight political backing. Something bigger than all of them was going on.

She held on to her phone, her hand covering the screen because she needed the darkness to think. Why would Lucy have police systems on her home computer? Why would Bill grant such a thing? And why would it be kept from their colleagues?

Lucy wasn't picking up. Dana tried three times, but it snapped to voicemail each time. Dana's finger and thumb twitched as she sat and her knee fizzed. It wasn't like Lucy to be out of communication range, and after last night Dana had no doubt Lucy would reply. She had no choice but to leave a voicemail:

Hey, Luce. Sorry to leave a message, but I can't get through. Thank you again for last night, and for getting to meet Tubs. I, uh, I understand why you would want that to be private from people, so thank you. Look, we have a new boss here. I think some crap is hitting the fan with Bill. Hope none of it is flying your way, but I fear it is. Call when you can – if not me, then Mikey. Take care, chick.

It seemed inadequate; as if there were some form of protocol she was supposed to be following. What, she wondered, would Lucy want me to do now?

The answer was clear.

Get on with your job, and find a killer.

Chapter 26

Lucy was shaking back more tears, mortified that Tubs had been seen. She was the guardian of his privacy and his dignity, and she'd failed him. Again.

Rita knelt beside her behind the door and squeezed her shoulder. 'What is it? Tubs? Is Tubs okay?'

Lucy nodded through the sniffles. 'Yeah, yeah. He's . . . he's the same as yesterday. Yeah.'

'Then what?' Rita defaulted to matters of the heart; Lucy would have split with someone, been let down or lied to by someone; romance gone wrong.

Lucy regained her composure, but her voice still juddered. 'Some-one from Ethical Standards, from work. Here. Just now.'

'Ethical Standards? What did they— Jeez, sounds like you need a lawyer, Luce.'

Lucy was certain that lawyers were never the answer: they created problems, they didn't solve them. Lawyers had nearly killed Tubs with their stonewalling; how could they be the solution here?

'No, I . . . I hate lawyers. There must be another way.'

Rita stood up and lifted a reluctant Lucy by the elbow. Lucy felt raw. The nurse was good people, but this was compounding her humiliation somehow. Rita, however, would not be swayed. 'Ethical Standards knock on your door, early in the morning? In my line of work, we reach for a lawyer. No ifs, buts, or maybes. *A. Lawyer. Now.*'

It came to Lucy that her distrust of the legal profession was crumbling: maybe her values were less rigid and unbreakable than she'd allowed herself to believe. It was sobering. She wondered what Dana would say. Crap. She knew what Dana would say: the same as Rita, in the same tone of voice.

Rita was used to people needing a push and saw what was required here. She ushered Lucy into the living room, took out her own mobile and asked for the name of the best lawyer Lucy knew. Then she looked up the number and called him.

'Hello, David Rowe? I'm going to hand the phone to my friend Lucy Delaney, and I'd like you to help her, please.'

Lucy's shaky hand took the phone. The apartment felt cold, clammy.

'Hello, David? Sorry to bother you.' Lucy ran her hand through her hair. 'It's . . . it's not about the case. I know better than that.' She turned to Rita for support; the nurse mimed a shoving motion with her hands. 'Yes, it's uh, it's a personal favour. I need to contact the best employment lawyer you know, and I need to do it quickly, please.'

'Okay. I'm texting you her number now. She's Nancy Foster. My firm has gone up against her nine times and lost each one. Look, give it ten minutes, so I can ring her and try to smooth the way for you.'

'Thank you, David. I wouldn't ask if I . . .'

'I know, Lucy, I know. That's why I'm helping. Ten minutes, then ring Nancy, okay?'

It took the ten minutes for a stuttering Lucy to tell Rita what had happened. Rita kicked the sofa, apologizing afterwards. Lucy was wise enough to know when someone was batting for her.

Nancy Foster picked up straight away. No chitchat; straight into it as Lucy outlined the basic facts. Nancy asked a few questions that seemed irrelevant, then agreed to meet Lucy at the station right away. As she put the phone down, Lucy felt less out of control. Less like a victim. But not much.

Chapter 27

Dana gave a tight smile to Martin Simpson as she entered his custody suite. The overpowering smell of bleach, tempered by an airborne attempt at implying a pine forest, floated through the air between the regular cells. Preparation for Friday-night spills, and Saturday-morning remorse. An IT contractor with a ludicrous gold watch played with a keyboard and frowned, while Simpson muttered and looked at the clock too often. One of the CCTV cameras had junked yesterday afternoon, and apparently the software was the culprit. A sizzling strip light added to the fractious atmosphere.

The Lecter Theatre was empty. Some discarded coffee cups and a tray of half-eaten microwaved scrambled egg in the backroom's kitchenette were testament to Marika Doyle's overnight in the suicide-watch cell. In front of the cell, just over a metre from the glass, was a full-length mirror. One of those that tilted and came on castors, it was angled so that the prisoner could see both themselves and the front desk. Several officers had remarked on it, with Simpson stoically ignoring their questions.

'How was our latest guest, Martin?'

Dana liked a view from an experienced old hand like Simpson; being a custody officer, he had no axe to grind about the case itself. He took his time replacing a file on the shelf – Simpson was big on colour codes, and woe betide any stand-in who messed with the system.

'Well, pretty quiet, generally. She did baulk at the mirror, though. I explained one of the cameras was out and I needed to keep an eye on her, but any glass would have to be placed outside the cell. After about half an hour she couldn't resist testing, and then she understood she could see herself in it. It got to her: agitated. Still that way this morning. I'm not sure she slept too good. You're welcome to review what footage we do have, but she was definitely rattled. I'll send whatever we've got up to Lucy: Doyle appears from time to time in one corner of it.' He ran a finger across his lips, thinking. 'How did you know? How did you know a mirror outside her cell would do that?'

Dana smiled. 'A hunch. It was a bit of a long shot, but I'm glad it seems to have worked. Thank you for arranging that.'

'No problem. Want it left there when she returns? Hopefully, the nerds will have fixed the camera soon.' He threw a pointed glare at the IT contractor, who deliberately avoided looking up.

Dana considered the message sent by keeping the mirror, or by removing it. 'Hmm. No, actually. As long as your camera's working, you can take the mirror away, please; it's served its purpose. I want her to realize now that it was set up purely for that reason, and that she gave us the answer we were looking for. Thanks again, Martin.'

He wheeled the mirror into a storage cupboard on his left. The success of her gambit lifted Dana as she walked towards Interview One. It vindicated going out to the cottage – Dana felt bolder about following through with other theories. Little victories: Dana savoured them when she could, and it felt good to already have some idea about Marika. It was equally possible that it would be the last one she'd get today, but it might give her leverage.

*

David Rowe had arrived at the station last night about twenty minutes after Marika was brought in. Once the doctor had completed his assessment David had held a discussion with Marika, preparing her for the cell and the process of being incarcerated overnight. Dana's willingness to leave the first interview until morning had undoubtedly helped David to deal with his client: Dana was watching Marika and her lawyer through the glass, hoping there would be some sort of pay-off this morning.

Although, right now, the young woman was animated, the occasional finger-point being met with a frown from David Rowe. Marika looked fidgety, and disgusted to be there. But not surprised. Her hair had dried after being out in the open for twenty hours; knotted dark curls with no discernible style. A freckled face with small and sharp features; snappy, reflexive movements. She reminded Dana of a fox near a highway: quick-witted, hyper-aware.

Mike stood beside Dana, shaking his head. 'She is nineteen, yeah?' he asked. 'Looks way younger.'

He would have guessed maybe fourteen – certainly younger than his own daughters. Marika didn't look to be on the cusp of anything approaching adulthood. Her gestures were gauche and cartoonish. She slumped back in her chair when her lawyer seemingly didn't comply. The sulkiness took Dana back to the impression Suzanne had first given.

'All records demonstrate she is. I thought she might appear smaller, younger, more frail when she was wringing wet – like Suzanne did – but she's the opposite. Yesterday she was wet and cold when she arrived here, but she looked resilient, aggressive even; like she'd been in her element and was all the stronger for it. Today she looks more civilized, but less rooted in something she comprehends. Weird.'

'You're not putting all your hopes on her, are you?'

Dana pursed her lips. 'I'm trying not to. If the Aryans are to blame, then Marika may know the thick end of nothing. On the other hand, she might hold a key; she might even hold it and not realize. Everyone seems to think she's a scheming little thing: as if that automatically means she must be hiding something. It's just as likely a defence mechanism.'

Mike dropped his voice to a murmur.

'I'm, uh, on to those rumours. Lucy? Bill? I'll have more by the time you come back to the office. And Luce'll be here by then, safe and sound, I'm sure of it. I'll take care of that crap. So park it while you go at this girl.'

Dana swallowed hard, held back a tear that welled at the corner of her eye. Then she quickly squeezed Mike's hand, surprising him, and moved towards the door. She halted and spoke softly to its frame. 'Thank you, Mikey.'

Chapter 28

David Rowe stood when Dana entered the room. Marika looked at him in surprise, then shook her head as if he were a kitten that couldn't be trained. Dana shook hands with him, then reached towards Marika.

'Good morning, Marika, I'm Detective Dana Russo.'

Marika's handshake was neither practised nor heartfelt.

'May I sit down, Marika?'

Marika glanced at David. 'No, I don't think so. You should stand for the entire interview.'

Dana stayed stock still.

'Uh, Jesus, of course you can sit down.' Marika turned to watch David sit, only after Dana had done so. The old-world courtesy seemed to both amuse and exasperate her. 'For God's sake, does everyone here belong in a Jane Austen novel?'

Dana ignored her and set out her files. Marika fiddled with a fingernail then gnawed at it until a gentle tap on the shoulder from David made her stop. The nails were ragged, the cuticles shabby and hard to see. Dana could see scratches on each of Marika's wrists, up her forearms and on the backs of her hands. Possibly from running through undergrowth.

Possibly not.

Dana went through the protocol of the recording mechanism, bor-
ing Marika still further, then switched on both recorders. She'd
reassessed how to introduce things, what to reveal: David Rowe would
know what had been in the media overnight, so there was no sense in
trying to hide that information now. All the same, Dana intended to
shield her own knowledge until she could gauge the extent of
Marika's.

'Marika, I'm the lead investigator in the murder of Curtis Mason
Monroe, which occurred on or about Wednesday night. Your sister,
Suzanne, has been with us for twenty . . . four hours now. Like you,
she was detained under the Close Proximity doctrine. I assume your
lawyer has explained the legal position to you?'

Marika sat back in the chair, which squeaked. She draped one arm
over the back, feigning indifference. Further scars up the milky forearm –
north/south, not east/west. The sign, Dana noted, of someone who was
serious about it. Dana's next thought: *not necessarily Marika.*

'Yeah, we did all that. Uncle David's big on procedure. Look, just
ask your questions and we can get done here.'

Dana was not about to let anyone dictate either her speed or her
direction. She sensed Marika was not impatient, but anxious. She'd
assumed Marika would have a plan for this, but perhaps she didn't.

'In a hurry, Marika?'

'Yeah, can't wait for another microwave meal. Your old-timer in the
cellar thinks he can cook.'

Dana folded a sheet back on a legal pad. 'Mr Simpson prides himself on the cuisine. I'll pass on your good wishes. I'd like to begin by
asking you a few questions about your earlier life, with your mother.'

Marika's eyes narrowed. 'Because?'

Dana kept her voice even and controlled. 'Because I'm in charge of
this investigation, and I feel it germane to the case. That's the reason
behind every question I ask in interview.'

'Uncle David already told you about it, though.' She tilted her head towards him.

'Your lawyer – because, in this room, Marika, that is precisely what he is – has provided some background information. I'll be asking questions that only you can answer.'

Marika looked to her left, grinning slyly. 'Uh-oh, she's kinda frosty about you. Sorry.'

David lowered his voice, understanding that Dana could still hear every word. 'Marika. You remember our discussion ten minutes ago? Don't believe I said those things for effect. Someone died. It matters. So wipe off the attitude, sit up, focus and answer the detective's questions. As I said earlier, you'll need all your brains for this.'

Marika sulked at being chastised, nibbling at her bottom lip and avoiding eye contact.

'David has told me some of the circumstances, Marika. And I wouldn't be asking if it wasn't important. I understand how difficult that must have been for you, especially after Suzanne left for university.'

Marika snorted, and Dana thought she detected a slight glisten in the young woman's eye. Not quite a tear – more an opaque melancholy. 'I doubt that, Detective. I doubt you have a clue.'

The first test. Dana couldn't afford to get it wrong. Dana was acutely conscious that everything she said in this room had many audiences. Definitely Marika and David, then Suzanne; certainly Dana's colleagues on the investigation team; potentially a courtroom and defence lawyers and thereafter the media; possibly now a cynical and impatient McCullough. It wouldn't be easy to appease and navigate all those audiences simultaneously.

'Hmm. Let me tell you what I think it was like. Then you can tell me all the ways I'm getting it wrong.' Dana took a deep breath and focused on a small mark on the wall behind Marika's shoulder. 'Each day, when you first woke, there was about half a second when you couldn't quite recall where you were, or what was going on, or who else was in the house. Just before the sleep cleared. That was the best half-second of your day. If you woke in the middle of the night – and you did, frequently – you jolted, shaken by uncertainty and fear. Darkness had the adrenalin already pumping. But daylight gave you a cocoon: barely longer than a blink, but it was there.

'After that moment, you knew what you'd be doing that day; what was involved, how much it would cost, what it would take from you. You were utterly sure there was no escape. There would be no saviour: no one would come to your aid. You wouldn't recognize them if they did and, in your heart of hearts, you couldn't be sure that you'd let them. Because being saved would, in itself, be a terrifying change. It would unravel how you defined yourself, and without that there was emptiness. That was a dreadful thing to know: that you were so used to it all that, even though it was awful, you couldn't accept anything else. A piece of you wanted your circumstances to be unique, and a sliver of you wallowed in it. And all that comprehension took place in the next second of the day.

'So now you're awake, and two seconds have passed. Your senses go berserk, but they only do one thing. You can't feel if your legs hurt, or if you have a headache; you have no sense of whether you're hungry or thirsty, or even still tired. Because now your senses only know how to do one thing: they know to search for *her*. For your mother, for the one thing in your world that matters. It's all about her. Your senses look for the only living thing in the house – your mother. You try to hear if she's scratching about downstairs, or if she's set fire to the sofa. If a shadow is lingering outside your room – waiting to hug you, or waiting to choke you. If breakfast is sizzling away, or if you need to fetch bleach and gloves and start scrubbing away the bodily fluids she left on the stairs.

'Once you know where she is, and what she might have done, it's time to drag yourself out of bed. You don't own a mirror, because she has BDD and any reflection will control her life. You've even scuffed glass and metal surfaces so she has no proxy of a reflection. But that means you don't know what *you* look like, either. You think that's for the best; that it's appropriate. Since you don't matter, you don't need to have an image of what that looks like. You get up slowly because any squeak of the bed might prompt her to start screaming. You need each fragment of solitude, because each makes you a fraction more resilient. So you creep about the room, breathing softly, terrified that her shadow will float into that light under the door; that there'll be a deceptively soft and craven knock; that she'll ease into the room before you've gathered enough will to get through the day without dying, or killing.

'You're already terrified, because each day is terrifying. No matter that you're there all day every day, no matter that you care – you don't have the skills or the knowledge to deal with her pathology. It's impossible. Yet, you feel you must. On that knife edge, all the time. That, Marika, was the first minute of each day of your life. For years.'

Dana turned to Marika. 'How am I doing so far?'

Marika's blinks didn't stop a few tears. They slid past her brittle defences, onto the table. Dana quietly shifted the tissue box nearer to her; she declined the invitation. Dana felt heady and gripped by concern, like watching someone free-climb a cliff. Her kneecap zinged. She'd blazed through the monologue, praying that Marika would sense the authenticity and connection but fail to see how much it wrenched from Dana to say it.

'Not bad. Not bad.' Marika sniffed. 'Few lucky guesses in there.' She tilted her head as she thought. 'The BDD? How did you . . . ah, crap. The mirror. That's why you did it. I was racking my brains all night.' She pondered her insomnia. 'Well played. Satisfied now?'

'We do genuinely have camera problems in Custody. But nonetheless . . . my intention was not to embarrass you in any way, Marika. I

understand the debilitating nature of those kinds of things, believe me.
But I needed to be sure Mary definitely suffered from it, and it will
help us to know that you have it. Though, I suspect, you have it less
strongly. Less overtly.'

Marika now took a tissue and blew her nose. Dana indicated a rubbish bin in the corner of the room, and Marika three-pointed it. David
coughed.

'BDD? Sorry, not up to speed.'

Dana looked to Marika to see if she wished to explain, but the
young woman stared at the table.

'Body dysmorphic disorder. An obsessive preoccupation with some
aspect of personal appearance. Often hair or –' she glanced across – 'skin
pores?' A nod from Marika. 'It can be highly debilitating, as I said.
Extremely difficult for loved ones to understand, or help. I wouldn't
wish it on anyone.'

Marika looked up sharply, then softened her expression, as though
grateful. The connection fizzed and the jolt in Dana's voice appeared to
pass unnoticed.

'I noticed the absence of a mirror in the cottage. And most of the
glass surfaces or shiny metal surfaces – the oven door, for example –
had been scratched comprehensively. That way, they couldn't provide
an accurate reflection. It's an attempt to control, or limit, the behaviour. Doesn't always work, but the idea was smart, Marika. Definitely
worth a try.'

'Didn't stop it. Phones started having that mirror app. Anyway, I
couldn't stop her buying little cosmetics mirrors. We fought about
them. I'd break 'em; she'd hide 'em. Became . . .'

'Emblematic?'

'Hmm. Good choice of word, Detective. Emblematic, yeah.'

It occurred to Dana that the two sisters would have learned differently; grown in different trajectories by different means. Suzanne was

the elder; indulged more, able to escape, given stronger signals all her life. She would have developed by recognizing broad brush strokes and large landmarks: hers would have been an adolescence of reacting to the overt, but ignoring whatever jarred. Marika, on the other hand, was always the younger, and then the carer in Mary's final slide from sanity. She would have needed to be more watchful, more wary than Suzanne. In those last years of Mary's life each flicker or word would carry more weight, with more at stake: Marika would have learned from the shadow of a gesture, rather than theatrical expression.

'And when Suzanne left for university?'

Marika considered her reply. She was fidgeting with a piece of scrap paper, rolling it into a tight cylinder then trying to dig one end under her fingernail. 'What about it?'

'How did your relationship with Mary change, when it was only the two of you?'

Marika shrugged. 'To be honest, in some ways it got better. I'd always thought Suzanne did the heavy lifting with Mum. I thought, you know, once Suzanne was gone, I wouldn't know how to cope. Which was why I got so angry at her leaving – at the *way* she did it. So . . . disloyal. Underhand.'

She looked to David, hoping for a sign of approval. She got nothing. David's stony face suggested to Dana that he was ahead with his thinking, reaching for fresh answers and not liking what he found. Perhaps a sense of foreboding about Curtis Monroe questions. Maybe a growing belief that he couldn't defend the sisters without their help. But Dana had to park that now; focus on what Marika was saying and, more importantly, how she said it.

'I thought dealing with Mum would be a nightmare but, after she'd vented a bit, she seemed to calm down. It might have been easier for her to have one young girl in the house, instead of Suzanne pretending to be an adult. I suppose . . . I suppose there were no border disputes, were there? I mean, I was twelve; so, I wasn't going to tell her how to organize her life, and I wasn't going to run it for her. I think she felt less threatened: more like she could – and should – control things.'

The picture was too rosy; Suzanne's account cut across it, and it was precisely this kind of anomaly that Dana knew she'd get once both sisters were in interview. Perhaps that was the cause of David's poker face. Being one to one with Mary had surely been, as Dana had laid out, an ongoing nightmare for Marika. But for some reason she wouldn't share that emotion directly. Not at this time.

'But that control went too far, didn't it?'

'How would you—? What do you mean?'

Marika bristled. Her eyes shone; her energy in a rising argument told Dana something useful. Conflict was where Marika felt on firmest ground.

'Hmm. I saw the door handles, Marika, in the kitchen. And the brick by the drain. I've guessed. Let's talk about how that went for you, shall we?'

The silence stretched. Marika opened her mouth, then closed it; looked away to the corner, then back with a sardonic smile. Dana's implacable look wiped it from her face.

'You can't ha— no, you're bluffing. Tell me what you think you've sussed, genius detective.'

Several emotions now fought for space in Marika's expression. Some shame, certainly – Dana understood why. Also, Marika's concern that she didn't seem to be the unreadable book she'd supposed; at least, not unreadable to Dana. Marika displayed a fear of the exposure and, as a result, a sense that her fences weren't so much falling as being dismantled.

'If I must.' Dana made a note in Pitman without losing eye contact, watching Marika's quick glimpse of the pad.

'At some time – correction, I think at various times – Mary put padlocks on the kitchen cupboards. Locked your food away.'

Dana looked first at Marika, who fought to keep her composure, and then at David, who was frowning. 'She would keep the key safe: I suggest, around her neck. You slept together: the necklace would be tight, so she'd wake if you stole the key. All the food in the cupboards would be distributed at her whim, or not. Perhaps it was a crude reward, or more likely punishment for disobeying. I saw the scratch marks on the door handles; the way they were periodically re-screwed to the wood. And I looked at the back of the house, behind the pallet. I saw the way you'd prised and eased a couple of bricks away from the wall, so you could reach through from outside and get some food when you were truly desperate.'

Marika was wide-eyed: the level of detail had caught her unawares and she wasn't used to being sliced open by others. She was presumably in the habit of wielding the scalpel herself.

'Of course,' continued Dana, 'you could have simply crowbarred the cupboards open. In theory, you weren't being starved, not completely. Notwithstanding the evidence you'd leave behind; the arguments and punishment that would have ensued. But beyond that was the pressure, Marika: the simple pressure of adult over child, mother over daughter. It defies all logic.' Dana could feel her own eyes water; sense the past clawing through time to drag her back. 'She held an authority over you that relied on your conscience to sustain it, and it did.'

Marika swallowed and looked down, then opened her mouth in a silent *aah*. It unnerved Dana, so she ploughed on to retain the advantage.

'A couple of further guesses for you to ponder, Marika. Mary never worked out *how* you were surviving; why you weren't withering, as she'd expected. But she ended up keeping a written inventory and noticing that you were getting more food than she was giving.'

Marika's quick scowl suggested this was accurate. Dana was wrenching memories she'd held back for a decade or more and using them as weapons now. It felt wrong: wrong for herself. Surely solving this crime wasn't enough of a pay-off for the pain? She pushed through. 'In general, I would think Mary's logic wasn't sharp; she'd jump all over the place and wouldn't hold a line of reasoning for too long, yes?'

Marika nodded at the table and picked at her nail with the paper scrap.

'So, I suggest the logistics worked in reverse to what one might expect. If Mary was having a bad time and struggling with reality, that's when she'd forget to control the food, and you had access to it. But when she was "better" – when she had some grip on normality – that's when she was organized enough to go about her business, to use the padlocks. It ran counter-intuitively: the more sick she was, the more food you could access. And that, of course, meant that sometimes you were willing her to go downhill. You had to.'

Both women heard an expletive from David. Both ignored it.

'You thought about reaching out to Clara Belmont; she lived nearby. But a combination of pride, shame, and the fact that she despised you when you were younger, prevented this. You didn't feel you had the right; though I think you were wrong about that. Some things transcend feuds and rifts, believe it or not.'

Dana waited until Marika closed her eyes, lifted her head and gave an imperceptible nod.

'The humiliation of reaching out to Uncle David would have been even worse: plus, it would probably have ended with Mary being taken away. And, strange as it seems to others, you didn't wish that. People don't understand; they see the obvious and think you must have prayed for that kind of intervention. They think you wanted your mother taken away, so it would all end. But they'd be wrong: I understand that, Marika. You didn't want your mother sectioned; you wanted her *well.* Your judgement was tainted by your love, even for someone being cruel to you. Happens all the time. *I know.*'

Marika was silent. When logic felt right – as it did here – Dana did her best to allow it to flow.

'So in the end your main tactic was give in. But each time you did so you hated yourself for it, and detested Mary even more. She won, and you loathed the pair of you for that. Suzanne didn't know; not for a long time, not until after it had ended. The padlocks came off each time Suzanne came home from university: you hated that only Suzanne could induce Mary's sense of shame. You associated your sister with a change in your mother, which disappeared whenever Suzanne did. Part of you wanted Suzanne home so that Mary would retreat, but part of you despised your sister for seeming to get the best of Mary. Besides, you already detested Suzanne for failing to notice what Mary was doing: something I spotted in under an hour. You felt Suzanne could, and should, and chose not to . . . you felt she didn't care enough to work it out. That anger, that frustrated rage, ran deep. It still does.'

Marika flicked the paper against the edge of the table. Dana had been expecting a fiery response: it didn't come. The reply was loose, weak, predictable.

'That's a lot from some scratched cupboards and a couple of loose bricks. In case you haven't noticed, Sherlock, the whole house is crumbling. It's a miracle it's standing up. And we haven't kept it in showroom condition, have we?'

'You haven't denied, or disproved, anything I've said, Marika.'

Marika ripped the paper before setting it aside. She seemed undone by the conversation: Dana's accuracy was a notch-cut, and more talk about Mary would bring the whole tree down.

David's voice came through her thoughts. 'I, uh, think Marika would like a coffee break now, Detective. And I need to speak to both my clients before we resume.'

The inference was clear: Dana had made progress, and David needed to reset. And, no doubt, tell Suzanne what Marika had said. He'd promised he'd defend both sisters against Dana, and here he was, proving it. Dana judged it was better not to push it at this stage.

'Of course. I'll have some coffee sent up. Please let the uniform officer know when your client would like to return to the cell.'

Marika looked shocked, and uncertain. Whatever Marika had expected from this first interview, Dana had turned the notion upside down and inside out.

Chapter 29

Nancy Foster was 156 centimetres tall at rest – which was never. She was 161 centimetres when she bristled – which was always. Three maroon milk crates sat on the rear seat of her car, files pouring like lush foliage onto the upholstery. She checked her reflection in the rear-view mirror and flicked away an errant morsel of All-bran. As David Rowe knew well, she liked emergency calls; relished the drama and fed off the energy and the urgency. It was when she was most useful to her clients and most dangerous to her opponents. Smart adversaries drew out the battle into an attritional war of clarifications and briefing documents. Because in the heat and whirl of the skirmish, Nancy was too good.

A flurry of red hair and ludicrous check-pattern jacket, she burst from her BMW and grabbed Lucy's arm in the car park, forcing the pace to the front door of the station. Drizzle was settling and the disabled ramp glinted. Lucy felt exposed and raw, hoping that no one would see her; certain that the gossip was already ricocheting around the building and beyond. Dana: she wanted to see Dana. But this was all going too quickly for that.

Nancy almost pulled her into the small conference room. Lucy got a glimpse of Miriam in reception before the door closed, hand raised to speak to her and then withdrawn. Nancy had a battery of questions for her new client, which she asked quickly. Lucy felt centred by the momentum; she'd been cursing herself for being passive. Nancy made notes in a childishly large and curved scrawl, nodding occasionally and twice harrumphing in what Lucy presumed was a triumphant way. She again asked odd questions – utility bills, bathrooms. When she read the warrant, the lawyer kept up a poker face.

'Nancy, you've probably noticed I'm not Bill Gates. I can't afford to—'

Nancy waved her hand dismissively as she passed back the warrant. '*Pro bono* to you. Nothing to pay, not even for coffee. Let's talk tactics.'

Nancy said it as if there was about to be a discussion, but Lucy had enough of a measure to understand that it would be instructions. Nancy leaned in confidentially.

'What I want you to do is . . . shut up. Don't say a word in there. At all. In any way. I can see you're a smart woman, so the temptation's great. And I can see you're angry, and rightly so. But say nothing. Leave it to someone who'd be hideously expensive if it wasn't for free. If I need clarification, I'll take you into a corner and we'll whisper.' Nancy grinned. 'Might do that anyway, to scare the crap out of him, so be prepared. But leave it all to me.'

She chopped at the table for emphasis. 'We go in: you stay silent, we kick his butt, we leave. That's what happens. Okay?'

Lucy still hated lawyers. She still wanted a way out that excluded the entire legal profession. But as they rose, it was clear that she'd have to ride this one out and trust a lawyer for the first time in her life.

Friday, 2 August 2019. 0915 hrs

Butcher stood when the two women entered, but couldn't bring himself to look at Lucy. Nancy narrowed her eyes, confident that she held the best cards, and equally sure that Butcher didn't know his ace from his elbow.

Lucy glared at him and dragged her chair backwards until she was slightly behind Nancy's shoulder: an echelon for protection. Nancy swept the glasses and bottle of water to one side, indicating her readiness to proceed. Butcher crossed his legs, ostentatiously declining to look at his own notes, and started the recorder.

'Thank you for coming in, Miss Delaney.'

Nancy lifted her hand and barked a response. 'My client was *forced* to come in, after you invaded her apartment this morning. Don't paint it as though she wandered in here, happy as Larry.'

Butcher raised an eyebrow, as if this room were a court of kings and such etiquette was both poor, and likely to lead to a beheading.

'Invaded? I did no such thing, Ms . . .'

'Foster. It's Foster. And it's customary to know the name of the people you're talking to.'

The tone was set, and it came to Butcher that Nancy Foster wouldn't be deviating from this path. He was prepared to defend his warrant and its execution, but the truth was that no one from Legal had got back to him with a definitive opinion. He was twisting in the wind.

'Ms Foster. I executed a lawful search warrant, as per the conditions of that warrant.'

Nancy sighed. 'Ah, if only you had. If your warrant had been lawful, maybe we'd be less upset. But it wasn't.'

Butcher wasn't sure whether to challenge. He was sure the warrant was fine . . . except, he had a nagging doubt. It wasn't just finding the old man in the apartment; there was something else jabbing at the back of his mind. Nancy took his silence as an opportunity to rattle forwards.

'Mr Butcher, you executed a warrant at whose home?'

'Miss Lucy Delaney. Apartment 122, Cicely Saunders House. Right there on the paperwork.'

'Hmm. Yes. The shoddy paperwork. Because the legal occupier of that property is William Delaney, aka Tubs Delaney: the man you burst in on. Lucy is his carer and is allowed to remain in the property solely for that purpose.'

'Are you sure? I don't think so.' Butcher cursed himself for seeming to back away. 'Anyway, so what? Given his . . . circumstances, you're splitting hairs, here.'

'Not so. I'm disappointed that you view civil liberties as "splitting hairs", but hardly surprised. You had a warrant to search William Delaney's address, which required his agreement to do so. You had no legal right of entry without his permission. Did you secure that, Detective?'

Butcher pulled a face, as though he expected Nancy to instantly retract. The idea was absurd; offensive, even. 'He could hardly . . . I had search rights, as contained in the warrant.'

'Except the warrant is a grade two.'

Nancy let that hang; not purely to stun Butcher, but to allow her own client to begin thinking it through. Then she continued. 'You and I know that if you have strong evidence, you're granted a grade one: you can enter the property without permission. If your case is weak or non-existent, you get a grade two: entry requires the expressed permission of the legal occupier of a rental property, or the legal owner of a private property. If someone is acting in that person's stead – for example a building concierge, or a dutiful daughter – you must get *their written signature* before entry. Lucy Delaney is not the legal occupier and cannot therefore lawfully grant you permission, *unless* she signs to say she has done so on Tubs's behalf.'

It was slowly dawning on Butcher. Nancy liked to run down wounded prey.

'What you did, Detective, was to look at utility bills for the property, which are in Lucy's name, and assumed she's the legal occupier. But she is not. The property is owned by the local authority: it's an alternative to hospital for those too sick to look after themselves. That's who Cicely Saunders was, genius: she started the hospice movement. Each resident in that tower lives with a carer. I'm sure you noticed the giant lift that can take a bed; the disability safety railings in the bathroom; the oversized doors for wheelchairs. Impressive detective like you spots these kinds of details in their sleep, right? Lucy is the live-in carer; Tubs is the occupier. If Tubs is unable to grant consent to entry, you must get the *written signature* of the proxy. Lucy says you didn't: I'm sure this Markos bloke can verify that you didn't. So your warrant is, uh, a piece of crap.'

Lucy was mortified she hadn't spotted all this at the time. It was shaming, how she'd panicked. Butcher was silent, so Nancy twisted the blade.

'Everything you found using that failed warrant was "fruit of the poisoned tree", so to speak. Nothing you obtained this morning is admissible, unless my client permits it.' She allowed herself a triumphant smile, then raised a palm. 'Now, we're happy to allow the police software, the audit trails relating to it and the files it generated. Have at 'em. My client is squeaky clean, and that evidence will exonerate her. As will the evidence we provide later today.' The palm curled into a finger-wag. 'But your fishing expedition on the emails and mobile? No sirree. Those are out; not lawfully acquired. And you'll sign the declaration to agree they're out. Won't you?'

Butcher had the bereft feeling of a leader turning around to find his team slinking away quietly. 'Uh, I'd have to check with Legal before signing anything. Assuming I sign anything.'

'Oh, I see.' Nancy was almost grinning. 'But just now, you were adamant that your warrant was watertight. Do you need an intern in

Legal to tell you where the leaks are? Fine.' She pulled something black from her pocket. 'We'll give you forty-eight hours to have the signed declaration sent over to my offices – here's my card.'

She peeled it onto the table and Butcher sneered at it. 'Needless to say, Detective,' warned Nancy, 'if you look at the emails or mobile in the interim, we will sue you. Quite extensively and painfully. And I should add that illegal snooping under those circumstances – in this state – carries *personal* liability: Lucy can go after you, not the department, and no tailored suit in Legal will lift a finger to help you. Just so you know. Feel free to discuss what that's like with Anton Schultz. Former police officer Anton Schultz. He tried this kind of stunt two years ago. Didn't go well. But if Anton puts in a good word, you can join him patrolling industrial estates for minimum wage. I'm sure it'll be fulfilling.'

Lucy noted how she'd faded into background wash. She didn't entirely object: things were going her way here, and she felt a growing sense that the whole charade this morning had been a fishing expedition for someone else's benefit.

Butcher was now a shade of flustered red; to be fair, Lucy thought, he hadn't completely caved. But Nancy wasn't finished: Lucy sensed her lawyer could roll like this all day.

'Detective, do you know what nominative determinism might be?'

Butcher looked mentally battered. 'Pretend I don't.'

'Okay. It's when someone turns out to do what's in their name. So a Smith becomes a blacksmith, a Cooper makes barrels, and so on. If you're a detective and you're named Butcher, you should understand and use your legal powers better than this.'

Butcher sensed that this had spiralled beyond his pay grade.

'We'll be sending you exonerating proof that my client has full and current permission for using that software and has used it appropriately and legally.' Nancy dropped her tone and volume. 'Ethical

Standards already has that proof, by the way. But you're being denied it, by your seniors and betters.'

Nancy let that sink in for both Butcher and Lucy, who exchanged a look of mutual confusion. She continued to speak to both parties.

'Perhaps you should be asking why that is. And who's being targeted today? Because it isn't Lucy Delaney. She's getting hit by weapons aimed at other people. Lucy is collateral damage. This Bill Meeks is also collateral damage. And so are you, Detective. Hung out to dry. That's why Legal won't return your calls. Think about it.'

'How would you know?'

'You mean, how would I know more than you? Well, first, by being smarter. Second, I don't always do something purely because someone told me to do it. Third, I always ask who has something to gain, and what that might be. Fourth, unlike you, I have contacts in Central who speak to me. Stuff like that. You're being moved around the chessboard by people who neither know you, nor care. Wakey, wakey, Detective. My client will get out from under this, as will her boss – eventually. But there'll be a human sacrifice required by the gods of bureaucracy. Right now, you look favourite. Have a great day, Detective.'

Butcher forgot to stand when they left; he sat and stared at the space from which Nancy had fired.

Outdoors, the air was energizing, the sun blinking through a milky sky now the drizzle had abated. They repaired to a sheltered corner of the car park under a Pandanus tree.

'That was awesome, Nancy.'

Nancy grinned. 'Aw, shucks, nothing you can't learn. I've heard you can tee off that way, given the right club. Anyway, you saw the best of me, because that's the bit I'm best at.' She checked her phone. 'Here comes the bad news. We've rattled Butcher: he'll do some digging of his own, now. Which takes the heat off you for a while. But the resolution is a distance away. Prepare yourself for that long game; they already have the means to clear you, and always have had. This whole thing is about people up at Central jockeying for prestige. You and your boss are ways into achieving that, and the up-tops regard you both as fodder. It's not personal; it's not about either of you, or your work performance. It's all about forms of leverage: the crap that people use to elbow their way to the top.'

Lucy had gained that sense while Nancy was talking, but it still made her nauseous and light-headed. She was used to doing her job well and being appreciated for it. Looking over her shoulder and second-guessing herself was new.

'What should I do now?'

Nancy shrugged. 'Depends. If you want to work today, you can waltz right in and carry on. Not a person to say you can't. If they do, call me immediately. But they won't. All this crapping around is currently financially free for the bigwigs. If they stop you working, they face a compensation suit which is out of all proportion. They don't want to spend cash, or embarrass the force publicly. So, by all means, go back to work. Or have a day off. Whichever. Yours to choose.'

Lucy didn't feel solid enough to make a choice; she half wanted Nancy to decide for her. 'They took my software, and the passwords. And my phone.'

'Yeah, they'll keep the software from your home, for now. The passwords shouldn't be cancelled, because they're an intrinsic part of your job and you have them lawfully: explain that to Markos and I'm sure he'll sort it. I'll get your phone back to you, and they can't do anything with your emails. Again, Lucy, if anyone threatens that, call me.'

'So I can work, but with this cloud over me?'

'Yup, that's the long and the short of it. Which is why the longer game –' Nancy reached into another pocket for another business card – 'is played by Gabby here, who is a completer-finisher *par excellence.* She'll keep the pressure up to clear you officially, but it'll take months.'

Detail was Nancy's lactic acid: the more it built up, the slower she became. Lucy didn't understand why it would take months, when she and Bill would provide conclusive proof within a day. Nancy intuited her confusion.

'Why so long, you ask? They'll fiddle around, pretend they've lost things, claim it's under review, awaiting consultation and feedback: all the standard markers for kicking a can down the road. Don't sweat it; they haven't got a thing and you *will* be cleared. Other processes about other people: that's what will take the time. Certain individuals have to be finessed, forced . . . finished.'

'Hmm. Stigma Central, then.'

Nancy could see her client was still ashen and worried. 'Stigma? Yes and no. People who know you will immediately discount any idea that you've done something wrong. Everyone else will form their own opinion. But within a couple of days, they'll forget this ever happened – assuming you don't go around reminding them every five minutes. It'll blow over quicker than you'd believe. People aren't that interested. Rely on their apathy; you'll be fine.'

Lucy looked away as her eyes watered. 'I could kick myself. A grade-two warrant. I deal with them daily. I wasn't reading it when I was reading it, you know? I was stalling and staring at paper, not reading. Idiot.'

'Hey, now. I saw that mistake because I was miles away and smart after the event and I was specifically looking for a clown move that we could shoot at. Aggressive lawyers like me don't care, Lucy: it's not in our clients' best interests. You were caring for your father. Your compassion made you misread, but compassion is exactly what your father needs from you. Am I right, or what?'

'I suppose,' Lucy mumbled.

'Suppose nothing. I'm correct.' Nancy stood on tiptoe. 'Now, is that dick about to give me a ticket, for God's sake? All right. Deal with Gabby until I contact you again, okay? It's been fun. See ya.'

Like anyone after a tornado, Lucy was lost and searching for anything familiar in the debris.

Chapter 30

Dana was passing the bathroom when she heard the familiar clink – Lucy's bracelet flicking the basin as she washed her hands. Strange, she thought, how a prosaic sound could be as resonant as seeing someone. She pushed the door open.

Lucy jumped, startled.

'Jeez, sorry, Luce. Didn't mean to burst in like that.'

Lucy's eyes glistened. She seemed softened around the edges. Dana opened her arms.

'Had a bit of a morning.' Lucy's voice was muffled in Dana's shoulder. Dana stroked her hair.

'Yes, sounds like it. God, I'm sorry. Couldn't get through, then I had to interview Marika Doyle. Should have been there for—'

'No, no. Really.' Lucy stood back, but held on. 'I had to sort out the lawyer, and have another meeting with that arse from Ethical Standards. No, nothing to apologize for.'

'But I like apologizing; it's what I do,' said Dana. It swept them both into a watery smile.

'Bless you and your hobbies.'

Dana rubbed Lucy's arm. 'Are you all right? What's the situation now?'

'Urgh, it was a total 'mare. A guy called Butcher from Ethical Stand-ards rocked up to the apartment, dragging Dennis the Tech and a warrant to search.' Lucy looked to the ceiling and blinked hard. 'I was a fricking idiot, Dana. I panicked. Couldn't bear the idea of Tubs . . . well, I didn't read the *grade two* and let the bastard in. Stupid.'

'So he . . .?'

'Yeah, saw Tubs. I lost it.'

'Oh crap, Luce, crap. He'll keep it to himself, though, surely?'

'I dunno. I made threats but, hmm, not obliged to, is he? Could stroll around telling anyone. Besides, he'd have to put it in the reports, so there's that. I let Tubs down. You – I'm so glad he met you. Dennis is discreet, I'm sure. But this Butcher: he got shredded a few minutes ago and he might be the vengeful type. Who knows?'

Lucy sniffed and dragged a sleeve across her eyes. Dana took hold of her shoulder.

'You did not let Tubs down, Luce. You did not. You hear? God, what you've done for him: I couldn't have done it, and I don't know anyone who could. Head up, now. Besides, Tubs would have told that guy to go screw himself, if he'd been awake.'

Lucy gave a half-grin. 'True. That would be the polite version, yeah.'

'There you go. So what happens now?'

'Oh, wrapped up in legalese, basically. I'm like Schrödinger's Admin Officer: no one knows if I have a job or not, unless they open the box and check.'

'Jesus, this is so not-right. What are they thinking?'

'Uh, not sure they are. At least, one part isn't talking to the other; people are getting hit by shrapnel.'

'So the software? I don't get it.'

'Oh, okay, long story short. Bill Meeks knew Tubs, actually – way back in the day. Bill used to play bass; met Tubs at some venues. When I started here, I had to tell Bill about Tubs's situation – I might have to rush off, or might not make it in, if the nursing cover crapped out on me. Anyway, Bill had the software put on my home computer, so I could still contribute. Plus, I can sometimes do stuff in evenings and weekends without leaving Tubs. There's a system for authorizing: each year a senior commander at Central has to agree the permission again. We have all the paperwork, and I have a spare copy on the cloud. It's all by the book.'

'So what's their problem?'

'Hmm. They're claiming not to have the paperwork, even though they do have it; have always had it. They even left Butcher out of that particular loop. They're implying software might have been used improperly, but that's complete bull and they know it. Apparently, it's all a lever of some kind for some other purpose. Poor Bill. I'm not even allowed to contact him.'

'Mikey got hold of him earlier, just after I started on Marika Doyle.'

'Is he all right?'

'Suspended, pending . . . pending I don't know what. He's pretty shaken, I think. It was like a dawn raid up there, and in front of half his peers. Shabby all round.'

'Christ. Other people's politics, huh?'

There was a knock and Mike sheepishly drew the door open. 'Thought I heard you, Luce. You okay?'

Lucy looked him up and down as he came in, beginning to recover her poise. 'Mikey. Are you trans now? Should we make arrangements?'

She felt his laugh as they hugged.

'Watch this space is all I can say.' He stepped back, appraising her features. 'How are you?'

'Like I was saying to Dana, I'm here/not here. That sort of thing.'

Mike acted as though that made total sense.

'You found out some background, Mikey?' asked Dana.

'Well, I did some digging with my sources at Central. They laid it out like this. The commissioner is going in a few months. That's over a year earlier than his contract. We have the World Student Games in the city soon, which is a terror threat; once he's seen that off, he's gone. So all those people who thought they had eighteen months to get in position – they now have three. The politics are that your ducks need to be in a row by launch time: you can't come up on the rails at the last minute.'

Lucy raised an eyebrow at Dana. 'Ducks can't come up on the rails?'

Dana put her finger to her chin, theatrically thoughtful. 'They'd be obscured by the horses; so, yes they could. They're tricky customers. But if it looks like a duck, and walks like a duck . . .'

'It could still be a platypus,' replied Lucy.

'*Précisement, chérie.*'

Mike watched the word-tennis. 'Anyway,' he resumed, 'it's not only the commissioner that moves. It's like a Rubik's cube, if you can remember such things. Moving one creates a gap elsewhere; filling that creates another gap. Lots of people eyeing up chances all over the shop. The problem, apparently, is McCullough. The guy's got dirt on half the hierarchy. He's nearly out of there, but enough of a powerbroker at Central that several people have no chance without his endorsement. So, it's better all round if he's moved. He has twelve months left before he retires, so they needed to park him. He was only prepared to be parked here because it's closer to where he's retiring on the coast. So they created a "reason" why Bill had to go on gardening leave for around a year.'

'Jesus. That's kind of what Nancy said. She's my lawyer, by the way.'

'I know. She's also my cousin, weirdly. Sort of my cousin. I've never understood what "once removed" or "twice removed" means, but she's one of those. Human Rottweiler, good egg. Anyway, if she thinks the same, then it must be true – you and Bill are caught in the crossfire. Unfair, definitely. But it means you should be cleared at some point.

We have to put up with McCullough for eight or nine months, I reckon: he'll pad out his last few weeks with long-service leave, fake sickness, that kind of rubbish.'

Dana frowned at Lucy. 'A year all up? God. But in the meantime?'

'Yeah,' replied Lucy, 'Nancy says I can carry on regardless. She says they daren't try to stop me working, because it might cost them money. So, I'd like to get back to work.'

'Are you sure? You could take a few days, if you want?'

Lucy threw a paper towel at the bin. 'I need some real life, to be honest: dead bodies, cruciform shapes, crazy sisters, Aryans. I'd rather be thinking about a murder than my own feeble career, thanks. Let's go to work. Thank you, Mikey, you're a star.'

Mike waited a beat, then left them to it. Lucy raised a smile. 'I'm your original high-maintenance girl, aren't I?'

'Hardly. I'm glad we could help in some way; I felt terrible when I couldn't get through to you.'

Lucy lifted herself onto the bench. 'Ah, I was a bit of a drooling mess at that point: Rita had to physically pick me up. I felt better after Nancy tore Ethical Standards a new one. Seems like it's moving in the right direction, at least. I, uh, just spoke to Nancy's assistant, Gabby. She said Nancy's fees were getting paid by a couple of people. Know anything about that?'

Dana looked away as she replied. 'Hmm. I believe that, as a member of the MDTU, you're entitled to their legal insurance. That's what I hear, anyway.'

'MDTU?'

'The Mikey Dana Trade Union, yes.'

Lucy nodded slowly. 'Oh, that union. Funny, I can hardly remember putting in the application forms.'

'Yes, it's more of an opt-out than opt-in kind of thing.' She looked firmly at Lucy. 'They always back you, Luce. Always.'

'Well, I'm very grateful to that union.' She smiled. 'It seems about as big as Brian Setzer's Orchestra.'

Dana laughed. '*I hope you won't judge the entire Brian Setzer Orchestra by my actions.* Yes, kind of like that. What else can we do for you?'

Lucy tilted her head. 'Another hug?'

Dana tried to ease into it.

'Jeez,' whispered Lucy, her voice thrillingly close. 'Your heart is going pretty fast.'

'Yes. I'm working very hard at being relaxed.'

Lucy let go, and smiled. The next three seconds were silent and thoughtful.

'So, what now? How do we catch a murderer?'

'Urgh, okay. I'm currently putting Marika in the crosshairs. So we need a team briefing to take stock. I feel like it's barrelling away from me.'

Lucy pushed away from the counter and held the door open. 'I can do that. I shall do that. Let's rock, chick.'

Chapter 31

Dana gave herself ten minutes in the dark. Sitting quietly in her office, blinds down and eyes shut, she closed herself off to the sounds of the corridor. Solitude had to be carved from the day.

She felt progress was being made with the Doyle sisters – Marika, in particular. While she granted due allowance for surprising Marika and getting inside her head, it was still throwing Dana off balance to find her so cooperative. There was a purpose to Marika's stance, and Dana had yet to get a handle on it.

Meanwhile, Suzanne had been holding out: Dana had heard it in her tone. Suzanne was still relying on David to intercede on her behalf, whereas Marika was cutting David out completely. The contrast might be less than it seemed: both sisters could be holding back from telling David all they knew, and that may be apparent to him. Dana needed to rethink how hard and how fast she could go with the sisters; David was looking to stem the impetus of the interviews for fear of letting down the women again.

Dana tugged open the blinds. She'd needed a short break to re-set; she'd also wanted to give Lucy a few minutes to get into the office and feel back in step with the day. Dana wondered how much involvement McCullough had with the events of the morning. Perhaps he was simply part of the general maelstrom and was being blown around by circumstance himself. But Dana felt that he was the type to relish these machinations; it would have been his bread and butter at Central. He was the senator with a dagger, the duplicitous courtier, the cuckoo in the nest, the dissembler. The whole thing reeked of his kind of politics, his view of people. He certainly knew all about Lucy – an admin officer at a station McCullough had never worked in – before he set foot in the upstairs office.

As she opened the door she saw Ali making her way down the corridor, headed for the briefing. There was something awry. It took Dana a moment to twig, then another to confirm it to herself.

'Ali, can you step in, please?'

Ali glanced at the briefing room as though it offered sanctuary. Dana sat down and indicated the door with a finger; Ali closed it and sat pensively.

'Are you feeling okay, Ali?'

It was a perfectly simple question, but Ali seemed unravelled by it. She shuffled the file of the prison correspondence from one hand to the other.

'I, uh . . . yeah, didn't sleep too well. Had some bad news. Uh, divorce, actually.'

'Oh, God, I'm sorry. Jeez. Do you need some personal time?'

'Uh, no, s'okay.'

There was something still out of kilter, and Dana wanted to skate past rather than confront it. She felt her own weakness wash through her. 'The letters, then. Ali?'

Ali was staring at a point over Dana's shoulder. 'Yeah, uh. Yeah. So I read them again, and again this morning. I, uh, have a theory. It's a bit way out.'

'Fire away.'

'Hmm. Okay. So, you know I usually work in Family Protection?

Well, part of my job is to understand how children are groomed. The techniques, the . . . methods. And, um . . .'

'Spit it out, Ali.'

'And . . . I think that's effectively what the sisters were doing. In the letters. To Curtis.'

It was something that, without being labelled, had sat in the back of Dana's mind. Now Ali had named it and pushed it forward.

'You think the sisters were grooming Curtis? To what purpose?'

Ali shuffled, and again looked across to the briefing room. 'Well, that's the thing. Not sexual. I mean, they weren't drawing Curtis into anything like that, I don't think. But all the same, they were, uh, using similar techniques. The way they establish rapport, common ground . . . the way they push and prod, then withdraw. That almost . . . catch-and-release: it's classic. They establish the friendship, and it's on their terms. They hold the power, including the power of withdrawing from it without notice, without reason. The victim's on tenterhooks; the victim fears the withdrawal of the relationship. It's not balanced, it's . . . one way. Then, later, there's basically a demand for proof of loyalty. Here.' She flicked at two Post-it labels within the pile of papers, two thirds of the way through. 'That's the key – once the victim passes that test, it's time to reel them in. It's . . . I don't know if it's learned behaviour by the sisters; I don't think so. It doesn't have that vibe. Maybe it's simply their instinct of how to handle people – some are born manipulators that way. But I feel . . . I feel that's what they did.'

Dana tapped her pen on the blotter. When she'd first read the letters, she'd been searching for evidence that one or other party was the leader. She'd felt it could play into the murder – assuming the sisters were involved. If Curtis had led in their letters, it might imply that he'd dominated their interaction in the cottage; therefore the sisters' move to kill him may have been a reaction to that – possibly, self-defence. Whereas if the sisters had dominated in the letters, they might have controlled the conversation in the cottage and the self-defence angle might well disappear.

But Ali had looked a stage deeper; as she should, Dana thought, given her background. Ali's antenna was tuned for someone manipulating from distance.

Ali opened the folder to the relevant page and paragraph. Dana re-read with fresh eyes. She could see it, now it was pointed out.

'Yes, yes. I think you're right. Great work, Ali. This changes things. Changes my line of questioning with each sister, certainly. I'd felt something was out of alignment, but you've nailed it. Well done.'

Ali tried a look of quiet satisfaction, but it didn't quite gel. They shared a look that said they both knew what was coming.

'Ali, did you drive to work today?'

A flush rose across Ali's features. 'No, I . . . got a lift from my sister.'

Dana leaned forward. 'That's good, isn't it? For all of us, I mean. For our safety.'

Ali swallowed hard and looked at the floor.

'I think,' continued Dana, 'that you're not quite well enough to be at work today, Ali, are you? So I think you need to Uber home and come back tomorrow when everything's . . . improved. That way, we can put this behind us all.'

Ali's fringe flopped down in surrender.

'Good,' said Dana. 'We're on the same page. But I do need you to work from home. I need you to go through these again, please, looking for something in particular. It's really important. In fact, I need you to email the answer as soon as you have it, straight to Lucy.'

As Dana pointed at the paper she saw Ali look plaintively a third time at the room opposite, hoping for an intervention that wasn't coming.

Chapter 32

Lucy had fired up the shared drive and located all the documents from yesterday, including the work she'd done shortly before she'd left for home. She'd hoped being back in the office would be a welcome re-set of the day, but she could feel an exhausting wash sweep across her. Mike made the mistake of crossing her vision.

'You're on my list, Mikey.'

Mike raised both hands in mock-surrender. 'Oh, is that the list of your favourite people in the whole wide world?'

'Sadly, no. It's the people who promised me info, but haven't delivered the last of the sisters' legals. Now, that membership is a precursor to my assassination list. Don't make that jump, Mikey.'

'You have a . . .? Of course you do, silly me. I'm waiting for the lawyers to send through final details of the will, then I'm done.'

'Hmm. That's what I call a *possum excuse*. It doesn't fly very far.'

'Good to have you back, Luce. I've missed your threats to my personal safety.'

She smiled and looked across to Dana, who was deep in conversation with Ali over the prison correspondence. Something important, Lucy guessed, and wondered why Dana specifically wanted Ali to cover it.

*

With Ali sloping off towards reception, Dana turned to see the rest of
the team looking across the corridor. She wondered what they'd seen in
Ali's body language; whether it appeared defeated or cowed or defiant.

She crossed the corridor and placed her file on the table. 'Thank you
for waiting, everyone. Ali's not feeling a hundred per cent, so I've sent
her home. She'll be going through the prison letters again in more
detail – I've given her a steer on exactly what I'm looking for now, so
hopefully she'll pick out some key aspects as we go.'

Lucy and Mike would know – would intuit – that the discussion
with Ali had been a lot more than that. They'd be too discreet to ask.
She wondered if Richard or Rainer would cotton on.

'Okay, I'm in urgent need of a recap. A lot of things seem to have
happened in the past twenty-four hours, yet not much obvious head-
way. At least we have both sisters now: I expect to accelerate that side
of things in the next few hours. It's frustrating: we've made significant
progress in some areas but the whole thing isn't gelling yet. I feel it,
too. But there are some angles that will open up soon: we only need to
prise them a little.'

As motivational speeches go, it wasn't the best. The kind of thing
she never felt good at, a reach to find the right words. She could pull a
suspect apart on the turn of a phrase, but she couldn't find the way to
enthuse people who thought well of her, who wanted to work and
wanted the team to succeed. She turned to the whiteboards more for
her own comfort than anything else.

'So what I want to do is go over what we know – what's in black on
the board – before we start looking at the red writing.'

Mike stepped in. 'Yeah, me too. We're all doing different parts here,
and it's not easy to keep overall track.'

Not true, but generous, she thought with a nod.

'Okay, then. Lucy has amalgamated all your work yesterday – thanks
to all of you for that. I've added my own, and the input from the

autopsy. It's all on the shared drive, but I'll paraphrase it now. This is what we know: jump in when I miss something.'

She pointed at the two photos; these had been culled from the station's custody system and replaced the earlier ones from the cottage. Instead of the perky teenager with a curly smile, a washed-out, exhausted Suzanne, pummelled by some aspect of her life into acquiescence of all kinds. Instead of the gawky pre-teen sulk, Marika was intent and intense, her stare bristling yet vaguely self-satisfied. The two evolutions should be telling Dana something; it hadn't fully percolated yet.

Dana drove them through their knowledge thus far, halting when someone had something to add.

Richard gave more details on the basis for the sisters' offer. 'We had the official prison documents this morning: the Doyles' accommodation offer was for seven days under what's called *first steps*. It wasn't seen as, nor classified as, anything more permanent. Curtis was supposed to use the time to sort out something longer term.'

Mike had had no luck pursuing the background on Aryan Force. 'Still waiting on Canberra Feddies to give any kind of steer. The extent and process of the Aryan Force drug trade took local and federal by surprise, and they're still feeling the professional embarrassment. We're not supposed to know any of this, of course. Likely outcome is that we'll get little help from Canberra without a viable suspect connected to Aryan Force, which we don't currently have.'

Rainer, now. 'My interview notes from the car rental and McDonald's are on the shared drive. The bottom line is remarkably dull. Suzanne paid for the rental car in cash – coins as well as notes. She was let off the credit card for deposit: the Nissan's an old clunker and she signed a legal waiver. Macca's kids noticed the square root of bugger all: they all exist on autopilot there.'

'Oh,' interceded Richard, 'the CCTV? I've looked forward and back each time we have the trio on screen. No evidence that anyone

looks twice at them; the only recurring person is a little old lady who's
on the street when they drive by and coming out of a knitting shop
when they leave Macca's. I'm guessing she's not closely linked to Nazi
prison subculture.'

'The phone we recovered from the cottage, Rich,' asked Dana. 'Any
news on its provenance?'

'No luck finding where it was bought. Luce and I hoped for some
CCTV footage of the transaction, or a witness. But nah, we have no
clue where they bought that phone.'

Dana inwardly cursed. In a case where no one appeared to telephone
anyone, she'd hoped for some kind of breakthrough from the mobile
itself, but it appeared to be clean-skin in every way: no calls, no history,
not even a semblance of where it came from and who bought it. Usually
telephones were rich pickings for who, where, when and why.

She finished off with the latest science. 'Forensics tell us a few things.
Evidence that Curtis set foot in several rooms of the cottage. Evidence
that he lay on the bed: the only bed. Evidence that he drank a third of
a bottle of vodka, neat. No evidence of any car approaching the cottage,
other than our own SUV for the search team on Thursday morning.
No evidence of a struggle at the cottage. No evidence of who, if anyone,
transported Curtis from the cottage to the crime scene. No evidence of
who struck the blows, or who cleared up afterwards. No evidence of the
current whereabouts of the following: the weapon, anything used to
keep the scene clean, the fluoro vests or the quadbike. No evidence of
any other vehicles – except Willie's pick-up – or any telephone calls
made, within three kilometres of the cottage, on Wednesday.

'I think it's worth reiterating exactly what we're dealing with here.
I've found myself underplaying it: process can rob us of basic compassion if we don't watch out. I know Curtis's original crime; I'm not
diminishing that. But, all the same. Someone took an axe or somesuch

and smashed it into him so hard it obliterated his ribs and split his heart. Even though he was probably dead immediately, they swung another two times. They'd have been covered in Curtis's remains. And they left him dead, tied to some posts in the middle of nowhere, as carrion. With seemingly no hesitation, backward glance, any sign of remorse, or attempt to cover up the body. That's the kind of human being we're chasing.'

Dana looked around the room. Mike raised an ironic eyebrow, but the other three kept their eyes down.

'Reactions to the forensics, please,' she asked.

'Hmm. It seems we don't know much.'

'True, Rainer. But I expect you to expand on that point, please.'

'Of course.' Rainer stood, but against a desk to avoid dominating the room. 'So, I think what normally happens is that, once a murder has been committed, we quickly fill in a lot of blanks about what went on before it. By which I mean who went where, and when: telephone records, bank details, cars going through cameras and freeway tolls, paper trails. That's before forensics produces fingerprints, DNA, fluids, drag marks, and so on. They quickly give us a fairly good picture of what happened, and therefore potentially who and why.

'But this – it produces next to nothing. Maybe you've seen cases like this, but I haven't. Because he was in prison, it's like Curtis had no existence until he walked out of the gates. The victim has almost nothing in his life we can verify that suggests he would be murdered, except the link to Aryan Force. But so far we can find no one connected to Aryan Force doing anything about Curtis Monroe; no sign of telephone traffic, money transfers, rumours, following the victim?'

Mike nodded solemnly, still inwardly smarting that zero had come back from Federal sources, or Wickham Watts, that they could use. 'Nothing, Rainer, no.'

'Likewise,' continued Rainer, almost apologetically, 'we have no independent corroboration for the sisters, or for what happened inside the cottage. They're dead zones.'

Lucy raised a finger. 'As pep talks go, Rainer, that's pretty crap. Try *yes we can*, or *search for the hero inside*, or something.'

'Sorry, sorry. I don't mean to sound negative. I suppose what I'm coming to is that we seem to be bumping up against limits of physical or electronic evidence: usually, they open things up, but not here. So I guess I'm saying that it's going to be solved once we break through on motive.'

He was right, and Dana had thought the same since early yesterday. They needed to know the starting point – the point of origin – to uncover a reason for the killing.

The sisters had opportunity, but seemingly no motive; the Aryans had motive, but seemingly no opportunity. Unless the Aryans pitched up in the dark and were careful: the sisters might be holding that detail back. Possibly, as Mike said yesterday, because they were scared to tell. Logic suggested that motive trumped all – she didn't have cast-iron reasons to rule out opportunity for anyone. And yet . . .

'Yeah, I was going to draw the same conclusion,' said Mike. 'Physical and electronic evidence seems to put us on hold; unless someone has some left-field input, which I'd appreciate. Motive is the best and quickest means of progress here. And I guess that means thinking laterally. The only people who currently have motive are the Aryans: the Doyle sisters have none. Do we have anything that breaks that view?'

. . . and yet, Dana couldn't shake the feeling that she was far closer than she could currently explain. The point of origin was tantalizingly close to her grasp.

'Not totally, no,' she replied. 'I think there's something there, but we have to build it with the sisters. They haven't broken easily or quickly, not least because each one has the other to think about. I suspect that if you grow up together in an isolated house, dealing with a mother who's unstable at best, sleeping intertwined each night for a decade, you have a pretty interesting bond. It's going to take me time to sever that connection; I had hoped something forensic, or some data, might perform the cut. So right now I'm prepared to look at anything, and I mean anything, that looks different to what we have now.'

The four of them looked sheepish; even Lucy, who was usually a fountain of positivity. Clearly, the incident this morning had shaken her badly; this was a chastened, withdrawn Lucy. Dana fervently hoped the change was temporary.

'Um, I have something that practically defines left field.' Lucy's voice was uncharacteristically distant.

'Excellent. Fire at will, Luce.'

'All right.' Lucy sat up straighter and turned her monitor to face the group. 'So, you might recall that I suggested a word cloud on the letters between Curtis and the sisters? Well, here's the first graphic. Now, here's the amended cloud, after I removed obvious words like Carlton, Du Pont, prison, and so on. Now it's clearer. See the word in the middle?'

Dana squinted at what seemed like a tiny and indistinct font. She missed Mike's *welcome to my world* smirk.

'Signs.'

'Yes.'

'Signs of what?'

'No, the film, *Signs*. You've never seen it? M. Night Shyamalan?'

'I heard he peaked at *The Sixth Sense*, and everything after that fell to pieces. *I'm a schoolboy, Sidney, teach me.*'

Lucy grinned and gave a thumbs-up for the classic quote. 'Okay, so Mel Gibson plays a priest. No, really. His wife was killed by a drunk-driver, a neighbour. As she was dying, she told Mel to tell his younger brother, Merrill – Joaquin Phoenix – to "keep swinging away". Mel sinks back to a farmhouse in the middle of a vast cornfield with his young daughter and son, and Joaquin. Mel's renounced his faith because of the tragedy, and his life is floundering. Joaquin is a has-been baseball player who was a prodigy at school level but failed in the major leagues because he swung madly at every pitch. With me so far?'

'I'm no baseball expert, but I assume that's significant later?'

'Everything is. That's what the film's about.' Lucy was warming to her task, and Dana loved the inklings of her old vibrancy. 'So, Mel's son has chronic asthma, and his daughter has this weird habit of starting a glass of water then finding some reason not to finish it; the house is littered with full glasses of water. That all matters, too: trust the director, guys. Okay, so then the Earth is invaded by aliens. Ironically, that's a minor issue: a McGuffin.'

'What's a McGuffin?' asked Richard.

'Oh, I know that one.' Rainer's film-buff girlfriend had taught him well. 'A plot device. Like . . . in *The Maltese Falcon*, they spend the whole film screwing each other over to own the Maltese Falcon. It doesn't matter what the prize actually is – could be gold, or diamonds, or cash. It's purely a device to show the characters' greed. Right?'

Lucy gave a thumbs-up. 'Spot on: say hi to Caroline for us.'

Rainer gave an appealing blush.

Lucy grinned. 'Yada, yada: crop circles, Brazilian kids, hiding out in a cellar, et cetera. So, aliens have invaded from Planet McGuffin, and there's one near Mel's house. It ends up with the alien holding the son, about to kill him. They realize the alien is burned by water, so Mel tells Joaquin to "Swing away, Merrill" with a baseball bat. He smashes the glasses of water; the alien's killed but fires poisonous gas into the kid's lungs. But the kid's asthma has closed his airways, so he survives . . . I'm paraphrasing and vastly undermining the film, here.'

Dana's radar was pinging while she stared at the carpet. She screwed up her eyes in concentration. 'Never mind,' she said. 'What's the message?'

'That all things have a bigger purpose; no matter what it is, or how bad it first seems. If the kid didn't have chronic asthma, he'd have died from the gas. If the daughter hadn't left water all over the place, they wouldn't have known how to kill the alien. If Joaquin hadn't been such a screw-up, he wouldn't have been living with his brother and there to "swing away". If Mel hadn't lost his wife, he wouldn't have been at home to save the rest of his family; he'd have been at work. And she wouldn't have given him the key to survival with her dying words. So everything – even his wife being killed – served a higher and greater purpose.'

'Hmm.' Dana had been hoping for something obviously connected to the case. A cruciform corpse; an attacker with an axe – something.

'It's a good film,' insisted Lucy. 'Underrated. Understated. Critics got hung up on minor plot holes. But at heart it's a spiritual film. It's about the circularity of events; all the major aspects double-back on themselves by the end and have another meaning. Even terrible things can turn to good. Anyhow, Curtis Monroe thought it was inspiring, clearly; by the look of it, so did the Doyle sisters. The word cloud says . . . this mattered to all three of them, somehow.' She shrugged. 'I told you it was left field.'

Dana pondered, then asked, 'So Joaquin found redemption at the end?'

'Yeah. Well, they all did, really. In a way.'

Dana's radar was still firing, but the signal was distant. She didn't have time to pursue it; all four were looking at her for direction.

'Thank you, Luce. Okay: next steps. Rich – thank you for looking at the CCTV footage after they all got to town. But now that we've located the sisters arriving at Du Pont in the Nissan, I'd like you to work *backwards* from that prison arrival with the CCTV, please. There should be some footage of them first arriving in town, getting to the car-rental place, and then travelling out towards the prison. I'd like that footage, please. Again, be on the lookout for anyone who seems to be taking an interest or recurs in the material. Oh, and also the images of Marika filling up with petrol early that day. Clara said . . .?' She looked to Rainer for confirmation.

'Between 0800 and 0830, apparently.'

'Thank you. I'm not entirely sure what we're looking for, Rich, to be honest. Demeanour, posture, gesture, visual clues: something. Anything that appears to show their state of mind, their level of organization, or the state of play between them that day. Thank you.'

Richard pursed his lips. Dana couldn't help feeling that she was asking her team to clutch at straws.

'Rainer, I think we need some more background on Suzanne: she's the one making occasional forays into the big wide world, which gives potential for the viewpoint of others. So please interview her colleague at the supermarket, this Brian Aroona. Wake him up if you have to; I'd like more on her state of mind over the past few weeks, and especially the shifts leading up to yesterday. Did she say something? Did she indicate future plans? Did she discuss anything that plays into Curtis arriving or her recent relationship with Marika? This was a watershed for the sisters, one way or another. Perhaps Suzanne let slip some sense that she knew what might happen and wasn't comfortable with it. Thank you.'

She wasn't confident Brian Aroona would yield much – not based on Suzanne's description of both Brian and their working arrangements. All the same, it was a base to be covered.

'Mikey: I'd like to discuss my interview strategy with you, please. If you can get any further with the feds or local about Aryan Force, all well and good. But I'll need to sit down with you in a minute and re-assess. Speaking of which –' she faced all four of them – 'Ali has uncovered something: I'd like your take on it, and what it might mean.'

She hadn't given Lucy instructions yet, and she knew it. Lucy gave a quizzical look.

Dana turned and spoke partly to the whiteboard. She was flush with the realization that, while Ali had spoken of grooming, the sisters' tactics within the correspondence had also resembled that of scammers and how they drew in victims. The 'grooming' that Ali described seemed to betray a similar pathology to that of con artists. The way they formed common ground quickly, keying in to language and tone immediately; the skill in drawing the victim part-way along the road then backing away; the sense that the victim ended up chasing *them*, not the other way around. The techniques were, she thought, similar. And familiar. A flash of her mother – a rare smile around her lips – pierced Dana's mind.

'Ali's view of the relationship contained within the correspondence is interesting. Here's her take. The sisters begin to write. The letters are quite formal initially; courteous and respectful. It's a lifeline for Curtis, one he never imagined would appear: a normal conversation, with normal people. Don't forget, he's 24/7 in a sex offenders' wing. There has to be a desperation to have some part of his life move beyond those walls, those predilections, those assumptions of him. The sisters offer that.'

She tapped their photos, then turned to face her colleagues.

'But they also appear to know their own power; they understand where that balance lies. He's beholden to them, even though they offer nothing concrete until the last few letters. Like an adult grooming a teenager – or a con artist bringing in a mark – the sisters draw Curtis out of himself until he's in an emotional no-man's-land. He's exposed his feelings to them: he's terrified by the thought of trying to build a life outside prison once he's released. The prison and Probation both thought he'd struggle with it, so he's probably right to be worried.'

Dana was wondering, even as she explained the practical details, how the sisters knew how to do this. As Ali had said, and Dana agreed, this didn't feel like a learned behaviour. Nor was there any evidence from the books in their home – or the library records Lucy had located and skimmed – of anything like research. There was an unpalatable truth here: one or both sisters were naturally good at this kind of manipulation.

'However, for the sisters, Curtis's vulnerability reads like leverage. Then, they threaten to withdraw. It's not an overt threat: there's no apparent malice in it. They simply imply that they might find all this difficult, that they might need to step back. That's all it takes – their potential reluctance panics Curtis. It's the equivalent of a conman seemingly walking away from the con then watching the victim trail after them, pleading. It's key in this type of relationship: when the *proof of loyalty* is demanded. They ask him if he truly wants to make amends for what he did, and he says in no uncertain terms that he'd do anything – *anything* – to make things right.

'Once he says that, there's no triumphalism. The previous tone from the sisters resumes – chatty, positive, non-judgemental. But I have to feel that the marker has been laid at that point. The terms of the relationship have been set in stone; all three of them know what those terms are, and will remain. From then on, they begin discussing his impending release.'

Dana looked to each of them in turn. 'Thoughts?'

'They have a plan, a definite plan,' said Rainer. 'As you describe it, there's no accident that the power lies where it does. It's intentional.'

'No,' interjected Mike. 'They have two plans.'

His idea jolted Dana, who'd been about to nod at Rainer. 'You have the floor, Mikey.'

Mike collected his thoughts; sequence mattered as much as content. 'It's been bugging me since I first read the letters. Initially, I thought I was finding them strange because, at the end of the day, it's two young women writing to a convicted rapist. I think I overplayed how important that aspect was. Once you park it and simply look at a collection of letters, it reads differently. Did to me, anyway. Let's assume that the basic plan is to draw Curtis in – make him beholden, as you say – and persuade him to come to the cottage as soon as he gets out. Let's assume that they organize the logistics that way. To what end? For what purpose?'

Mike left a pause and open hands.

'There's a few logical options, it seems to me. There *are*, sorry. One: they're nice people and want to give a criminal a bit of a fresh start. Possible, but incredibly naive: look at *his* crime and *their* demographics. But then, people can do naive things: sometimes they hope for the best and it turns out the worst. Option two: they have a morbid fascination. Again, possible. Some people are junkies for the details, the grimmer the better. There is such a thing as a groupie for violent crimes, twisted as that is. Option three: to kill him. I can't currently think of a reason for them wanting to do that. But hey, he's dead near their cottage, so it has to be in the mix.

'Option four is some combination of those, and that's the option I believe in. It's a combination because there are two sisters; two people with different personalities but incredible proximity. They practically melt into one person in many ways, but their differences are stark, and all the sharper when they're side by side. One might have the plan to help Curtis and see him on his way; the other might have the plan to execute him. One might be interested in the gory details; the other might be repulsed. Given how the sisters seem to be capable of fundamental similarities and differences in the same space, I think there's – *there are* – two plans going on in these letters, both at the same time. But don't ask me which is which, or who had the upper hand. Because I plain don't know. I don't think any of us know.'

Dana was pondering when Lucy cut in.

'So you think, Mikey, that there was more than one motive for writing the letters at all?'

'Yeah, I do.'

'But we can't distinguish those, can we?' asked Lucy, turning to

Dana. 'The letters are written all of a piece: I can't detect changes of tone. I can't see where one sister's contribution ends and the other starts. In fact, while both sisters sign it at the bottom, the letter is always *I* and *me*: not *we* or *us*. It's as if they're one person for the purposes of the letters – indivisible.'

Dana had noticed the pronouns on the first read; it had led her to initially suspect one writer. But Lucy had hit the mark, she felt – both sisters had been involved in the writing, and it didn't even occur to them to use a plural. Which perhaps spoke to their bond and the loyalties it would surely engender. But also how explosively it might shatter.

'Yes, that's true,' admitted Dana. 'And that first-person pronoun freaks me out, to be honest. All the same, I think Mikey's right; there are two plans. Even if the letters' content suggests one plan: each sister had her own idea of why they were writing, what would result, and what the outcome might be. Each thought the letters reflected that. Whether by skill or luck, the letters – taken as a set – manage to tread a line. Each sister saw the letters as validation: that her plan was the one they were executing. Although, like Mikey, I have no clue which is which.'

'And no idea about their ultimate motivation?' asked Richard.

'No, sadly. Not there yet. Although . . . I feel I'm very close. I have no way of backing up that statement, by the way; it's an instinct. Please have a think about all that and kick around ideas. All right, thank you. I'll be back in with one of the sisters shortly, then we'll probably meet up again. Thanks.'

Mike's phone buzzed and he frowned as he saw the caller ID. He turned away and moved towards the corridor to take the call. Dana wondered if that meant something was wrong at home – it wasn't Mike's usual demeanour. Richard and Rainer headed for their desks, and Dana beckoned Lucy towards her office.

Lucy collapsed into a chair and ran both hands across her face.

'I checked the data off the transmission towers from the last twelve months against Suzanne's shift patterns. All the telephone calls indicated in that district are from late afternoon, so either sister could have made them. Probably more to do with when Curtis was around to receive them, I suppose. And Rich checked a few outreach workers on Marika being a regular at the railway carriages overnight. Nope, not seen there before last night. Sorry, I'm not helping much today.'

Dana noted an email from Randall Crawley – his editor had downgraded the murder story for now, so there was no need for a 10 a.m. press meeting. Thank God. Presumably, Randall's contacts hadn't told him the dead body was in a cruciform, or that two sisters had written to a rapist.

'You're always helping, Luce.'

A faded, tired smile. 'What, by explaining M. Night Shyamalan films?'

'It all ends up being useful at some point. That was the message of the film, wasn't it?'

'Hmm. For example?'

Dana realized that a tiny mechanism was clicking into place: a small piece going where it should. Her finger and thumb tapped together.

'Well, yesterday, you didn't think Suzanne being a top-class showjumper was relevant, but you still threw it in.'

Lucy shrugged. 'The killer used an axe, not a horseshoe.'

'Ha. But seriously, it does matter. The showjumping is a marker. It demonstrates how Mary treated Suzanne differently – better – than she treated Marika. That would have burned. I bet Marika brings up the subject even now when they're going at it, and I bet it plays into how they are with each other. So, something like that can be useful, even if you think it isn't.'

It also occurred to Dana, for the first time, that this aspect wouldn't hurt for Marika alone: Suzanne would have scars as well. She was close to being an Olympic pick, until Mary's death forced her to give it up and take care of her teenage sister. Dana hadn't fully appreciated how that timing represented a life-changing sacrifice for Suzanne. Without Suzanne quitting college and returning home, Marika might have been taken into care; lost in a system and the family rent asunder, possibly permanently. But the cost to Suzanne was the chance of competing in Rio de Janeiro; palm trees and podiums.

'Okay. I appreciate the intent,' replied Lucy, 'but I'm not convinced. Label me sceptical.'

'I physically cannot imagine that.' They both grinned at the requisition of Mike's catchphrase. 'Look, you noticed that I didn't give you a task in the meeting.'

'Yup, I was going to ask.'

'Okay. I held it back because it's easier if only you know about it.' Dana was loath to keep anything from the whole team, but on this occasion she needed to spare Ali's blushes and credibility. 'I want you to do the same thing I've asked Ali to do, but I don't want Ali to know that. She needs feeding up a bit, one way or another. I've asked her to email some details through to you this morning, so if you integrate those with what you find, she'll be none the wiser.'

Lucy frowned. 'You don't entirely trust her?'

'Hmm. I think she's, uh, not as on the ball today as she might be. So we'll go belt and braces.'

'All right. What am I looking for, and where?'

'These letters. There's something missing and I want you to identify the gaps. I think that Marika – not Suzanne – was talking to Curtis via a mobile telephone. A device she's stashed somewhere in the swamp. Merely talking a few minutes, every few weeks: the calls you've just analysed. So my idea was this: there might be things referred to in the letters which haven't appeared in previous letters. Some will be non-sequiturs just kickstarting new subjects, but some will be a continuation of the

phone conversations. So, if we identify the new elements in various letters . . . we should be able to work out what was said in the telephone
conversations, without having access to the phone. The subject matter,
at least, if not the detail. See?'

'I get it. That's how they identify black holes: by omission. What
should be there, and isn't. Same thing with planets they can't see – how
another body's orbit wobbles. That's so clever.'

Dana held up her hands. 'Thank you. It's only smart if it works;
otherwise, it's too clever by half and we've wasted some time. But I
think it's worth a shot.'

'I'm on it.'

Chapter 33

Mike was halfway along the corridor before he realized who was speaking.

'Yes, sir. Sorry. It's quite a bad line.'

'Hmm.' McCullough's voice sounded pinched by crackling distance, but his impatience made it through the static. 'I hear you have a fresh angle on your murder.'

'Sir?'

An irritated sigh, perforated by the clinking of ropes against masts – the soundtrack of a marina. 'Don't stall me, Francis. I was getting enough of that from your quiet little friend. I won't tolerate a repeat effort. The Aryan connection?'

Mike almost muttered to himself a mantra to protect Kasparov. 'We got wind that Monroe ratted out some drug-dealers in Du Pont prison, sir. Thought it might make a viable motive – revenge. It also fits with the issue that the body was left public, when it could easily have been hidden for ever in the marshes.'

The silence drifted so far that Mike considered smacking his phone against his palm.

'Hmm. No. Stop looking at that angle. There's nothing to it.'

'But it's surely credib—'

'Shut. It. Down. Francis.'

Mike was sure that his fuming breath was audible at the other end. 'Sir.'

Another pause; he saw Dana pass towards her office, giving a worried thumbs-up query as she took in his expression. He blinked slowly, which she understood to mean *no, I'm not okay.*

'Right. I have a different job for you, Francis. No need to help Russo any more. She has her deadline for trying to make herself look good. Clearly, those girls did it and Russo is stalling. You're needed on something more important.'

This had felt like the lie of the land since dawn. He'd spoken briefly to Bill Meeks, to commiserate. Bill had seemed tired and shocked at the same time and Mike had arranged to visit him that evening. He'd also asked what McCullough was like. There had been some further feedback from a couple of friends at Central. The hallmarks of Anton McCullough on a major investigation: bizarre, contrary but definite shifts in direction – seemingly prompted by special information that he never shared but implied was there. *Twelve months, max*, he told himself.

'But there's four of us investigat—'

'Francis.' The voice was soft, but used to being obeyed. 'I'm aware of Billy Win-Win's slackness. It no longer applies. Do not – repeat: do not – aid Russo in any way. I'm going to get a grip on crime here, and that means going after Miguel Alvarez. You lot have done nothing in that area worth reading. That stops, now. We're going to crack down on the drug dealers responsible for ninety-five per cent of the crime in this little backwater. Put a new plan together for that. I want to see your ideas tomorrow afternoon, and for God's sake try to come up with something original. I don't want a re-heat of crap that hasn't worked.'

The one clue Mike had that McCullough had gone was the dead tone.

He realized his hand was shaking as he pocketed the phone. There was something infantilizing about McCullough's disdain. And that's what it was – with no hint of personal clash or identity politics: Mike received the same lack of basic respect that anyone would.

Dana was in her office, poring over the letter transcripts yet again, sure the concealed door into the case lay within.

'Mikey. Bad news?'

Mike slumped in the chair and Dana noticed his fatigue. It wasn't like him – Mike was the positive counterpoint. But if the call had been about his family, he'd probably be on his way home by now.

'Yeah. The Aryan Force angle. I had a phone call.'

'From whom? Canberra? From that guy Baker?'

'Ah, no . . . leastways . . . no. From McCullough. From our illustrious new overlord. No, he, uh, well, it wasn't a cosy chat. More of a monologue.'

Dana frowned. She'd hoped McCullough would stay true to his word and back off until tomorrow morning. She should, she decided, take note of that. McCullough's promises were worthless; his threats were anything but. 'What did he say?'

'Basically, he said I was wasting my time with the Aryan Force angle; it wouldn't be a runner and I should use my time better.'

She raised an eyebrow. 'He said that?'

'Pretty much, yeah.'

'But he can't know what we have, or suspect; nor what we've done. He's been out of that loop. You're holding out, Mikey. Spill. More verbatim, less precis.'

He should have known better, he thought, than to try to ease around the subject. Dana was scrupulously polite, but that didn't mean she fought shy of harsh reality.

'Ah, lots of crap about being a new broom, things are going to change. I tuned that part out, pretty much. I was too fixed on him telling me to drop the Aryan Force line, exactly when it was getting interesting.'

'You think . . .?'

The insinuation hung in the air. They were well synched: Mike had considered the same thing.

'Well, that's a longer bow. We don't know how far up the Nazi networks reach, do we? McCullough might be a dickhead off his own bat, no help needed. He did make it extremely clear that it was an order, with all the discipline code behind it: ditch the Aryan Force side of it.'

Dana wasn't used to having a limb of the investigation amputated, not without a reasonable discussion.

'A bit left field, isn't it? I can buy him finding out about a potential Aryan connection without us telling him. He has that kind of network. But to slice it off as a viable option? Why not let us play it out, see where it goes?'

Mike tapped out a rhythm on his knee.

'Well now. A couple of potential reasons. The first is benign, the second, not so much. Idea one: he's simply a belligerent and fundamentally annoying person who injects random switches of direction into cases. I was told that by at least three people in Central, so this wouldn't be out of his wheelhouse. Idea two: either he has a personal interest – or he knows someone even more senior who has – in making us drop the Aryans. Kaspar thought the tentacles reached high up: the Aryans have a better screening process for customers than ASIO has for spies. That kind of juice implies someone high up, who knows the countryside up there, can move around unhindered, ask whatever and whenever without question . . .'

'Yes. Yes. Both of those are viable. His personality suggests the first; his behaviour suggests the second.'

Dana had to keep her mind in check here. It was tempting to start linking disparate events – a possible link between McCullough and the

Aryans, plus Bill's sudden suspension, for example. Maybe Bill's removal was a response by the Aryans to their own leadership coming under attack? Did the Aryans want McCullough sent here to punish him for failing to protect them? Or to position him to cut down any further probing of their structure from this end, or any attempt to link them to Curtis's murder? She realized Mike had resumed speaking.

'Whichever, he said I wasn't to assist you any more.'

'What?'

'Again – adamant. Cut off my objections. Said we had bigger fish to fry and I was going to lead on those things, so I should stop working on the Monroe murder. He said, and I quote, "Clearly those girls did it and Russo is stalling." Sorry, Dana.'

Without Mike pursuing the Aryan Force angle, it would simply have to be parked: none of the others had the security clearance to go prodding around. Dana could go back to it tomorrow – maybe contact Kasparov herself – but that could only happen if the Doyle sisters became a dead end. In some ways it simply made up her mind for her. She had a fait accompli for a road she'd been ready to take for some hours. The 'choice' was now no choice at all – she was all-in on the Doyle sisters. She'd ride that until the trail went cold.

It crossed her mind that McCullough might have anticipated that conclusion. He might have been directing her towards his own pre-ferred outcome for the case while cleaning up the trail for the Aryans at the same time. At any rate, his decision would suit him: everyone else had no option but to adjust. McCullough was all about McCullough.

'All right. I'll leave anything Aryan until tomorrow, but I reserve the right to try that angle again. He hasn't told *me*, has he?'

'Sound career move, Dana. There's no possible way that can go wrong for you, is there?'

She grinned. 'Anyhoo. How's my driving? With the two sisters?'

'So far so good, I reckon. From what I've seen and read. But let me ask you something. How you are with them: you're cosying up to Marika, but kind of distanced with Suzanne, yes?'

'That's a fair summary.'

'So what's the thinking around that?'

'Hmm. Okay. So my current reading is that Suzanne is seen by both as the indulged one: the sister who got the best of, and from, their mother. The golden girl with the dimples, heading for Olympic glory while her younger sister sulks and whines in the background. Marika is the sufferer, the endurer; the recipient of Suzanne's leftovers. Now I could simply continue along those lines, but I think both of the sisters would relax into that. They're expecting warmth from me towards Suzanne and indulgence at best for Marika. They'd slip into their roles like climbing into a coat.

'Whereas, if I do the exact opposite, it provokes. I'm bonding with Marika, but leaving Suzanne out in the cold. I'll be illuminating by contrast – the shadows showing the limit of the light. Both sisters can see that how people respond to them doesn't have to be that way: that things can change, that others might view them differently. I'm hoping Marika sees the chance and grabs it; she's the one who can open this thing up, because I believe that, ultimately, she wants to. That's why I'm cosying up to her. I have to create a potential new scenario where that isn't simply possible, but desirable.' Dana dropped her pen back onto the desk. 'But I think I misjudged it, Mikey, with the sisters. Made a mistake.'

Mike frowned. Dana's description of her approach seemed psychologically acute to him. She frequently delved deeper into that than he did.

'The plan you've outlined sounds right to me.'

'When we first got hold of Suzanne – when I was planning the interviews – I'd thought Suzanne would be the easier to crack. She seemed amenable, malleable: she wanted to be onside with whoever was in the room. I thought the breakthrough would come from her. We quickly got past any attempt by her to roadblock proceedings and I became lulled into thinking she was the route to success here.

'Whereas Marika, well, they all said she was difficult. Clara Belmont, David Rowe, Suzanne herself; they were all sure Marika was aggressive, smart, controlling. And I think she was, *is* – but to some extent, only in that house.

'But here's the thing; here's what I forgot to factor in. Marika's experience is in one house, with two people. That's been largely her world for fifteen years. Everyone's opinion of her is based on seeing her there, in her comfort zone. There, she knows which buttons to push and when, and what will result. But take her out of that setting and some of her advantages dissolve. Whereas Suzanne, for all that she mirrors what's around her, has lived in the rest of the world – the real world. She knows how to navigate new places and people.

'Marika doesn't know how to do that. She's still being the same Marika; doesn't comprehend how much of a fish out of water she is. So she keeps ploughing on with what worked before; what has always worked since Mary died – before, even. And she's baffled when it doesn't work now. There's no plan B, because she's never been anywhere that's needed one. When all's said and done, *Marika* is the way in here. Marika is the one who can buckle, if I strike at the right angle. Suzanne's the corroborator, or not. Marika's the One True Source.'

'There's a corollary to that.'

'Which is?'

'Marika needs to be held to two different standards. If you're right then in here, she's vulnerable and hasn't quite worked out how to play the game. She might, though, before you're done: she seems like a quick learner. But back at the cottage, she'd have been smart, aggressive, controlling. So we need to consider her behaviour around the murder night completely differently to how we see her now. We can't judge her behaviour on that night based on how limited she is here.'

'Yes, I sort of thought that, in the room, but I hadn't laid it out. Good point, Mikey. And a similar thing for Suzanne – but reversed. She's more confident, more proactive and better equipped out here in the real world. We should downgrade how much control we believe she could exert when she was in the cottage, shouldn't we?'

'Yup. So your error . . . your *perceived* error, was to initially come at the sisters exactly as others have always done? You've had to switch tack later on?'

'Yes. I've been inconsistent. I started treating Suzanne in a certain way – the way she's used to, in fact – and then shifted once Marika showed up. I've changed strategies halfway through, and I'm sure David Rowe has shared enough information with each of them that they'd notice my shift.'

Sometimes, Mike felt, Dana let perfection be the enemy of success.

'Hmm. Okay. I humbly suggest you're overthinking that element. Here's why. They've spent, what, fifteen years being one and a half people? For much of that time they've been so intertwined it would often be hard to distinguish one from the other. They only felt like separate people when their mother treated each differently, or in their rare hours out of the home. Now, bar David Rowe, each is in a room alone with you. They're each there as an individual; not as half of . . . *Suzika*. They won't pay a whole lot of attention to how you treat the other sister, they'll be focused on how you're treating *them*. Don't obsess about what the other sister is being fed, and whether they spot inconsistencies: they won't. All their focus is on themselves, and how you're playing it now is feeding their . . .'

'Solipsism?'

'I was going to say ego, but once again, you beat me at Scrabble.'

Dana smiled. 'It still feels like an error to me.'

'Yes, it does, but it isn't. Don't be a perfectionist, Dana: it's getting in the way of your interview rhythm and your approach. You have three options, don't you? One: talk only to Marika and let Suzanne stew some more. Two: talk to each individually, but accept that each will know a fair amount of the other's conversation. Or three: get them both in a room, and watch the emerging friction between them do your work for you.'

He was right, Dana thought. Those were the main chances. She was prepared to talk to both at once, but only when she had enough ammunition. Going in without her own firm idea of exactly what had happened would invite them to throw her off. Any ambiguity at that point would also be fodder for David Rowe if it came to trial: *Hell, even the cops didn't know, Your Honour. There's your reasonable doubt; thanks and goodbye.* No, she needed more weaponry than she currently had.

'I want to talk to both sisters in the same room, but not quite yet. When I do that, I need to have most of the story, if only in my head. One more push at Marika, to make sure the door is open with her and she's prepared to spill. One more push at Suzanne, to stoke her fear about what Marika might do. With any luck, Ali and Lucy will be back with some more data. Then, I'm willing to risk a conversation with both sisters.'

'Okay. Personally, I'd go in with both sisters now, while the iron's hot. But you're not me, luckily for you. I see why you're doing it your way, though. Happy?'

'Will be. Thanks, Mikey.'

As Mike left, he low-fived a smiling Lucy, who was waving three sheets of A4. She presented them with a flourish.

'Your black-hole-hidden-planet idea? I think it paid off. Ali sent through hers, and I joined them with mine. Between us, we found twenty-three *inexplicables*, as I now choose to call them. I've put them in date order, with the dates there, in bold. Is that what you had in mind?'

Dana scanned the pages, fairly sure that most of this evidence came from Lucy. A few inexplicables were obviously non-sequiturs that were kickstarting a subject for the letters: she wouldn't need those. But there were others; about every two or three months throughout the period. Those, Dana was sure, were the results of telephone chatter; they implied knowledge that wasn't in any prior letter.

'This is great. Thank you.' She looked up. 'Lucy Delaney, you may now consider *yourself* a legend.'

Lucy laughed. 'Waaay ahead of ya.'

Chapter 34

'Have you spoken to Suze?'

Marika tried to make it sound breezy; she glanced towards David and popped the final segment of a tangerine as she spoke. Both sisters had begun using shorter versions of names. It felt like a truer version of each woman was emerging.

She was trying to guess Dana's strategy. Dana had already anticipated Marika's zero-sum assumptions about power. It was, in Dana's view, practically baked in by Marika's childhood. She would, Dana predicted, try to go on the offensive. Perhaps she could be lulled into pushing too far.

'Since we last spoke? No, Marika. Suzanne will keep. I'm gaining far more from talking to you.'

Marika found the gambit childishly obvious. 'You don't think that, Detective. We've chatted about my mum, that's all. Big deal. There are bigger things out there, and you haven't even started.'

'Yes, and no, Marika. On the one hand, you're correct – there are other matters that we need to discuss in time. And we will, when I choose to do so. But on the other hand, you're missing the obvious evidence. Because where and with whom I spend my limited time is a good indication of how things currently stand. Time is a resource – I

don't waste it on avenues that lead nowhere. If I'm talking to you and
not Suzanne, that has significance: don't kid yourself that it doesn't.
Since you arrived in the station, I haven't even seen Suzanne. That
should tell you something, Marika. It certainly tells me something.'

Dana had no doubt that Suzanne was an intelligent young woman
and had been capable of debating with Marika. Over the years there
would have been plenty of fights, sullen silences, tears and reconcili-
ations. Yet, judging by the short silence and ashen look, Marika was
not used to someone fighting back in quite this way.

'Sure. You tell yourself that, Detective. I don't see what you gain by
chinwagging about our mothers, to be honest. Speaking of which –'
Marika smiled thinly – 'I noticed, you know.'

Dana affected puzzlement, but inside she was swamped by heat.
Although part of Dana had meant to give Marika the opening, part of
her feared it now. Others, beyond this room, would begin to know or
guess: Dana's childhood traumas would emerge into more public view.
She was even, possibly, risking being recognized in her new guise: the
text of this conversation might leach out eventually.

'Noticed?'

Marika adjusted her posture, sitting straight and true, as if she were
beginning an exam. 'You've been to our cottage, Uncle David says.
Seen the bed, the mattress. You know there was only one.' She tilted
her head, almost as though she cared about Dana's welfare. 'But, earlier, your little speech, about my day? Very good, don't get me wrong.
Very, uh, accurate. But you talked about my mother standing outside
my door. I didn't have my own room, Detective, did I?'

She leaned forward slowly. 'But I bet you did.'

Dana heard David's sharp breath as Marika's eyes sparkled with triumph. She focused on maintaining eye contact. 'Yes, I did. Fair
exchange is no robbery, Marika. Understand?'

Marika's vision lifted to the ceiling and she took a deep breath. 'Yes.'

Dana scribbled in Pitman, aware of Marika's attempts to work out what she was noting. A bridge had been traversed – Dana had held out her hand and Marika had allowed herself to be pulled across. While Dana wrote, Marika tried to press her imagined advantage.

'What was she like?'

Dana understood that she could take this in any direction she wanted. It would be easy to play down her childhood and her mother's sadistic streak and protect herself from the memories flooding back. Easy to deflect others who would have access to this transcript. But she felt it was better to be authentic. That notion made her stomach twist, even as she formed it.

'Hmm. She was, from what I can gather, quite similar to your mother. Hence our degree of overlap. Like Mary, never quite diagnosed with something that would stick. Her pathology was unambiguously transparent, it seemed to me; but the cause of it was blurred, apparently.' Marika nodded almost subconsciously. Dana continued. 'Unlike your mother, however, mine refused all medications. And unlike your mother, she was indulged, rather than ostracized or restrained. It made her bolder. Gave her free reign. So while we're not in a game of pain one-upmanship here, you and Suzanne should know that I understand the toll such a life can take.'

Dana took a deep breath and added. 'What it can make people do.'

The last sentence drifted like smoke between them, the full implication never floating across to David. They watched each other carefully.

Marika raised an eyebrow. 'Are you sure? Maybe you don't want to go down that road, Detective. Sounds tricky for you.'

This was a route map for the rest of the day, Dana felt: challenges that might be merely a ploy.

'Yes, I'm sure, Marika. And we will go down that road, when I'm ready to do so. Be prepared for that journey.'

Dana detected a frisson. A sixth sense that Marika's bluff had been called.

'So, Marika. Let's talk about Curtis Mason Monroe. Why did you write letters to a convicted rapist?'

'Jesus, Rika.'

David couldn't help himself. Apparently, client and legal representative hadn't covered that ground: it marked out Marika's trust as a glittering prize. Dana had assumed the sisters would tell David the lot – he'd need it for their defence and he was their closest living relative. But it appeared his efforts to protect the Doyle sisters were being undermined. By the Doyle sisters.

Marika shot a glare at David. 'What, Uncle? What? That I'd write to someone like Curtis, or that I didn't tell you?'

Probably both, thought Dana as she watched David cave and look away. He couldn't rein her in, or face her down, like he could with Suzanne. Marika's look was poisonous.

'The question still stands, Marika. When you're ready, please.'

'Hmm. I read in the newspaper about the case. Sort of. It was a story about a lawyer who'd just made High Court judge somewhere, and it said she'd been known as the prosecutor in the Curtis Monroe case. Weird how often they name those cases after the attacker, not the victim. I didn't remember it; I was a kid then. So I looked it up, at the library. It's all a matter of public record, as you'd know.'

'So you were aware of what sort of person he was?'

'Yeah. "Was" is the operative word here. He confessed. He knew what he'd done and he didn't hide from it. Wanted to make amends in some way – and I figure confession is the first step in that. What do we do with those people, Detective? Come on, you deal with them all the time. What should we do? Throw them on the scrapheap for ever?'

Sometimes, yes, thought Dana. Some of those people were irredeemable. They didn't want to be changed, or saved, or whatever. They wanted to be free, because they regarded other people as toys. Curtis Monroe had known what he was doing and had done it anyway. Mike had returned shaken by Louise Montgomery's present state, nearly a decade after the event. The rip currents of Curtis's crime were still pulling people under.

'So your decision to make contact with Curtis Monroe was some form of altruism?'

'Yeah, you could say that.'

Dana made certain Marika could see her make a note. 'And was this a mutual decision, with Suzanne?'

Marika stared at the table, looking for the exact words. 'We both agreed on the course of action.'

'Did your agreement come before writing to Curtis, because you both wished to do that? Or did it come after you, Marika, had begun writing to him?'

'Why does that matter?'

'Because one is Suzanne's voluntary action entered willingly; the other is a fait accompli and indicates reluctance.'

'Suze is always reluctant when it comes to my ideas. Big-sister syndrome. She always comes around in the end.'

'Hmm. So, before, or after?'

'During. I was just finishing the first letter and she asked what I was doing. A robust discussion followed. Frank views were exchanged.'

'She thought it was foolish? Dangerous?'

'Suze didn't see the point, until the point was explained. Then she didn't see the purpose, until the purpose was explained. The first letter – and each letter after that – went out in both our names.'

'What did Curtis think, when he got your letter?'

'Oh, he was nervous. No one had even tried to write in that way before; his family had disowned him. I'm certain he was worried he'd blow it. Hope being worse than resignation, see? You know this,

Detective; so do I. Better if no one even tries to be kind, than to have someone reach out and you screw it up. It gives you something to lose, doesn't it?'

Too true, thought Dana. Marika had a keen eye for the psychology of the guilty and desperate; maybe it was something she had in common with Curtis.

'What did you write about?'

'Don't insult me. You'll have read them by now, I know you will.'

'You're right. I apologize, Marika. So, Suzanne needed to be . . . brought up to speed, before she came on board?'

'Yeah, she had to be told.' Marika shrugged. 'Some people think each answer's in a book; they think each book's an answer. Can't relate the knowledge they have, to people in front of them. You know the type, Detective.'

'I know the type that thinks they know the type, yes. Let's talk about some of the content of those letters.'

Marika affected disinterest. 'You're in charge, apparently.'

Dana could hear a flutter at the end of the sentence; an ambivalence about whether to sound assertive or not. She waited a beat before drawing Lucy's efforts from the file.

'Here, on 3 March, you write that *red is, of course, the fashionable colour this year.*'

Marika smiled. 'It's a joke, Detective.'

'Yes, I know it is. As we both understand, the compulsory jumpsuits at Du Pont are red. I get it. But that isn't the point I was making.' Dana sat straight and leaned forward, mimicking Marika's posture from earlier, and making sure she knew it. 'My idea is this: at no point in any previous letter did Curtis intimate that the prisoners wore red.'

The smile faded, and Marika defaulted to slowly tearing another piece of paper. David was paying closer attention now, and Marika flickered as he came into her vision.

'Another example for you, Marika. On 22 August you say this: *I guess it's your turn for the film choice on Tuesday, and we all know what that'll be.*'

'Yeah, we'd got to know each other a bit by then.'

'No doubt. But I'm sure you get the real point. Curtis hadn't written about which night was film night, or the dates when he chose the film for the rest of the unit to watch. He hadn't told you that information. *In writing.*'

David tried to help. 'Is this leading somewhere, Detective?'

Dana looked to him, and back to Marika. 'It already has, Counsellor. Marika knows what I'm talking about.'

There was a flash of resistance in Marika's eyes. 'You'll never find it.'

'We probably will, and sooner rather than later. It will be the sole piece of metal for some distance; you'd be surprised how easy that can be to detect. Since there's no rock around there except in the quarry itself, we can quickly narrow down the options to tree trunks or fallen logs. Anything else, like burying it in the ground, is too exposed: rain, animals, and so on. It won't be that far from your house; that would be too inconvenient. A kilometre, at most. See how quickly the search parameters narrow, Marika? My guess would be it's wrapped in a plastic bag, a sealable waterproof one. I think you threw a handful of rice into the bag: it would soak up any condensation that accidentally got in. We already know the dates and times of the phone calls – we get that information from the transmission tower data: from two towers, in fact. Yours will be pretty much the only phone calls made from inside a swamp, won't they, Marika? And I've now demonstrated how we can understand what you discussed in those calls, by plotting the logic gaps in the letters between you and Curtis.'

Marika shrugged, but Dana noticed her feet were turned down, almost pressing herself away from the table. As if in pain. 'I don't see where that gets you. *Teenager has phone*. Whoopee. Great headline, Detective. It'll go viral.'

She was trying to manoeuvre Marika into thinking that there was an inevitability about further discovery. That way, she might fold and yield.

'It tells me that you planned Curtis's visit from at least twelve months before. Which doesn't make it an ad hoc, informal thing; you weren't simply providing food and shelter for a few days. You had a specific reason for offering. It was organized: preparation went further than the minimum required. Secondly, it tells me that you were telephoning Curtis, and he was speaking to you; it's a different magnitude of communication than a few bland letters. Thirdly, *you* are telephoning Curtis. Not Suzanne. I doubt that Suzanne knew you were doing it. Or, if she did, she understood that she was specifically excluded – arrangements were being made that affected her but she wasn't party to them. A bit of a wedge between the two of you; one deliberately crafted by you, Marika.'

Marika pulled a sour expression. If felt to Dana as though a mask was being lifted; beneath was uglier, angrier. 'Perhaps the wedge was needed, Detective. Perhaps being an indulgent younger sister wasn't getting the job done. Some people won't see unless you show them; unless you grab them by the scruff of the neck and push them forwards.'

She made it sound like training pets, rubbing their noses in their own crap to make them learn.

'I understand your anger towards Suzanne, I do.'

'Hmm. You'd like me to think so. You keep acting like you have empathy, or we have some common bond here. But maybe you're simply a good actor.'

'These emotions you're displaying now, Marika: they are the ones you weren't allowed to show when Mary was alive. Because your

emotions were subservient to hers. It takes a lot to swallow them down,
I know. The resentment doesn't dissipate, it calcifies inside you, goes
hard and cold and feels like something alien. They aren't emotions you
can then conveniently access when it's appropriate: you can either
carry them inert, or not at all.

'Therefore, in a future time – when you do want to express
emotions – you find you can't do it. At least, not properly. Not appropriately. So you might continue to hide them, deny them. Or you can
try, you can *risk*. But your emotions are like wildfire – barely contained
and usually damaging. You can't set them at the right level because you
don't know how; you push people away when you want them to stay;
you overwhelm, you frighten and seem unstable. Even those you think
are close to you sense your lack of calibration. People like Suzanne.'

Dana assumed Marika would need to ponder this entire conversation later, roll it around in her mind and assess the texture. But if Dana
could fit the key in the lock, Marika would surely turn it and open the
door to the whole thing.

'When Suzanne quit university, after Mary died, you poured your
emotion towards her. You gave of yourself, for the first time in your
life. You told her what Mary had been like; what you'd endured.
You showed her how impossible it had been; how it had to change.
She recoiled, didn't she, Marika? She refused to engage, treated you
like a whiny child. She blocked your feelings, and your right to have
feelings.

'Let me guess. You talked about Mary's spiral, about you being victim and carer at the same time. The shame of the starvation was too
much to tell, even to Suzanne, but you probably gave broad hints. She
could see the degradation of your body and spirit – you knew she
could see the scars – yet she refused to engage. She was aloof, above it
all: she'd moved on with her life and didn't want to be dragged back by
you. Dragged back? By her own sister? Instead, it was clear she saw her

PRISONER   343

return as temporary – a necessary evil until you turned eighteen and she could leave. *With a clear conscience about it all.*

'You felt appalled and angry and hurt that she'd turn her back and retreat. After all your sacrifice, all your endurance: Suzanne responded with revulsion and disregard. So instead of building bridges, you started planning how to burn them. Your departure from the cottage, when it arrived, would be scorched earth. You'd take Suzanne down with you. That was your new plan. And she never had a clue.'

For such a critical decision, the signal was subtle. An incline of the head, before Marika reached for the water bottle. Dana had her pact, her covenant.

'You provided Curtis with a cell phone.'

Marika scratched her hair. 'Yeah, he didn't need it.'

'Because?'

'Because he had no need of it.'

'Because he had no need to make a call, and therefore didn't make one that day?'

'Well done.' Marika sat forward again, her face more fox-like than ever. A keen, forensic intelligence that she used almost exclusively to skewer people. 'Do you own a phone, Detective?'

'Yes.'

Marika made a show of looking around. 'Where is it, then? Most people don't let them out of their sight.'

'On my desk, while I'm giving all my attention to you.'

Marika mock pouted. 'Too kind. I bet you hardly use it, do you?'

'Why do you say that?'

Marika waved a desultory hand at the pad to Dana's right. 'Because of this. The shorthand. I mean, no one learns that stuff any more, do they?'

'Don't they?'

'No. People record stuff with their phone. They don't draw a series of squiggles they have to translate later. Watch them spot a notice in a window: they don't write down the details, they take a photo.' Marika pointed to the tape machines. 'I mean, you have, what, two recorders going here? No need for a third record, is there?'

'Maybe I'm writing down what I think of you.'

'Hmm. That would be interesting. Do you have to show that to Uncle David, one day?'

'No, it's not disclosable. And yes, you would find it interesting.'

'Still, this; it's unnecessary. A silly habit, a comfort blanket.' Marika opened her hands, evangelical. 'Do without, Detective. Live your best life, and all that.'

'Have you lived your best life, Marika?'

'I've lived the best life I was allowed.'

'That's not what I asked.'

'That's what I've done, though. We all have. All of . . . us.'

Us could now mean two or three people; Marika's language was starting to drift. Barriers were dissolving, slowly but surely.

'The swamp, Marika. I've seen a bit of it; I can't fathom how you navigate through there.'

Marika pondered. David frowned at his notes.

'Ah, well. Lots of practice. I mean, over a decade wandering around. I don't even need a long stick now. When I started, I'd have a pole like Gandhi had – prodded in front of me all the time. Slow progress, but you learn.' She gifted herself a smile. 'Place gives up its mysteries slowly, Detective: it rewards patience, time spent. What a particular shade of green says about what lies beneath; how branches turn when they grow below the surface; what different types of bubbles imply. It's got its own language – you have to listen.'

'But it's constantly shifting, changing. How can you be sure that something that was safe last week is safe next week?' Dana thought back to the floating grass, roiling up to the back fence of Marika's garden.

'Ah, it slithers and sways, but that's all a bit misleading. Fools the newbies like you. It slides about, but usually it stays within its own confines.' She pressed hard into the water bottle. 'Where I live, there are borders you can't see, Detective, invisible rules to follow. Like most things, it's predictable within a certain range. Sometimes there's a breach, and it tips over to where it shouldn't be. It can only sustain what's natural for it, Detective: it slowly reverts to type.' She sat back again. 'Like people. Swamps are like people.'

Certainly, thought Dana, like Marika. It was time to fire a shot; see what might be exposed.

'All the same, knowledge can't be bulletproof each time, Marika. Some things get trapped in the mire. You must have seen that, witnessed the suffering?'

Marika stopped, stared at Dana. A nerve had been hit. Dana glimpsed the clock on the recorder and made a note. She'd have to analyse later the exact nature of that reaction.

'Oh yeah, happens.' Marika clearly hoped that would be enough, but Dana left a peaceful silence that eventually worked. 'I mean, a while back I saw something floundering in there. Too far out for me to reach.' Marika's hands twitched as though she wanted to re-enact the scene, but she pulled herself back. 'No chance of a long branch or a rope to it, and I might have died myself if I'd tried. Nothing to be done. All very sad. But if you live out there, it's also very *circle of life*, isn't it?'

There was a bitter slap to the final sentence.

'There was nothing you could do but watch?'

Marika narrowed her eyes, wondering how much Dana had already intuited. This was dangerous ground: she could be harming herself by replying, depending on what was running through Dana's mind. Or perhaps she was committed to the telling, and merely surprised herself by how little she thought of the consequences.

'Not a thing. It was night: all I could see was where the light fell. Little flashes of thrashing limbs in the darkness. Classic mistake: when you're in a swamp, don't move. Don't try to fight the flow; you can't win. Your circumstances always drag you down.' Marika was staring at the middle distance beyond Dana, drifting back in time. The reverie animated her; light sparkled in her eye. 'But this . . . fought. Scuffed and kicked and fought for life like you wouldn't believe. All the while, big, wide eyes looking back to the bank. Such desperation, Detective, such a will to survive. You'd think it's in us all, but it isn't. But that night – well. It took her a while. A slow, lingering death that was more due to exhaustion than anything else. If it had been simply down to willpower, there would have been no death at all. But there was.'

Marika closed her eyes and her voice fell to a whisper. 'Eventually, the ripples stopped, the bubbles ended. It all went blissfully quiet when the surface was smooth again. I found it . . . soothing.' Her eyes opened. 'So yes, I know what the swamp can do.'

'What was that animal? A dog?'

Marika was non-committal. 'Mmm.'

'Marika, was what you saw male or female?'

Marika shrugged, as if she neither knew, nor cared. 'Well, already, uh, *parts* under the waterline. Why?'

'Because when you described watching something drowning in the marsh . . . at one point you said "her".'

'Hmm. Well. For the record, then. I must have watched a bitch die. Satisfied, Detective?'

Yes, thought Dana, *I am satisfied*. More than satisfied, in fact.

She was about to bring the interview to a close when David did it for her. 'I really need to speak to my client now, Detective.'

'Of course. Interview suspended, 1050 hours.' Dana snapped off the two recorders and closed her notebook. 'I'll have some refreshments sent down to the custody unit for you.'

She glanced at David, making sure that Marika heard the final sentence. 'Oh, and Counsellor? I'll need to speak to Suzanne Doyle shortly. Shall we say, forty minutes?'

Chapter 35

Dana emailed Rainer, asking him to coordinate a search for Marika's hidden phone. Stuart was able to help with the piloting of a drone. She set parameters: trees and hollowed-out logs, within a kilometre of the cottage, the drone to focus on any semblance of a well-trodden patch of ground. She also warned Rainer to be careful: the whole area was treacherous.

She considered again the possibility that McCullough had some kind of connection with the Aryans, and had halted the investigation down that line to preserve or hide something. She decided that, in the short term, it didn't matter: she needed to pursue the Doyle sisters to a result or a dead end. But it did mean, she reflected, that time was of the essence here. If the murder *was* committed to avenge Curtis's prison revelations, McCullough would charge the sisters tomorrow anyway; that would protect the Aryans. At which point the investigation might have bypassed the killers and charged the innocent. She had twenty hours to tackle that.

Next, she searched online for famous film quotes. M. Night Shyamalan was a rich source – mainly for *The Sixth Sense* and seeing dead people. But she found what she was looking for. Ideas and theories were coalescing: a compelling picture was emerging.

Dana could feel a chill calm descending through her body. It was a strange but welcome feeling. It told her that she'd reached the point in an investigation when she was at her best. Professional golfers called this sensation *the zone*; the few golden minutes when you couldn't miss, when muscles were fluid and strong, when decision-making was clear cut. The biggest problem Dana had – like the golfers – was getting out of the way of her own moment.

She was aware that Suzanne was a few hours shy of her thirty-six-hour review: the compulsory reassessment of whether she still needed to be held under Close Proximity rules. Another district commander elsewhere – probably Talbot, or Dukic – would have to be contacted in the afternoon. With that in mind, Dana wanted to push Suzanne in particular.

The dynamic of the sisters had become clearer. It went back, way back, at least a decade, though it had accelerated in the past few years. The peculiar fermentation of emotion that could take place in an isolated house, a solitary bed and a mother's oscillating sanity. The unique mix of pressure, desperation, helplessness, obligation, betrayal and pain. The echoes were painful shards for Dana, but tapping into the feelings of Marika in particular had opened the door.

She read again through the list that Lucy had uncovered – with Ali's assistance – of the tell-tale gaps in the logic of the letters. Leaving aside the two she'd used on Marika and the ones that weren't offering anything novel, she had twelve examples left on the page. They'd been listed according to the letters' chronology, but she'd rejigged the sequence to find the narrative within. They told a clear story: the direction was apparent and the trajectory fitted all the other evidence. The courting – or *grooming* – of Curtis Monroe. The CCTV pictures. The use of fluoro vests. The absence of weapon, quad bike or blood spatter. The leaving of the body in a public space. The lack of a motive.

First, a tilt at Suzanne. Then the challenge of the Doyle sisters together, in one room for the first time. There was a prize within reach: Dana felt she could grasp it. She just required their confessions.

Chapter 36

Mike needed a break from his report on the Alvarezes – the letters were starting to swim, and his left shoulder hurt. Middle age: it even left him unfit for typing. Lucy had been working on Dana's latest interview with Marika, adding it now to the shared drive.

'Are you up to speed, Luce?' He waited while the skittling fingers came to a halt.

'Yup. Just finished transcribing that last one.'

'And what have you noticed?'

Mike knew that Lucy didn't want to simply type; she wanted to understand.

'Well, now. Something occurred to me, as I was transcribing. Dana hasn't asked anything about the night in question, or the crime scene. Not in . . . five interviews?'

'Yes, true.'

'Which, firstly, makes me wonder how much David Rowe currently knows about those things and how much we're obliged to tell him.'

It was a valid point. It depended partly on how much the sisters knew: which, in turn, depended on how much they'd been involved in Curtis's death. Even so, Mike had noticed that David Rowe didn't seem to have been told much by his clients. It was dumb to leave your legal adviser unaware of basics. Yet the sisters seemed prepared to keep their own lawyer out of the loop.

'Ah, good question. At this stage, nothing and nothing. Since Dana's not asking anything about the crime – or the crime scene – we're not obliged to disclose details about the body or the forensics. Dana won't go any further than the current media reports, which she herself briefed. Recent evidence is a need-to-know; she's reluctant to lie out-right, but nor is she obliged to show and tell. David Rowe knows what's on media websites and whatever his clients have chosen to share with him, which appears to be little.'

'I thought not. Hmm.' Another notion had floated to her while she'd been dealing with Dana's interview. 'Okay. Can I ask you a fur-ther question?'

'Sure. Is it about your assassination list? Because I thought I'd done enough to stay off it, to be honest. And I don't do contract kill-ings of lawyers, or Ethical Standards bods, however justified they may be.'

Lucy laughed. 'No, you're gold, Mikey. For today, anyway. No, it's about how you each interview people. I noticed that you more sort of, I dunno, dive in there about the day in question. Whereas Dana starts with their biographies. In a manner of speaking.'

'Yeah, Dana and I have discussed this before. So my take on it is, as you say, to start with the recent past. The interviewee may be in a heightened emotional state. They might spill something which, if they had a chance to collect themselves, they wouldn't otherwise tell. The first hours of an investigation can give you that edge. Second, those memories are fresher and more recent: they could tell me something that can exonerate them – so I can move on to other options – or direct what I'm doing in the investigation. Third, I figure if I get a sense from them about what's happening now, I may catch them in a lie when I go back to talk about their past. That's because people think forwards, and they find it harder to line up their stories if they're, essentially, telling them backwards.

'Dana's take is that talking about themselves is something they're often good at, experienced in. They can pace it, they feel at ease; it's familiar and comforting, when the situation may have them agitated. Also, by starting at the beginning, so to speak, she doesn't have to reveal to suspect or lawyer what we currently know or what we've recently found: she can withhold that information longer than I can and release it when it suits her. As you astutely noticed, Luce. My technique works if you're being more aggressive, confrontational; you're trying to catch the lie, and that's a good way of inducing pressure. But Dana's aim is more to get them spilling generally and then recognizing the error when they make it.'

'Wait, back up,' said Lucy. 'You use what we know currently about the case, in the interview room – it's leverage, I can see that. We know something they don't; knowledge is power. But Dana doesn't refer to it. So isn't she throwing away a key advantage?'

'I see where you're headed, but no, she isn't. She's still using the advantage, but in a different way. Because she isn't giving them specifics about our current knowledge, they have to guess what she knows. It shapes what they say, and what they don't. She's using her current knowledge of the evidence as a tactical asset: by not using it. So here: neither Marika nor Suzanne – or David Rowe, for that matter – is aware of exactly how we found the body; what state it's in; what the forensics told us; if we got something from blood or fingerprints or tyre marks; what we've subsequently discovered. Marika and Suzanne have to guess what Dana knows and frame their answers accordingly. And David Rowe can't guide them any better than that, because he doesn't know, either. Until Dana chooses to reveal our forensic and investigative evidence, she can quiz two people who are largely in the dark.'

It's clever, thought Lucy. For all the Doyle sisters knew, Dana might have chapter and verse and was engineering them into incriminating themselves. Or Dana might hold next to nothing and was simply on a giant fishing expedition. How could either sister frame an effective approach around that uncertainty?

'Dana and I both assume,' continued Mike, 'that the murder is always the last act in their story. It comes at the end. The reason for the murder – the reason *there is* a murder – comes before. It might come an hour before, when a fight blew out of proportion. Maybe it was a day earlier, when someone saw their partner with a lover. Perhaps a year ago; a decade. People can have long memories and deep scars. Killing someone is almost certainly the defining moment of a person's life. It has a gestation, sometimes a long one.

'When Dana talks to them, it's with that idea specifically in mind. She's starting way back because she's trying to ascertain exactly when murder took root – the first step on the path. Because if she can find that point in time, then she believes she'll find what drove them. The opening minute of the route to murder is where the motive is born, and that matters – it speaks to why, when and how, as well as who. Just like investigating a bushfire: all the data there is historic, so you look for where the fire started. That *point of origin* is the thing she absolutely has to know.'

Did she know? he wondered. Did Dana now have the key, that point of origin she was looking for?

'Then, like me but from a different start line, she goes forward in chronological order. We both do that because that's how we all live – it's a sequence that's part of our existence. We don't live outside of that structure; we can't. And it's how we tell stories. If I ask you about last week, you don't dance around the chronology. You won't tell me all about Friday, then the preceding Monday, then Wednesday night, then Tuesday morning. You remember, and recall, and live, in the same direction – forwards in time: always forwards. So talking in that same direction feels natural, feels right. It engages them – whether they want to open out or not. The trick is spotting the anomaly, the admission, the mistake, when they make it.' Mike raised a finger. 'Then there's the chips.'

Lucy had been concentrating, letting it all soak in. The final statement jarred. 'The chips?'

'Ah, okay. We came up with this last month, having this very discussion. I use bargaining chips in my interview technique: little ways to leverage information. Like the current knowledge on this case, for example. Might be something I have on the person – their fingerprints on something, a CCTV image – that gives me a bit of clout. It *pushes* the interviewee into giving up further information.

'Whereas Dana doesn't work that way, not often. I call her technique "empathy chips". She lets the interviewee into a piece of her world which they recognize. Or, perhaps, they see that she's on the same mental or emotional plane as them and what they spill will be treated in a certain way – maybe more benevolently. Don't be fooled, though – she often makes it up: they aren't to know and she's not obliged to be truthful about it. But the perception of shared emotion or experience means they open up. Dana steps across the chasm and then offers a hand to help *pull* them across. So, I push, Dana pulls.'

Mike was privately adamant that his approach was less psychologically damaging. Even invented empathy took an emotional toll: Dana's method was, despite her natural caution, often a high-wire act. It exacted a price: he could see that.

'Which one's the better way?' Lucy now had a pen and half a page of notes.

'Ooh, trick question. Well, we'd each say our own, and we'd both be right. They each suit our personality. I can do direct and confrontational better than Dana; she seems obstinate and cold if she tries it. But she doesn't get restless if the interviewee wants to talk around the subject, so her technique fits her. Therefore, the polite – and accurate – answer, is both. Piling in like I do can leave you exposed: you have to share what current knowledge you have, rather than hold it back. On the other hand, being direct means you seize control of the room immediately – that can be a priceless advantage if you follow through. Plus, because we have different techniques, we can critique the other. That's vital; we need to keep each other on track, so it helps that we're doing things differently. And if we have to, we can switch interviewers on someone and give them something fresh to deal with. Teamwork. Like I always say to the kids: *that's what winners do.'*

They began moving towards the listening room between Interview One and Interview Two.

'Ha! Mikey, do you really raise your kids with homilies from the back of cereal boxes?'

Mike gave her a serious, stern look. 'Yes, Lucy Delaney. Yes, I do.'

Chapter 37

Nearly twenty hours without being interviewed had granted Suzanne plenty of space for doubt and suspicion to seep in. She'd been given a pen and paper before David Rowe arrived and the notepad was already filled with doodles: concentric circles with stars firing to the corner of the page. Dana noted the deep indentations from the pen.

Suzanne's nervy distress was clear in her skittish body language; she was agitated, anxious for the interview to begin. She scratched, as if her hair were itchy, and kept glancing at David's manicured fingers. She had, undoubtedly, a *her side* to be put forward, and put forward vehemently. Denial of the opportunity had ramped the urgency.

Dana took her time laying out her files and pen, feeling the impatience billow from Suzanne. From David, too, she noticed. She now felt that he should have recused himself from both sisters at the very start: he was far too close to this case on every level, and it was hampering him. She'd also calculated that, while David could relay the gist of her interviews with Marika, he'd be unable to tell Suzanne all the nuances; what was left unsaid or was visible through the cracks.

Dana slowly covered the early formalities of the interview with a calm stillness that made Suzanne fidget. The best way into this conversation was via Marika: to imply that Dana was only interested in the younger sister.

'At school, was Marika bullied?'

Suzanne edged back as though nonplussed by the question, both its timing, and its existence. 'Bullied? Ha. That would have been nice.' Suzanne caught herself, then shrugged. 'I mean, no, Rika was not bullied. She established her rep pretty early on, and . . . that did her for her school life. It rang true, so people backed away.'

'Please explain.'

'So, when I was at uni, I once saw a fight between two men. One of them was huge – some rugby player, I think; all muscles and Polynesian ink. The other was a skinny little wretch: greasy hair, that pale skin that looks a bit blue; neck full of acne. To look at him, you'd think I could take him. And, for a while, that's what Polynesian muscle-boy thought as well. Except this little guy, he kept coming. Constantly. Never stopped. Broken nose, blood spewing, clothes ripped: didn't matter – he didn't care. And he won, eventually. By the time the police arrived he was throwing punches unhindered. Took four cops to take him down. He won, Detective, because he had complete disregard for his personal safety, or for consequences. He literally didn't care if he died, whereas the other guy clearly did. That total loss of control – it's surprisingly effective.'

Suzanne seemed happy to leave it at that. It took Dana's patient stare to make her explain.

'That's what Rika has; total loss of control. Try getting her truly angry – you'll see. If she loses it, she goes right off the scale. When she was eleven, three girls started taunting her – she was wearing last year's school uniform and they called her *povo*; said her mum was nuts. Well, Rika gave one girl a black eye, shoved another through a plate-glass window; chased the third the length of the running track and pulled out lumps of hair at the roots. No care for her own safety, or for consequence. Word got around. No one bullied Rika.'

Once again Suzanne was inviting Dana to think of Marika as the amoral threat, the instigator; the guilty one of the two sisters. She'd been trying various forays and incursions on this track since her first interview: Dana still wasn't finding it quite convincing.

'Were you scared of her?'

'My sister? Nah. She was very . . . *forensic.* Dished it out to those who started it. We were always fine. Constantly arguing, but always fine.'

Dana felt that Marika's resentment of her sister ran deep and long: four years alone with Suzanne had merely scratched the surface of reparations. Dana severely doubted that the two were always fine; that seemed a wilful misreading by Suzanne.

'Until?'

'What do you mean, until?'

'Hmm, you two are not like that now, are you? You're not *fine* at all. I've interviewed you both, and I consider you poles apart.'

Three blinks, an open mouth, a stuttering breath. 'Bad bluff, Detective. You're nowhere near.'

Suzanne lacked her sister's artifice and punch. Dana could feel the momentum change; she sensed the room tilt and everything beginning to slide away from Suzanne.

'On the contrary, I'm on the money. I'm the first to admit I don't always get sibling rivalry; but right here, right now, I'm spot on. I'm surprised you can't see it, Suzanne. Don't you see? It's all over bar the shouting. Don't you understand what Marika has done to you?'

The slight frown seemed to indicate that Suzanne was vaguely aware but in denial. David stayed silent.

'Done to me?'

'She's painted you into a corner. Oh, she's in the corner with you,

Suzanne, but your problem remains. Marika wants to be there. More importantly, she wants *you* to be there with her. She views your previous behaviour as reprehensible and thinks this is the endgame.'

Dana didn't have all the pieces yet, but what she had was slotting together with every passing minute. And, just as vital, she'd spotted what Suzanne didn't know.

With the Doyle sisters, the gaps always mattered most.

'Let me give you an example, Suzanne. The kitchen cupboards. I noticed them as soon as I looked. They had scuff marks and screw holes where the padlocks and handles came on and off. Your sister had doctored the brick wall outside, so she could get into the cupboards in dire emergency. The cupboards that Mary kept locked, denying Marika food.'

Suzanne looked almost concussed; Dana reached to her own childhood to drive the point home.

'The secret, shaming, insidious effect that lack of nutrition brings. The awkward stares at school lunch, the foggy excuses she made. The slow and clumsy movement, the dulling of the senses; the squeezing twist of the organs. It invited ridicule and scorn on to Marika – that's why I asked about bullying at school.

'The impotent brew fermenting inside Marika at that point was this: desperate hatred of her mother, yet the stubborn love of a daughter. The combination would burn like acid, believe me. Marika went through all that regularly. But only when you were away at university. *Mary wouldn't behave like that when Suzanne was around* – that was the subtext. Marika doesn't blame you for it happening in the first place; she understands Mary's pathology better than anyone does. Instead, she blames you for not noticing. She blames you for drifting through visits, blissfully unaware. She blames you for lying entwined with her each night and never asking. Because, in her eyes, you chose to be ignorant.'

Suzanne blushed with shame. 'Yeah, but I . . . I . . . who would think of that? Who would imagine that a mother would do that? What sort of a person would you have to be to comprehend that, straight off the bat? What would . . . *what are you*, Detective?'

'I'm someone who pays attention, Suzanne. In Marika's eyes, the fact that I noticed within an hour of visiting your home for the first time? That cements how obvious it was, and therefore how deliberately oblivious you were. And now she's hanging you out to dry, Suzanne. The first step in that? She's told a total stranger how you left her to suffer Mary's worst, most uncontrolled years and then waltzed back into the home wearing blinkers.'

Suzanne flung a hand at Dana. It was an empty, flimsy gesture. 'She's played the victim card with you, then? Ha. And there was me, thinking you were a sharp operator. So Uncle David said, anyway; guess we both have to rethink that. What was it? A bit of a snuffle? She can make her eyes go red on demand, Detective. Give her thirty seconds and you'd swear she'd been up all night, in fear of her life. It fools a fool, I'll give her that. But I expected better from you. Thought you'd see it for what it is – a con. But this isn't about food. It's all about justifying her own subsequent behaviour. All the things Rika did – I bet she's spared you those details, eh? That's her magic trick. She needs to pass her guilt on to someone else, and you and I are sitting here – so she passes it on to us. You've fallen for the martyr act, like I did.'

More cogs turned in Dana's mind. *All the things Rika did.*

'You set a lot of store by how devious your sister is, Suzanne: a Machiavellian mind, a Napoleonic sense of strategy and a serial killer's morality. Why should I believe any of that?'

Dana did believe. She was counting on it to be true.

'Why shouldn't you, Detective? Check the facts.' Suzanne scooted forward, desperation in her eyes, and counted off two fingers. 'Mary is dead. Curtis Monroe is dead. I'm the one person who's been in the same house as Rika . . . who's still alive.

'Her name? Marika? It's an offshoot of Maria, which is a derivation of Mary. So she's diminutive: twice. And it means bitter disappointment, or sea of sorrows, depending on the language. My mother was an intelligent woman, before it all went wrong. She knew what she was doing back then. So, Marika – the name's not an accident. *Sea of sorrows*, Detective.'

Suzanne, in the final analysis, couldn't manage to nail this. Marika's groundwork, Dana decided, was too smart. Marika was brilliant: her dazzling ability had left Suzanne like a defeated bull in the ring – maddened by embedded swords it couldn't reach, whirling and bucking but merely exhausting itself, and fading fast.

Dana quickened the pace. 'Writing to Curtis Monroe: her idea?'

Suzanne snapped out of a stare. 'God, yeah. I mean – what the hell?'

'What reason did she give?'

It should have been a quick and simple answer. Instead, Suzanne coughed to play for time, looked up at the ceiling and down to Dana's Pitman notes.

'Some crap about doing some good. Something simple: writing letters. Initially, we'd assumed he'd be in there for years. So it was, you know, two people writing to someone they'd never meet. It wasn't in our – *my* – plan to ever meet him. Yeah, not in mine.'

Dana scratched another note. 'But then?'

'Then I find she's *talking* to him. Telephoning him. Some mobile she keeps in the death zone out there. I don't know how, where she got the money. Or the phone. She's . . . resourcefully weird. Anyway, she talks him into trying to get parole and, bugger me, he gets it.'

A crucial element here was, Dana felt, the degree of planning by each sister.

'Weren't you frightened, given his past?'

'No, I . . . no. Something about Rika's view of him. Something she got from the phone calls. I knew she'd . . . made arrangements. There was some kind of understanding, and she was so calm about it, so certain. So, no; never got as scared as I should have been.'

'But unnerved.'

'Yeah. A convicted rapist and us, in an isolated cottage. Yeah, of course.'

'So you both got yourself some weaponry. Which you threw away and thought we'd never find. Didn't you?'

Suzanne couldn't resist a smirk, as though this was the first step onto firmer ground. Once again, the need to be right – to win at something, *anything* – couldn't be contained. 'You tell me, Sherlock.'

'A Taser.'

Suzanne blinked way too much.

'It was a Taser, Suzanne. You tested it on the back of the sofa, at the base; there's a tell-tale burn mark there. Or at least, it's tell-tale if you're a detective. We have the photo from Forensics, by way of proof. I assume that the Taser was dropped into the swamp on the night in question, once it became clear it wasn't needed.'

Suzanne seemingly couldn't work out how Dana knew all this. She was trapped, and now all she could see were fences, tripwires, bindings: it was all becoming hideously clear. Now, Dana was certain, she could push further. Because Suzanne was ready to lash out at Marika.

'Just so you know, Suzanne, bluffing has ceased to be an option. Total cooperation is your sole course of action now. If you don't believe me, check with your lawyer.'

Suzanne looked to her left, where David gave a slow, heavy-lidded, defeated nod. Suzanne shuddered, as if her bodyguard had just walked away. When she turned back to Dana, she looked younger.

'Cooperation about what?'

'The night Mary died. Tell me.'

David jolted, but Suzanne didn't appear to notice; she kept staring at Dana. Something seemed to click in Suzanne's mind.

'I was supposed to go home that weekend. It'd been arranged for weeks. Every time she called me, or messaged me, Mary mentioned it. Pleaded about it. Her language got more desperate: she couldn't cope without me, the pills weren't working, Marika was . . . there was always something. Always building up to the bigger questions: why didn't I give up the degree and come home? Why did I leave? Why did I wreck the family? Why did I crush that perfect little existence she thought we'd had?'

A quick glance of apology to David.

'I didn't want to go home, Detective. Ever. I'd escaped, you see, I'd done it. I'd got far enough away and seen enough of the rest of the world. It didn't have to be that way; trapped with Mary and Rika and constantly dealing with my mother's swings, paranoias, *issues*. My life could be better. I was headed for an honours degree; I was competing in equestrian nationals; I had a shot at international comps, maybe the Rio Olympics. All I had to do was resist the guilt trips, the veiled threats. All I had to do was stay strong.

'So this weekend, God, it loomed larger and larger. I had no real excuse for not going home. Only that I didn't want to and it would harm me to do it. The whole weekend had started to become a line in the sand for me, and I think Mary picked up on that. She was fighting, in her own strange way. Fighting to keep me.

'Jesus. Stupid, weak me. I relented. I gave in and came home on the Friday afternoon. The bus dropped me in Earlville and I thought Mary would be there at the bus station. She wasn't. I got a strange feeling, right then. She should have been meeting me with a rambunctious bear hug and pretending to do what real parents do. It was always a horrible act, Detective, when she did it: a hideous am-dram mess, and everyone could see right through it. Strangers gave her this look of pity she never noticed. Anyway, when she wasn't there, I knew something was off balance. Took me two hours to walk home in the rain.

'When I got home, she was off, distant. Like she hadn't wanted me to come at all. Like I was some unwanted guest she was obliged to feed; I'd outstayed my welcome as soon as I arrived. I was used to her sudden swings – we both were – but this felt different. I asked Rika if there were new meds, if something had happened. Rika shrugged. I felt like a pariah.

'About nine, Mary kicks off. She'd been simmering, frowning, muttering to herself all evening. We're watching TV – some film from the seventies, some guy in space: Rika wanted to watch it. Mary switches it off, digs in her armchair cushion, and produces a hammer. A bloody hammer. I'm confused, but Rika jumps up and says no. She says they discussed this, and Mary had promised. Mary looks right through her. Mary's zoned out, and she has a hammer in her hand. I get up, ask what's going on. Mary shakes her head slowly, starts moving towards me.

'There's something, Detective: I'm sure you've seen it. Something in someone's eyes when they're serious: when it's not a tantrum, or a trick, or an aberration. Something about their look says this has been building; it's the end of a long and bitter process. And that's what I see. Mary means it. Mary's had enough, and she's going to settle it now. I've pushed her too far. Or, more accurately, she's been pushed too far. Because she screams that Rika told her; Rika had told her I was never coming back. Rika had said she should get used to it – Rika had said I'd be postcards and memories, occasional texts, a name and a photo; something to mutter about if anyone ever asked. Rika had sworn I was ashamed of Mary.

'She swung at me, hard. I could feel it touch my hair on the way past when I ducked. Rika grabbed at her from behind. The route to the front door was blocked, so I opened the back door and ran. Of course – you've been there. Where the hell can I run in that back yard? Ten metres, then the swamp starts. I turn around, and there she is, narrowing the angle and blocking the route back to the house. Swamp at my back, and both sides. Can't see Rika. Can't see her. It's dark; most of Mary is the silhouette from the open door. A big, long block of light from the house, under her feet, to me. That hammer, swinging slowly. She hefts it a bit, to get a better grip.

'I've got nowhere, Detective, no way out. The swamp: I wouldn't get three metres. But it's looking better than being smashed in with a hammer by my own mother. I edge towards it. I can feel my foot nudge the lip; it's slippery. She's still walking towards me, the hammer's still swinging. Her eyes have dulled, like she's on autopilot. I'm calling, begging, anything – but she's not *there*.

'She's a metre away when Rika strikes. Rika runs at her and gives an almighty shove. She's smart – as though she's planned it. She doesn't push at the shoulder, no. She bends a bit and pushes Mary at the base of the spine. More momentum, see? More . . . impetus. Smart, like I said. Mary piles forward. She half swings at me as she goes past – it hits my shoulder but it doesn't hurt. Because Mary's past me now, and crashing into the marsh. The swing's tipped her further off balance. She hits the surface and it just opens its arms, welcomes her in. Like we always thought it would, if anyone fell in. Because now, Detective, our mother has simply fallen in when we weren't around, hasn't she? We both understand that, even as she rolls over and stares at us.

'She thrashes around a lot. I hear it; I can't bear to look. But Rika can't keep her eyes off it, drinks it in. Her face is in shadow, but it's shining from within. The splashes stop. I look back, and all we can see is Mary's hand. Totally still. Just above the surface, like a piece of porcelain. Elegant. She was never elegant, Detective, except in that moment.

'Marika killed our mother. And she was very, very happy to do it.'

Chapter 38

David slowed in the corridor, looking forward as Dana limped towards him, trying to catch up despite her fizzing kneecap. She put a hand on his shoulder. 'David, I'm so sorry about your sister.'

He still refused to look sideways at her and she understood why. Tears sparkled in his eyes. 'Yeah, well. Always had . . . well, it never sat quite right with me. Accidental, you know? Always thought there was something more than that.'

'Look,' she said, 'we currently only have Suzanne's word. It might be different when we ask Marika.'

David sighed. He'd composed himself, but the effort of doing so seemed to make him sag under the fluorescent lights. 'Yeah, Rika might have a different version. Though I can't read her right now. She's gone to a very different place, to be honest. But . . . ah, this whole process, Dana. I should have stepped back.'

Yes, thought Dana, *you should*. What he'd done was worthy, but it hadn't worked. The Doyle sisters hadn't trusted him or let him in, so he couldn't do his job. Another lawyer would have demanded the truth or threatened to walk. That wouldn't have worked against Marika, but it might have done with Suzanne.

'You still can, David. I could hold off a further interview, if you want to call in a colleague.'

David considered the option. 'No, no. We've come this far. Steep learning curve for whoever came in, so I doubt it would achieve anything in the short term. It would spook the girls to change this late. Even though they don't . . . yeah, no; I'll stick with it until charges, or the seventy-two hours. If nothing else, I can be the best help to whoever comes next.' He looked across. 'But thanks for offering. I appreciate it.'

'As you've guessed, I'd like to talk to them both together, in about half an hour, please.'

'We'll be ready. Hmm. *They'll* be ready, anyway.'

Chapter 39

Brian Aroona's street was one hundred metres long, bounded on one side by some scraggy eucalypts that half screened a run of cinder-block industrial units with rusted metal roofs. The structures had high-set windows spliced by steel bars; razor wire topped the wall between tree and building. The eucalypts withered in the barren topsoil, hindered by two abandoned fridges and a rusted V8 block. Their sloughed bark formed a scrappy covering for tawny grass. Behind them, the graffiti tags seemed half-hearted; one colour, repetitious. The street's drain was blocked by a nest of fallen leaves, darkened by a sludge that may have been engine oil.

The terrace of homes itself wove; the shared roofline undulated, the façades were blistered and crooked. Several homes had relinquished – or lost – their guttering. They leaned into each other like a group of drunken girls looking for a taxi.

If only, thought Rainer, these houses were slightly different. If the front elevation of the terrace were elegant sandstone, rather than fractured, crumbling HardiePlank. If only their age were defined by slate-and-gold plaques, rather than wearing their decades on their sleeves. If only the front yards – *courtyards* – were bound by elegant nineteenth-century wrought iron, rather than chicken wire. If only the seating these yards contained were hand-crafted Adirondack chairs, rather than half-chewed sofas bordered by rat droppings. If only the front windows held elegant plantation shutters offering a filigreed orange glow beyond, rather than slanted and broken venetians heralding a tsunami of discarded toys and cigarette butts. If only the cars outside were sleek European SUVs glinting in the sunlight, rather than a motley collection of blistered eighties Japanese mediocrity.

In short, if people with money owned these houses, then these houses would be worth money. That was how it worked, he thought; you either spiralled upward, or circled the drain.

He heard the Aroonas before he saw them. Snarky yells and a slammed door made him stop at what passed for the gate. A girl – maybe three or four years old – watched him from the upstairs window, choking a cuddly rabbit and pawing at a chocolate stain near her lip. He picked his way past two empty cardboard boxes that had wilted in sun and rain and tapped on the door.

The door was answered by the matriarch. Mrs Aroona was mum, grandmother; auntie by blood and by community consent. A wide, flat nose and a body like a folded quilt. She was wiping flour from her hands with a tea-towel stained by raspberry juice.

'Yeah?' Her voice was resonant and tar-coated.

'Rainer Holt, Carlton Police. I need a quick word with Brian Aroona, please.'

Mrs Aroona looked skyward, then threw the tea-towel at the bottom stair. 'Again? Jesus. What now?'

The *again* referred to a series of interviews about a stolen Subaru; Brian had been seen in the rear seat using his hand to make *shoot-you-dead* gestures at a cousin. It was all written up as largely a family argument going nowhere, among kids who watched too much crap on TV. The Subaru had started a minor grass fire by the football oval when it burned.

'Oh no, nothing like that. Brian works with someone who might be a witness; we need some background, that's all.'

Rainer's face was young and blemish-free and it often won him a free pass of credibility. Not this time. Mrs Aroona squinted; her eyes receded completely in her crumpled face.

'Yeah, sure.' She turned and near-screamed, 'Briiaaan!' Then turned back and shrugged. 'Has his headphones on, see?'

'Ah, right. Anything I'd have heard of?'

'Nah,' she replied, leaning back and taking in all of him. 'Right age, wrong colour.'

She wandered off as Rainer digested that. Arrhythmic clumps on the stairs preceded Rainer's view of dusty Steel Blue work boots, jeans with wiped grease on the thighs and a lumberjack shirt. Brian looked dishevelled but not sleepy. His hair was a thick mop, tilted sideways in a way that appeared to Rainer as more accidental than styled.

Brian raised an eyebrow. 'Yeah?'

Rainer showed his badge and pointed to a rickety iron bench across the street. 'A quiet word in the ornamental garden, please, Brian.'

Brian flashed a grin, clearly used to sarcasm after working nights with Suzanne Doyle.

They sat upright, so that the sun was shaded by the lowest tendrils of the eucalypt. It made them look oddly formal.

'You work with Suzanne Doyle, is that correct?'

'Yeah. We're shift buddies. Why?'

'Uh, Suzanne is a witness. We're running background.'

Brian lolled his tongue in his cheek. 'Riigghht.'

'Unless you'd like to talk about torched Scoobies and threatening behaviour? Acquisition of an illegal Taser for another party? We could do that, if you prefer.'

'Nah, you're good. Suze, then?'

'Correct choice. What's she like to work with?'

Brian looked down the street. 'Yeah, nah, she's a top chick. Better than most of the dickheads down there. She's . . . fussy. She'll only work with me, actually. Cancels her shifts when I'm on holidays.'

'Hmm. How come?'

'All the others annoy her. Playing around, throwing stuff, on their phone for hours. So's you know, there's no manager on the night shift. Just the two stackers. If one of them is a dick, well, your whole shift's a pain. Who wants to work all night with someone they want to stab?' He checked himself, flustered. 'That's, uh . . .'

'An imaginary stab.'

'Exactly. So Suze only works with someone who doesn't mess around.'

Rainer gave him a sidelong look. 'And you're Mr Serious?'

Brian shrugged. 'Compared to them, yeah. Look, it's a game is what it is. The stacking usually takes about five hours: it's the same number of pallets each night. But if you did it in five hours and sat around the rest of the shift? We're on camera every step: they'd take a look and then cut our hours, or cut people. No good, is it? Suze is a genius at making it last the exact time. We always look busy for the cameras, but it's nice and . . . comfortable.'

Rainer understood. Standard fare on mundane jobs, he thought: make it fit the time and the resources, no matter how much you have to stretch it. Simultaneously unprofessional yet altruistic.

'How has she been, the past few weeks?'

Brian shrugged again. 'Yeah, okay, I guess. Not much . . . well, a bit different. A bit . . . I dunno.'

A burbling Falcon showed its nose further down the street, then reversed behind a wall. Word of police presence had spread in under a minute: he never quite knew how.

'Let's picture a planet, Brian, where you can try harder than that.'

Brian had also clocked the Falcon and shifted on his bum uneasily. 'Yeah, sorry. She's been quiet, even for her. I only asked once – she looked daggers a bit, so I shut it. Something bothering her, but I don't know what. Soz, mate.'

'Did she mention any future plans?'

'Nah. We don't really have chats about stuff like that – Suze doesn't like lots of chat. She did say she was going back to uni, but that was a while ago and I wasn't sure if it was still on.'

'Does she ever talk about home life? Her sister?'

Brian smiled. 'Mental Marika? Yeah, occasionally, when she's really steaming about things. Look, I have three brothers and we fight all the time. But, like, end of the day, we've always got each other's backs: no ratting out, no running out. Our code, see? Suze and Marika – got no code. Same house, same mob – but got no code.'

For someone who came off as laid back, thought Rainer, Brian could be psychologically astute. They'd all been reaching for that definition for twenty-four hours; Brian had it in his pocket the whole time.

'How does Suzanne feel about that?'

'Yeah, we don't do too much feely-talk. But if you ask me what I reckon? Suze did something wrong, somewhen; she doesn't talk about what it is, but it kinda sits there on her shoulder. Doesn't know how to make it right. Wants to get to uni and finish her course but can't quite bring herself to leave.'

'Hmm. Have you ever met Marika?'

'Not as such. Seen her round town, and on that quad bike a few times – she looks pretty cool. But tough as. Totally tough as. She'd kick my arse, no trouble. You can tell.'

Rainer raised an eyebrow. Brian was chunky, to say the least. 'Big guy like you?'

'Uh-huh. She'd fight like a cat – a *mad* cat. Something in her eyes – like, desperate. Any defeat about anything and it would *all* be gone. That kind of thing.' He stared at the gutter. 'Yeah, I steer well clear of Marika.'

Chapter 40

Dana watched as Marika was brought into the room. She'd given special instructions to Custody – Suzanne first, then ten minutes before Marika arrived. Give the older sister time to brew suspicion, to infer deals had been done, or information passed, no matter what David Rowe denied. By allowing Suzanne ten more minutes of anticipation, Dana had manoeuvred her into full paranoia: Suzanne no longer trusted anything anyone said.

David Rowe could barely look at Marika: mutual disaffection clouded the air between them. All the same, she pulled a chair away from the wall and sat in the middle space. Dana caught how this created a physical barrier between Suzanne and David – the former would have to go through Marika to reach the latter. It also affirmed the dynamic suggested earlier, when Suzanne had dragged her seat away to create that space. Marika would be the central figure of the three in every way.

Suzanne kept glancing at Marika, maybe for reassurance, maybe for clues. But the younger sister simply stared at the mirrored glass, contemplating her own reflection. Her breathing was slow and steady, her eyes clear. Suzanne, by contrast, was exhibiting the red-eyed, sniffling martyrdom she'd earlier accused Marika of faking. Suzanne was fraying at the edges; Marika looked pin-sharp.

'Good afternoon.' Dana sat and began to lay out her notes. She had three files stacked together, each with Post-it notes peeking from the wad of paper. Rainer's report from his latest interview sat on top. 'Did you get enough time speaking to the doctor, Marika?'

'Yeah, all good, thanks.'

'Excellent.' Dana indicated the recording equipment. 'Then I think we should begin.'

She looked at the three in turn: Marika looked ready; David clicked his pen in assent; Suzanne stared at the table and wound a piece of thread tight around her index finger.

'I want to start by reading Curtis's final letter. The one he sent days before he left prison.'

'Why?'

She'd expected Marika to be the one objecting, somehow. The query came from Suzanne.

'Well, David clearly hasn't read it and has no idea what was going on at that point. But mainly because we're about to talk about something profound here, and I don't want Curtis himself to get lost in the complexities. I think it matters that we hear from him. These letters are the only part of Curtis's voice that remains. You don't have to do anything Suzanne, just listen.'

'But I don't—'

'Suzanne.' David intervened. 'I want to hear the letter. If you don't, then, as Dana says, just be quiet.'

Suzanne chewed her lip but didn't have anything further to say. Dana slid a photocopy of Curtis's last written words onto the top of her file.

Dear girls,

It's almost here. The last day. Coming up. All the days get slower the nearer we get. I keep thinking a guard will tell me it's all off – that they were only kidding and it's crazy to think they'd let me out. But here we are. Thanks to you. Thanks to your decisions. Because you know when to push someone.

You're my family. I don't mean to pressure, but you surely know that by now. Everyone else backed off. Everyone else left. They all had that look on their face – that I was dirt, I made them feel ashamed. In the papers, for that: it humiliated them. I disgraced them in the court with what I confessed. They couldn't take it, and they didn't care what leaving would do to me. You did. You spotted that straight away. Together, we've mended stuff. I'll never forget that. I owe you.

What I did before was unforgiveable. I took what wasn't mine. I hurt someone. I didn't stop. It can't be forgiven, or forgotten. I can't change the past. I know what I did, and I saw enough at the trial to know the damage I caused. I'd give anything to change that, to make good – I told you so, early on. How can I make good, though? I've struggled to work that out, but you knew. You knew what I could do, and now it's close enough to touch. All I can try now is to make something in this world better.

Some of these guys in this unit had it real tough – terrible, some of them. They're in here because they got so many scars they couldn't help themselves. Every time they did something, they were trying to push away what had happened to them. I wasn't like that. And I wasn't like some of the others – the real bastards. I didn't want it, plan it like them. But I'm here because I should be – you know that and so do I.

Now I have a chance to do something – something important – to make up for it all. You've shown me things can be different. You've helped me to see that if I try, I might make it. And the most import-ant bit of that is to keep my promises. It really matters that I do. Matters to me. I've got to step up now, right?

Got a meeting with some guy a few hours before I walk out. Some guy who can act, make sense of what I tell him, use the information for good. Terry says it's stupid – to put myself at risk and all that. But he's wrong. The risk matters, doesn't it? If there was no risk, the promise wouldn't mean anything. That's a way you set things right, isn't it? Got to do the right thing this time. I used to skate through life when I was a kid. School, home, everything – I just drifted, took what came, never really tried. Can't do that now.

After that, hopefully, I get to meet you both. Not for that long, but all the same. Get to meet you at last. The only person in here who really talked to me was Terry and to be honest that's his job. All the guards, the other prisoners – I feel like they put up with me. I've always felt like that – people are okay while I'm there, don't miss me if I'm not. You've been different from all of them. You didn't have to write at all. You didn't have to stick by me.

Your friendship. It kept me alive in here. Gave me a place to store my heart. Made me see sense. It's meant everything to me, to find good people who believe.

Don't worry. I know what to do. I'll keep my word. All I ever wanted for the last nine years is exactly what you're giving me now. Everything I could ask for. It will all make sense then, I know it will. Payment made.

Thank you. Thank you. You're the best,
Curtis

Marika had her eyes closed. Suzanne shook her head. David was frowning, unable to filter all the information quickly enough to form a judgement. For Dana, the letter said everything, but only if she processed it backwards: if she started by knowing what happened and the letter filled in the blanks.

'Let's begin,' she said quietly, 'with Suzanne's statement from her previous interview. Her description of the death of Mary Doyle.'

David sniffed loudly and squinted. Suzanne fidgeted. Marika now looked evenly at Dana, as absent as if she were hearing how to creosote a fence. It unnerved Dana: Marika had a poker face to die for.

'Is there any aspect of Suzanne's description, Marika, that you consider inaccurate or untrue?'

Marika smiled. 'Hmm, no. Well, I mean, she's described what physically happened. I can't argue with that. When we called Uncle David and then the paramedics, we told them Mary had wandered off while we were watching telly, and just fallen in. She often snuck out there for a ciggie; kept telling us she'd quit, but then she'd need a lot of "fresh air". Preserved her fading dignity, I suppose: neither of us called her on the lie. Often she was too zonked to notice we didn't believe her about most things. We had whole weeks like *Sunset Boulevard*. Anyway, yeah, what Suze said. All that really happened, in the sequence she said. Yeah.'

Marika moved closer to Dana, relegating Suzanne to her peripheral vision.

'I pushed her; I admit that. But Suze caused Mary's death, Detective. I was trying all that week to make Mary face up to reality, but I failed. Mary lost it: she was going to kill my sister. A hammer, for God's sake. I had to do something. That was the one thing I could do.'

Was it? The *one* thing? And was it inevitable? Dana believed she would never know: it was too long ago and there was little evidence beyond the sisters' explanations. In one sense, it didn't matter. What counted right now was the perceived cause and effect.

Dana's planning for this interview had included a review of the notes around Mary Doyle's death and post-mortem. Mary had drugs latent in her system but was deemed *compos mentis* at the time of her death. Forensics had seen nothing that suggested malice on the girls' part. Each aspect of Suzanne's account – now supported by

Marika – fitted all the available evidence from that time. Dana had no wedge to open it up further.

Marika's statement was an admission of manslaughter: she'd given away several years of her future in less than a minute. Yet, legally, it would be a reach to say Marika *murdered* Mary. Dana could suggest Marika knew that falling into that swamp would be fatal. But Marika's defence would be that she purely intended to push Mary away, stop the hammer blow. *A maximum of three to six years, serving two; maybe less* was a calculation Dana made on the spot, and understood Marika had made some time ago. Possibly – probably – before the push.

'You'd like to say something more about the cause of Mary's death?'

Suzanne thrust out a hand; it hovered over the table, inarticulate. Beads of sweat on her wrist emphasized her frustration. 'Woah. Hold on. Leading question, or what? Does *my* lawyer have anything to say?' She looked past Marika's profile, at David.

Marika sat back, amused, giving a wry raising of the eyebrows to Dana. David put down his pen slowly. 'Suzanne, we're not in a court, so the issue of "leading questions" doesn't apply.' David's voice lost its quiver as he got onto the firmer ground of legal definitions. 'The detective is, I suspect, asking about something she already knows. So does Marika. Detective?'

'Thank you, Counsellor. The question still stands, Marika.'

'Thank you, Detective.' Consciously or not, Marika was beginning to mirror Dana's cadence and speech patterns. She sat up straighter, as though a sermon was coming. Suzanne winced.

'Yes, Suze is downplaying her role a bit, you might say. Like I say, she caused it. She breezed out of our lives, Detective. All that summer, after she left school: not a hint she was going to uni, nothing to let us know anything might be changing. So we wasted our time, Mary and I. All summer we didn't prepare; couldn't prepare.'

Dana had imagined the sisters arguing about this for years

afterwards; tantrum after tantrum, fight after fight, reconciliation after reconciliation. But now she wondered if she'd been partly wrong: aspects of it seemed to be happening now for the first time. Marika turned to her sister.

'I get it, I really do, Suze. But . . . you should have trusted me. You should have told me ahead of time because I needed to work out alternatives. Even at that age, I could have done something – reached out to Uncle David, or whatever. It was selfish. It was hard-hearted and brutal, and I never forgot it. And now look where we are.'

Suzanne wound the thread tighter around her finger, cutting circulation. Marika gave it a moment, then resumed speaking to Dana.

'When Suze left for uni, it was a betrayal. Mary and I both felt it; I mean, it even sank through the fog of Mary's mind – not much of the real world managed that. We were bereft in every way. We had no money, Detective. Centrelink would take months to put any welfare into the bank account, and who the hell was going to employ Mary? We got Uncle David to sell our car for us. It was clear to him that we were struggling, but Mary wouldn't have any *charity* from him. They had an almighty row: Mary told him to eff off and banned him from the cottage. I had to fill out our Centrelink forms: Mary hated the idea of handouts, but it was all we had.'

Dana made a Pitman note.

'We limped along after Suze went,' continued Marika, her gaze now fixed on the wall beyond Dana's shoulder. 'It hardly helped Mary's health, did it? I mean, she had to dump three-quarters of her meds because we couldn't afford them. I can't say if they were helping but, at minimum, they were placebos that made her feel she was trying to win. And that's what matters, hey? Not whether you win or lose; but whether you felt a useless old wreck along the way. Dropping those meds gave Mary the final sting of failure. She gave up. She got worse. Her paranoia got out of control.'

Suzanne was still refusing to even acknowledge what was being said. Perhaps, Dana thought, this was how she'd argued for the past four years – by shutting down, by withdrawing. If so, no wonder Marika's anger never abated; it was ramping up right now.

Marika slid her sleeve up past her elbow. Some of the scar tissue glinted in the light as she rotated her forearm back and forth. David watched, astonished. Ashamed by his astonishment.

'You noticed these, Detective. First time we met, if I recall. You were too smart to ask about them; besides, you knew. I'm sure you wouldn't have taken any lame excuse about me scraping against thorns and bushes. Not like *University Challenged* here, who swallowed that line without a squeak. No, you know these for what they are, don't you? Cuts on a human arm, made by someone else.'

Marika stared at Dana's arms and raised an eyebrow: Dana nodded imperceptibly. Marika's gaze returned to her own scars, almost respectfully.

'She made the wounds carefully, oddly enough; Mary took a lot of care over these. Had to get them just right. See?'

She thrust a forearm into her sister's eye line – Suzanne looked away.

'Look closely, Suze. There's no hesitation marks. None whatsoever. A woman who could barely make a coffee without spilling it, but she's millimetre-perfect on cutting her daughter. You know why? Do you? Because damaging me *inspired* her, Suze. It made her eyes shine, it felt like success for her. I tried to tell you. But all you cared about was *me, me, me* and *oohmaybeRio.*'

The last sentence was spat, and Suzanne flinched. Marika gave a half-smile of triumph. Dana saw how precious that currency was: even a sliver of comprehension from Suzanne was a trophy for Marika. Yes, Dana concluded, Suzanne avoided the sibling battle by withdrawing.

Each time she did it, the stance would have maddened Marika a little more. Until she snapped.

'Anyway, Suze had caused us the biggest problem, then strolled away humming a tune. Mary and I were trapped in the cottage – no car, no money, reduced meds and one bed. See where this was headed, Detective? We simultaneously loved and despised each other. As you rightly said; for all that I hated what she did to me, I simply wanted my mother well. Not incarcerated, not even punished, just healthy, and not suffering any more.'

Marika didn't notice David's scrunched eyes. Given what he'd already heard, he'd clearly been expecting nothing now but toxic amorality: he hadn't anticipated compassion. Marika continued.

'Mary and I were two chemicals that shouldn't be mixed, yet we were in the same space and the same time. All the time. Days bled into each other. We lost track: we'd get up at midnight, stumbling around, wondering why it was dark. We ate ingredients, not food. Every semblance of normal life – the routines, the interactions – it all got mislaid. Oh, and tired. We got so, so tired.'

Marika lost herself, drifting towards the miasma of the cottage. Dana coaxed her back.

'Was this when the problems with food began?'

'Hmm? Oh, yeah, it was. When she wasn't cutting me – bloodletting for my own good, to let my poison out – Mary had the idea of starving me. Not to hurt me, but to *help*. It was basically all medieval mumbo-jumbo: purging the body of toxins and demons. Cutting or starving – they were the same thing to Mary. She was certain that what ailed me also surely drove me; she could control that by releasing my blood or making me ill.'

Dana swallowed. Mary would have been too out of it to realize that cuts on a forearm were often visible to outsiders. Dana's mother had been smarter, more strategic: her cuts had been to Dana's upper arms and so easier to hide; cuts re-opening existing wounds, to minimize the scars. Dana's shame was hidden, and all the more painful for that. Secrecy made it sting more.

Marika raised a finger, as though offering a point of order, and directed it at the side of Suzanne's head. 'And here was a bonus, Suze: when she made me ill, I needed her. She could play at being parent. She could feel wanted and needed and adult: even basic first aid seemed a wondrous thing to me. In that fog of hunger and fear, I was a good little daughter who appreciated her mum. Mary couldn't resist provoking that gratitude in me. It was a drug, Suze: Mary was addicted, and content for those few hours. So we can add Munchausen's to her list, can't we?'

Suzanne slapped the table. No one jumped. 'You'd have been in a children's home if not for me, Rika. A bloody kids' home. I sacrificed two careers for you. Two. And I paid. I bloody paid you, Rika. Like you wanted. Why are we here?'

Dana zoomed in. 'Paid?'

Marika looked at Suzanne. 'Want to tell the nice lady, Suze? Want to talk economics? The price of everything, and the value of nothing? Hmm?'

Suzanne shook her head like a toddler.

'Thought not.' Marika's voice was brutally metallic.

She turned back to Dana and softened it. 'Don't worry, Detective, we're coming to that real soon.'

'Very well. You were saying, Marika, about the food?'

'Yes, I was. Well, the food itself was almost secondary, to be honest. I could steal a bit through the loose bricks – good spot, Detective. You also worked out that Mary went for the starvation approach when she was well and forgot it when she was sick; she'd be on her game whenever I was stealing food back. So not too much, or even Mary would notice. Anyway, as you said, there was a yawning gap between what you noticed immediately about the food and what Suze refused to see. Back then, I was still inclined to give Suze the benefit of the doubt; maybe she didn't realize. After Mary died and we discussed it more . . . forcefully, I saw that she'd simply ignored it. The whole thing didn't suit her, so she didn't bother with it. Did you, sis?'

The heat between the Doyles was smouldering. Marika had side-lined David here, to be certain that her narrative prevailed. She faced Dana when she had to, Suzanne when she chose, and David not at all. Her control of personal space was impressive.

'I was stunned, Detective, when you noticed the cupboard doors – and what they implied – straight off. That last little bit of leeway I'd granted Suze? It vanished, right there and then. No more. It was obvious how easy it was to see, and how Suze had *refused* to see it. I'd been right: to be that angry and to act on it.'

It wasn't quite that simple, thought Dana. She'd noticed the cupboards, and followed through with the bricks outside, because that experience resonated with her. With Dana it had been mainly medicines withheld; she'd needed to break through a wall at the back of the cupboard to reach her tablets. The scars of the experience remained: her recognition of the situation was unusual.

Dana couldn't afford for this to be purely a soliloquy from Marika: she was looking to convict both. A totally silent Suzanne could claim that Dana never gave her a chance to explain.

'*Did* you notice the cupboard doors, Suzanne? Back then?'

Suzanne chewed her lip. 'Not . . . no, I . . . not as such. No. I mean, who thinks their mother would do that? I didn't. Most of what was wrong with Mary was internal, and directed at herself. If Rika had said Mary was starving herself, I would have believed that. But I thought . . . I thought Rika was making it up, to force me back home. I thought it was a way of guilting me. Don't think this sweet adorable thing here isn't capable. You're getting duped now, Detective. We can all see it.'

Was she? Dana checked herself. She had a narrative in her head about what had happened. It was one sharpened by the previous interviews, by forensics and other data; by her intuition. She couldn't afford to listen only for confirmation of that narrative; Suzanne was correct in that sense. But no, she didn't feel she was coasting here. Marika was being precise in what she explained: all that she said squared with all that they knew.

'So Marika's assertion – that back then you refused to accept the evidence of starving – is factually correct?'

Suzanne's nod was barely visible.

'So, Marika, after Mary died and Suzanne returned to the cottage from uni, how *did* you act on Suzanne's omission?'

Marika took a swig of water. Now they were getting to the elements that Dana couldn't currently fully prove. Marika had more opportunity, and more reason, to skew things her way when she talked. Dana focused more sharply.

'For a while after Mary died, I stewed. And, if I'm honest, I was glad Suze was back. I thought it was a fresh start. I thought life might improve. Suze was moaning about giving up uni to be my legal guardian; she always held up *her sacrifice* as if I should be forever grateful. But for that short time, I was relatively content. It soon became clear, though, that Suze intended to go back to uni once I turned eighteen. She'd *deferred* her course, not quit. She was still planning a future where I could go to hell. I was fifteen, coming on sixteen. I needed to either get what I wanted before Suze went back to uni or have her tied in to something she had to follow through. I had almost three years, maybe a bit longer. As it turned out, nearer four.'

The air conditioning hummed.

'And what did you want, Marika? What did you want from Suzanne? For the record.'

'I wanted her atonement, Detective. I wanted her to pay her debt: the debt she owed me. She'd saved herself by making me kill our mother. I saved her life: Suze owed me a life. As you said before, Detective: *fair exchange is no robbery.*'

They stared at each other, comprehension washing back and forth.

David tapped his pen on the table. 'I really must speak to my clients now, Detective. Immediately.'

Chapter 41

Dana moved to the viewing room, where Mike and Lucy were watching. Lucy was typing the transcript into a laptop as she heard it on headphones; Mike watched the Doyles with their lawyer and swilled some orange juice in a mug. He turned as Dana entered and gave a thumbs-up.

'I don't think I've seen David Rowe panic before. It's quite something.'

Dana smiled at Mike. 'One for the ages.'

David was indicating with a palms-down motion, followed by a pointed finger towards the mirror: *button down everything because they're watching*. Suzanne had looked and baulked; Marika hadn't even glanced. Now David was asking, hands spread, for information. Suzanne was instantly stayed by Marika's hand at her shoulder. Marika spoke briefly and David spun towards the wall, running his hand over the back of his head in exasperation.

'Where do you think we're at?' asked Mike.

Dana perched on the edge of a table, sneaking a smile at Lucy.

'How much of Mary's last night was planned by Marika, we'll never know. She isn't going to say, not even obliquely. I suspect very little was truly off the cuff, but we'll never be sure. That means manslaughter, not murder: Marika knows that very well. The end result is that Marika did indeed kill Mary to save Suzanne. At minimum, that's what both sisters believe, and it's dictated their actions since then.

'Here's where Suzanne could have got out from under that rock. Had they both played nice and built a life together when Suzanne left uni, I think Marika wouldn't have sought Suzanne's overt apology. Living a good life, supporting her younger sister, that would have been reparation enough, I believe. Marika would have nursed that grievance, sure – played on it from time to time – but it wouldn't have required full compensation.

'However, when Suzanne returned to living in the cottage and didn't want to learn about the abuse she'd chosen to ignore, it stoked Marika's fire. That is one angry and calculating grudge-bearer, and she's good at manoeuvring Suzanne into corners. Dangerously good, in fact. A piece of me thinks she's that good because Suzanne lets her – unconscious guilt, playing out – but all the same, Marika's a talented young woman in all the worst ways.'

'Why kill Curtis Monroe? And how does Marika get him to the cross-thingie so that they can kill him?' It was Lucy who asked, but they both looked to Dana for an answer.

'I have a theory, but right now it's hard to back it up. We'll have to see what the sisters say. I've got about ninety per cent of the whole crime in my head, but a fraction of that on tape. Oh, have they stopped?'

Marika had sat down again. Suzanne was leaning against a wall. David asked Marika another question, but Marika simply blanked him. He sat wearily, shaking his head.

Lucy's phone rang. She answered, and passed it to Dana. 'It's Rainer. Sounds like a bee in a jar.'

Dana smiled. Rainer was now out among the swamps, so she was surprised he could get a signal at all. He must have wandered around the rare patches of dry land, phone in the air, counting bars.

'Hey, Rainer.' She listened intently as Rainer spoke. 'It's wholly intact? Good. Perfect. Yes, send the phone to Dennis, but bring that in to me personally, please. That's a diamond. Don't let it out of your sight. And . . . very good work, well done.'

She passed the phone back to Lucy, who looked at her expectantly.

'Good news, I take it?'

'The best. Final part of the jigsaw.'

She faced the interview room. Three people avoiding each other's space. Frigid air, and two recording devices. Dana felt now was an excellent time to move in.

Chapter 42

Back in Interview One, the recording equipment settled, Dana resumed. She now had enough ammunition to know if anyone was lying, or embellishing, or holding back. It was a rare feeling. She could let this unravel as it may, knowing she had the means for conviction.

'So, Marika, the choice of Curtis Monroe?'

'Yes. Well. It *was* accidental, in many ways. Or, at least, it was fate. I prefer that description myself. I needed a particular soul, in a particular condition, and along came Curtis.'

'You needed his soul?'

'Yes, I believe so; I'd put it like that. Suze might not agree. But I think, when you hear the full circumstances, you might at least see why I felt that way.'

'You have the floor, Marika.'

Marika straightened her posture.

'Thank you. It began as I described to you earlier. It was nearly two years after Mary had died, and I was getting frantic. I was already seventeen and, after my eighteenth, Suze would be looking to move out. The clock on Suze resuming university was ticking, and I could hear it. I mean, the urgency felt tangible to me. I'd floundered a bit in those two years; I'd flailed around and grasped nothing. It was all so . . . unscientific.

'Then I read the article – about Curtis's case. Louise's case, in fact. I had a dim and distant memory of it, to be honest. Even Suze didn't recall much: a lot of sirens and people going past; a couple of journalists who took one look at Mary and backed off. So I can't say it awakened old feelings, or was unfinished business in any way. I imagine that's what you first thought: there was some connection pulling me or Suze back to the past in that way. But there wasn't. We didn't remember much; either Curtis or Louise could have walked past us and we wouldn't have recognized them.

'Anyway. I read the article about the prosecutor, and back then we had the internet. Got enough details from that, and old newspapers through the library, to build a picture of Curtis. Here was the sort of person I wanted, Detective. Someone who'd done something terrible and who, frankly, wouldn't be missed. A person whose own family had turned its back – the world wanted him to fade away. Because, when all was said and done, I wanted Suze's penance. So the soul of a man who'd forfeited his rights by his own actions seemed appropriate. It was the minimum harm to achieve the correct result: that was how I saw it. As it turned out, he was better than I could have imagined.'

Dana wasn't one for fate, or the universe providing. There was no guiding hand, no all-seeing spirit; she was adamant about that. She believed people created what happened to other people: it was that simple. Yet Curtis Monroe and Marika Doyle were two people who should never have met and should never have had such carefully intertwined destinies: their congruence seemed beyond mere human control, somehow.

'Of course, I didn't tell Suze any of that,' continued Marika. Suzanne sighed quietly and regarded her hands as she listened intently. 'She didn't need to know until . . . she needed to know. So I framed it as a personal project of conscience: I wanted to write to a prisoner and we might as well start with a nearby crime. Suze didn't like it; but I was still under eighteen and the prison would baulk at someone that young writing to a prisoner. Especially, of course, one convicted of rape. So the letters had to come from us both. Suze owed me, though she failed to realize at the time how much. She saw, and believed, what she wanted. And I was diligent – including Suze in each letter, asking her to vet it. *The big, clever sister who went to uni* . . . it was dispiritingly easy.'

Suzanne flushed – no one liked being described as that gullible. Dana could picture the manipulation; Marika was a natural. She'd ask about the meaning of a word, getting it wrong so Suzanne felt superior. She'd deliberately break the rules in a draft, so that Suzanne's corrections felt like an older sister controlling the process. And all the while . . .

'I began getting this *melancholy* from Curtis. I can't fully describe it; you might have picked it up yourself from the letters. I could sense his anxiety and his exhaustion. He could never get away from what he'd done; it would always haunt him. He was drowning in prison, Detective: he belonged there because of his crime, but in another sense he didn't belong there at all. He felt out of place in that unit: didn't share their attitudes, their warped priorities. Yet he'd created his own situation – it actually *was* all his fault. He couldn't square the circle: how could he be exactly like those people, when he wasn't?'

And, thought Dana, Marika's plan distilled around then. The synchronicity of it: Curtis's feelings about what he'd caused and how he was being punished, contrasted with Suzanne's apparent indifference about what she – in Marika's eyes – had set in motion. Curtis had done something unforgiveable, but got it. Suzanne had done something unforgiven, and then seemed to be skating. The contrast would ignite Marika's righteous anger.

'After a year of letter-writing, I felt I had enough trust from Curtis to move things forward. Again, the time imperative, Detective. My eighteenth had come and gone: Suze was getting itchy feet and had a return date set. I made an agreement with Suze: we would keep writing to Curtis until he reached eligibility for parole. He needed our support until then; we'd started something and had a moral obligation to follow through that far. That tied Suze to the cottage for a final eight or nine months. She'd already started preparing for uni; she got her deferral adjusted. In fact, if not for all this, she'd be starting back in about six weeks. It was a close-run thing, one way or another.'

At this point, reflected Dana, Marika would have needed her 'proof of loyalty' from Curtis. Ali had identified it in the letters and, now that she knew about the background, Dana could envisage the moment herself. The fulcrum of Curtis and Marika's connection occurred then: after that, Curtis was on an inexorable slide that would kill him. His proof of loyalty was admitting to Marika that he'd 'do anything' to set it all right, to make amends for his crime.

'So I began to telephone Curtis: a mobile I kept out in a tree stump. Yes, rice and all – well done, that was freaky intuition. It was amazing that the prison allowed calls. Was a bit stilted at first, but we began to connect. We were both sure the calls were being recorded, even though he'd been told they weren't. But it felt from the start that we were on the same page. It was strange, unnerving; to feel so attuned to someone who'd done that. I never forgot what he'd done, Detective; don't think I got complacent. I understood. But his ideas of what he'd do if he was ever released were feeble – he'd already decided they'd refuse parole. He wasn't even going to try. I convinced him that simply an attempt might look good later on; it showed willing, and showed he played by the rules and learned.'

'And of course,' said Dana, looking deliberately at Suzanne, 'your letters and offer of temporary accommodation got him over the line. He would have been refused without that assurance; would never have set foot outside the prison.'

'Seriously?' uttered Suzanne, looking left.

'Of course, sis.'

Marika relished being several steps ahead and, Dana thought, probably surprised herself that she enjoyed Dana being alongside her.

'I assumed you'd worked that bit out, Suze. So yeah, Curtis got parole. Now it all got real for the three of us, didn't it? He was getting out, and he was spooked. He was terrified by outside life, by all it entailed. He didn't want to play; he wanted to tell them to forget it. But they weren't going to forget it, were they? So we talked some more. I planted an idea – one that he gradually came to see as good sense. I knew he would. It was an open door: all I had to do was push. I know how to push.' She smiled. 'The stars aligned.'

Dana knew for sure now. The document in Rainer's hand, wending its way to the station: it was born when Curtis was especially vulnerable, and Marika had struck.

'We know what you suggested to Curtis, Marika, what you pushed. We found it, about twenty minutes ago. God bless drone technology.'

Marika's hands clasped like an unconscious prayer. 'Ah. Fair enough. I was keeping it as insurance, but you might as well have it.'

'I understand. Please continue.'

Marika took a sip of water. Suzanne faded into the background as Marika told everyone's past, and everyone's future.

'So, at that point, Suze wanted to sever contact with Curtis. After us being his life raft for eighteen months, she wanted to cut the rope and watch him drown. I mean, Jesus. Now he was an actual person who might really stand in front of us, she refused. All her compassion was fake again, wasn't it? Once there was *work* to be done, she didn't want to know. It was all so familiar, Detective. Suzanne redux: talk a good fight, then run from the battle. Well, not this time. Because this was her redemption. I was dropping reparation right into her hands. All she had to do was play along.'

That was true, thought Dana. But Suzanne didn't know what she was signing up for.

'We'd saved up for the car rental – two hours' worth. Suze's mate at work, Brian, his half-sister works at the car-hire place and got us a deal. We drove out to the prison. Jeez. What a place. What a . . . location. Curtis came out and got into the car. We knew there were cameras on us there, so we all said nothing. No clues for you, Detective, not just then.'

Marika's decisions about evidence still felt arbitrary to Dana. Sometimes withholding and hiding evidence, sometimes laying it out for all to see. She couldn't yet explain each forensic decision the young woman had made.

'But you put on fluoro vests before you reached the end of the causeway?'

'Yeah, my little flourish. It's mainly camouflage: who looks at three people in fluoro? Tradies, workers in a crapped-out Nissan; nothing to see here. It was especially important to Curtis – he was feeling conspicuous. Apparently, prisoners do that a lot, the first few weeks: they feel like people can see they don't belong, that they're out of practice with the world. Fluoro makes you invisible, I figured. Curtis became . . . *all of them, one of us.'*

The Unknown Soldier, thought Dana; she caught the subtext. The fluoro was sold by Marika as a form of hiding Curtis in plain sight: *fluoroflage*. That would placate Curtis and Suzanne. But it also made it almost impossible for the police to miss when they investigated. The more subtle consequence passed Suzanne by: she missed the trail of crumbs Marika had laid out. Dana glanced at Suzanne, who was feigning indifference but wondering how and when to intervene in Marika's statement. Something had told Suzanne it was going to end badly, but she was now too far behind to catch up.

'Curtis wanted a burger: he'd told us that in the letters. A Big Mac, to be precise. The car-hire place was around the corner from Macca's, so it suited all three of us. They dropped me off near the railway sidings – I'd hidden the ATV there. They got the burgers, and we sat by the trees and ate. I can't stand Macca's, personally, it tastes like wet cardboard, but Curtis loved it. I think he liked the novelty of it: prison's forbidden food, eaten with a breeze on his face, for the first time in years. Moving air can be a luxury – who knew? After that, we dribbled back home on the ATV, taking off the fluoro near the service station. It was really slow, three-up. I'm not even sure it's supposed to carry three people, as such – it can carry that weight as hay, or grain sacks, or whatever, but the weight distribution was all wrong. Nearly canned it, up by old Clara's place. She'd have loved that, watching me squelch my face into the tarmac. Anyway, we got back to the cottage as it started to spit with rain.'

So far, nothing Dana could query. Everything fitted with the evidence they had – the CCTV footage, the sightings, the timings, the logistics. She wondered if Marika would try anything that departed from the truth, or whether she intended to simply barrel through, irrespective of the consequences. It looked like the latter. Consequence was not something Marika was avoiding here – it was her goal.

'We ate some toast. We watched some movies. I thought he'd want to watch *Signs*, but apparently he'd watched it as a last-day treat in the unit. Didn't need any reminders of content. Hmm.'

Another piece slotted into the puzzle for Dana. She was relieved: it was a vital element, and she needed to know she was correct. Marika stopped, allowed herself a smile of recollection.

'And he drank – part of a bottle of vodka he'd asked us to get. It was a bit tricky, him drinking. I mean, we could do with him drunk enough that he'd be cooperative, but we couldn't carry him if he got pissed. And after a while, the anaesthetic effect doesn't get any better, does it? So a delicate balance, Detective. Curtis and I had discussed it, though:

all for the team, all for the common goal. The room got warm. I was edgy, to be honest; I wanted everything to go well for him. I wanted him to travel well. Suze was skittish, staring at her watch a lot and fumbling around with her hands. She looked like she was about to take an exam. None of us had much to say, but for Curtis and me it was . . . *amiable* silence. Suze let the side down – grumpy little teenager attitude. Eventually – about half ten, I think – Curtis is pleasantly half-drunk and we're ready.

'Back onto the ATV: it was raining heavily and I was glad, because then no one would be out there. I had all the equipment in a rucksack; Suze had the spare clothes in a waterproof bag. We stopped at the old boom gate. I spread out a tarp, pointed to the ground, and he sat, a bit groggily. Then he lay down and closed his eyes.'

Now Dana could picture the crime scene. It had bugged her at the start, not to have a mental image of the scene. Now she could picture a groggy Curtis lolling around on a rough tarpaulin, the rain lashing down. Marika's pounding heart, glorying in the anticipation. Suzanne's sinking sense that this would define her, but lacking the strength to walk away before it did.

'It was cold, that cold drenching rain. The lights on the ATV drain the battery really quick, so I switched them off. The only light we had now was a torch thing strapped to my head. For reading, not for . . . what we were doing. Pissy little white light; it was like trying to do surgery in the dark. I had so much to do, and Suze was no help. The light moved around like crazy. We got subliminal little flashes of Curtis: dozy, like a sloth. The rain eased off to drizzle. The soil around there really grabs at you; sloppy sounds from each footprint, and the mud fizzed as it subsided. It gives off that earthy, metallic smell; kinda like blood does. I could hear the swamp behind us: it rolls when it rains, like it's turning over in its sleep.

'Suze couldn't do the ropes. She never could. We'd practised them at the cottage for days, but she was all thumbs. Her hands were shaking; mine weren't. I could tell she wanted to run, so I grabbed her arm and looked right at her. The torchlight made her squint, but she stopped shivering. In the end, she nodded. I did the ropes for her; they had to look professional, didn't they?

'After a few seconds, Suze said, "You do it." She might have said please; can't recall, but I doubt it. Twitchy little coward, even then. She wanted a way out again, she wanted me to do the difficult thing. I wasn't taking that crap. I told her she had to do it; that it had to be her, and it had to be now. I wasn't having her ruin all my work. She had the easy bit; something practical and simple, and I would do everything else.

'I had the scenario I'd worked for. There was no fight from him; no struggle. He was tied in a cruciform and there was no one within cooee. He wasn't someone anyone would miss. I handed the axe to Suze. It was her job now. Her responsibility.'

Marika stopped mid-flow.

'I'm doing a lot of work here. Once again, no help from Suze. Perhaps I should know how much you know, Detective. I mean, we're exchanging here, aren't we? It's not a one-way street.'

That was true, thought Dana. She would have to offer up something from her side. She was frantically trying to reassess the forensics – why Marika left a trail leading to both of them but carefully hid other clues.

Suzanne looked quizzically at Marika; David sighed. The elder sister was still trying to fathom exactly what Marika had done and not done, and why they were there. David had, it seemed, largely caught up to events, and regretted having done so.

Dana took great care to line up her papers in a neat pile. She and Marika understood the implication; each had, during the course of the morning, used a formal posture to indicate something important.

'If I can tell you Curtis Monroe's last words on this Earth, you tell me the details of how it happened.'

David made a move forward to interject but was halted in his tracks by Marika's raised palm. Suzanne looked skyward, as though she couldn't halt a tragedy. Marika looked intrigued.

'I get it. Thank you. But perhaps we should tell these kind people why I should do that.'

'Firstly, because you have the information. We all know that.' Dana looked at each of the three in turn. 'So does Suzanne, for the most part, but you want to be the one to tell it. And you know things she doesn't; I'm sure we'll come to why that is. As for the reason you should tell?' Dana shrugged, as if the reason were inevitable. 'Well, if I guess the phrase correctly, then I must know basically what happened: who did what and, most importantly, why. You'd be fleshing out the details, wouldn't you? Putting the two of you in the best possible light, helping your lawyer. And besides, you want to. You really, really want to. Right?'

Marika's face said she did. Suzanne blinked a tear to the corner of her eye, clasped a tissue tighter and spoke through gritted teeth.

'Rika, it's not a game. Don't be stupid.'

Dana calculated that the 'stupid' was an error. She'd spent all the interviews pandering to the sense that Marika wanted to be considered smart. David leaned forward again.

'Suze is right, you should—'

'Shut up. Both of you.' Marika folded her arms. 'Go ahead, Detective. Your side of the bargain.'

Here was the moment. Everything led to this: a statement that would either solve or stall the entire investigation.

'Ready, Marika? His last words were . . . *Swing away, Merrill.*'

'Oh, Jesus, Jesus.'

Marika didn't move a muscle. The shocked whisper had come from

Suzanne. She'd stared at her sister's reaction and realized Dana was right on the money. The whisper curled around the room.

'Well,' said Marika. 'Label me impressed. I didn't think you had that bit, Detective. Kudos.'

Suzanne grabbed at her sister's arm and was shaken off. 'For God's sake, Rika, this is not a game.'

Marika whipped a look at her sister; venomous, self-righteous. 'Yeah, yeah, it is, actually. It's the *endgame*, Suze: it's the game we play at the end. That thing we would always come to, and now we have? It's . . . what we both deserve. You know it. Now, she knows it, too.'

Suzanne recoiled, horror-struck. A motive that Dana now comprehended had never even occurred to Suzanne. It was pouring through now; what Marika had done, and what it would do to Suzanne.

'God, you always . . . always meant to . . .'

Marika's features were dead. It was a bitter mask. 'Yeah, I did. I always meant to. Don't worry, Suze; we're both going down the same road now, for the same reason. That's a form of togetherness, isn't it? That's our *special bond*, intact.'

'Did you . . .? For God's sake, did you leave him out there? Have they got the body?'

'Of course. I meant it, Suze. All of it.'

Suzanne recoiled; her hand drifted to her mouth. The utter betrayal, mixed with a rising sense of her own stupidity, her own naivety. Marika spread her hands wide, as if it was all obvious.

'I meant for you to kill Curtis, you know that. But I also meant the police to find the body, to have the evidence to convict you. Of course I did. Because atonement isn't a private act, Suze. It can't be done on the quiet, with no witnesses, no fall-out. Why did you ever think it could?'

She pushed herself nose to nose with Suzanne, who wilted. Marika's voice fell to a furious whisper. 'Atonement *is* the shame, the guilt: it only exists when it's witnessed. Don't you get it yet? Everyone knew Mary was dead. That was *my* shame, *my* guilt – I knew I'd caused it. Our mother, for God's sake. If you kill Curtis but he's shoved into a swamp and no one even knows he's missing, what kind of reparation is that? You haven't *paid* unless others see what you've caused. Like I had to.'

An eye for an eye, a corpse for a corpse: Marika's credo ever since Mary had died. Nothing but an identically public consequence would do. Suzanne's reparations would be Marika's too; they would pay for Marika's weakness in not confessing at the time to killing Mary. Marika had told Suzanne that killing a convicted rapist would be her penance: Marika would deal with the forensics and consider honour satisfied on both sides. Suzanne had been so desperate for her life to move on, so suffused with guilt over Mary, she'd believed her sister.

Marika took another swig of water. 'It mattered, you see. The process mattered. Curtis and I had agreed it would be done right: you can hear it in that last letter, can't you? Suze was standing over him. The axe looked heavy in her hand. Rainwater was running down her, drenching her shoes. Her hair was slung forward; she looked Gothic. Every time my flashlight swept past the blade, it gleamed, winked at us all.

'Curtis coughed, spluttered really. He couldn't open his mouth properly with the rain falling and him lying flat. I put my hand under his neck to help his head lift a bit, and leaned really close. Almost gathered him to me, I suppose. Inches away from each other. In that silver light, in the rain, his wet face was sparkling. I wiped his mouth with my finger, just traced across his lips. That moment, Detective: that moment. I asked him for the magic words; just to be sure. He whispered, but he said them. *Swing away, Merrill, swing away.* I needed to be sure, and now I was. I let him down easy. Settled back on my heels, behind Curtis's head, out of range.

'I pointed the torchlight at Curtis's heart. His breathing was hammering now. He had his eyes shut. He needed mercy; Curtis needed sweet release. It was cruel to wait. Suzy dithered. She tried to step away, and I grabbed her ankle. She got it together a bit then. I couldn't see the swing coming through the darkness; all the light was on Curtis's heart. Suze's foot lifted slightly, her hip swayed. The blade ripped through the light, through the skin, the bone. It crunched, Detective. Crunched. Right first time, our Suze. The rest would be for display.'

Suzanne slumped forward. David ran his hand across his mouth, stifling a sob. Dana and Marika looked at each other; the only ones who could stand this. Marika continued.

'Suze believed I would dump Curtis's body in a swamp, tied to the ATV. There's a pool of deep marsh about two hundred metres from where we killed Curtis; the locals call it *Miller's Ruin*. The gases from the swamp sometimes produce shimmering lights above the waterline. Back in the day, they thought that was the ghost of an old bushranger, Harvey Miller. He's supposed to be in there, someplace. No one knows how deep Miller's Ruin is, but you could hide a bus in it. Double-decker, maybe. So plenty big enough. That's what we agreed – Curtis roped to the ATV, and the whole shebang six metres under Miller's Ruin. Well, everything but Curtis and the ropes went in there. Curtis stayed exactly where he was.'

David and Suzanne had the same perplexed furrow on their forehead. Marika looked triumphant.

'To explain,' began Dana, addressing Suzanne and David, 'we found Curtis Monroe's body still tied to the posts in a cruciform. We found the ropes, but not the tarp. Our forensics told us that Curtis died from the first of three blows to the abdomen, which severed his heart. We established time and method of death from that. Suzanne, a question.'

Suzanne hesitated, her reflexes hammered and reeling. 'Hmm?'

'When Curtis was lying on the ground, and you'd tied him up, and Marika had handed you the weapon, Curtis said, "Swing away, Merrill." Didn't that strike you as odd?'

Suzanne frowned. 'I . . . no. I didn't hear the exact words. It was raining and dark; Rika had the torch, and she was nearest to his mouth. I saw his lips move, but he might have been mumbling anything. A prayer; sorry; mother; I don't know. I couldn't hear anything. I had a sort of tinnitus sound in my ears, and I couldn't even feel the axe in my hand. I felt so . . .'

'Disembodied?'

'Yeah. Yeah. Wasn't . . . *couldn't* be me. Even though it was.'

Dana turned to Marika. 'Would you care to explain to your sister?'

Suzanne was shaking now with the shock.

Marika smiled. 'Please save me the effort.'

'Very well. Curtis couldn't get over what he did to Louise. He wanted to die. He wanted to commit suicide, but he worried he'd fail when it came to it. Marika offered him a way out in their phone calls: we worked out what they'd discussed from analysing the letters carefully. She would arrange for him to be killed in a way that he couldn't duck or escape. Marika told you, Suzanne, that he needed to be tied so he couldn't squirm and make things awkward; really, it was to stop him reneging on their deal. But, in case freedom made him change his mind legitimately at the last minute, they'd agreed a safe word; a code only they knew. If Curtis said the line from the film *Signs* – *Swing away, Merrill* – then he still wanted to die; the deal still held. Marika was checking.'

Marika grinned. 'I'm genuinely impressed, Detective. I had no idea you'd be so good at this. I thought we'd be here for days.'

Marika saw no moral disgrace, no carnage, no damage even in this room; she merely saw a chess game in the final stages.

'So, Marika, you got your atonement. Suzanne got hers, by paying a corpse for a corpse. Curtis?'

Marika sparkled, as though she still held a secret Dana hadn't fathomed. 'Ah, maybe you missed a bit?'

'I believe that was through the Aryans?' Marika nodded, so Dana continued. 'Curtis felt he'd done nothing positive in his life; not simply

because of Louise, but everything. The one way he could show peni-
tence was to tell all about the Aryans' drug empire to the authorities.
Curtis knew – or believed – that he would be dead before dawn anyway, at Suzanne's hand. He could do some good before then, by
disrupting a major drugs ring. The advantage for you, Marika, was that
his staged death threw even more suspicion onto the Aryan Force
inside Du Pont. The cruciform imagery suggested message-sending by
a powerful group.'

'Yeah, you're pretty close. Curtis said it would be a win–win. The
Nazis would get attention because he'd spilled on them, then his suicide would look like they'd killed him, causing them more grief. So the
more staged it was, the better. But if I'd left the tarp and the fluoro
there, you'd have connected us to the crime quicker and the Nazis
would have had a free pass on it. Ultimately, I knew you'd come looking for us – for Suze – and I wanted that, of course. It was my payment
to Curtis to delay your investigation swinging towards the two of us.
He wanted you to think it was the Nazis long enough to give them
extra hassle. He hated having to do the Aryans' legwork in that prison:
believe it or not, given his crime, he felt it was morally wrong. And yes,
he wanted to die: he gave me a signed letter stating that. Which you've
now found.'

Rainer had read it to her over the phone and, while lawyers might
pick holes in it, the document backed Marika. Curtis's own hand said
that he wanted to end it, Marika and Suzanne were helping, and he'd
wanted it blamed on the Aryans for a while. He hadn't mentioned
Louise Montgomery's name.

'The other details, Marika?'

'She'd straddled him and swung. Perfect, first time. She stopped and
asked if he was dead. I would have said yes regardless, to be honest, but
yeah, there was no pulse from the throat. I told her two more swings –
Nazis wouldn't stop at one, would they? So; face the other way. Backhand.

'She was shaking by the third. I told her to drop the axe on the tarp; didn't want blood anywhere else. Fresh clothes on the ATV; she changed into them and I kept hers. She wanted to go, then; wanted to walk away. Someone else would clear up after her. Same old, same old. If I was ever going to deviate from my own plan – if I was ever going to stick the body in the swamp with old Harvey Miller – well, that idea evaporated. My sister doesn't like dealing with anything that doesn't suit her, you see. And besides . . .'

'The weight?'

'*Exactly*, Detective. Thank God someone gets it.' Marika turned to face her sister. 'How did you imagine, Suze, that I was going to lift the dead weight of a grown man onto the ATV? Hmm? Acquire some mystery winch from somewhere? Or magic up some superhuman strength? Two of us would have struggled. One? Impossible. Pretty obvious, I'd say, but no, never occurred to you. Walking off down the road because that was convenient to you.'

Marika's breathing remained steady; Suzanne's was starting to judder. Dana only had a couple of minutes left before shock fully engulfed Suzanne. She nodded at Marika to continue.

'So yeah, no chance I would hide the body after that, and no chance that I could. Suze had got changed and dropped the bloody clothes onto the tarp. Then she just . . . faded. I don't know how else to describe it, Detective. Once she'd changed clothes, she just walked away. We still had just that tiny head lamp, so she went from bright light to darkness in three or four steps. Something ghostly about it, something unreal. As if she'd never really been there at all.

'Took several goes to get the tarp out. Then the tarp, the axe, the Taser we hadn't needed, the fluoro – all wrapped up. Changed my blood-spattered clothes for fresh ones. All the evidence bundled up and tied tight to the ATV. Blessed night – it started to sheet it down right then: washed all my sins away. Then back down the rise a hundred metres – there's a turn to the left between two large bushes. On to Miller's Ruin, and let the ATV cruise down into it. Sorry to see the thing go, but . . . didn't think I'd ever be driving it again.'

'Clara Belmont had seen the three of you riding back to the house that afternoon. How did you plan to explain Curtis's subsequent absence? Blame it on the Aryans?'

'My agreement with Suze was that Curtis would go into the swamp and we'd look to explain the ATV going missing. It was insured, so we'd end up with some cash. We'd say that there was a knock on the door late at night; Curtis answered it and wandered off with whoever.'

That had been the working hypothesis for a long time, Dana thought. In truth, most of them thought it the most likely scenario. Until Dana had started to talk with Marika Doyle.

'But your agreement with Curtis?'

'His body would be staged; the focus would be directed onto the Aryans for a while, as he wanted. But once you had the footage of the fluoro, I knew you'd put it all together eventually. Just not this quickly.'

'Then you stayed away from the house?'

'Yeah. The plan Suze and I agreed was that I'd come back to the house and we'd alibi each other for the night. Then we'd go to the police the next day and say someone stole the ATV overnight. Clara had, as you say, seen us both on it the previous day. *We woke the next morning to find it gone, Officer. No, the keys were still on the hook in the house; they must have taken it without starting it, somehow.* That kind of thing.'

It would probably have worked. The proximity of two crimes: Dana would have believed the people killing Curtis had also 'acquired' the ATV at the same time, probably to transport the body without getting forensics in their own vehicle. Following that logic, she'd then assume the killers arrived and left by car but dumped the ATV in a swamp after killing Curtis. Yes, Dana thought, that theory would have held water for a long time.

'But I changed the parameters, Detective. I simply stayed away. Time for Suze to take responsibility, for once. Something tricky that didn't involve a book or a horse – how would she cope? I knew you'd take her in for questioning. That was your chance, Suze. To confess. To tell everything – uni, Mary, the letters, the axe, everything. But ah, even twenty-four hours later, you'd told them none of it. Uncle David said you'd bottled it – not in so many words, of course, but I got the impression. Still hoping to skate away and go back to university. Still hoping every problem in your life goes away, without you doing anything. Just turns into smoke behind you, right? So, in the end, I had to tell you, Detective.'

'Your absence generated extra time for you: it gave us more time to develop the Aryan angle.'

'Ah yes, true. I tried to abide by Curtis's last wishes, so yeah; you had enough time without me around to really think about the Nazis.'

David's pen rapped on the table. Dana had virtually forgotten he was there. 'I think you have more than enough, Detective. My clients need to rest now.'

'Of course.' Dana moved towards the recorder, until Marika lightly touched her forearm.

'I'm not a monster; please don't think that, Detective. I mean I tried, with my mother. You know: you know what it's like when someone's unreachable.' Now, at the last, Marika began to tremble. 'No one could get to Mary Doyle's heart, Detective, no one. It wasn't possible. I got nearest; I was on the right path. I got under her skin.'

Chapter 43

Dana had reached her office when Mike called out. They exchanged a thumbs-up in the corridor. Dana closed her eyes: the tension of the morning was pulling her energy away, peeling back layers and making her feel suddenly vulnerable. They hugged.

'I'm lovin' your work, Dana.'

'Thank you, Mikey. I think I was pushing at an open door, there. Marika wanted to spill.'

They sat in Dana's office and, not for the first time, Mike noticed the absence of anything personal in it. As though Dana expected to be called up, or called out.

'Ah, well. She spilled because, firstly, you'd done the right legwork; secondly, you got *her*; and, thirdly, she knew you'd worked everything out already. McCullough will be delighted: a solved murder on his second day.'

McCullough. Was it really only a few hours ago she'd been in his office?

'Urgh, he'll take it as confirmation he was right all along. Guess which one of us will feel vindicated by today's events? Clue: not me.'

'I wouldn't knock yourself out trying to guess what's in his feeble brain. It's mostly air, or methane, I think; just the word *me* floating around in a void. Still okay to see Bill at seven? He swears there's . . . *there are* . . . no armed guards at his farm gate.'

'Definitely. Count me in. I'll have to be ambassador for Luce, as well: she's not allowed near him. Yes, I'd like that. Thanks, Mikey; covering for me today, making sure Luce had some help.'

Mike spread his arms. 'That's what very large families are for. Besides Nancy-twice-removed, we have several other lawyers, a plumber, carpenter, doctor: we're ready for Armageddon.'

Dana smiled. 'I'll keep you on speed dial. Hey, Luce.'

'Hey, chick. Congratulations.'

Lucy hung on to the door frame. Mike read the runes and departed. Dana beckoned her in.

'Thank you muchly, Luce. A bit exhausting, to be honest.'

Yes, thought Lucy, the strain was on Dana's face. 'I'm thinking Lily's Tea Rooms?'

'Cool, I'll get my coat.'

Lucy wandered off down the corridor while Dana went to the locker and fetched her coat and handbag.

She thought Lucy would be waiting at reception but, as she neared it, she spotted a figure in the kitchenette. Lucy, reaching for what was obviously a second chocolate-chip cookie.

'Really hungry then, Luce?'

Lucy crammed the first segment in and pawed at the crumbs. 'Ah, well, yeah. Hmm. You see, I run *towards* cookies, when everyone else is running away.'

Dana mock-bowed. 'You're the hero we need right now, Luce.'

'Not all of us wear capes.' Lucy dusted her hands and they headed towards the main door. 'Who makes these, anyhow?'

'That would be Miriam. In training for the CWA competitions across the summer. You're eating her early limbering-up, there.'

As they crossed reception, Lucy held up the rest of the cookie and gave Miriam a thumbs-up.

The road was slick with just-fallen rain, which left gossamer rainbows on the surface as Rainer drove through the puddles. The acacias sparkled and shivered off raindrops from the backdraught of the car. Ahead, the house glowered, almost a silhouette now against the greying sky. He parked at the beginning of the driveway and traipsed up the gravel, looking towards the living-room window.

The door opened as he reached the main step. Clara Belmont peered cautiously around the door, her fingers like spiders clawing for grip. She'd lost the abrasiveness of yesterday; it suddenly hit Rainer that this extra visit had rattled her.

'What's wrong?' she demanded as he approached.

'No problem, Clara. I thought you'd want some juicy details on Marika's case. And, look.' From behind his back he produced a plastic tray of cakes, covered in cellophane. 'If you insist on choking to death on a cake, young lady, it should be a Lamington: the Belmont name demands it. Nothing could be more Australian.'

Her lips curled into a smile despite herself. He thought he detected a slight blush.

'And if you insist on seeing me off, young man, the least we can do is eat from the good china, yes?'

She eased back and allowed him to cross the threshold. He took off his jacket as she hummed back into the parlour, talking over her shoulder.

'I hope you know how to make coffee, Rainer. Properly, I mean. And the fireplace needs a good clean. And I bet you're handy with a screwdriver . . .'

Someone up there was pulling strings: they got Dana's favourite table, set into a nook overlooking the gardens, obscured from most of the café by two large potted palms and a rattan screen. Lucy sat down and smiled.

'I took the liberty of ordering for you, Dana: a green salad, some olives and some sort of *amuse-bouche* involving paprika, kale and quinoa, I believe. You are a foodie, aren't you?'

'It's neither big nor clever to mock the afflicted, Luce.'

'Ha.' Lucy sat and unwound a scarf. 'I find it big *and* clever. How about cheese sandwiches, no garnish whatsoever?'

'Thank you.'

Lucy was getting used to reading Dana's features now; not so much the expression as the change around the eyes, the skin. 'You look absolutely wrecked by this morning's activities.'

Dana inclined her head. 'And again, thank you. None taken.'

Lucy laughed. 'No, I mean I can see that took a lot of effort. Did you spot all of that right at the beginning?'

The start of the case seemed a world away now. It jolted Dana to recall it was less than thirty-six hours. Not just the case, but the rest of it – what happened to Lucy and Bill, McCullough's arrival, the Aryans, David Rowe's deflation, Marika's confession. All in barely a day.

'Not all of it, no, Luce. The original crime scene looked staged, of course, but the mere fact that the body was public and not in the swamp threw me off. We spent too much time looking for people who would want to send a message by leaving Curtis's body visible. My fault: it didn't occur to me until today that the message-sender could be Curtis himself.'

Lucy felt that Dana was running herself down there; it wasn't as if she'd missed something obvious. The truth had to be put together piece by intricate piece: that took time.

'So what tipped you off? I still thought this morning it was the Aryans.'

Dana fiddled with her spoon; Lily's did proper crockery and

utensils. The hum of other conversations fell away, as it always seemed to do when Lucy was near.

'The letters. It was always the letters. They were the one solid indication we had of the victim's state of mind. And eventually, of course, those logic gaps. I didn't pay enough attention early on; I treated the letters as some novelty adjunct, because Curtis the convicted rapist was corresponding with two women.'

Lucy frowned. 'Didn't we *all* do that, though? Focus away from Curtis? Mikey included? I mean, first and most likely was some fallout from Louise: it was his first day outside the prison after a nine-year sentence. You had to clear away that option before looking at anything else.'

'True. But then I couldn't find a reason that would make the sisters the killers; none of us could. Because part of the real motive for his own murder was inside Curtis, and part of it went back years for a pair of sisters we'd never met before.'

They'd all been thrown towards the Aryans by the lack of apparent motive from the Doyles; plus, the sisters knew the country and how to hide a body in it and there had to have been a reason why the body was left in the open. Marika and Curtis had chucked in some very effective false trails.

'But Marika wanted you to find out. She wanted to get caught, ultimately.'

Exactly. Dana wondered if they would be anywhere near solving the case if she hadn't keyed in to what Marika wanted to happen. Without that fizzing connection to what Marika had endured in her childhood, Dana doubted they'd be here now, celebrating.

'Yes, she did. It wouldn't have been atonement – in Marika's eyes – if we hadn't caught both sisters *and* secured confessions and supporting evidence. There's a specialist team arriving tomorrow to trawl Miller's Ruin; Marika said the crime scene evidence was all tied to the ATV and sunk, so it should be recoverable.'

Dana wondered if, given only a slightly different trajectory, she might be even more like Marika. The degree of overlap between her and a proven killer didn't bother her that much; she knew herself well enough to comprehend it. No, her consideration was more intellectual than emotional.

'Marika's extremely tired. Exhausted, in fact, by her own life. She wanted it all done; then she wanted it all over. We were a vehicle for that final phase. Marika left . . . *spaces*, individual points of light which, viewed from the right angle, made up a constellation.'

'Why didn't Suzanne spot her sister's game and counter it? She was here, in custody, before Marika. Suzanne could have got ahead of all this: at least planted reasonable doubt.'

'Yes, she could.' Dana waited while the waitress laid tea on the table. 'Thank you, Mandy. And for a while I thought she was doing exactly that, if I'm honest. I think she dabbled with the idea, and that was what I picked up on. But she couldn't sustain it. To do it effectively, she had to supply – or at least *imply* – an alternative theory which fitted the basic facts but exonerated her. She couldn't. Partly because she didn't know what we had: she assumed the body and all the evidence were at the bottom of a swamp, because she'd agreed with Marika that it would be. So her tactics were limited: she didn't want to give up things she was certain we hadn't discovered. But also, she isn't capable of that kind of Machiavellian thinking – Marika got all those genes.'

Lucy could see that. Marika held herself like someone who was constantly working out angles of attack and escape. The more she thought about it, the more Lucy considered that Dana had not so much outwitted Marika as joined forces for a mutually advantageous outcome. That required creating a sense that nothing could escape Dana, and Marika therefore should – *must* – yield and confess all. It also required the kind of empathy that couldn't be faked; could only come from common experience. But it couldn't be said that Dana had been truly ahead of the younger Doyle at any point.

'So they're both guilty, Detective. And they've both killed someone. Which one is more guilty?'

'In the eyes of the law, they're equal. A conspiracy is judged to be as serious as the act. They each took part in both aspects on both occasions, before and after the fact. It doesn't matter whether one persuaded the other, or what emotional blackmail was used. Marika killed Mary, but Suzanne was part of the conspiracy. Suzanne killed Curtis, but Marika was part of that conspiracy.

'That was why Suzanne was so supine in there for that last interview – it finally dawned on her that Marika had woven her as tightly into this crime as Marika herself. She finally worked out what Marika had done to them both. The full facts, especially once they're known, are ropes binding them together. They're entwined again, like each night in that bed.'

Lucy finished pouring and passed the cup across. 'But Suzanne wielded the axe.'

'Thank you. Yes, Suzanne struck the fatal blow, but others were complicit.'

Dana paused, stirring the tea slowly. Perhaps when the case was cleared, it would be one of those where she looked back and saw the whole scenario in a different light.

'In fact, now that I mention it, I think everyone was complicit. Everyone. For example, the whole medical system – for diagnosis after diagnosis, test and re-test, across decades: nothing that helped Mary a damn. David Rowe – for not pushing into the sisters' lives and for being studiously polite as Suzanne and, especially, Marika were hanging by their fingertips. Mary Doyle – for translating her own fears and imperfections into abuse of her children. She cut and starved a child and, in her more lucid moments, knew that should be unacceptable.

But she never stepped away. Suzanne – for running when Marika still needed her help, and for shutting her eyes when they should have been open. That created the conditions for Mary's death, and started the machinery that led to Curtis's death. Curtis himself, of course – filled with self-loathing for what he'd done to Louise, wanting someone to end his torment for him. And Marika – planning a murder because she wanted some reparation: a price that would never be sufficient, for a debt that never actually existed. For all that she suffered, Marika had no right to invoke murder as compensation.'

'What a mess.'

'Indeed. Who'd have thought that signing a university application would lead to two homicides?'

'Ah,' said Lucy, smiling. 'Your point of origin for the murders?'

Dana frowned. 'Has young Mikey been giving away trade secrets?'

Lucy raised her hands in mollification. 'Oh, thumbscrews, white noise, no sleep for a month, his kids hostage, et cetera: he took ages to crack.'

Dana grinned. 'Sure, that sounds like him. If you'd just given him a paper cut, he'd have cried and spilled everything.'

'We talked about the empathy chips, as well.'

Dana stalled. 'Hmm?'

They paused again while the sandwiches arrived. Mandy smiled at them both and pulled the rattan screen tighter behind her as she departed.

'Some of those exchanges with Marika – not faked for the occasion?'

'Ah. Well.' Dana felt the heat of disclosure. 'Quite often I do. You shouldn't accept what I say in there at face value every time. But I sensed Marika wouldn't take to being conned. And the resemblances were uncanny enough, and frequent enough, that my genuine responses were the best option.'

Just that admission alone chilled Lucy. She could see again Marika's scars shining under the lights, a mental image of a shivering, terrified Marika scrabbling at bricks in the dark, desperate for food.

'Jeez, I'm so sorry.'

Dana had previously intended this discussion for somewhere at some point in the future. But last night – Lucy's courageous telling of Tubs's story, her reaction to Dana's revelations – had changed Dana's mind. These things were for saying directly, face-to-face, she'd now decided. The relief and the shared intimacy: part of that came from taking a chance in the telling.

'Thank you. Cuts heal, but the scars remind you, as they should, I suppose. People usually wonder how the kid could allow that: why they don't fight, or squirm away. But you get frozen, is what happens: one way or another.'

Dana grabbed at her shoulder, suddenly itching. In every sense, her scars ran deep.

'Mary would have kept Marika still through fear; Mary was unpredictable and therefore dangerous. So Marika would probably sit, paralysed by fear, while the cutting took place. For all her bravado, Marika isn't beyond being terrified. No one is. Unlike Mary, when my mother went at me with the knife she always re-cut along existing scars, so it would look like I'd literally opened old wounds. She got extra cruelty for free. I was incapacitated by all the ropes; the only thing I could move was my finger and thumb, tapping them. It was the one control I had; the sole thing I could do, to know I was still there.

'I was a bit luckier than Marika. Yes, luckier. The starving, in my case, was a one-off from my mother; her friend's suggestion. Because I don't think it brought enough visceral reaction from me and therefore instant gratification for her. My mother liked sharp, vivid responses. I could enrage her by just shutting down, blanking emotions. That's one reason I'm so good at it, I'm afraid, beyond natural talent. But with the starving I just became slower, fuzzier, clumsy and careless; like I was drunk. She wanted me wide awake and totally aware.'

Lucy shook her head. 'Christ.'

Deep breath. 'But if you and I are going to . . . well, I want you to understand some more things. Up for that?'

Lucy blinked once, held back the tear, then sat up straighter. 'Yup. Medicine in one big gulp, Tubs always said.'

'Okay. Seven years ago: the twentieth anniversary of Dad, plus one day. I was back at Pulpit Falls. He used to take me there when I was little, so I could taste the waterfall. There was a way through the bushes that ran behind the water, onto a small ledge at the back of the torrent. He'd hold on to my arms and I could lean out, feel the water on my tongue. Tipped forward like a little ski-jumper: total blind faith that he would keep me safe. It was our secret.'

The warmth of the memory bloomed out from Dana's heart and soothed her. Strong hands that would never fail, cool air beside the tumbling water.

'Anyway, seven years ago, I was there again. The route was long since closed: that part of the cliff was partly clay and it was slowly crumbling. I found the entrance hidden in the undergrowth, though, followed it down. There was just about enough of a path to access the ledge, if you were very careful.

'I was standing behind the falling water, watching it rush headlong into the river. Pulled down by gravity, sure; but there was something exhilarating, freeing, about it. The water just went, just kept on coming; it had a sense of, I don't know, *liberty*. I closed my eyes and felt the vibration of water on rock as it crashed below. When I opened my eyes, there she was. My mother. On the path. She must have waited there every year, around each anniversary, believing I'd have to come back to it one day. She knew I couldn't resist.'

Dana recalled the heart-fall, the plummet from warm memory to cold reality. Now she clutched a nebulizer and squeezed hard.

'Our eyes locked, then she grinned. I knew that grin – the slight curve of it, the malice, the intent. I knew it was bad for me. She could see through all the defences and . . . *alterations*, and recognize her daughter; I couldn't pretend to be someone else when she glared at me. I turned to liquid inside; it was instantaneous, a drag-back of those years, and I couldn't control it. She lunged at a piece of timber someone had set against the cliff – one of the old fence posts, I think. She started hacking at the ground, gouging out lumps. After two pushes a big chunk cleaved away: already a one-metre gap. She was locking me in. If she ripped more of the path away, I couldn't escape. No way out but back the way I came, and she was destroying that. No one would hear me scream for help above the roar of the water. Jumping would be fatal. She was killing me. She was killing me at the one place on Earth where I'd felt peace and trust and love.

'I leapt towards her. Had two knees back then. Landed half on the path, half over the edge. She swung the wooden post and, thank Christ, she just missed. I hauled myself up. Her hate, her exhilaration, made her sloppy – she wasn't balanced. I stood up and threw my hands at hers, hoping to deflect the next blow. I grabbed as she tipped; she fell as I toppled; we both went over.'

The fizz as air was displaced by roaring water; the two of them joining the headlong descent; the white of the water and the black shreds of brutal stone below, looming up at dizzying speed.

'Chance, really. And karma. I landed on a sloping rock that tore my kneecap apart, and slid into the water. The cold numbed the pain. She fell head first onto a sharp outcrop. It split her brain in half. She floated past me as I scrambled for land. She was serene somehow, but carved in two.'

The sound of the waterfall receding, the river coiling maternally around her, and her mother's body, borne away with a bubbling red trail to the nearby reeds.

'There should have been a full inquest. If not a trial. We all should have faced the music; it was only right. The local council: no fences, no warning signs on their property. The Church: what they did to her, with her, for her – what they allowed to be done. And me, of course: my involvement. But there were too many people with too many reasons to suppress. The inquest was opened – then adjourned, for ever. I'm the one who could unlock that now, I suppose. But I was weak, and selfish. Still am. I didn't want to testify about what had happened. As far as they knew I was Dana Russo, an innocent person attacked by a mad woman. Which I was, in some ways. But not in others. I couldn't be sure, you see: maybe I pushed her, or pulled her. Perhaps I wanted her to perish. Or possibly, I wanted us both to die. Still haven't . . . still haven't decided.'

Lucy was silent, stunned. Then she reached around the side of the table and took Dana's hand. 'I'm so glad you made it.'

Dana's smile, tears glistening. Overwhelmed. A stuttered whisper.

'You're like a benediction, Luce. You're luck I don't deserve.'

Acknowledgements

Last year my debut novel, *Hermit*, was published. This was a lifelong dream for me and it was heartening that the people charged with supporting it were not only professionals, but understood how much the moment meant. They could all have cited the pandemic and walked away blameless: they stayed and got behind my book. They are stars.

I need to thank my agent, Hattie Grunewald, who could have chosen any of literally thousands of manuscripts, and chose mine. I was then picked up for publication by Headline, who brought my ace editor, Toby Jones, and his team in London. They've refined each book to within an inch of its life. The reason lots of readers even pick up my books is the cover designs of Patrick Insole.

In Australia, Hachette ran a wonderful support campaign: special thanks to Ailie Springall and to Anita Crompton. Hachette could have just paid lip service but instead they dived in, to an extent that I could never have dreamed.

Most of all, readers took hold of the book. To be honest, I don't mind what readers read: as long as they do read, and discuss, and recommend. Especially now, bookstores need help; they're a civilizing influence in a dog-eat-dog world. But naturally, I'm thrilled when anyone chooses my book. So, thank you, to everyone who stopped at the crime section of their bookshop or library, and started reading.

Author's note

This book is fiction. Hopefully it's fiction that is so vivid and compelling you'll swear it's real life, but it's all made up. Except for the bit about Athletic Bilbao – that's true.

The joy of this, for me, is that I can invent useful aspects of legal process that don't actually exist. Australia does not have level one or two warrants, nor does it have a doctrine of Close Proximity.

What I'm saying is: don't rely on this book, or crime authors, for legal advice. Oh, we'll be all pleasant and confident, but in the end you'll get crap advice and we'll have eaten all your biscuits. Better to find someone with certificates and that all-important professional insurance.